The Bridge of Years

Books by May Sarton

POETRY

Encounter in April
Inner Landscape
The Lion and the Rose
The Land of Silence
In Time Like Air
Cloud, Stone, Sun, Vine
A Private Mythology
As Does New Hampshire
A Grain of Mustard Seed

NOVELS

The Single Hound
The Bridge of Years
Shadow of a Man
A Shower of Summer Days
Faithful Are the Wounds
The Birth of a Grandfather
The Fur Person
The Small Room
Joanna and Ulysses
Mrs. Stevens Hears the Mermaids Singing
Miss Pickthorn and Mr. Hare
The Poet and the Donkey
Kinds of Love

NONFICTION

I Knew a Phoenix
Plant Dreaming Deep

The Bridge of Years

A NOVEL BY

MAY SARTON

W · W · NORTON & COMPANY · INC · *New York*

Copyright 1946 by MAY SARTON

SBN   393   08652   6

Library of Congress Catalog Card No. 76-162709

ALL RIGHTS RESERVED
Published simultaneously in Canada
by George J. McLeod Limited, Toronto

PRINTED IN THE UNITED STATES OF AMERICA

1 2 3 4 5 6 7 8 9 0

L'héroïsme est essentiellement une vertu, un état, l'action hero-
ïque est essentiellement une opération de santé, de bonne humeur,
de joie, même de gaieté, presque de blague, une action, une opération d'aisance, de largesse, de facilité, de commodité, de fécon-
dité; de bien allant; de maîtrise et de possession de soi; d'habitude
presque pour ainsi dire et comme d'usage, de bon usage; de fécon-
dité intérieure; de force comme d'une belle eau de source de force
puisée dans le sang de la race et dans le propre sang de l'homme,
un trop plein de sève et de sang.

CHARLES PÉGUY

Contents

PART ONE

Spring: 1919

Chapter I

On a country road near Brussels stood one of those small family estates so dear to Belgian hearts: a large vegetable garden; an orchard; a white table and chairs in the shade of an apple tree; a couple of meadows; a little duckpond; a formal French garden; and the house itself thrusting its tiled gable through a bower of trees. Here lived Mélanie and Paul Duchesne and their household. Here they had stayed all through the war of 1914–18 while their neighbors of the big summer estates on either side of them fled to safety in Holland or England. But those houses were hidden behind hedges and formal lines of trees so that the avenue itself looked like a country road and, as a matter of fact, ended by being one: half a mile from the Duchesne place it opened out to fields of oats and wheat, rolling green pastures where the Percheron horses were bred, real country dotted with sturdy stone farms.

Even before the war the Duchesnes, alone in their part of the road, lived here all the year round. They did not feel themselves city people, although their business was in Brussels. And while the big estates fell to pieces during the four years of war—the paths overgrown with weeds, the orchards unpruned, the artificial ponds dried up—the Duchesne estate stood fast, a small human fortress in a wilderness of neglect, intimate and secret.

It was 1919, the first spring after the war. In Belgium, as in half the world, people felt the necessity to be born again, but, like babies who have made the long struggle from darkness into light, their first reaction was protest. It was a rainy spring—armies of slugs materialized to devour the vegetable gardens. Even the weather failed to celebrate the end of the war. And people who had gallantly endured four years of semistarvation, misery, and humiliation became irritable and forgot how to joke. They had waited for this spring so long . . .

"After the war" was to have been a brilliant sunlit place where everything would suddenly change; where children would be all at once as plump and healthy as prewar children; where the cows long since consumed in Germany would make a miraculous reappearance; where in one night the poor sawdusty flour would become rich and white, the ruins be rebuilt, and work, happiness, and love shine out from all the faces. Each had his dream. But now the unified courage which had sustained them as one people broke up into a million private struggles. Now one had no longer to wait and hope, to endure: one had to act.

In the darkest hours Mélanie Duchesne had found comfort in the garden, and now in the spring she got up early (it was just after seven) and rejoiced in all there was to do. This morning she was determined to finish scraping the paths round the box-enclosed parterres of the French garden; they were covered with a green film of moss, and great tufts of goose grass threatened to choke the tiny hedges.

Every now and then she leaned on the scraper to catch her breath, to smell the misty morning air, to think, to see if she could catch sight of the thrush singing in the hawthorn, to listen for her little girl's voice upstairs.

But the first sign of life from the sleeping house was the creak of the pump and then Louise throwing water out into the courtyard after sloshing the tiled kitchen floor. (Oh dear, that would wake Paul, that slam of a door!)

As always, working in the garden, she felt happy and at peace. The sun burned through the veil of mist, opening the sky, making the trembling leaves on the tops of the poplar glitter as they swayed. All around her the earth seemed to breathe—the air was drenched with the fresh smell of it.

Paul, half asleep still and suffering from a migraine headache, had been listening to the scrape-scrape of the hoe, irritated when it stopped, more irritated when it started again. When the kitchen door slammed a second time he flung off the covers, stumbled to the casement window, and looked down at his wife, half furiously, half tenderly.

There she was, barelegged, her feet thrust into sabots, sturdy, boy-ish, determined—with an air of victory about her even at this time in the morning.

"Must there be so much noise in the morning?" he shouted down angrily, and closed the window before she could answer.

But while Mélanie was still looking up (it was a lovely house, she thought—it had such a homely air with its walls all covered with vines; and bother Paul anyway for being cross) another case-ment window came to life and there was Françoise leaning out of her nurse's arms, calling in her clear thrush voice:

"Good morning, Mamie!"

"Good morning, my precious!" They waved at each other and smiled and nodded, as if the house were a boat and Mélanie stand-ing on the dock, and then Bo-Bo carried Françoise off. The child still looks pale, Mélanie thought. She had had diphtheria in 1918, and even now it was hard to get her enough rich milk.

The day had begun. Mélanie took one last look at the garden, pulled up one last tuft of goose grass, and then went into the shed to put away her tools and to get Moïse, the goat, and put her to pasture.

"Come along, old lady," she said. But Moïse sat down implacably in her warm bed of hay and refused to budge. Finally Mélanie managed to push and pull her to her feet and then (such are the ways of goats) the perverse creature suddenly made up her mind and backed out in such a hurry that she all but knocked Mélanie down.

Louise and Marie, the two Flemish maids, laughed to see them go past the window, Mélanie shouting in her high, commanding voice: "Moïse, Moïse, a little decorum, *sacré animal!*"

She came back laughing herself, walking into the kitchen in her bare feet, having left her sabots at the door.

"Hurry up, you two," she called in Flemish as she ran upstairs to wash and change into city clothes. "Monsieur will be wanting his coffee. One of you had better milk Moïse. I haven't time." And with that she was gone. She could be heard all over the house, pouring out energy in every gesture, in every word.

"Hurry up, Paul, I have to get into the bathroom—— Hello, my darling, my precious—— But you *have* to have your hair combed; you are not a little goat, my precious——"

Fifteen minutes later the family had all gathered at the breakfast table, somewhat subdued by Paul's migraine. He sat in his dressing gown, sipping his café au lait, refusing to eat anything, disapproving the day.

The room was full of sunlight warming the orange walls, making pools of ruddy light on the copper pots and the shining blue-and-white plates that stood on a shelf at the back, but not dissipating the melancholy face, in the portrait on the wall, of a thin, thoughtful little boy wrapped up in a blue scarf, who was Paul twenty years ago.

Bo-Bo, lean and wiry, who had been a terror to the Germans, addressing them in pure Prussian (she had been a governess in Germany), Bo-Bo alone was not afraid of Monsieur in his terrible moods. She was old enough to be his mother and she now said:

"You had better have a piece of bread and butter," and firmly passed him one on a thin wooden leaf.

But Mélanie looked at her husband as if she had never seen him before. His thin aristocratic face, his perpetual air of intellectual suffering, of enduring all because one must endure, filled her with amazement. She felt often like a peasant in the presence of a tyrannical king. And yet he could suddenly be so gay, so wildly, almost brutally gay, playing preposterous practical jokes (only last week he had put a frog in Bo-Bo's bed). He would always be a mystery, and for that among other things she loved him. But it hardly seemed like marriage, she thought, to be in such constant peril. There was nothing settled or everyday about their relationship. Would there ever be? She had thought of marriage as a great calm coming to port, but perhaps it was never like that, but always a difficult journey undertaken in ignorance.

She resisted the longing to talk and, resisting it, felt an impulse to giggle like a schoolgirl in church. But that would never do. So after gobbling down a piece of bread and butter and cheese she disappeared into the kitchen with her coffee. There she could be heard explaining in Flemish that today the downstairs floors must be waxed, the copper in the *salon* thoroughly shined, and the tiles round the fireplace washed.

Paul sipped his coffee and sighed after each swallow like an exhausted man being slowly revived. Françoise, sitting on the bench beside him, her hair pulled straight back and still damp, the pigtails firmly tied in two red ribbons, watched and waited for the moment when she could slide over and sit in the crook of his arm. For Paul was the weather in this house, and today, in spite of the brilliant sunlight that poured down on the blue-and-white-checked tablecloth, on the pewter coffeepot, on the big blue cups, and there found itself reflected in Bo-Bo's fiercely azure eyes—today the weather was dangerous.

The cat broke the silence of breakfast by suddenly jumping onto the table, and now for the first time Paul smiled.

"Ah, Filibert, *ma vieille,* that is not done, you know," he said, lifting Filibert gently down. "Go down and behave like a decent cat and you shall have your milk." And then he called, "Louise, a saucer for Filibert, if you please."

"What are you going to do today, little one?" Françoise turned to Bo-Bo, for this was her chance to get anything she wanted.

"Oh, Bo-Bo, can we go to the big farm and see the foal?" Françoise was five years old but she spoke very precisely and clearly already. Paul couldn't stand sloppy speech. He had himself taught Françoise to speak and now was teaching her to read.

Bo-Bo resented any suggestions. "My child, I have a dozen things to do this morning. Perhaps later on, if you are very good and don't come and bother me till then."

"Oh, I won't. I have things to do too, Bo-Bo. I have to make a nest for a mouse."

"You have to have a short lesson with Papa. Come up to my study in half an hour." Paul went upstairs, elegant, disdainful as a heron, to gargle, to take an aspirin, to wonder why he felt so tired and dull, and finally to dress.

The minute he was out of the way the whole atmosphere in the breakfast room suffered a violent change. There was an immediate clatter of dishes, sound of running water, banging of doors, as if the dishes and taps themselves felt relieved. Mélanie hurried through the room calling after her.

"Françoise, help Lou-Lou clear the table, will you? Bo-Bo, come and talk to me while I put on my hat. What do we need from town?"

Françoise ran up to her mother and threw her arms round her legs. "May I come to the end of the road, Mummy? May I?"

"Oh, darling, there are still tramps around—I'm afraid you can't this morning. Bo-Bo hasn't time to come with us. But come to the gate and we can wave at each other from a long way off. My precious," said Mélanie, feeling suddenly as always the wrench of leaving, as if it were a real departure, "have a good day. Be a good girl. Take care of Papa—see that he gets some warm milk when you have yours in the middle of the morning. Good-by, Paul," she called upstairs—and, bending down to kiss Françoise, Mélanie thought with terror, How pale she is, poor mite.

And then she must run, she must run. There never was time enough in the morning.

Françoise stood at the green gate and waved and waited for her mother to turn at the bend of the road and wave back. Then she was really gone. The garden felt empty. There was a great hole in the day. Moïse in the meadow gave a disconsolate whinny, as if she too knew that Mamie was gone. And Françoise walked down the path and under the weeping willow, slowly, slowly, and when she pushed open the big front door felt suddenly frightened. Where was everybody? She stood in the dark chilly hall and listened. Not a sound. She pushed open the swinging door into the breakfast room. It was all shining and empty and neat; even Filibert had disappeared. The heart had gone out of everything.

And then she heard Bo-Bo's feet moving about in the nursery overhead. So that was all right. But Lou-Lou? Marie? It was very important to know where everyone was. Then and only then could she go and make a nest for the field mouse she had startled yesterday in the far meadow.

So she tiptoed, silenced by the silence around her, through the kitchen and out of the back door. There was a loud quacking: Lou-Lou must be giving the ducks their breakfast. So that was all right. Françoise ran around the house through the French garden and out into the meadow, just in time to be present at the daily battle between Marie and the goat.

"*Allons,* be quiet!" she admonished, but the goat cast a wary glance in her direction and sidled off. The trick was to keep away from the horns, to get behind her and begin milking before she decided to butt. Stout Marie was flushed already with the chase, but she too enjoyed being out in the sun, feeling the dew from the thick damp grass on her legs—for Marie too it was a game.

Just then Moïse made a quick turn and stood up on her hind legs only to have her horns caught in Marie's strong hands.

"Now I've got you, you devil." She threw the goat off and called to Françoise to bring the wooden milking bench. The fun was over; Moïse decided it was time for serious business. Moïse had suddenly become a domestic animal.

For Françoise it was a real spring, her first: last year she had been too ill, and before that too small. This year she examined each flower and bud as if it had been made for her—she laughed with delight to look around her and see the thousand delicate pink and white faces of the tiny daisies scattered in the lush grass. She looked up and saw for the first time the branches of the apple tree laden with thick rosy buds.

"Look, look," she called to Marie, "are those little apples?"

To Françoise, to Marie (whose fiancé had come back safe from the war), this spring was a beginning, a festival, a release from winter; but to Bo-Bo, upstairs beating out the pillows savagely as she made her bed and Françoise's, it was a battle, a new battle coming at the end of many others. For four years she had held dirt and disintegration and weariness at bay. The house had seemed to her (and to Madame, of course; but she did not have to fight rheumatism as well as everything else)—the house had seemed a fortress. If one of the copper pots had ceased to shine (though there was no more polish), if the floors had ever worn a particle of dust (though for four years they had struggled with little or no wax, using it only once a month instead of every day), if the windows had not shone like diamonds in the sunlight—then they would have been beaten. Then, when the Germans came to requisition the very food on the table, she could not have faced them as she did, at the door of a fortress, a place where people might suffer, but they would not give in. They would not cease doing anything that they had done before. They would not leave in a panic. They would stay and maintain their life, hold it together, keep it intact. Yes, take our ducks; you have the power to do it (but for two years she had managed to hide them in the cellar, letting them out only when there was a guard at the gate to warn if anyone came). But, yes, finally the ducks had to go, and the goat, and even one terrible year the potatoes as well. They could take them. But they could not take the life from the house, from the people in it. The house was a fortress. It stood. It withstood. It kept its secrets well—the false partition in the attic where they had hidden two English airmen for three weeks until they could make their escape; the chest in the upper hall which had concealed a French spy the Boches were after. And even when the masters of it had to go, even when it was their turn to be requisitioned and taken off to prison, accused of helping prisoners to escape—even then the house had stood fast. The house had maintained itself. The best teacups, after all, saved Monsieur and Madame's life, thought Bo-Bo with satisfaction, and with the deep inward humility which was the secret of her outward arrogance—for it had been she, of course, and not the cups, who had saved their lives.

A perfect stranger, dressed as a beggar, had come one night to warn them that they were under suspicion for helping prisoners to escape. They stayed up till two in the morning making up a story to cover every one of the steps, every one of the places where they might have been seen. They had invented the story step by step and then rehearsed it over and over to be sure they would not break down when they were questioned separately. It was then that Monsieur had proved his mettle. His command of the situation had been perfect. Madame had the courage of a lioness, but it would only have served her to die bravely if she had not been armed with Monsieur's clever story. Only there was one link missing, a link they had left undecided because they were so worried about Françoise, ill in the nursery, with her fever still rising, her glands swollen, patient and flushed, saying she couldn't swallow.

At five o'clock in the morning the house was surrounded: it really did seem like a fortress. Bo-Bo had to laugh: all the Boches needed to do was walk up the front path, but instead they crept mysteriously through the bushes getting their faces scratched on the twigs. The twigs had not needed to be taught to resist.

She went down and opened the front door, trembling with fear and laughter so that her voice sounded shriller than usual. She addressed them in German:

"Come in and tell us what you are doing. Don't go sneaking around in the bushes. You'll break the branches, you ruffians."

They had gathered then, rather sheepishly, and waited for an officer to stride up and order the arrest of Monsieur and Madame, pushing Bo-Bo aside and striding up the stairs before she had a chance to warn them.

At that moment the thought of the best cups came to her like an inspiration.

While the officer waited upstairs, keeping a vigilant watch over Monsieur so that he would have no chance to communicate with his wife, while Madame hastily dressed and packed a little bag with toothbrush and nightgown and a volume of Napoleonic Memoirs, Bo-Bo was taking the last of the chocolate—real prewar chocolate, hidden in the pantry—down and making a pot of cocoa. She set the tray with care, laying on it the best linen cloth, shining the spoons, and finally taking down the fine English cups covered with bright flowers.

She was ready when they came downstairs.

"It's so early, won't the Herr Ober-Lieutenant take a cup of hot cocoa before he goes?"

He had hesitated a moment. This was against regulations, of course. But the smell from the pot was irresistible.

"Very well. If we hurry." They had gone into the salon and sat there at five o'clock in the morning like three old friends, Madame talking volubly in German, Monsieur smiling affably, as if this were the most pleasant diversion in the world—a delightful, unexpected visit.

As Bo-Bo passed the cups she deliberately let one fall and smash. It was a terrible thing to do, but this was a matter of life and death.

"*Voyons,* Bo-Bo, butterfingers," said Monsieur impatiently. Bo-Bo pretended to be overwhelmed. She knelt down shamefacedly and picked up the pieces.

"Get a rag quickly, Bo-Bo, or the cocoa will stain the carpet!"

When Bo-Bo came back with the rag she asked innocently: "I believe it can be mended, madame. Could you tell me the address of the little man down in the city who mended the blue jar for us last month? I will take it today. I am so sorry."

This was the final link, the reason for a visit last month to an address way down in the city. And of course Monsieur and Madame understood at once. Bo-Bo wrote down the address on a piece of paper. She would go immediately with the broken cup and warn the man that he must pretend to be able to mend it, if questioned.

And then they were gone, Madame calling last-minute advice and directions about Françoise. There had not been time to weep.

Yes, the house and everything in it was the visible sign of their endurance and their victory. Many times the mended cup would be brought out in the years to come when Françoise asked to hear the story again. For Monsieur and Madame had come back safely, after three months, very thin and pale, to be sure, but alive.

Bo-Bo sighed remembering all this. They had been terrible days and yet great ones. Now the days held no terror, but they seemed diminished. Or was it only that she was growing old? She stopped dusting, suddenly galvanized. The girls were undoubtedly scratching the linoleum, the way they pulled the furniture about in the salon, too lazy to lift it. In a second Bo-Bo was running down the stairs.

"How may times have I told you to lift the chairs? Look at that scratch! Heavens, there would be nothing left of this house in a week if you were left to yourselves!"

Soon there would be real wax again to wax the floors, and real soap—heavens, what a delight to be able to fill a dishpan with real soapy warm water and make the glasses shine! If she did not give in now to tiredness and pain, if she could just get over the next few months, it would be all as it had been. Already Françoise had forgotten the war and all about it. Already it was all a story to her, a story she never got tired of hearing.

Chapter II

But there was one room in the house which escaped Bo-Bo's vigilance, and in that room a kind of life went on which was as different from Bo-Bo's ideas of life as night is from day. Here the dust accumulated. Here the windows were opened only on the warmest days, for Paul Duchesne had a terror of drafts, believing that they brought on his migraines—so that the room had a peculiar smell of leather bindings and ink. Here, with rows of neat notebooks before him, surrounded by many little pads, in a solitude of books, of pencils always kept perfectly pointed, Paul lived his own life of meditation, aware of the active life of the house only when it impinged on his silence—when someone dropped a dish or clattered a dustpan, or if the draft from an open window made a door bang.

Here he would sit for hours on end, hardly moving, except to drop the ash from a cigarette. Nothing seemed ever to have happened or to be happening in this room. It never changed. But in its changelessness, in its silence, a continual drama went on, an exhausting, constant struggle, which Paul in his own mind had often compared to the travail of Sisyphus rolling his stone up the mountain only to have it always fall down again to the bottom— and this struggle was the struggle of thought, the struggle of a man to give his ideas precision, to arrive at a system, a pattern by which he could live. Paul was a philosopher, a philosopher who was perhaps intended to have been a poet, if his tenderness had not been sealed up in the labyrinth of his mind, his violent, imaginative humor reduced to find an outlet in his occasional practical jokes, his humanity fearfully channeled and restricted. Perhaps it was the rebellion of his nature against this enforced strict discipline that had made him grow more irritable and difficult as the years went on.

As a student, when Mélanie first met him, he had had a wild fantastic charm and above all a sort of panache, a sense of his own destiny, of his own power, which she had found irresistible, which she had worshiped with the whole force of a clear and violent heart. But since then a great deal had happened besides the war. She still worshiped him, but she felt that he was withdrawing into places where she could not follow.

He had left the university without getting his degree, while they were engaged, saying that he could learn more by himself, declaring himself bored with having to attend the lectures of second-rate men, although they numbered among them professors of very high reputation. But without a degree he had set himself apart from the whole academic world and made his own path infinitely harder. Now, at thirty, he had ceased to be a young man of promise, an "original," and it was time that he had something to show for all those days and hours of work and meditation.

For Paul the end of the war meant at last the chance to be published by a Paris house, meant making the great effort of getting into shape, writing down consecutively, polishing, ordering, the work of five years. There was no excuse now not to get it done. There was no possible escape.

Also he had had before the war a small income of his own, enough to feel that he was doing his share of maintaining the family, but now, with the franc what it was, all people who had lived on income from investments were more or less ruined, and Paul's fortune had diminished to almost nothing. They had had to mortgage the house heavily during the war, and the whole burden of pulling their affairs out of the depression was falling on Mélanie. But this material dilemma seemed to make things even more difficult for Paul. He could not, he would not give up the work of his life, and yet what if he were on a false track? What if he never succeeded in saying what he meant? What if "what he meant" even was all a delusion?

For Mélanie there was never any doubt. She had from the first believed in his work blindly and implicity. She was, he knew, proud to be able to help him. But what if he should disappoint her?

He was full of scruples, doubts, self-questionings, remorse, arrogance, and at times a furious resentment against Mélanie, for whom life was such a simple affair of right and wrong, where one did one's duty heroically and gaily whatever it was—and where, above all, one could always recognize one's duty. This certainty made her at times intolerant in her dealings with people, intolerant in a way he would never be. But it made her solid and absolutely to be trusted. She had many friends. He had none. He had gradually withdrawn from them or alienated them with his *"esprit critique"* so that he felt himself sometimes a monster. And yet—and yet——

The house, the business, the whole material fabric of life was as nothing, a handful of dust compared to what he had in his head if he should ever come to the end of it and express it fully.

To Françoise, who had tiptoed to the door and now stood watching him, he was the most magnificent and beautiful creature in the world, the very angel.

He felt her presence at the door and was glad of the interruption. "Come, little soul, come and say good morning all over again to your bad-tempered papa—come, my bird." And she ran into his arms.

Everything in life conspires against pure thought; that was what his mind registered as he held her fast against him and kissed the top of her head just at the part in her hair. She asked nothing, and yet by her very existence she asked everything—to be supported, sent to school, taught, somehow helped to grow up, kept in good health, above all, *loved*. Here she was then, total distraction, laughing delightedly as he tickled her ear. But what a blessing!

Already she was trying to lift the big pile of books they always put in her chair so she could sit beside him and pick out the letters of the alphabet, the big ones on the title pages of books of poems. Quick now, and agile, aware to the tips of his long delicate hands, he was at her side.

"Too heavy, little one. Let me help you." She sat at his side, frowning with concentration and then pouncing with delight as she recognized

"T, Papa! T and O—no, Q." When they had finished the title page of one book they went on to words spelled out in big letters on cards he had painstakingly made.

"P-A-P-A," she spelled slowly, and then stopped.

"Well, say it again, Françoise. Say it slowly and see if it doesn't turn into a word."

"Pay—ah, Pay—ah." Her whole face was a frown of effort. She gave him a desperate glance and suddenly said, "Pa!" Then she beamed with happiness. "Pa-pa! Pa-pa!" she said it over and over triumphantly.

"There, you see, you can read now. In a few weeks you will be able to read a hundred words, then whole sentences. We are doing splendidly. How happy Mamie will be when she comes home."

So the lesson went on until Françoise began to feel that her chair so high up in the air was a prison; her behind started to go all prickly, and she wanted to laugh or cry. It seemed impossible to decipher another of the puzzles on the cards.

"Just one more, sweetheart, and you can get down. You have done so well now, don't spoil it at the end. I know you are tired, but just one more," so spoke her inexorable angel in his tenderest voice.

A bee buzzed against the window. Outside everything was free —she could see the willow tree like a green promise outside. There was so much happening out of doors; the letters looked so far away and strange; she could never guess them.

"Try once more."

But it was too much. She burst into tears. She wanted to get away, to hide, to hide herself somewhere under a bush where no one would ever find her except the birds. She beat her father off and kicked and screamed as he lifted her off the chair. She didn't want his tenderness and love. She wanted to be free and wild and alone.

"No, no, no!" was all she could say through her sobs.

But he would not let her go. She had to come back and sit quietly on his lap while he rocked her gently and talked to her about how she was five years old now and she must begin to be able to do things even when she no longer wanted to, about how Mamie went into town to the business every day, even when she was very tired, and how everyone must learn to discipline himself. So he talked to her in his ceaseless, gentle voice. But she did not want to listen, and when her sobs had stopped shaking her she just waited, like an animal waiting patiently to be set free while a human being caresses it, enduring, knowing it to be useless to struggle.

It was an immense relief when Bo-Bo's sharp knock at the door set them back into a matter-of-fact world again. She was bringing up two glasses of hot milk.

"Hm," she sniffed. "Little girls don't cry at their lessons when they are your age."

That sounded simple, and clear, and reasonable. She could accept that. She held the glass in her two hands and looked at Bo-Bo speculatively over it.

"Come along, drink it up, Françoise. Don't dawdle."

With Bo-Bo she felt perfectly secure. But then she did not love Bo-Bo so much.

Chapter III

At nine o'clock sharp the bell on the great door of the Maison Bernard tinkled and Mélanie made her entrance into the life of the day. At home, in the presence of her husband, she might be humble and even shy; here she was in command.

As soon as Mlle. Zumpt, the accountant, and Mlle. Louvois, the

salesgirl, heard the bell they leaped to attention and ran out into
the hall where Mélanie was already giving her orders while she
hung up her coat. The very tone of her voice had changed. It was
sharp, ringing. It electrified the cool, still atmosphere of the old
house packed with treasures brought from the East Indies, the
Congo, Liberty's in London—its floors of magnificently furnished
exhibition rooms, its model nursery, its paneled library.

"We must pay the printer's bill today, Mlle. Zumpt——"

"Yes, madame."

The two demoiselles followed Mélanie from the hall to the old
roll-top desk; she went on talking while she glanced through the
morning mail (all bills, as usual, bills and advertisements).

"Write a letter to the textile people—that order is a week late."

"Yes, madame."

"Have you got the accounts on the past six months? Let me have
them, please. The electric bill is too high. I must speak to Jean."
But the peremptory tone and its meek reception was really a sort
of game. After all, she was the *patronne,* and it was quite fitting
that she behave as she did.

The only person who refused to enter into the spirit of battle
and emergency, who would not regard the business as a constant
brave attack on superior forces, was Jean, the caretaker, who lived
downstairs with his wife and little boy.

"What is a woman in business?" he would growl to his wife.
"She makes such a fuss, but what is accomplished by it? The
business is going to pieces. Anyone can see that." And then he
would grumble his way upstairs and put the rugs in moth balls or
pack a jug for some customer in Ghent, muttering to himself that
it was hardly worth the bother for a mere hundred-franc sale. For
the present clientele he had nothing but contempt. He remembered
the carriages and the footmen who used to stop outside the door.

And then he did not like Mélanie's air of a woman who liked
to garden better than anything else in the world, her short, un-
fashionable haircut, her shabby old blue suit. Mlle. Louvois, on the

other hand, looked like a Parisian. That was as it should be. She piled up her red hair, made up heavily, and in her black dress and pearls would have done credit to any house on the Avenue Louise (the avenue of couturiers and jewelers, of bookbinders and costly tobacconists).

Mélanie had inherited the business from her mother. Mme. Bernard herself died in 1913, leaving her daughter the big house on the fashionable avenue, a large stock of furniture, hangings, *objets d'art* of all kinds, her two faithful assistants, and the good repute of the Maison Bernard. More personally Mélanie had inherited her mother's roll-top desk and her mother's nature. They were both artists rather than businesswomen. The business itself was an art, composed as much of a genius for personal relations as of a genius for color and texture, for dressing a house as if it were a person in its own character and still in perfect taste.

Their relation with clients was a curious one: they were, after all, merchants, and that meant that there was no question of social equality. But furnishing a house involves a great deal of personal contact, and Mme. Bernard had warm friends among people who did not receive her but who loved to invite her to lunch on some business matter and reveled in her humor and kindness.

Also she had courage. She was one of the first tradespeople in Belgium ever to have a carriage and pair, not for social reasons, but because she loved riding in the park. But the first day she drove out she was insulted and even stoned by people to whom this seemed the beginning of a revolution. She persisted. She ignored the insults and the stones were poorly aimed. Within a year her carriage and pair were taken for granted. Her business flourished.

When she died she left her daughter a firm foundation on which to build—but she had not counted on the war. When Mélanie took over she had a definite aim, the dream of making the Maison Bernard a center for designers, artisans, and craftsmen—a Guild of the Arts and Crafts—as William Morris had tried to do in England. The war put a stop to all that.

Now they kept going by taking small orders when they could get them (the old clientele was faithful) and by gradually selling off the stock. Every day Mélanie felt she was just holding off bankruptcy by a miracle.

Once in a while the bell tinkled and a customer asked for Madame. Then Mélanie would spend half an hour helping some woman select (from the great multicolored piles packed away behind sliding doors in the downstairs rooms) a few yards of material or a sofa cushion—spending her fire of energy recklessly—after ten minutes, deep in conversation about the client's children, her husband's fear of spending, her longing for gay colors, and so on and so on. In half an hour Mélanie had accumulated an unlimited amount of good will and fifty or one hundred francs to hand over triumphantly to Mlle. Zumpt as if it were a thousand.

"That poor woman wanted a sofa cushion, one of the embroidered ones, for a hundred francs—imagine!"

And Mlle. Zumpt would smile grimly and say, "And I suppose you let her have it?"

"Well, what could I do?" Suddenly Mélanie would look delighted. "She has such a mean husband and she really appreciated it." And then a second later the Mélanie who had made a new friend became the patronne again: *"Allons,* children, we are wasting time. Ring for Jean, and ask Mlle. Louvois to come here—these samples can wait. I want everyone here in five minutes."

While she sat at her desk, jotting down figures, she was thinking of other things—of that early summer of 1914—how they had worked, and what hope there was in the air! For August 1914 was the date set for an international exhibition of furniture and decorating, and the Maison Bernard was to be represented by a suite of rooms, specially designed and built for the occasion. What love had gone into the dyeing of brilliant emerald-green curtains!—into the great bunches of flowers inlaid in the doors of cabinets (they had imported craftsmen from Austria for this work); into the furniture itself, perfectly finished in every detail (the drawers themselves opening as if they were oiled and, inside, shining glossy as chestnuts). It was all imaginative, gay, elegant, and precious; the Queen herself had come to see it before the exhibition opened and was rumored to be interested in buying.

But August 1914 was the date set for other international affairs! The suite was packed away in the cellar of the Maison Bernard, and with it Mélanie's dream.

But always when they felt most depressed they remembered it. It was the symbol of hope and faith. It was, in a way, the heart of the business still. If they had done this really beautiful thing once, they could do it again. And mightn't it still come out and be shown? And mightn't it be the beginning of new life someday?

Now Mélanie had decided to break it up and sell it piece by piece. This was the bomb she threw into the assembled group.

"But, madame," Mlle. Louvois protested at once, "you will have to let it go for a song. Break up the suite! Why——" She was speechless before such a calamity.

"Yes, let's wait," Mlle. Zumpt instantly interrupted. "Things will be better in a year."

"My poor children, in a year we won't exist unless I can raise fifty thousand, a hundred thousand"—Mélanie was always rather vague about figures—"by next month. The mortgage is due, and this time they'll tell us the war is over and we have to pay." She shrugged. "Have you any other ideas, then?"

There was a painful silence while Mlle. Louvois polished her nails absent-mindedly and Mlle. Zumpt frowned and looked down.

"The war may be over for the Americans, but as far as I can see, for us it has just begun," said Mlle. Louvois bitterly.

And Mlle. Zumpt sighed.

A sigh was one thing that Mélanie could not endure. It suggested defeat and capitulation. She spoke to them both sharply, as if they were school children who had forgotten their lesson.

"No, I won't have these long faces. We've never failed to pull through and we won't now. As for the Americans, they may not have to struggle as we do, but also they have never made furniture to compare with that suite. Come, a little courage. Perhaps we can find an American to buy it," she added with a chuckle.

But they were not to be comforted. The suite had become the image of what might have been; it was the one thing left which really represented the honor and prestige of the house. It was one thing to sell off the remnants and small objects and an odd piece of furniture here and there—even to take orders they would have turned down five years before—but to break up the suite seemed sacrilege. For once they refused to rise.

"There must be some other way out. What about a sale?" said Mlle. Louvois with false brightness. They had tried that so many times before that it hardly seemed worth taking down the *Soldes* sign.

"Perhaps an order will come in today," Mlle. Zumpt suggested diffidently. "What about that firm in Antwerp?"

"They wanted an impossible price," Madame answered shortly. The fact was that this firm had collaborated with the Germans, making their money on the black market for diamonds, and she had not been able to bring herself to deal with them. "No," she went on inexorably, "there is simply nothing else to be done."

The time for discussion was over and the time for orders had begun.

"Mlle. Louvois, find the shears. You and I will undo the curtains and cushions—heaven knows what state they'll be in! You, Mlle. Zumpt, find the old accounts and we'll make out a price list piece by piece. Tell Jean to come down to the cellar at once with his tools. He will have to get at the packing cases."

Now that Mélanie had made the decision, she felt quite cheerful. The worst had been breaking it to the help. But she herself was glad to think that at last the pieces of beautiful furniture would have a life of their own, be admired and cherished, have the place of honor in some modest drawing room. More and more she was coming to think that their whole attitude must change, and if the business could survive, it must survive by looking in a new direction. They must try to catch the clientele of the big stores like the Bon Marché, which sold ready-made suites at cheap prices. If they could make beautiful things at low prices, they would really be able to pull themselves out. Mélanie would have liked nothing better than to be asked to do a small house for a change. But the problem was how to attract these people.

The very Maison Bernard was wrong. They should have display windows like the big stores. The atmosphere of elegance, the small unpretentious sign, belonged to the past.

But down in the cellar, busy with Mlle. Louvois, as they shook out the magnificent curtains, she felt a wave of pride and of regret. It was something even for a year or two to have produced really beautiful things, stinting nothing, neither material nor craftsmanship. There was nothing cheap or tawdry or poorly finished anywhere. She let her hands run over the marvelous finish of the desk and turned to Mlle. Louvois.

"It feels like satin."

"Heaven knows what will become of workmen who could make things like that." Mlle. Louvois came and stood beside her, looking at it and then touching it with a sort of homage.

Mélanie suddenly put an arm around her and kissed her.

"Dear Mlle. Louvois, just wait and see. We are going to have work for them—if we can just live through this year!"

As always, by the end of the day, when they sat, disheveled, dirty, triumphant, on the empty packing cases, drinking a tisane, the two demoiselles felt comforted and Mélanie herself cheerful and full of hope. For Mélanie pulled herself out of fears and doubts, not by thinking, like Paul, but by action.

Heaven knows, she thought, surveying the mess, there is enough to do.

Chapter IV

The trip into town on the streetcar was a preparation for the day, her time for making decisions; rocked from side to side, Mélanie sat very straight and hardly noticed the people around her or the conductor blowing his shrill and melancholy horn. But from the moment she stepped onto the old trolley on the way home, it was an excursion.

In the evening light the familiar suburbs, the shops and streets she knew by heart all seemed to greet Mélanie with affection; she kept her eyes open in case one of the little shops might have some cheap candy in bright paper cornets, or a few cigarettes (they were sold singly as a great luxury now), and she could bring home a surprise to the family.

The conductor's horn sounded shrill and gay; now she was on her way home. And she felt a great oneness with the hundreds of silent cyclists speeding past, leaning far over their racing bicycles, calling good night to friends as they turned off or waving triumphantly to the crowded trolley as they passed it. Their families were waiting for them too, far on ahead in the small towns and villages.

First the street passed through a long string of suburbs, then there began to be country houses, one or two large estates, and, on either side of the road, country cafés—the Chasseur Vert, the Brabançonne—where men and women resting under the arbors drank what, after a hard day's work and on a spring evening, they could imagine was beer.

But quite suddenly all this human bustle was left behind them as they reached the edge of the great forest and, even over the loud rattle of the trolley, felt its deep breath. A coolness, a hush fell upon them. Mélanie watched eagerly to see the wood anemones making patches of white and green on the bronze carpet of beech leaves. High, high overhead the tops of the trees wore a foam of green. It was all still, empty, gravely beautiful; now the whole weight of the city and of the day fell from her. So that by the time they were in sight of the avenue she felt as if she were coming back from a long journey, felt suddenly anxious, as if the last few minutes were unbearable. What might not have happened while she was away?

And for half an hour before, almost from the time she had stepped joyfully onto her trolley, a wave of expectancy and impatience lifted the world at home. Bo-Bo was already in the kitchen admonishing Louise and Marie not to start the omelette too soon. Françoise had reminded her father three times to put on his shoes and hurry or they would miss Mamie.

From far off they saw her striding along, swinging her brief case, her smile reaching out to them before anyone spoke, and everyone resisting the impulse to run—as if there were a thread pulling them together step by step and if they ran they would break it. And finally Françoise couldn't wait and leaped ahead and threw herself at her mother like a little dog, to be picked up and covered with kisses.

"My darling, my treasure!"

Paul felt the sap of joy rise in him as he pulled his wife's arm through his, taking the brief case from her, and they set out together, all three hand in hand, for home.

The open green gate welcomed them, and Mamie, while they chattered on about the day and what each had done, greeted each tree and bush with expectancy—so much happened in a garden in a day!

"Look, Paul, the Japanese cherry next door—isn't it early this year?" she interrupted him constantly, but nothing interrupted the stream of happiness. It flowed between them like the evening air. They were completely alive again, alive to the marrow of their bones, all that had been scattered and broken in the morning brought home again to their clasped hands.

Now, while Françoise got ready for bed, Paul and Mélanie walked all around the garden. From far off in the kitchen Louise and

Marie heard the voices rise and fall, the quick laughter, the silences.

They talked first of all that had happened in town, Mélanie still speaking with a little of the nervous energy of her business self, Paul asking questions, nodding his head, sympathizing, advising, setting the worries and triumphs of the day in their true perspective—so she felt.

But little by little the garden caught them in its multitude of spells, wound them round with its thousand lives, and business affairs simply didn't seem worth talking about as they reached the far path and stopped to examine the peach buds on the espaliers, to exclaim at the great orange slugs out for their evening ravages.

"Paul, wait here, I must get some salt to put on them—the garden will be devoured!"

And when she came back, running, breathless, so young, Paul felt moved to speak of his work, to share the burden of his thinking, to feel it touch another human being, take on reality, *sound* . . .

The dusk was there, making the garden mysterious and big—one could get lost in the shadows under the oaks in the far meadow. The marguerites shone like stars in the thick grass. The birds were singing their evening songs.

And as she listened, while the words flowed out without stopping in Paul's grave insistent voice, Mélanie stopped to pull up a weed, to note that a tree needed pruning, to remind herself to cut back the periwinkles, to listen to the cry of a heron far off——

"Listen, Paul, the heron——"

For her, happiness was made up of a thousand different things, and this moment was as much listening for Françoise's voice calling her to come upstairs as it was coming back to her garden, observing every detail and bud and leaf, as it was feeling Paul near her, his physical presence which moved her so deeply, as it was listening to his voice and following his ideas; in and out of them all her being flowed. And would Louise know just how to make the omelette perfectly? she interrupted herself—while Paul inexorably pursued the mounting curve of his thought.

"You see, what I have been coming to realize is that without all these tensions, these extremes, this constant ever mobile antithesis, there could not be a unity. The unity is in these very things which seem to negate it."

Mélanie didn't dare to interrupt, but she was thinking, I am like a little donkey and he is always holding a carrot in front of my nose but I can never quite reach the carrot; I can never quite understand. Did he completely understand himself? She stopped short of that question. One must live by faith, by instinct, by love. A negative answer to that question would have destroyed the whole fabric of their life.

They had made the whole journey round the garden and had arrived at the *potager,* with its neat rows of promises, the tiny lettuces, the sturdy radishes, the frail tops of the carrots. Mélanie stooped down to look into the cold frames, where great thick green bunches of cress were waiting to be picked.

"Here, darling, taste this. Isn't it delicious?" She stood and looked up at the trees and the sky. "How Mother loved it. Do you remember the sandwiches she always made on Sundays? Cress sandwiches——"

"Ah, how I love you, my darling," said Paul quietly. "What would I do without you?—even though you don't listen when I talk to you and have no idea what I mean."

"But, Paul, I do listen"—she smiled guiltily and pleadingly as he lifted her up (she had been stooping over the frames)—"and sometimes I understand——"

He laughed one of his rare truly gay laughs with no mockery in it. "It's all nonsense anyway. Why should you understand any more than the trees understand, though they are strong and beautiful and well-rooted in the earth like you?"

It was better than understanding, Mélanie decided, to love someone so much, so much that she could never say it, never tell him lightly and easily as he could tell her a hundred times a day. She did not have the words, but how much she admired him for having them!

It was almost dark.

The smell of nasturtiums was overpowering, the nasturtiums that climbed all over the bench and up the wall by the kitchen window.

Suddenly the lights went on in the house.

"Heavens, Françoise must be in bed waiting for me. Come out of the damp, Paul. You'll catch cold."

So they went in to the light, to the warmth, and a half hour later, when Françoise had been told her story and called Mamie back twice for a glass of water, for a kiss, they were gathered round the supper table, with Bo-Bo.

"The soup is cold," Paul said in frigid tones. Cold soup was an offense to the spirit. Mélanie herself got up and took it back to the kitchen. She had hoped that Paul's terrible black mood of the morning was past. What had happened between their magical moment in the garden and now? But there were no answers to these questions. He was as unpredictable as a summer sky.

When she came back with the steaming plates, he and Bo-Bo were having an argument about Françoise. She looked from one to the other of these old antagonists, whose respect for each other was well established after many battles, and laughed.

"My children, drink your soup first and then argue." But it was she herself who began it again by saying:

"I am worried about Françoise, Bo-Bo. She still looks so pale. Is she getting enough to eat?"

Bo-Bo, forthright as always and incorruptible, answered sharply: "She gets plenty to eat, but the poor child needs companions of her own age. She lives here like a princess locked in a tower, alone most of the day."

"She has a rich nature," Paul interposed quickly. "She finds plenty to do."

"Of course she has." Bo-Bo's hair seemed to stand straight up with irritation. "That is exactly the point, monsieur. She is much too intense and too sensitive for her age."

"I don't believe one can be too sensitive."

But this was too much for Mélanie.

"No, Paul, that's not true. She must grow up normally. One *can* be too sensitive. She will suffer terribly when she's older."

"She will suffer in any case. If she's sensitive she will have far more means to cope with her suffering—and other people's."

These discussions, which began with simple practical problems and ended in metaphysics and long arguments on the conduct of life, seemed perfectly preposterous to Bo-Bo, who always tried to bring them down to earth.

"No one wants her to be insensitive, but she will grow up a perfect monster if she doesn't have some contact with children her own age. You must admit, monsieur, that it's a bad sign when she bursts into tears in the middle of her reading lesson."

"Why did she do that, Paul?" Mélanie was instantly alert. "You didn't tell me."

Paul looked at them both with long-suffering patience. "I am trying to train her to concentrate. She must begin to do things even when she doesn't want to. She got a little tired, that's all."

"But, darling, she's only five."

"At five I was learning Latin." Paul's memories of his childhood, Mélanie always thought, had become slightly out of proportion in perspective. More likely he was nine and had forgotten it now.

"Well, if so, it was monstrous, monsieur." He was certainly not a good example. He had never learned to play with other children, living in that dark house alone with his silent father and the servants. Sometimes the power parents had over their children and wielded so ruthlessly frightened Bo-Bo.

"Besides," she went on inexorably, "she is too much wrapped up in you. You play on her emotions as if she were an instrument."

"Bo-Bo," warned Mélanie quietly. But Paul had turned to ice.

"If Bo-Bo thinks that, by all means let her say it. I myself never had a father who was the slightest bit interested in whether I learned to read or not. I longed to be loved." He shrugged. "Well, it seems Françoise is loved too much. There you have the human story, Bo-Bo, in a nutshell, eh? We spoil our own children in revenge against our parents. It's a vicious circle."

Everything, it sometimes seemed, was a vicious circle to Paul. And yet he was wise, he was right—that was what was so terrible. He was always, from one point of view, in the right. One could not argue with him. One could only, as Mélanie did now, as she always did, attack the whole problem from a different angle.

"Listen, darling, I have an idea. Let's have little Pierre Poiret as our guest for the summer. He's just a year older than Françoise, and Suzanne needs a rest. We would be doing them a good turn. Please, let us do that," she ended.

It was logical. It was simple. It was irrefutable.

"Do whatever you think best, Mélanie," he said with a sudden radiant smile, as if there had never been an argument at all. "Yes, let us have little Pierre, by all means."

But Mélanie could not answer his smile. It was a cruel smile. For after all, the real answer, the human answer to this problem, was something they had talked over and over. Mélanie got up from the table to hide the tears in her eyes. She wanted another child. She had always wanted a whole tribe of children. But on this subject Paul was adamant. He refused, he said, to bring another creature into this sorry world—a boy, perhaps, who would just be old enough to be killed by the Germans in the next war.

This was the wound in their marriage.

But now the war was over, they must have another child, make a new beginning, believe. To Mélanie his attitude was a betrayal of life itself. They could not give up now.

And after all, she reminded him, what had they suffered compared to many of their friends who had lost husbands, sons, seen their houses razed to the ground? To her it was a concrete personal problem. To him it was an abstract one. His pessimism was impersonal, which only made it the more impossible to fight.

To Mélanie it was simply impossible to conceive that there would be another war in their lifetime. To believe that there would be seemed like tempting fate. They must hope and believe, help to make a world in which it would not happen. They must bring up strong brave children who would be ready to make friends with the German children when they grew up—unembittered happy children, responsible children, magnanimous children.

How could one go on living otherwise?

Chapter V

Saturdays were Méla-
nie's days of Freedom. This one began with a great wind making the windows rattle early in the morning, rushing through the trees so that the forest echoed like an ocean and the roar of these airy waves reached the house on the Avenue. Mélanie was up with the birds—to be exact, *a* bird, the woodpecker who had begun tapping one of the elms just outside the window, insistently, as soon as it was light. Soon he was joined by a chorus of sparrows, cheeping busily in their nests in the wistaria that covered the house, by the blackbird sending his cool spring song out from the willow. The whole garden was alive with birds. Moïse answered them plaintively from her stall. Mélanie couldn't stay in bed with all that going on outside. Besides, there were a thousand things to do—these were the days, these April days, when the garden claimed her whole attention. The house might fall to pieces (but Bo-Bo would see that it didn't!), she herself must be out sowing and planting and cultivating, transplanting vegetables from the cold frames, cutting back the bushes, uncovering the flower beds, trimming the hedges. It was simply endless.

Croll arrived at seven, and while she got him a bowl of goat's milk and put Moïse to pasture, he began already to open the big cistern from which he would draw up pailfuls of human manure to put on the garden.

Croll was over seventy and seemed to have grown into his clothes as if the dark brown corduroy were the bark of a tree. His chin wore a perpetual thick stubble that never turned into a beard. His fly had lost all its buttons. He was practically deaf, and as he stood in the courtyard, drinking the milk, holding the bowl awkwardly in his two gnarled hands, he looked primeval, like some spirit of the earth, Mélanie thought, hardly human. But he knew this garden as if it were his own and cared for it with irritable passion, complaining all the time, accomplishing the work of three younger men. He seemed to feel with the plants and trees, to know what they needed as if he had roots in the earth himself. Mélanie hardly ever gave him any orders. They worked together, serving the garden, slaving for it, talking little. He was not interested in the life inside the house, ignored M. Paul. Only Françoise followed him around like a flirtatious kitten, and to her he sometimes talked, telling her his troubles and angers, but all in Flemish so, though she listened gravely, she understood only a word or two. No doubt that was why he talked.

Croll's wife had died twenty years before in childbirth. That much Mélanie knew from hearsay in the village. And his son had come back a few months before, having fought before Liége and later with the Belgian armies in France.

All around them the garden seemed in movement, alive—the burnished leaves shining and waving in the sun and wind, the last year's autumn leaves blown wildly down the paths, while with bent backs they slowly (for how heavy and earth-bound a human body is!) went about their tasks. Mélanie was transplanting lettuce from the cold frames. She could see Croll coming up the path wheeling the metal container with its rich excrement to pour on the garden.

Something was the matter with Croll this morning. He stopped rather often on the way and sighed quite audibly. When Filibert

wound herself round his legs purring, he flung her aside roughly
—a strange and violent gesture for him.

Mélanie wondered what was wrong. She asked him over to help
her for a few moments and talked of this and that while she handed
him the little plants one by one. Finally she said:

"What is your son going to do now he is home again?"

Croll went off with the plants and set them down near the beds
as if he hadn't heard.

But Mélanie followed him and shouted the question again.

This time he stood up, took off his cap, and scratched his head
in a bewildered way. It seemed a hard question to answer. Finally
he looked down at his sabots, kicked a bit of dirt, and said shortly:

"He's a lazy good-for-nothing."

Mélanie remembered the pride with which he had brought his
son to see her in 1913 when Jacques was called up for military
service. He was a fine gay boy with a red face and the rather bold
good humor of the Flemish peasant, quite unabashed and natural
as he joked with Paul. What had happened to him? He had been
working as a delivery boy for a big dairy in the neighborhood
then and was proud of his horses. Instantly Mélanie decided to go
and find him right after breakfast. She never doubted that she
could help people, that she knew what was good for them, what
they needed.

Croll had gone back to his own job and they did not talk any
more. It was time anyway to go in and wash before breakfast.

A couple of hours later, with Françoise skipping like a lamb
with spring fever beside her, Mélanie walked toward the village
across the great fields at the end of the avenue. The skies over
these fields were always magnificent, and today, with immense
white clouds sailing across them, the earth itself seemed lifted up
and to be soaring through space. It almost made one dizzy.

Françoise never stopped asking questions.

"What is that man over there doing, Mamie?"

"Sowing oats for the horses, darling. See what a great gesture he makes with his arm as he walks—and that big sack over his shoulder is full of seed."

"Who lives in that little hole, Mamie?" and she bent down to peer inside it.

"A rabbit, my treasure."

"What is that singing up in the air? Where is it, Mamie?"

"That's a lark—he's so high up we can't see him."

But Françoise was so busy with her questions that she couldn't be bothered listening to the answers.

When they got to the village Mélanie stopped at La Grand Louise's (as she was called to distinguish her from La Petite Louise who worked for the Duchesnes). La Grande Louise came every two weeks to do the heavy laundry.

"Hé, bonjour!" she called from her tiny vegetable garden.

Françoise had never seen her except bending over a big wooden tub in the courtyard at home. She stared now, full of amazement to think that La Grande Louise ever did anything else.

"Run along to the end of the garden and look at the rabbits, darling."

Immediately the two women began an animated conversation. Even Mélanie's gestures became the gestures of a peasant when she spoke Flemish. She might have been a neighbor from across the road. After she had asked about the garden, and about Louise's family and they had spoken of the cold spring, she came to the point.

"I have come to find out what is wrong with Jacques, Croll's son."

"Ah, madame"—Louise shook her head—"he's changed. He has the war sickness——"

"You don't say." Mélanie frowned and nodded back, one hand on her hip. The people of the village loved her. She felt somehow like family. She was not proud. She had none of the airs of the small bourgeois who came to jerry-built summer villas in the late spring and looked down on the peasants.

"And where could I find him, Louise? Let me have a talk with him. I've known him since he was Françoise's age."

Louise nodded her head in the direction of Croll's house. "Likely he's in bed still. Old Croll is helpless. The boy is too strong for him. What he needs is a good beating first and then a mother, someone to look out for him, that's what he needs," she said, smiling a broad smile with her wide mouth as Mélanie went off, only calling back:

"Keep Françoise with you, Louise. I'll be back in half an hour."

Croll's house was the poorest in the village, but his garden was always neat and he had two fine rose bushes Mélanie had given him on either side of the stone front doorstep. Instinctively she looked them over to see how they had survived the winter. Inside, the little stone house was dark with the dank smell of a hearth where the fire has died out and of Croll's abominable tobacco which he made himself out of weeds. It had only one room. Jacques was asleep on the double bed, half dressed, with a dirty old quilt pulled over him. Mélanie longed to get at it and give it a thorough scrubbing. But she had not come for that.

She went over to the bed and looked down at his sleeping face. He's nothing but a child, she thought with instant compassion. And heaven knows what he's been through.

Mélanie went to the hearth and started to light a fire with the few pieces of sticks and wood lying about.

Suddenly Jacques sat up, still half asleep, and shouted:
"Who's there?"

"It's all right, Jacques. It's Mme. Duchesne, your old friend."

As he woke himself up, his face became sullen and empty.

"What are you doing here?"

For a moment Mélanie hesitated. She had had no plan when she arrived, but in that moment of hesitation she made up her mind.

"I need an extra man, Jacques. We are in the middle of the spring planting. I wondered if you would come and help."

"Why should I?" He yawned and reached for a shirt hanging over the end of the bed. The tone was insolent.

"You mustn't speak to me like that, Jacques," she said firmly.

For the first time a glimmer of his old face slid over the new mask, like a faint light that came on and then went off.

"I'm no good for work, madame. I don't like work," he explained rather patiently.

"Nonsense. I never knew a harder worker than you. You're going to come along with me now and have a try. Do it for me. Remember how you used to come over and steal the apples? We were good friends then."

But as Mélanie talked to him with brisk assurance she felt more and more that there was a real barrier between him and the world. The war sickness, that was what Louise had called it. Well, they must get him well. And the first thing was to get him away from the demoralizing atmosphere of the house.

The fire was burning brightly now, and she looked around for some coffee to heat in the one saucepan hanging on a nail by the hearth. While she made coffee Jacques stumbled out to the pump and threw cold water over his face. He looked a little more like a human being when he came in. His clothes, Mélanie thought, exactly expressed his state of mind—somewhere between army and civilian life. He still wore army pants and boots but had taken one of his father's blue shirts.

"Come," she said, "let's have our coffee out of doors in the sun."

He followed her to the step and sat down, bringing two tin cups with him. It was easier outside. They sat still in the sun, silently, and drank the hot brown liquid which was mostly chicory and tasted bitter. There was no sugar in the house.

"It's been a long time, eh, Jacques?" Mélanie spoke out of the silence.

He looked away and didn't answer. Somewhere, somehow the light had gone out of him, the desire to live had gone out of him. He was passive. There was no time, long or short, in the place where he was now.

If she could only get him to laugh, just once, Mélanie thought, that would be the beginning. He was looking at her sideways now.

"I'll come with you," he said. "Might as well," he added.

"Come along, then. Half my morning is gone. We'll have to work like beavers to catch up."

From behind the tiny windows in the stone farmhouses the neighbors watched them go down the street and nodded to each other. Trust Mme. Duchesne to know when she was needed. She was better than a priest.

At Louise's house they stopped to pick up Françoise.

"Oh, Mamie, can't we take one with us?" she begged, hating to leave the rabbits, but then stopped and stared silently.

"Françoise, this is Jacques, Croll's son. He is back from the army now and he is coming to help us with the garden."

As they began the walk home, Mélanie talked about the garden and the animals and told Jacques something of what had happened while he was away. He didn't answer or seem to be paying attention, and she observed him curiously.

He was tall and gangling, the very opposite type from his father, and he had grown thinner. Mélanie suspected that he didn't get enough to eat. Later she would get the family doctor over to examine him.

After a while, as they came up into the great rolling fields, they were silent. Françoise clung to her mother's hand. Jacques looked out on the familiar land as if he were a stranger.

All around them, as they reached the high plateau, the larks were singing loudly. Jacques stopped and took notice for the first time.

"It's good to hear the larks again—that means we are really in the spring," she said.

"They sang over the guns," he answered shortly. "Stupid little creatures."

But once more the glimmer of light came and went in his eyes. Then they trudged on.

Later, in the garden, when Françoise had gone off for her lesson (Mélanie arranged it so that Jacques would be out of earshot of his father), she tried to get him to talk about the war. He worked badly, stopping for no reason, as if lost, hardly in thought, but in a sort of stupor. And she did not push him. She knew she mustn't force things or he wouldn't come back. And her whole plan depended on his coming back.

In the middle of the morning Paul came down to find Mélanie, to get a breath of air, to tell her that today Françoise's lesson had gone very well and he was pleased with her; and in her turn she took him to see the quince bursting out into pale pink flowers and already buzzing with greedy bees. She told him about Jacques. Paul was interested at once. Their house was always the haven for some lame duck or other, and the minute people were in trouble Paul could be unbelievably patient and kind as well as understanding.

A half hour later Mélanie was delighted to hear laughter from the far corner of the garden where she had left Jacques to trim the paths. Paul was telling him long grotesque stories of how the Belgians had teased the occupying forces all through the war. The universal weapon had been mockery of all kinds, from the broad humor of stealing the pants of a group of officers who had gone for a swim in the lake in the forest to more subtle and daring jokes like that of seeing that a copy of the chief underground paper, *La Libre Belgique,* found its way every morning to the commanding general's desk in Brussels. "And if there's one thing the German can't stand, it's being laughed at."

But when Paul had gone back to his study, Jacques lay down in the grass among the daisies and looked up at the sky until he fell asleep. Croll's anger and Mélanie's imperious maternal solicitude could not touch him yet.

There Françoise found him; she stood a long time looking down at this strange man lying in the grass. But when he opened his eyes and stared at her as if he didn't see her at all, with a goat's blank gaze, she ran, ran away to find Bo-Bo at the top of the house, cleaning out the attic.

"What is it, my treasure? What's the matter?"

"Oh, Bo-Bo," she said, hiding her face in Bo-Bo's clean cotton skirt that smelled so safe, "there's a soldier—he's sleeping in the garden."

"Well," said Bo-Bo matter-of-factly, "no doubt he's tired. Let him sleep, then."

"It's Croll's son, Bo-Bo." And then she burst into tears without knowing why and sobbed, "I don't like soldiers. I hate them!"

Chapter VI

Sunday was a special day, and although the Duchesnes were not churchgoers, they honored the day with certain formalities. Mélanie put on what she called her "chatelaine's dress," a green dress of heavy cotton material, the square-necked bodice fitting tightly and the full skirt falling in great folds to her bare sandaled feet. It was her day for writing letters, for sewing, for sitting long hours in the garden and *not* working. Françoise wore white shoes and socks, and even Bo-Bo, going to visit her sister in town, appeared in an old-fashioned and charming dress with an elaborate lace vestee and high collar.

After midday dinner Louise and Marie, transformed into peacocks, walked carefully down the avenue in their high-heeled shoes, their natural color pasted over with rouge, and Lou-Lou even carrying a parasol. They would meet their young men at the café at the Corners about a mile down the road. There they would sit outdoors and drink beer until they grew sentimental and held hands or went off to find privacy in the forest while the long spring afternoon melted away.

As soon as they were off, a great peace descended on the house and the garden. Mélanie could putter about the kitchen freely; she loved preparing the tea, bringing out the best china (which the servants were not allowed to touch) and the best silver, and on this Sunday, in a burst of happiness and to welcome special friends, making a cake (which was really a magical feat considering that there was no fat, only two eggs, and two spoonfuls of brown sugar at the bottom of the tin). The house felt cool and clean after the dazzle outside. Filibert sat with her paws tucked in on the window sill, sleepily watching the birds. Françoise helped by licking the spoon and running errands. Paul came down in his old straw hat and linen jacket; Mélanie thought, He looks like a planter in some West Indian island who should have a great number of black slaves and a café au lait child to fan him while he sits under a palm tree.

"Yes, it's Sunday," he murmured, and kissed the back of her neck. "My wife is in her Sunday dress, my little girl is in her Sunday shoes so she will have to come out and walk sedately down the paths with Papa and never escape like a little goat into the grass." And then, with a sudden change of voice, "There they are! There's Francis——"

The silence of the sun and the bees was shattered by loud welcoming cries and laughter.

"There you are, you old tramp, just the same as ever."

"Come in, come in! Look, Paul. She's elegance itself. Simone, you put us all to shame. Oh, how glad I am to see you!" The warm French kisses first on one cheek, then on the other; and Françoise lifted up and turning her face away from Francis's mustache; and Mélanie calling them in to take off their coats; and the inevitable argument as to where they should sit; and would they catch cold out of doors, what did Paul think?

They decided on the salon, or rather the cloud, which just then covered the sun and made the whole garden dark, decided for them. The salon was the most Sunday place in the house. It always smelled of wax and velvet and leather-bound books, the smell of a rarely used room.

To Françoise, who had followed them because she noticed at once that Francis had a little package in his hand—and could it be chocolates?—to Françoise it was a magical room. It was here that the books of poems in their fine bindings were kept—de Musset and Verhaeren and Ronsard and Hugo, which Papa loved to read aloud. Over against the wall an eighteenth-century cupboard with glass doors had all sorts of treasures. Sometimes she was allowed to stand on a chair and look at these one by one: a doll you could wind up and who then turned, making a funny clicking sound—a jade rabbit (this was Françoise's favorite, and once she had stolen it), a Russian wooden peasant who opened to reveal another inside her and another and another, until finally you came to a baby in swaddling clothes; and lots of other things: lacquer boxes, the finely woven Congolese baskets, and a miniature of Papa when he was a little boy. There was no end to the treasures in the big cupboard. On the other side of the room stood the old-fashioned piano where she and Mélanie sang *"Sur le Pont d'Avignon"* and *"Malbrouk s'en va-t-en guerre"* and *"Ron-ron-ron petit pat-à-pon."*

The two men settled themselves in the corner sofa and were soon enveloped in the smoke of the cigars Francis had brought. (What a disappointment when the present turned out to be cigars!)

Meanwhile, in the kitchen, there was so much to say all at once! The winter had been so long! And they hadn't seen each other for months, these two old friends—Simone, delicate and elegant as if she were sensibility itself with her wide gray eyes and look of an English girl, and Mélanie, brown and sturdy, her straight hair caught back with a round comb, her rather near-together brown eyes flashing out her will, and her small beautiful hands, the hands of an artist or a fine horsewoman, proving the delicacy of her heart.

They had gone to school together and been passionately attached ever since, so much so that it had seemed at times as if neither of them would ever marry or be able to break the silken cords of their mutual jealousy and love.

"My darling, we are forgetting the tea—our men will be wondering what has become of us!"

"But it's so good to see you, it's so *good*," Mélanie said with the love pouring out of her eyes. And then, in a sudden complete change of voice, the voice of catechizing interest, "How is Francis? Is he more cheerful?" For Francis had gone through a time of black rage and despair when the American Congress denied the League of Nations and withdrew its greatest strength, had even at one point threatened suicide, seeing all he had worked for and believed in smashed.

"You know what he's like; at heart he's the greatest optimist in the world—he has persuaded himself now that it won't make such a difference, that the Americans might after all have been more trouble than they were worth."

Just then Françoise pushed open the swing door, and Simone bent down to kiss her again.

"Hello, little soul, did you think we were never coming?"

A half hour later, when they were all settled—Simone on the chaise longue, Mélanie sitting behind the table, the two men comfortable in their corner, and Françoise on the floor playing with the jade rabbit—the talk, which had been stopped like a brook by twigs and rocks and sudden bends in its course, evened out, a smoothly flowing river.

Francis, a lawyer by profession, a playwright in his spare time, was an enthusiast—sentimentalist, Paul called him, and in return he accused Paul of being a cynic. The fact was that they were natural opposites. Whenever they met they argued incessantly. Now they were at it again, so the two women communicated to each other with a smile, as Francis in a paroxysm of impatience turned to Paul with both hands outstretched, shaking with emotion.

"But *voyons,* Paul, you simply cannot *live* and believe that all this horror of the war was for nothing. We *have* to believe!"

Mélanie found herself almost always on Francis's side in these arguments. "We have to believe." Yes, that is what she thought, what she lived by. But Paul seized his advantage at once.

"My dear Francis, don't you see that you give your whole argument away when you say 'have'? There I am in perfect agreement with you, in order to live, to go on living at all, we may *have* to believe. That is metaphysics. We are talking politics. Politically, it is quite clear that immediately after a war it is impossible to put into effect any sort of just international organization. You would have to eliminate the fallibility of human nature first—to eliminate revenge, to start *tabula rasa,* as if there had been no war. But that is just what none of us is capable of doing. We are inextricably involved in the past. It affects our every thought; it's in the stream of our blood."

Here Francis interrupted.

"And just because of that we can learn from the past. Won't everyone be willing to make sacrifices to ensure peace? Aren't we sufficiently aware of the horror of war now? Isn't that the greatest and most potent thing in the stream of our blood, Germans and Belgians and French and English alike?" He finished triumphantly, looking to his wife for agreement.

And Mélanie turned eagerly to Paul for his answer. How little we ever talk to each other, she was thinking. One had to see one's husband with strangers to learn what he was thinking and when one lives very close to someone one really knows almost nothing about him.

But Simone was hardly listening—she was looking out of the window at Moïse, quietly chewing her cud, in the meadow outside.

"We would be willing to make any sacrifice if we were certain of the outcome. But the only certain thing is that Germany will take any opportunity to repeat her past performances. Say we had been generous, really generous. Say we had been able to draw up a peace which would give Germany every chance to grow strong again, would that ensure the safety of our children, do you imagine? You cannot be such a fool, Francis. The only realistic thing politically is to crush Germany once and for all. And you see, with our idiotic halfway idealism, we are too sickly in conscience to do that."

This was Francis's chance and he seized it, taking the last sandwich and eating it in two mouthfuls in his excitement.

"But, Paul, *mon vieux,* there is an alternative. The alternative is such a strong international organization that if Germany rises again as an aggressor, she can immediately be put down. Don't you see how logical it is?"

"So logical that the only power capable of making this possible has withdrawn before the game is even begun," said Paul shortly. "The Americans are already sick of Europe and European affairs, and one can hardly blame them. Why should they inherit our problems and our old medieval troubles and feuds when they are lucky enough to be three thousand miles from the sources of infection?"

"Because if there is another war, as you believe, they will inevitably be drawn into it and lose millions instead of thousands of their young men, that's why."

Françoise had stopped playing and was looking from one to the other, disturbed by the undercurrent of anger and misunderstanding in the air. She went and stood by her mother, who put an arm round her and whispered something in her ear. But Françoise shook her head decidedly. She wanted to stay here.

"Alas," Paul answered with a sigh, the moment of irritation over, "nations don't learn from experience any more than men do. We learn to live with our limitations, with our neuroses, with our sicknesses—we do not alter them or cure them."

This was more than Mélanie could take. "But, Paul, human beings are capable of growing, surely, of learning from experience. You must admit that," she said passionately.

"Possibly, but it takes a long time, and in the lives of nations that time is infinitely longer than the lifetime of a man. It is centuries. You see, Francis, I am really on your side, but my ideas of time are different. I do not expect things to change for the better in my lifetime or even in Françoise's."

"Look," said Simone quietly, turning toward them a radiant face, "how beautiful the light is in the garden, how peaceful it is —and all you do is get on each other's nerves. What does it all matter?" she said with charming melancholy. "We shall die in any case."

"What's dying, Mummy?" Françoise asked. It sounded nicer than anything they had been talking about.

"It's what the sparrow did that you found in the path, the other day, my treasure."

"I don't like it," said Françoise decidedly. "It's eyes were open but they couldn't see. It looked horrid."

But just then a clear voice called, "Anyone at home?"

The Poirets had arrived from Namur. New life poured into the salon. Mélanie and stout, vague Suzanne went off to make a fresh pot of tea. But Pierre went right up to Françoise and tried to get the jade rabbit away from her. He was a fat little boy, a year older than Françoise; as soon as he saw the rabbit he wanted it. Françoise was purple with anger. Before anyone could do anything she and Pierre were on the floor, kicking each other lustily.

"Children, children," Emile remonstrated in his soft gentle voice, quite helpless before such violence.

Paul had not moved. He was fascinated by this unexpected demonstration of temperament in Françoise, amused, delighted. It was Simone who rose to the occasion, surprised the two children with a hearty smack each, and took them out into the hall to make the peace. Actually nothing could have been a better beginning to a friendship. They had earned each other's respect. Françoise, wiping her tears of rage away, looked at Pierre and smiled a mischievous and delighted smile. "Shall we go and see the ducks?" she said magnanimously.

"Yes," Pierre said, and they ran off together.

Simone went to the kitchen to tell Mélanie and Suzanne what had happened. The men were left alone.

Emile Poiret was the most perfectly gentle person in the world, so much so that always, wherever he went, he called out in both men and women a desire to cherish and look after him. He seemed as helpless as a saint, was in a way a saint, teaching botany in a little country school, hiding his real learning from the world, and gradually building up his collection of the flora of Belgium. With his full brown beard and his thick-lashed brown eyes, hidden under a large black hat, going out in all weathers with his specimen box and his trowel, he was treated by his neighbors with the deference given in older times to the village "simple." He had married a village girl, and his whole life had the quality of a Francis Jammes poem, pure and devoted and with its sources deep in his religion, for he was a Catholic. Even Paul was silenced by the simplicity of Emile's faith, and by his own tenderness for this old school friend, who had made such a poor match and, alone among them all, seemed to have found the secret of happiness.

"While it is still light, let us go into the garden," said Emile. "Are there hepaticas this year? You know, Suzy and I have tried and tried to get them to grow. How does Mélanie do it?"

"Oh, you passionate gardeners," Paul teased him. "The world might fall to pieces, but if there were hepaticas coming out, you would manage to hold the Last Judgment back an hour or two!"

But they were all glad to get into the open air, to saunter slowly up and down the big path in front of the house, where they could walk three abreast, smoking their cigars, stopping to listen to the bells ringing the angelus. Paul and Francis were soon deep in discussion, while Emile listened with one ear but left them every minute or so to examine a bush or a plant, to pull the dead leaves off and release the young shoots of the daffodils, to see how the grapevine in the arbor had survived the winter.

Meanwhile, in the kitchen, forgetting all about the tea, while the water in the kettle boiled away, the three women were discussing the little scene between Françoise and Pierre.

"How is Pierre, Suzy?"

"Well," Suzanne answered timidly, "Emile believes that he is going to be brilliant—you know he can read already. But he is a very violent nature. We have been worried about his temper."

"Well, why not?" Simone interposed. "He's a healthy, lusty little self-willed boy." Simone's whole attitude toward life was laissez faire. She could not really understand Mélanie's wanting to change everyone and everything.

"He needs discipline," said Mélanie quite severely.

"I know"—Suzanne smiled deprecatingly—"but you know Emile, how gentle he is. He can't bear any sort of violence. He says we must not impose our will upon the child."

"Nonsense. Let us have him for the summer, please do. Françoise needs a companion and you need a rest."

Suzanne looked a little troubled. What would Emile say?

"Come, don't say no, don't hesitate. It would give us so much pleasure."

At this moment the peace of the evening was interrupted by a loud quacking in the duck yard as if all the ducks were being attacked at once, as indeed they were, for Françoise and Pierre had at last succeeded in climbing over the wire fence and were chasing them first to one side and then to the other.

"Françoise!" It was Mamie's most severe voice, and Françoise stopped in her tracks and waited for the storm. Pierre, quite unconscious of the danger they were in, was laughing loudly, standing like a king among his slaves, completely absorbed in this new game.

"Saperlipopette"—this was Mélanie's worst swearword, ejaculated with fury—"come out at once, both of you. Pierre, stop that immediately!"

And while Emile took his son off, knelt down, holding his two hands, and explained to him that he was being cruel to the poor

ducks and they might die of fright, Mélanie had hauled the screaming Françoise off into the house to give her a good spanking.
"Now go to bed and I'll come up later and talk to you. Mamie is
very disappointed."

But spanking did not have the intended effect on Françoise,
to whom it was a fearful humiliation. She put the covers over her
head and spent the next hour plotting revenge upon her mother.
She would pull up all the flowers. She would kill the ducks. She
would never speak to her mother again.

The afternoon had gone, quite suddenly. It was evening. The
long sharp shadows against the brilliant spots of sunlight in the
grass now melted into a dusk. A white veil of mist hung over the
garden. It was time to go, to go back to the city, back to work. It
was time for friends to part. How short it had seemed!

Now they were putting on their hats, Mélanie suddenly couldn't
bear it that she had seen so little of Simone, of Emile to whom she
was devoted.

"Emile, we haven't been round the garden once!" she said de-
spairingly.

"But I saw the hepaticas. I saw everything. The garden is beautiful, as beautiful as ever." He smiled his gentle smile.

"Well, well." They were gathered now in the hall, and Paul,
standing one step up on the stairs, looked down on them. "You
must come again—soon. After all, the war is over; you no longer
have any excuse at all not to see us," he mocked.

"How can we bear to see such hopeless pessimists!" Francis
teased. "It will take me a week to get over your dreadful ideas."

"Good-by, dear Mélanie."

"Good-by, Suzanne." And then, with imperious insistence,
"We'll expect little Pierre next month, around the fifteenth, eh?
You won't forget."

And then they were gone; only their voices floated back, far
away already, and the click of the gate. They were gone.

Mélanie sighed. She and Paul went up the stairs slowly arm in arm, pausing at the landing for a last look out and to listen to the sleepy chirping in the wistaria.

"Tired, Mélanie?"

"A little, darling—we'll have supper soon." She leaned against him for an instant. "Go in and speak to Françoise—she's in bed. And tell her I'll come and kiss her good night and bring her some milk. You know she was really terribly naughty."

But when Paul pushed open the nursery door only the lambs gamboling on the wall were awake. Françoise, with her hands folded prayerfully under her cheek in the immemorial gesture of children, was fast asleep. Or so he imagined.

Actually she was wide awake. She was already putting up her defenses against them. She did not want a long talk about what was right and what was not. She wanted to be left alone and to think about her new friend. Françoise was already a stubborn little girl who knew her own mind. Already she was not to be possessed.

Chapter VII

On Sundays the texture of their lives was woven of one piece, but on Monday morning all the threads seemed to separate. Each member of the household had to meet his own problems, to go back into his own life, and these lives were so separate and distinct it seemed at times as if they were hardly related at all. For what had Mélanie's business worries to do with Paul's questionings of the universe, or his careful perfectionism in expressing them with her voluble telephone conversations to old clients to tell them that the suite was to be put up for sale? And what had either of these to do with Bo-Bo's painstaking darning of the beautiful old linen sheets which were beginning to fall to pieces? Or with the multitude of secret occupations Françoise set herself in the garden—the nest of a mouse?

The daffodils faded and the tulips and bleeding heart came out. The buds on the lilac burst into leaf. The willow put forth long yellow leaves. The robins built their nests. And in the house the curtains were taken down and washed and put up again. Lou-Lou began to wonder if her fiancé would ever seriously consider marriage. Marie broke off with one young man and took on another. Croll worried about the snails eating his cabbages and began to train the beans up the long poles.

Only Jacques had no problems, because he seemed to have no life of his own, nothing that drove him one way or another. He missed the army, missed regular meals—too lazy to forage for himself—missed his pals and the leaves in strange towns where no one was critical if he felt like getting drunk or going to a whore. He came to the place every day because it was nicer there than at home; he got a free lunch and a few francs if he worked (Bo-Bo kept strict account of what he accomplished and doled out small sums when he deserved them). And he liked being around the child. Françoise, after her first timidity and hostility, was now his adoring slave. It was pleasant to be worshiped like this, like a god, a worship having no relation at all to what he thought of himself or what anyone else thought of him. He made her a kite and they used to go out sometimes to the far fields and fly it. It was a pleasant enough life while it lasted, but sometimes he wondered how long Madame's patience would last. He couldn't really make out why she hadn't sent him off weeks ago.

But while his son amused himself as best he could, Croll worked on like an ant, never stopping for an instant, lifting the plants into life as if he literally were creating them, and talking to Filibert now that Françoise was rarely around. Filibert sat between the rows of carrots and onions with her paws tucked in and listened unwinkingly to the long tragic complaints. Filibert was very quiet these days and had grown noticeably stouter.

"No one knows what's going to happen," Croll would say, looking up at the sky and then bending heavily over his spade—was it a storm or a revolution that he envisaged dimly? "It's all at sixes and sevens. The young'uns come back and they're good for nothing. The new mailman stops for an hour in every farm, is nothing but a gossip—the price of food would make my grandfather turn in his grave. Ah yes, Filibert, it's a bad time. It's a bad time—at least when the Germans were here, we knew where we were, what it was all about, had something to live for. Now they're gone, it's no better. No one can eat that American bacon, and where is the flour they talked so much about?"

Only after a long enumeration of the things he had picked up at the village café, where he went once a week on Sundays in a clean shirt to drink a glass of port with some cronies, only when he had repeated this litany, did Croll utter what was closest to his pride. Attacking the snails on the cabbage leaves, he would mutter:

"Spoiled, spoiled, rotten. What is in their minds to let him take his ease in the grass when the garden is going to ruin? Craziness," he muttered savagely. "What's to become of him now? What will he do with himself? No pride, no pride," adding with a kind of satisfaction: "He'll come to a bad end. Ah yes, Filibert, no good will ever come of him now. He'd better have been killed out there by the Boches, eh, Filibert?" And the old man, suddenly cheerful now that he had said it all out to someone, scratched the cat's neck and her arched back with a rough tenderness.

For once Françoise had come to the end of her ideas: what to do?

Jacques was lying outstretched on one of the white benches under the apple tree, but when she crept up behind him and tickled him with a piece of grass he told her to mind her own business and leave him alone. But what was her own business?

She tried to think of something wonderfully exciting and wicked, but it was too hot to chase the ducks. Inside the house it would be cool and dark and still. That was the answer!

A few moments later she called softly to Jacques, and her tone sounded just secret enough to make him sit up. She was standing

at the window of the salon. He was rarely invited into the house
and he was curious about what it was like in there. In a second he
had swung himself up over the high window sill and was standing
in the room. As if by agreement, they were as quiet as mice. Françoise had drawn a chair up to the cupboard—every time there was a
creak on the stairs her heart beat as if it would jump right out.

Everything in the cupboard was magic, everything had its own
secret; that's what made it such a wonderful place. The Russian
woman had her secret inside; the doll had her dancing secret,
though she looked so stiff and frozen forever into her pirouette;
even the Congolese baskets had a secret woven into the fine design.
For Mamie had told her that these baskets were never sold; they
could not be bought. They must always be given to a friend. Françoise herself was full of secrets as she showed Jacques each of these
treasures, one by one.

At first he was more interested in looking around him, at the
books, the shabby velvet armchairs, the rugs and brightly colored
paintings. He felt he was in a museum, not a house. But Françoise
demanded his attention, and he was forced to join in her game,
nodding his head, looking properly awed and excited like a tourist
being shown a town by an experienced guide. She could say a few
words in Flemish now and she whispered excitedly.

But when she finally showed him the jade rabbit, the treasure of
treasures, the quality of Jacques's attention changed suddenly. This
was not a toy, a child's game—this was a jewel. This, he thought to
himself, had value. It could be sold.

Françoise beamed. He was showing an entirely proper awe of
the king of the cupboard.

The postman's shrill horn interrupted them. Bo-Bo would come
down in a second. Jacques was as quick to sense the danger as she.
He lifted her down from her chair, slipped the rabbit into his
pocket, turned the key of the glass doors of the cabinet, and
jumped out of the window before Françoise knew what was
happening.

She crept out of the salon just as Bo-Bo reached the top landing and heard the door of the salon click. Peering down, Bo-Bo saw a little figure in a pink pinafore tiptoeing through the hall.

"What are you doing in the house, Françoise?" she asked severely. "And in the salon, what's more! Run right out into the sunshine. It's no day for a little girl to be indoors."

Françoise was only too glad to make her escape. . . .

Two days later the theft was discovered and the household questioned. Mélanie was upset. The rabbit itself had no importance, but the idea that someone in the house would steal was important. It was a betrayal of trust. It seemed almost like a personal attack. Hadn't she dealt justly with everyone, always? And now injustice and dishonesty filled the very air she breathed. The worst of it was that as long as no one was accused, everyone felt accused and Marie and Lou-Lou behaved very sullenly. It was like an infection.

As usual Bo-Bo did what she thought best without regard to Madame's ideas. She was quite sure that Françoise had stolen the rabbit (she was the only person known to have been in the salon that morning), and, fiercely protective, she wanted Françoise to have a chance to own up to it without the moral inquisition which would be sure to follow if she told Madame and Monsieur.

For Françoise the three days that followed were a nightmare. She longed to throw herself in Bo-Bo's lap and confess that she had stolen it—that would be a relief. That would be much easier than bearing all the guilt and yet knowing that she hadn't stolen it and that therefore Jacques must have. But how could she confess without getting Jacques into fearful trouble? People were sent to prison for stealing. The worst was that she had to pretend that everything was all right. Mamie had immediately asked her to tell the truth. And she had answered honestly that she hadn't taken it. No one except Bo-Bo doubted her word.

Oh, it was a terrible time. It seemed unbelievable that the rest of the world went on as usual, that the pigeons never stopped cooing, that the sun shone and Filibert purred when she scratched her under her chin. Nothing had changed, it seemed, and yet the whole world was black.

She waited anxiously for Jacques, but he hadn't come since the day of the theft. And how could she face him now? The only person who was any comfort at all was old Croll, who hadn't even been told of the affair since he was obviously not guilty: he never set foot in the house. With Croll she could feel safe; she followed him about like a little dog, fetching his tools, watching him silently, comforted beyond words by his cracked, lined old face when he gave her one of his rare smiles. He did not know that she was a criminal.

Bo-Bo's patience was almost at an end. She scrubbed Françoise's neck and ears much harder than was necessary and combed her curls ruthlessly in the morning. She dropped all the little pet names and called her simply "Françoise," as if she were quite beyond the pale.

By the time it came to her lesson with her father on the fourth day and still Jacques had failed to come, Françoise felt violently sick to her stomach.

"My darling," Paul said, caressing her cheek very gently, "you're so pale. Don't you feel well? Shall we give up the lesson this morning? Come and sit in Papa's lap."

This tender concern was too much. All the anguish she had been carrying around with her, the lonely burden, was suddenly too much to hold. She gave a great wail of despair, buried her face in his shoulder, and shook with huge sobs.

Paul, completely bewildered by this enormous grief, couldn't understand what she was saying, but let her cry it out, rocking her gently, until she began to be quiet.

"My bird, my little soul, nothing can be as bad as that, nothing in all the world."

She had told him through her tears, but the worst of all was that he hadn't understood. How was she to do it again?

"Papa, Papa," she was crying again, beating her fists against him now, hysterically.

But finally he understood. And when he understood he was terribly angry. The theft didn't matter, but that Jacques, whom they had taken in and trusted, should put Françoise through such an ordeal, that was unforgivable. Hardly conscious of what he was doing, for his anger could be like a seizure, Paul went to the desk, almost dropping Françoise on his way, and took a pistol out of the drawer. Bo-Bo was horrified to see him running down the path a moment later, like a madman, with a pistol in his hand. Luckily for him, Jacques was nowhere to be found, and before he could reach the road, Bo-Bo had caught him and was scolding him with a fury augmented by her fright.

"Monsieur, you must be out of your mind. What has happened? What is it?"

Croll too had been roused from his pruning and came to see what on earth possessed the master.

All of this Françoise watched from the window, shaking with fear. But she couldn't hear her father shout at the bewildered old man.

"Your son, that's what the matter is! Your son is a criminal. He should be locked up."

Croll shrugged his shoulders and bent his head. It was beyond understanding what had happened, but it was all exactly as he knew it would be. His son had got into some trouble.

Bo-Bo's first thought was to find Françoise, the little treasure, the poor little soul whom she had so wrongly suspected. She found her being sick in the bathroom, and put her to bed.

Never had cool sheets and Bo-Bo's rough hand stroking her forehead seemed so sweet to Françoise. It was all over at last. She could go to sleep.

The whole business was sickening—that's what came of all this irrational good will of Madame's. They would have done far better to let Jacques work out his own salvation, that is what Bo-Bo privately thought.

But all this was the beginning and not the end of a long story. Mélanie would not give up her lost sheep. She refused to call in the police: "If he once feels he is being hunted as a criminal, he will become one." That's what she thought, and the marvelous thing about Mélanie, what set her apart from most people, was that she acted on what she believed. She did not talk about things. She did them. She waited until word came from the village that Jacques was back again and then went off and fetched him, scolded him fiercely as if he were her own son, made him thoroughly ashamed of himself for what he had done to Françoise, and then took him into town with her to the business. There, she thought, she could keep an eye on him, give him odd jobs to do and keep him out of mischief.

Also there were a hundred precious little objects lying around the salesrooms which anyone could put in his pocket; she wanted to prove that she still trusted him. Mélanie was not going to give up yet.

More than that, the whole affair had roused Paul. He liked Jacques. He always felt a great sympathy for the sinner (not, like his wife, as an object for reform, but intrinsically and out of a feeling of identification) and, after his first rage, found himself thinking more and more about the whole problem. After all, a man who had been through the fighting at Ypres, at Dixmude, and then the four long years after those supreme battles of the Belgian army, to such a man whose whole adult life had been spent in mud and filth and boredom and danger, what did stealing a rabbit mean? What standards of behavior could he have? And how could those standards be given him now? By what means?

The truly heroic struggles come after the war is over, thought Paul, the struggles to solve the millions of human problems left in its wake. The full ugliness of war, the waste, the destruction is visible in the living rather than the dead, terrible as their numbers may be. And this responsibility, these ideas he could fully share with his wife. After months of lying apart, each reading a book until they fell asleep, he and Mélanie now had long talks about the whole matter. Jacques had become the symbol of a national responsibility. What they could do individually to help one soldier must be needed on a gigantic scale, must be organized and the problem fought as one fights a contagious disease. Lying side by side, late into the night, Mélanie resting her head on his shoulder, his arm around her, they found again something of the intimacy they had almost lost.

For Mélanie it was a blessing to have this positive creative work to think of and to take her mind off the constant petty strains of the business and the mortgage which they had managed to put off for another three months.

Now she was always running out for an hour to consult with their psychiatrist friend Charles Bockman, to make inquiries of the various existing organizations as to what exactly was being done to rehabilitate the soldiers, of what could be done. From her friends and clients she heard of other cases, similar to Jacques's. She went to the judge of the Children's Court, for some of the soldiers returning were still minors. She got in touch with officer friends and tried to make them interested in helping to seek out the men who most needed help. She talked to all her business relations, urging them each to take on at least one returned soldier, even at a sacrifice. And she was outraged to discover how little some of them were anxious to co-operate. The fact was that the whole country was in a state of depression and financial chaos. Businesses were retrenching rather than expanding. Everywhere people waited for times to change, feared the growing power of the Left in politics, were anxious to pull what they could out of a bad state of affairs.

Why were people perfectly willing to give money and time to curing the physically ill but always unwilling to face the problems of the mentally bewildered and disabled like Jacques? Already the reaction against the soldiers had begun. A uniform, which had

been the symbol of the country's pride and resistance, was now becoming the symbol of all that everyone wanted to forget. They were
tired of making sacrifices, tired of giving time and energy and
money and heart to the needs of the community. Each wanted to
be left alone to work out his own destiny as best he could.

Tirelessly Mélanie poured her passion and energy into the meetings she addressed, and the more she poured out, the more seemed
to flow into her.

"We can lose the war in the next twenty years," she would say.
"We cannot afford to have a lost generation. We cannot afford to
grow a crop of incompetent neurotics who will be in the positions
of power when our children are twenty. More than that, are we to
abandon these children of the nation, as if they were dead? Thank
them and wash our hands of them?" So she spoke in the small
shabby halls of parochial clubs, in the elegant salons of the rich
and noble, everywhere where there were a few people gathered together who might listen and help.

Paul accepted the presidency of the Brussels P.E.N. club partly
at least in order to be able to use his influence with the writers and
intellectuals.

The affair of the jade rabbit was assuming large proportions.

Chapter VIII

But what of Jacques
himself? What really went on inside him? What in human and
not theoretic terms did the "delayed shock" Dr. Bockman so glibly
diagnosed mean?

He did not, of course, know himself. He kept trying to find a way
back. Having money to spend had seemed a way, but when he had
a little money what was there to do with it? You couldn't buy decent liquor. He wasn't interested in girls. He didn't know himself

what happened when he started doing up a package and then stopped in the middle and just stood there, without the will to tie the string.

Only one thing had happened. More and more he felt safe with Madame. He didn't really listen to what she said, but her energetic exhortations, her unfailing good humor, something simple and powerful in her which he felt strongly, made him happy to serve her. It was perhaps a little like being in the army to be ordered around and scolded. He did not remember his mother: now he was allowed to be a child.

"Jacques, fetch me my bag, will you? I left it upstairs in the library." He might be gone a long time, but eventually Madame's imperious voice would remind him.

"Jacques, hurry up! I asked you for my bag fifteen minutes ago! Have you fallen asleep up there?"

For her sake he shaved in the morning and put on a clean shirt, twice a week, which Jean's wife washed and ironed for him. He ate his meals with the Jeans, as they were called, and they fed him well. It meant a little extra money, and they could do with it. And after Jean's initial grumbling, he grew rather fond of the silent hulk of a boy to whom he could boast a little and who was useful around the place if you kept after him.

Jacques liked it in town. He loved the feel of the silks and the soft cushions and the bright colors upstairs in the salesrooms. He liked to polish the furniture and the parquet floors. His moments of happiness came when he was using his hands on these jobs that had to do with fine surfaces and beautiful things. He did not have any desire to steal—that one moment in the salon seemed to him like craziness. He was part of the family now, at least of the working family in the business. He did not have to climb in the window to get into a salon. He had his own key to the front door.

He had not seen Françoise since that day a month before. Madame had asked him to come, but it made him uncomfortable even to think of it. He tried to forget Françoise. He slept in a soft bed in a small storeroom on the top floor of the house in town. On Sundays he went home to see his father because Madame insisted on it. But Croll puttered about in his own tiny garden and hardly spoke to him.

The old man was convinced that he was being spoiled and stuck stubbornly to his own ideas about his son. The love in him had burned out when his wife died. He did not have any to give to human beings any more. Only the rose bushes and the grass and trees felt the gentleness of his feet and hands, the gentleness of his heart.

But for Mélanie, Jacques was a comfort and a distraction—thinking about him, she could put aside for the moment those pressing anxious thoughts of accounts and sales.

How was she to keep both the demoiselles on, as well as Jean, unless things got better soon? It was unthinkable to turn them out. She knew all about Mlle. Louvois's long and unhappy love affair, about Mlle. Zumpt's tender care of her mother, who had been paralyzed and semiconscious for five years. They had gone through the good times and the lean times, taken salary cuts on their own initiative, lain awake at night just as she had. They were not employees really—they were partners. The business was in their blood.

The more Mélanie worried, the more Napoleonic she became, the more severe, the more commanding, setting a higher standard for herself and everyone else. If things looked very bad indeed, there was always the tonic of hard work—cleaning out the cupboard of remnants and repricing them, making an inventory, or going over all the bills with patient Mlle. Zumpt to see if they couldn't pay off a little here, a little there, and so satisfy the growing list of creditors. They needed new stock badly, but at present they simply couldn't afford to buy any.

The sale of the great suite did bring in a little cash, enough to get through the month of May at least—thirty days' reprieve, Mélanie thought grimly. And a few small orders came in, partly as a result of her speeches about the soldiers. Old customers were beginning to come back. There were one or two nibbles on large orders—a country house near Knocke, a town house for which two other decorators were making bids. But the fact remained that something radical had to be done.

What? What? She asked herself the question over and over again, sitting at the old roll-top desk, masses of papers piled around her, looking out at the greenness (the trees were in full leaf now) in the courtyard outside.

What would her mother have done? Her mother, with her fierce gaiety and sweep and confidence, her mother, with that business sense which was as much a part of her as her Liberty-silk scarves, as the beautiful brilliant linings to her sober suits. What would she have done? But she didn't have to keep the business alive through four years of war and how many years of depression after it. The tide was flowing in, not flowing out, when she brought her splendid cargoes in on the waves.

"Madame is worrying," said Mlle. Louvois sympathetically as she came in to ask how far Madame would be willing to mark down a table a customer was interested in. She had stood at the door several seconds before Mélanie turned her head.

"Take three hundred francs off the marked price, but no more— we're selling at a loss." And then Mélanie suddenly laughed. "We are not going to give up, you know. I'm going to think of something one of these days. Never say die, as the English put it."

It was the old, almost mechanical reflex of pumping courage into her associates when she most needed it herself.

Mlle. Louvois shook her head and sighed as she went back to the customer. Madame was wonderful, but, looking at it objectively, what could they do? What was to keep all the businesses going in this long period of "after the war"? And would it ever end? She could hear Madame calling "Jacques!" as if she hadn't enough to worry about already without that one!

"Get your coat, Jacques. We are going out." Mélanie always took the boy with her, if it were at all possible, when she had an errand to do, and today she had suddenly decided to go and look at the ready-made suites the Bon Marché did up in such attractive packages and sold for their immediate slick appeal to young married couples, to the people who needed to furnish a place to live in quickly, the soldiers, home and at last able to marry, but with no money to marry on, the tradespeople, and even the farmers who were rebuilding hideous red brick houses on the ruins of beautiful old farms.

So Jacques and she found themselves part of the great staring, milling crowd in a big department store.

"Look, Jacques! Look at that nice young couple—do you suppose they will buy that hideous suite and live happily forever after in it?"

A ribald laugh went up from the crowd as the serious young man, flushing fearfully, sat down on the bed to try the springs.

But what brought all these people here? Mélanie wondered. Perhaps just the greed of seeing what was new, of feeling part of the bustle and business, of imagining that it was the sign of better times —as, who knows, perhaps it would be? As she looked attentively at the faces, middle-aged women with too much make-up on, servant girls with their young men, an occasional stout bourgeoise pulling a wailing little overdressed girl behind her—as she looked at the faces, she was appalled by the greed in them, a sort of cruel avidity. Everyone pushed and clamored, as if they must get there ahead of everyone else—but where were they going? What was driving them on?

She turned to Jacques to see his reaction. He was smiling, the queer boy. For him too this pushing and clamoring had the illusion of life. But how empty it all is, she thought to herself, suddenly tired. Somewhere very far off, miles away, was the green gate, the cool silent garden, and Croll down on his knees among the onions —Moïse basking in the meadow, and Françoise having her lesson. How long had she stood there thinking? A second, a half hour? Mélanie was suddenly panic-stricken. She could not afford to waste time. She was here on business.

Pulling Jacques after her, she charged through the crowd and went over to an ugly, badly finished commode, opened the drawers, and ran her fingers over the rough finish inside. She was interrupted by a shopgirl who asked, a little insolently:

"Can I help Madame? Madame is interested in this suite? Five thousand francs including the lamp." Mélanie turned to see the lamp. It had a mermaid as a base and looked as if it were made of plaster.

"Everything is so badly finished," said Mélanie, half as a question.

The girl shrugged her shoulders. "Well, what can you expect for the price? People are not interested in quality any more. They expect to refurnish in a few years, anyway." She talked glibly and a little condescendingly. In her faded blue hat and serge suit, Mélanie didn't look like a very promising customer.

"Even so," Mélanie went on, "I don't see how you do it."

The answer was sharp and cynical. "They are made in Germany. We are importing hundreds of them, madame."

"Let's get out of here." It was Jacques's voice behind her. His face was dark red. He looked as if he were going to hit someone.

"Yes, come along. I invite you to a cup of coffee in the café across the street."

They didn't talk as they left. They didn't hear the girl say something nasty about people who nosed around and had no intention of buying. They didn't see the young couple, radiant and frightened, carefully counting out their money.

Mélanie's own astonishment was quickly changed to concern for Jacques. She had never seen him angry, and now he was in a real rage. He swore loudly and spat as they came out into the air. Later, when they were sitting drinking bitter coffee, as unlike the real thing as the furniture upstairs had been, Mélanie tried to calm him. She too had been for a moment shocked. That "made in Germany" seemed a slap in the face. But she could rationalize this feeling and Jacques could not. To him it was obviously a real betrayal.

"The swine!" he said over and over again. "The swine!"

"But, Jacques"—she felt forced to remonstrate, though she half agreed with him and she was arguing with herself as well as him, "the war is over, has been over for months, and people have to live."

"The Boches have to live, you mean. You see," he said, suddenly eloquent with the broad Flemish eloquence that has so much physical power behind it, "for four years I have been taught to kill the Boche, not to help him to live. And for four years he has been trying to kill me. Let him stay home now and live as best he can and let me alone."

People in the café put down their newspapers and stopped talking. It was turning into a scene such as Belgians love. If there were only some real opposition, it might turn into a good fight.

"But, Jacques, we have to live together, that's just it. We can't live alone. That would mean years and years of depression. And trade is one of the first ways of building up again, all of us. You haven't asked what the Germans are buying from Belgium."

"And I suppose they're paying in those worthless marks of theirs," spoke the silvery voice of an old man in rather halting Flemish.

"*Ja.*" Jacques turned to him for support. "We have paid for everything Germany has or ever will have in blood." This romantic statement, spoken with such passion—Jacques had brought his fist down on the table, rattling the cups, as he said "blood"—this violence brought a few "Bravos" from the listeners.

Mélanie didn't want to make matters worse now by arguing with Jacques, but he must be reasoned with. It was no state of mind to be in, and she was astonished at his violence. In general the soldiers had come back with an almost complete lack of hatred. It was civilians who talked as Jacques was talking now. What had happened to him, then?

But behind the violence there was an idea. In all those weeks of puttering around the business, silently, he had come to respect the workmanship and the beauty of that furniture.

"What about us? What about the Belgian workmen who made the furniture you have? I suppose they are unemployed? I suppose they are starving, while some German factory turns out this rubbish!"

It was not the war that had done this to him; it was something that had happened since. He was speaking out of love, not out of hatred, Mélanie saw suddenly.

The old man had gone back to his paper. No one was interested any more, now that they were talking about furniture and had stopped using the magical words "blood," "Boche," on which imaginations had been inflamed for so long. Who was interested in furniture?

"Jacques," said Mélanie firmly, "come back now, and when you're in a more reasonable state, we'll have to talk about this. You've given me an idea, and if it works"—she smiled broadly, as if this were a joke because it seemed too good to be true—"we may have something to show the Bon Marché one of these days."

Jacques walked beside her, his face closed, somber, furious. But Mélanie was on fire. Why not try to get her own workmen to build furniture like that? Why not beat the department stores at their own game? Her mind raced ahead to the cheap checked material she could get by the bolt for curtains, to the Congolese matting that was being imported again. She would have to find a designer first, someone who would understand the problem, and then (and this would be more difficult) persuade old M. Plante and his workmen to turn out quantities instead of making one perfectly finished piece. Would they be able to do it? It would mean a larger place; it would mean investing in materials; it would mean a gamble. It would mean the old beastly question of capital. She would have to talk it over with Paul—he was the expert on financial affairs. He understood money and the peculiar juggling that went on about banks, mortgages, estates, capital, revenue—words that meant nothing to Mélanie's concrete mind.

They were walking down the Avenue Louise now, and Mélanie felt as if a weight had been lifted from her chest. She walked fast, enjoying the great spaces around them, the lines of chestnut trees bearing their heavy white candles of flowers, the horsemen riding past on the bridle paths, the light, the air, the majesty of the avenue flanked with tall cream-colored houses. It seemed suddenly so beautiful to be alive, to be walking fast, to be dealing with the future again, to be making plans, to be marshaling her forces for a battle. She had almost forgotten the lost boy at her side. But with a quick maternal gesture she pulled his arm through hers. It was going to be all right.

"You know, Jacques," she said, "you have been a real help to me today."

It was like a decoration (this was the quality she had of making people feel suddenly honored as if in battle). The light flowed back into his face. For the moment he too knew, for the first time in months, that it was good to be alive.

A flock of pigeons wheeled over their heads, the white under the wings flashing. He looked at them with delight.

Chapter IX

Mélanie soon found out that it would be quite impossible to meet the prices of the German factories and employ any of her old people to do the work. It would mean starting a factory of their own, and Paul said that at present they simply didn't have the assets to borrow the huge sums necessary. Also, they both felt a certain reluctance to go into big business. But what were these material problems compared to the hope? Mélanie said to herself. She had turned a corner, inwardly; she was going forward instead of simply trying to maintain the dead past. The lift which she had waited for so long had really come. There was a change in the atmosphere.

And something like it was happening to Paul. His manuscript was half written in its first rough draft, and (while Mélanie sometimes ached with sleep) he now often read parts of it aloud to her after dinner, not so much wanting her advice as to hear how it would sound, explaining the difficult passages and reclarifying his ideas as he did so. It was not to be a formal philosophical treatise. It was written in the form of notes, often using long expanded metaphors as a device. It will be, he used to say when he was feeling optimistic, a series of keys to certain ideas, rather than the elaborate working out of the ideas themselves. A poetry of ideas.

Even Mélanie could see its accomplished beauty of form and marveled at his wisdom, felt all her old humble wonder at his brilliance and depth, so far out of her reach except as a sensation, as a release for her imagination, as a secret new value in her heart.

Only for Françoise these early weeks in May held no promise. The very first delicate roots she had put down into life, the first strong love for a person of her own choosing, had suffered a blight. It seemed that Jacques was not coming back. At first every morning she expected him and made plans of what they could do when he came. But the kite stood in the cupboard abandoned with her father's old tennis racket; the green gate never gave that long-awaited click; no one named Jacques ever called her name.

She was five years old. People are rather apt to think that a person five years old hasn't great capacity for suffering. And it is true that her grief for Jacques would not last very long (besides, Pierre was coming in a week, and that, the grownups all knew, would distract her). But for Françoise there was no past and no future, only the intense lonely present. Once Bo-Bo found her standing at the gate in the middle of the morning, standing quite still with the tears streaming down her cheeks.

It was high time the passionate little being had a friend of her own age, thought Bo-Bo, carrying her off to help sort out the mountain of socks and stockings in the mending basket, telling her a long fairy story to distract her. But Françoise, after listening attentively and sorting out all the socks, had asked:

"Do you think, Bo-Bo, that he will ever come back here?"

Then she had climbed into Bo-Bo's lap and listened to a long quiet explanation, of how Jacques was sick and very tired from the war and after he had a rest he might come back. It sounded very far off. It was now that she wanted him, now, this minute. How could she wait any longer? "Sometime" sounded like "never," she thought while Bo-Bo stroked her hair and finally gave the little pigtails a pull.

"Run along now, little angel, go and play in the garden."

What was "the war"? she wondered when she was safely hidden in her house under the rhododendron bush? And why, if the good people had won, did they seem so sad when they talked about it and often get angry like Papa with M. La Grange? And why, if the Boches were so wicked, was one coming to see Papa this afternoon? Why were there so many ants in the world? she wondered, for she was driven out from her house by a great army of big black ones.

Indoors in his study Paul was asking himself some of the same questions in slightly different terms. This afternoon he would for the first time face a German friend. He had often reminded himself of Gerhart Schmidt during the war, wondering what had become of him, wondering if he would turn up in Belgium as some petty official, for his myopic eyes had certainly kept him from active service. They met ten years before in their student days. Schmidt was a member of a debating team; he and Paul spent several evenings together drinking beer and arguing; kept up a philosophical correspondence and met every two or three years, once in Paris, once at a congress at The Hague. Those were the days when ideas and people flowed back and forth across boundaries needing no passport. What passport to friendship, to communion, would they have to manufacture now?

Schmidt, Paul remembered, was shy, rather gauche, very conscious of his defective eyesight, a little apologetic, a brilliant dialectician. He had married sometime during the war, for in his letter he spoke of his wife and a son Françoise's age. All this was human, believable, even touching.

But Schmidt was a German. Tacitly, at least, he had invaded the country of a friend, taken it by force, and finally been driven out and beaten. What sort of German would Schmidt be? And what sort of Belgian shall I seem to him? Paul wondered.

By four o'clock Paul was pretending to walk around the garden but actually was keeping an eager nervous watch on the gate. It was absurd to be so nervous, he told himself. After, all Schmidt is a human being, an old friend, and there is nothing so terrifying in that. We can always talk philosophy, and indeed that's the only thing we can do.

But when the old friend hadn't turned up at half-past four, Paul's nervousness turned to irritation. He wished the whole thing could be called off. Why try to build bridges over the immense and cruel abysses? Why does he have to come and bother me at all? he said to himself.

At that second the gate clicked. Eagerly, like a boy, he turned and ran, took both Schmidt's hands in his, stood looking at him.

"So here you are, you old devil."

Schmidt had tears in his eyes. These sentimental Germans, Paul thought, but he was near to tears himself.

"Come along, come along. Welcome to our house—you see it still stands."

"It is charming," Schmidt answered in his halting French. "The garden—the house," he added vaguely. And Paul thought, He hasn't changed at all. He's just the same. It seemed suddenly incredible that millions of bodies lay in the fields of France and Belgium, cities had been razed, children starved—and yet here they were again, the same two old friends. What madness!

But after the first few moments, in which embarrassment and the passage of time could be covered with the simple questions and answers and the simple acts like relieving Schmidt of his brief case and hanging his worn coat in the cupboard, when at last they were sitting in the salon opposite each other, and before Bo-Bo brought in the tea, there came a silence, the silence that couldn't be filled any more, the silence of strangeness and fear, of love and hatred, of grief and joy.

"Yes—yes," Paul murmured, tapping his knee with the fingers of one hand, a gesture Schmidt remembered well.

Schmidt glanced nervously round the room and then sighed.

Paul looked at him keenly and kindly. It was, after all, poor Schmidt who was at a loss. "You haven't changed, old man—you're just the same, even, I'll wager, to your misbegotten ideas of philosophy."

But his sally brought hardly a smile.

"I am so glad to see you," Schmidt said simply, and shook his head, back and forth, back and forth sadly.

"Well, you see, we haven't done so badly, either of us. We've survived. Your little boy must be just Françoise's age—you must send him here for a summer sometime."

It was good to see Schmidt, better to think of their children growing up without the shadow between them, learning each other's language.

"That would be fine—yes, that would be fine. So kind of you," Schmidt murmured. What was behind all these hesitations? But suddenly he spoke; the shy silent man spoke, and once he had begun it was like a flood.

"Duchesne," he said, "it is terrible in Germany. Terrible. You have no idea. No order, no peace, no food. Hans has lost weight in the last year—ten kilogs. We are so worried about him. I shouldn't say this to you"—and again he shook his head miserably—"I don't know what is the matter with me. But, Duchesne, it is hell in Germany. I try to hide myself in my work——"

"Yes." Paul was glad of the interruption. "How is the great work? It must be nearly finished. You are holding out on us, Schmidt."

But, having begun, Schmidt found it impossible to stop. "But there is no hiding from the chaos. The soldiers have come back demoralized, ready for anything, defiant, sick——"

"Well," said Paul quietly, "my poor friend. That's war. So it has always been. So it will be."

But Schmidt said earnestly, "Not again. Never again."

Paul looked out of the window. Never again? He wondered.

Bo-Bo with the tea was a welcome interruption: she had been governess in the house of people Schmidt knew slightly in Frankfort. One of the boys had been killed at the Marne. One forgot sometimes that Germans too had been killed at the Marne. But Bo-Bo was not a sentimentalist. She shut her mouth tight to keep from saying, "Served him right. Why didn't he stay where he belonged?"

"Will you have sugar, Herr Schmidt? We have only brown sugar. But it sweetens."

Sipping his tea, Schmidt relaxed for the first time, asked about Paul's work, listened attentively to Paul's long, sinuous, and perfectly articulate analysis of it, while Bo-Bo sat and knitted beside them, stiff and erect, the comforting solid presence of a woman doing the eternal things women do, war or no war, maintaining the balance of life.

Paul knew he was talking too long, but it was rare to have a listener who really understood what he meant; he was attracted to and touched by something sensitive and receptive, a discreet warmth emanating from Schmidt. Never, never could they afford to be enemies, the very few in the world who understood the same things, who worked secretly and alone at the development of ideas, so Paul thought as he talked. He was on the point of speaking of it when Mélanie opened the door.

"I hurried home from the office, I was so afraid I would miss you." She turned to Paul with a little laugh of relief and pleasure. "He hasn't changed at all, has he, Paul? He is just the same. Oh, it is good that you came," she added warmly. "We needed to see you."

With Mélanie home, philosophy flew out of the window. Without the slightest hesitation she plied Schmidt with questions, about his family, about his little boy—about Germany. Her interest, her absolute friendliness, the heart so visible under her curiosity made it all simple.

She was horrified to hear what conditions were like.

"But something must be done, Paul. The children are hungry." Must the children always suffer for their parents' sins, world without end? Starving people would not educate them, change them, bring about a real peace, a chance to build. Oh, did the chain of suffering and destruction, destruction of lives, wearing down of hearts, have to go on forever?

In contrast to her energetic dismay, Schmidt was very quiet. She insisted that he send the boy to stay with them as soon as possible.

"Not this year," he repeated, "but perhaps next. It was by a miracle that I got a passport," and he smiled wanly. Now it was his turn to ask questions. He felt very tired. These people seemed so full of hope, faith. That was it. In Germany the faith had gone. All was bitterness, resentment, fear, and after the huge fruitless effort and sacrifice of the war, a terrible empty fatigue—as if literally the blood had been poured out of a body.

"I suppose the feeling here in Belgium is very bitter?" he asked when he had found out something of how the Duchesnes' own life had been managed during the four terrible years.

Paul glanced at Mélanie, but she left him to answer. It was better to be honest. It was, he felt, the only way to honor friendship now, to be quite honest.

"Yes," Paul said shortly. "It is."

Of Schmidt's real feelings about the war they knew nothing. Would they ever know?

There were these gaps in communication. There were these strained moments when there seemed nothing to say, when there was no bridge possible, when each for the other stood as a human figure against a huge background of suffering, separated suffering, lonely suffering. In such a moment Mélanie sent Bo-Bo for Françoise. Then at least, she thought, they would be in the presence of the future and not the past.

Françoise had been very curious to see this German friend of whom Papa had spoken at the lesson that morning. What would he be like?

When she had said how-do-you-do and made what she thought was a very good curtsy she withdrew to her mother's chair and stared at Herr Schmidt with unembarrassed curiosity.

He talked to her gently about Hans and about the goat. "How old are you, Françoise?" he asked in his quiet, apologetic voice. But Françoise couldn't answer. He was just like other people, only more gentle, that is what she thought.

"She is shy"—he turned to Mélanie—"but she is charming—so fair, so silent," he added poetically.

He was not wicked at all, Françoise decided. He was very nice. Her stare broke into a smile and then, overcome with shyness, she hid her face in Mamie's dress.

"Come here and talk to me a little," he begged, and without a word she ran into his outstretched arms and in a moment was sitting rather precariously on his sharp thin knees.

"You have made a conquest," said Paul. The ice was broken. Mélanie insisted that Herr Schmidt stay to supper. They could not possibly let him go so soon.

They had talked about bitterness as an abstraction. Now right here in her own house Mélanie was forced to face it in reality. Marie and Lou-Lou refused to serve a meal to a German. Bo-Bo scolded them but they would not budge.

"Wait on one of *them?*" Lou-Lou had said with passionate scorn. For once they were unmoved even by Madame's furious *"Saper-lipopette!"*

"Very well, then," she said when it was obvious that anger would be useless. "Go up to your rooms and stay there until he is gone. I'm ashamed of you. Good Catholics as you are," she said, making a final appeal, "you don't seem very able to forgive your enemies."

But Lou-Lou was too angry to care. "He didn't have to come here. Can't they leave us alone?"

"He is our guest and an old friend of Monsieur's," said Mélanie icily. "Go up to your rooms, both of you." It was a command.

Lou-Lou sat at her window watching the night come, firm in her righteousness and anger. But Marie lay face down on her bed and wept savagely, burning tears of pain and rage. Her father had been shot as a hostage in the first days of the war. "If they think I'll ever forget," she sobbed over and over. "If they think I'll ever forget!"

These were the wounds that never stopped bleeding, the wounds of the ignorant, the simple, the brave, the foolish—all over Belgium, where the farmers would go on digging up skulls and bits of shell for years—the wounds in the flesh. They would never be healed by reason. They were physical facts. What would heal them? Time, perhaps? But how many bloody stories told at the hearths of farms in the long winter evenings would keep them alive; how often would the blood again drip on the stone and imaginations burn with hate!

The war was over. New babies were being born every day who would not remember, but their fathers remembered and their mothers, feeding them at the breast, remembered. The millions of Lou-Lous and Maries remembered, and for one Francis and for one Mélanie they were counted in millions. Besides, what was there to prove them wrong? Germany was a great evil mystery too far off to be recognized as human. They did not see the starving children in the streets of Berlin. They only knew and repeated that no single German gesture raised one demolished farm, no single German hand was stretched out to make reparation. Hospitals, universities, whole villages and towns were rebuilt with American money, by American generosity. But American generosity would not heal the wounds. Justice, not charity, was what the Lou-Lous and the Maries and the millions like them demanded. Though even to them, starving other people's children would not have seemed like justice.

The fact is, Mélanie and Paul agreed, lying awake and talking half the night, the fact is that suffering does not make for generosity. Only imagination makes for generosity, only the acceptance that revenge never was the answer to human suffering—but only sandpaper on an abrasion, keeping the wound raw.

But also—and this they did not admit even to each other—Schmidt himself, with all his sensitivity and gentleness, was still thinking in terms of Germany and German suffering. Even he was hemmed in, imprisoned, in his own pain. The hand he had put out had not asked for forgiveness. It had asked for pity.

Chapter X

It had done Paul good to see Schmidt again. In the region where they were neither Belgians nor Germans, but philosophers, he could communicate with Schmidt as he couldn't with any of his more intimate friends; as he watched Schmidt's attentive face, something happened. Something fused. The ideas which he had struggled so hard to possess possessed him. He was ready to write the whole thing down. He was intensely happy. This was the true spring, the true end of the war—when ideas were free once more to flow between all human beings, the boundaries lifted. They had been starved for each other, the vital flow frozen; what a relief to see the flicker of approval, the flicker of doubt in Schmidt's eyes—what a relief to know that such exchange was still possible.

It was as if all through these four years he had been stopped, he had been unable to work, to make the final effort of writing, because Schmidt was lost somewhere, because he could not communicate with Schmidt. Now the whole book had suddenly become a letter, a communication, an act of love. And this love was so concentrated and exclusive that nothing outside it counted or perhaps even existed.

For three weeks Paul worked, seeing nothing except the work—free, flowing, wholly alive as he sat at his desk. But what the household saw of him was an exasperated, nervous man who rushed out in a fit of temper if a door slammed, who came down to meals and sat with his family as if they hardly existed, who, if he asked politely some question of his wife or little girl, didn't seem interested in the answer. To them this man who had in himself been released, who was full of love, who had come into his full power, to them he had become an inhuman tyrant, hardly a person at all.

At first Mélanie, happy that he was working, identified herself completely with his struggle. She invented special dishes that would be easy to eat and nourishing. She came home every evening with a great excitement and yearning to find him, to know how he was getting on. But she soon realized that he didn't want to talk about it, and even if he had wanted to, she would not have been able to follow him, so she stopped running up the stairs and bursting in for the reassurance, for the joy of being with him again. Instead she worked furiously in the garden; she spent more time with Françoise, taking over the reading lesson as Paul couldn't be interrupted.

She waited for his ordeal and her own to be over. And in the daytime there was so much to do that all this was quite easy. It was the night she dreaded. Very often Paul never came to bed at all; the light under his door would still be shining at four o'clock when the first birds were waking up.

In her mind she recognized that being separated from one's husband for a few weeks really had no importance, but in her flesh she was hurt. They had often quarreled before, and then she had sometimes thought that lying in the next bed to someone, within touching distance, separated by anger, was the worst suspense she could imagine—when the invisible wall looked so high and formidable it could not possibly ever be scaled. But at least then she knew that she was, even as an irritation, very present for him, that she existed. Now it was as if she had ceased to exist. When he kissed her it was an automatic gesture, a brushing-off, the thing you did out of habit before getting into bed.

How can I be so selfish? she asked herself. But there it was. He had shut her out of his mind, and that somehow she could accept in her humility. But now she was shut out in the flesh. Filled with love and longing and passion as she had never been, love asked of her to do nothing, to be passive, to cease to exist.

In the night she felt fearfully alive, as if all the sunlight of the day, the early morning, and the evening was poured into her and held there in suspense. Running her hands down over her breasts and thighs in a gesture of exasperated self-knowledge, she hated herself for trembling.

"I'm not like this. This isn't me," she said to herself. And marriage seemed to her then the most impossible thing ever asked of human beings, the insoluble problem.

In a second of horrified illumination she understood what could drive a woman to take a lover. And then, revolted at herself, filled with rage against her own sex, she buried herself in books, read a long dull history of Rome, doggedly, to stop thinking.

Paul was not blind. He knew what he was doing. But he shut the knowledge out. He had to write his book; everything else must wait. Mélanie must wait. He had not meant it to be like this. It was not his will, but the tides were turning another way, and he had to let himself be carried on them after all these years of waiting and hoping and thinking. He felt that if he once let the tension drop, if he relaxed, if he came back to the peace of the body even for an hour, he would never be able to climb back to the high peaks where he stood. When he stopped writing he was too tired to mind very much what might be happening to other people. Only sometimes, when he finally came to bed, he would stand and look down in the cold morning light, as if from very far off, at this woman, who was his wife, abandoned in sleep.

So it went on, the deep war within the ordered, outwardly peaceful house. And in the morning light the tortures of the dark diminished. Mélanie could cheerfully call herself an idiot, laugh with Françoise, give Croll orders about clipping the big hedge, wish they had a hive of bees again as they had had during the war, and even plunge gladly into the business in town.

So it went on until a Sunday when they had had a long-standing invitation to walk over to a neighbor's for dinner in the middle of the day. Mélanie had forgotten all about it, so she had to knock on Paul's door and warn him that she, Bo-Bo, and Françoise would go and she would leave lunch for him on the stove.

He didn't answer her knock; she opened the door softly and stood there.

"Paul . . ."

"What is it?" he asked without looking up.

"We were supposed to be going over to Blanche's for dinner, and I thought——" But she didn't have time to finish.

He turned on her with the accumulated frustration and passion of all those days and nights. "I can't possibly go out. Can't you understand, I've got to get this done. Can't you leave me alone?"

But this was too much for Mélanie. Leave him alone? When she had hardly spoken to him for a week. Leave him alone? No, that was too much. Selfish, mean little man whom she had married in a moment of weakness.

"Listen, Paul, it doesn't matter what you do at home. I don't care that you hardly know any of us exist. But you must behave like a human being where other people are concerned. Blanche will have taken trouble to cook a dinner——" But this wasn't what she meant at all, and how did she ever say that, when she had never intended Paul to come?

"To cook a dinner!" He stood up now and threw his pencil down violently on the table. "My God, Mélanie, don't you understand anything?"

"Yes, I understand your selfishness, your complete lack of moral responsibility, your arrogance—I understand that very well." At last, she thought, knowing the wickedness of the thought—at last we are talking again. At last he knows I'm here. And with that she burst into tears and ran out.

Where to go? Where to go in her own house where no one could see her or find her? Where to go in her own house to rage and cry? Bo-Bo was in the bedroom. Françoise would run up to her if she went into the garden. Downstairs? Where? There being nowhere, she locked herself in the bathroom, sitting on the seat, rocking back and forth as if the motions of dealing with a physical pain would help this pain in the heart. She felt fearfully ashamed, lost, beaten. As if she were no one, any more, no one's wife, no one's love, or mother, or child.

Paul sat down savagely at his desk with his head in his hands. Let her cry. A man with work to do was crazy to marry. How could one ever get down to the truth if one was expected to live at the same time, to live with a woman and a child, what's more? To be polite to the neighbors? That was really the last straw.

But he would work in spite of her. He would finish the book. He would not be stopped now. No, not if the house burned down over their heads. He picked up the pencil from the floor and wrote on:

"To try to make an accord between thought and life is to square the circle. That is man's state and the tragedy of his destiny. There is no solution to this conflict; the only solution is in recognizing the incompatibility between the 'life of the spirit' and 'the spirit of life' and their indissoluble union in us. Taking this knowledge as point of departure, we can only try to accept ourselves as steeped in a radical contradiction. Then it is for us to decide where we shall put the emphasis, on life and by so much we betray the spirit; on the spirit and by so much we betray life."

And meanwhile Mélanie sat in the bathroom and gave herself a severe talking-to. Outside the life of the house went on with sudden piercing reality—Louise and Marie clattered down the stairs on their way out, calling good-by to Bo-Bo; a door opened and shut;

the creak of Françoise's little wheelbarrow went by under the window. All her thoughts shifted gently like the pieces of bright glass in a kaleidoscope and came to rest in a new sober pattern. Marriage, she told herself severely, surrounded now, sustained by the fabric of life in the house, marriage is as much a matter of self-denial as of self-fulfillment. Not to see this, not to recognize the space in which she and Paul moved like twin stars, always together but always solitary, was to miss the point.

But while she bathed her eyes in cold water and put on a fresh dress, Mélanie suddenly wanted Simone, her darling Simone, who understood everything, on whose shoulder she could lean her head and rest. In those far-off days before they were each married, all had seemed bathed in radiance, all tenderness and flowers; there were no walls. Everything was to be shared like the two halves of an apple. Could marriage ever be like that, so much more difficult and harsh? Marriage, she thought, was living with a stranger. Even now, after all these years, Paul was a stranger; never did she feel really safe, never quite off guard, never wholly accepted.

I am a grown-up person and I am married to Paul, she admonished herself as she took out a fine lace collar from the Florentine box and pinned it at the back, as she fastened her mother's diamond brooch at her throat. It was all very well, but the fearful thing was that at this moment she knew she was married to Paul but she did not love him. She loved Simone. She wanted to be with Simone.

It's the devil to be a woman, she said to herself suddenly, and felt much better at once.

Late in the afternoon, in the house emptied of all human life, the garden itself stilled and drenched in sunlight, as if even the bees were taking a nap, in the center of absolute silence, Paul put down his pencil. It was finished.

He sat and looked at the neat pile of sheets before him and at the motes in a wide beam of sunlight that crossed the room. He yawned and stretched and for the millionth time wanted a cigarette more than anything in the world. It was finished—five years of thinking and questioning, five weeks of intense concentration, of writing. Now he was empty, empty, empty, emptied out into two hundred sheets of paper with little gray squiggles on them. Finished.

The silence which he had not noticed before was suddenly tangible. There was nothing to be heard except the steady tick of his watch, marking each second as it passed. Time flowing away into silence. Life flowing away into silence.

Paul got up quickly and went to the head of the stairs. Silence. He called loudly, "Mélanie! Mélanie!" No answer. Then a questioning cry from Moïse. Then nothing.

Where were they? Where was everyone? He ran down the stairs and into the salon where Mélanie's book lay open on the chaise longue. He threw open the window and called into the garden:

"Mélanie, where are you?" There wasn't even an echo. His voice lost itself, was absorbed into the silence, a cry that might have been a pebble cast into a magical pool without a ripple to mark its descent.

Oh, now he wanted her. He must have her. He must hear voices and feel the clasp of a hand. He must have food and drink, hot coffee and soup. He must have love. He must live.

How could she not be here when he needed her so much? He went softly through the swinging door into the kitchen. Filibert was asleep on the table in the sun. At least here was a living being he could talk to. He scratched Filibert under the chin and felt the slow sleepy purrs begin in her stomach.

"That's right, old Filibert. That's right, old Filibert. You know," he said, gently scratching Filibert's neck in the back and stroking her with knowing hands, "I want my lunch, Filibert. I want my wife," said Paul. There would be no end to the tension. There would be no safe landing until Mélanie came home.

He had forgotten all about their fight in the morning, but now he remembered. He had let her go. He had not kissed her good-by. Brute that I am, selfish creature that I am!

But just then the gate clicked. He heard Françoise laugh delightedly and then Mélanie saying, "Shh—Papa——" So that's how it had been all this time for them, walking around on tiptoe, not daring to laugh.

He was at the front door to greet them. He shouted and waved as they came down the path:

"Darling, it's finished. It's finished! I'm a free man again."

They were holding hands, Françoise looking at him with wide eyes, Mélanie smiling radiantly as they came nearer and nearer down the path; and then he caught them both in his arms, lifted Françoise up to his shoulder in a great swinging gesture, took Mélanie's hand, and said:

"Come round the garden. I've seen nothing. I know nothing. Oh, darling, it's finished," he said quietly, putting Françoise down again. She was giggling with surprise and happiness to have Papa back again. She ran into the garden and pulled up a little carrot and brought it to him.

"Oh yes, my darling, I'm starved. Thank you, little soul, thank you." He talked on and on, squeezing Mélanie's hand, smiling at her, full of gaiety. His tide was full in. He didn't notice her silence.

For Mélanie felt suddenly exhausted, as if she had come back from a long and terrible journey. She needed a moment to recover, a moment to adjust herself to this new Paul, a moment to prepare for meeting him. She sent him with Françoise to put Moïse to bed and went into the kitchen to prepare a feast. Here, doing the immemorial things, breaking the eggs, taking the milk from the pantry, feeling Filibert wind herself round her bare legs, going out to the garden to find the most delicate and perfect little lettuce, mixing the salad dressing, she was back in her own life. She was safe. She was a woman getting supper for her hungry husband.

The jays in the garden screamed. Moïse called her evening call, plaintive and obstinate. She wanted to be milked but she did not want to be put to bed yet. And then Françoise's laughter spilled over the garden, over the air, piercing, delighted, as they went careening past the window, Moïse, as usual, having suddenly decided to run just when she looked as if she would never budge again. They burst into the kitchen out of breath, delighted with themselves. Paul seized Mélanie in his arms and began to waltz around the kitchen.

"Paul, Paul, the omelet!" she cried.

"The book is finished, my darling," he sang to the tune of the "Blue Danube," and she answered, carrying it on, "The omelet is burning, my love." He led her past the stove and snatched the saucepan off with one hand and went on: "The book is finished, my darling," the omelet, Mélanie, and he in a fine swirl all around the kitchen.

Françoise, standing in the doorway, watched them gravely. She felt uncomfortable. She wished they would stop. They were her father and mother and she wanted them for herself. But now they seemed to have a secret all their own and she didn't like it. Suddenly she started to cry before she knew what was happening to her.

"Paul, the child," Mélanie whispered, and in a second he was kneeling beside Françoise, drying her tears with his big handkerchief, making her laugh before she had finished crying by turning it into a rabbit with long ears. All through supper she sat in the crook of his arm, eating little bits of omelet from his fork, while he and Mamie smiled at each other over her head, while he talked about his work, about publishers, about Paris, about getting it typed.

"Oh, Paul," Mélanie sighed at last, stretching her hand across the table to him, "it seems as if we had really come through, as if the war were really over—at last."

"Yes, it's strange, but you know, it was Schmidt's coming that did it. I had waited for that without knowing I was waiting."

"Dear Schmidt," Mélanie said, looking down.

"Poor old Schmidt, the war isn't over for him, I'm afraid."

"But it will be, Paul. It will be," she said, willing it to be so, because how could they have this happiness, this peace, this fruitfulness alone—and if just a few hundred miles away there was no happiness and no peace?

"I wonder—about Germany," he answered thoughtfully. It was a question left in the air, left in the kitchen with the empty dishes and the cold fire, as they went upstairs together, to put Françoise to bed.

And when the child was safely tucked in, when they had walked round the garden almost without talking, absorbed in the secret they held in suspense between them—when finally Paul said, "Let's go to bed," then the tides which had ebbed and flowed so separately at last rose together in a great flood, taking them far out and beyond themselves to where Paul's carefully considered convictions were swept away by the force of the tide, bringing new life with it.

PART TWO

Summer: 1930

Chapter I

Now in the height of summer, ten years later, the house was almost hidden in all the trees; the poplars had grown so high you could see their tops from the meadow, over the red gable. Silent, stifled by the heat, the garden felt like a jungle—the cosmos, zinnias, and Canterbury bells all tangled up together in the flower beds, the boughs of the apple trees, heavy with green apples. Only the two baby goats, lying beside their mother, cooling their bellies in the long grass, looked comfortably pastoral. It was not, after all, an abandoned garden. It was a civilized meadow with a table and chairs under the apple tree. It was almost teatime in late July, and the silence would soon be broken.

For the family had grown in ten years—there were new child voices in the garden, the voices of Colette and Solange—Colette, the child of promise, the child of passion, conceived when Paul's first book was finished—dark like her mother, intellectual, sensitive like her father; and Solange, whom no one expected, thrown in like a radiant joke two years later, Solange who should have been a boy and was instead the most feminine of little girls, blue-eyed, fair-headed, a dazzling flirt, shamelessly spoiled by the whole family.

It was a long time since Paul's book had come out, to be greeted by indifferent silence. It had been rejected by every respectable Paris house, and in a moment of impatience, of arrogance, he had had it privately printed in Brussels. The attic was stacked with copies of it—half the edition. His friends had bought it, of course; there had been a few letters, a remarkable one from Schmidt, one from a professor at Montpellier with whom Paul kept up a correspondence. It had reached and touched ten or twelve people. Could he justify his existence with that?

After much heart-searching, after three black years, Paul had decided not. He had made the compromise between the life of the spirit and what he called the spirit of life. He entered the business in town. He bought an automobile so that Mélanie could put Solange in a basket when she was a baby and take her in with them every morning. He spent hours tinkering with the car, an old open phaeton which continually broke down; he was delighted to discover that he could do things with his hands.

Partly because this kind of self-confidence came to him so late and he was tapping a side of his nature which had never been used before, he got great pleasure from being part of the everyday world. He helped Mélanie find new quarters for the Maison Bernard, a house where they could have a showcase and cover some of the overhead by renting furnished apartments. He even went to night classes to study furniture design and drafting and now had a studio over the shop where he designed for their own clients. He enjoyed it all immensely, enjoyed his own skill, enjoyed his relations with the workmen, felt often like a prisoner released from jail—and he was delighted (as he had never been by praise of his books) at his clients' amazement to have a desk designed by the philosopher, Paul Duchesne.

Life was not lived at the point of intensity—the point which he looked back to find, the point ten years ago when he finished his first book, when Colette was conceived. Life might be conceived there, but it was sustained on another level, less pure, less violent, closer to earth, difficult, gradual, asking above all the ability to endure. He wondered sometimes if that promise held out so long ago, that fierce sense of power and glory, could not be won back, like innocence which one loses young and finds again when one has lived a long time. But what compromise might be fatal to that end? What compromise necessary?

Only love could tell—so that a man like Emile, who seemed pure love, never had to ask the question at all. And Mélanie, in her straightness and clarity, did not ask it either. But Paul asked it constantly, enduring moments of raging despair when he realized how much time he was spending away from his real work.

So, looking out on the green willow, in the summer of 1930, he realized that now he was forty he still did not have any answers, only questions.

Around him, stretching to the sea on one side, to the mountains on the other, the little low country spread out. In ten years all traces of war, or nearly all, had gone. There were no ruins to be seen; only, worse than ruins, the jerry-built cheap houses lining the country roads.

And the deeper scars of war were healing: Germany had been admitted to the League. It looked as if there might be years of peace ahead. The air was full of inventions and plans—Lindbergh flew the Atlantic, capturing the imagination of the world. The lines of communication, severed for so long, were set up again— American books translated into French, German students traveling in Europe again, so that the Lindbergh flight seemed the perfect symbol of a new time, the symbol of hope. Francis was bubbling over with good will and enthusiasm, an admirer of Stresemann's, a convinced believer in a new Germany, in a new Europe, full of admiration for what the Soviets were accomplishing.

But Paul, hunched over his radio for hours at a time, listening to the voices of Europe, was unconvinced. The seeds of nationalism were sprouting everywhere: in Italy they had become aggressive and imperialistic already. For one Francis who thought in terms of a United Europe, there were a hundred clamoring patriots in every country. Even in Belgium the Flemish movement, begun as a fight for a language and a culture, was growing into a fight for political power, for a state within the state. There were fights in the streets. It was said that if you asked for a spool of thread in a shop in Ghent, *in French,* you would be told it was not in stock. Belgians were as anti-French as they were anti-Dutch and more anti-British than they were anti-German.

The great willow in the Duchesnes' garden, shutting them out from the world, shutting them in closer and closer to their own life at home, was a pattern repeated everywhere and on every level. Its gentle green tears shut out the world.

Here in the garden very little seemed to have happened in ten years. The paths were still in need of scraping, but the tiny box hedges in the French garden were as prim and precise as ever. Only under the willow tree there was one startling proof of the passage of time—Françoise sitting in a deck chair. Now she was a gangling fifteen-year-old, reading Tolstoy. Her thoughtful gray eyes moved from the book to a large furry caterpillar inching along at her feet, as if she were thinking not about the book but about something else. After a moment she looked at her watch, half rose from the deck chair, then thought better of it and sat down again with a slight frown.

Jacques was coming to tea—he had been coming to the house now for years and behaved like one of the family. But there was always a slight strain between him and Françoise. Among all the people who came to the house he was the only one she really respected. But when he came she never could think of anything to say and her shyness made him shy.

When she saw it was nearly four she thought of running up to put on a clean dress and then changed her mind. It might be noticed, commented on. No, she would stay here.

And while she waited, listening for the click of the gate, hidden under the long green leaves of the willow, the house was beginning to wake up from its after-dinner silence. Bo-Bo and the little ones were in the kitchen making sandwiches, Colette cutting thin slices from the big loaf, Solange spreading apple butter on them sleepily. They were beautiful children, Solange very pretty with fair curly hair and very pink cheeks, Colette with a pointed quick eagerness and very large dark eyes.

"Heavens, my doves"—Bo-Bo threw up her hands in mock despair—"we are not feeding a herd of elephants!"

"Jacques is coming to tea," said Colette matter-of-factly, and Solange went off into a fit of giggles. He was apt to eat rather a lot.

Bo-Bo went out to ring the bell while the two children spread the cloth on the table under the trees and carried out the trays. From all over the house and the garden the family, scattered to sleep, to read, separated for a few hours, now came together excitedly as if they had been parted for weeks.

First Mélanie herself walked across the meadow and had to be embraced by Solange and pulled over to the table to admire the sandwiches. She had grown stouter in ten years, but she still wore her chatelaine's dress and there was no gray in her straight hair caught back with a round comb.

Then Papa followed in his old straw hat, as thin and heron-like, as elegant as ever, as cross as ever, for the bell had woken him from a nap.

"Where's Pierre?" Mamie asked, counting her flock. Bo-Bo was already seated in her usual corner of the bench with her perpetual basket of mending.

"Pierre! Pierre!" everyone called together like a flock of parakeets, their voices shrill and imperative.

"My children," Paul said when he had borne it as long as he could, "you are deafening your poor old papa. Please go and find him and stop shrieking." At forty Paul amused himself, mocked .at himself, by behaving like an old man.

But Mélanie had no feeling of age. It startled her to remember

she was forty, a grownup. Time had taken this great leap ahead—
she had not changed. She was not ready for the leap. Where had it
all gone? she wondered half humorously as she poured milk into
the children's cups from the big blue jug.

Paul looked over at his daughter sitting dreamily in the grass.
"What have you been doing all day, Françoise?"

But she didn't answer. He and Mélanie exchanged a look as if
to say, "Well, she is thinking—she doesn't answer—our funny little
daughter." It was too hot to talk. Only the cicadas' shrill conversation buzzed on in the trees.

And then the little ones appeared round the corner, dragging
Pierre after them; he was rubbing his eyes, looking ungainly and
sheepish. For the last three years Emile and Suzanne had sent him
to the Duchesnes for the summer.

"He was asleep! Fast asleep!" the little ones chanted. And
Solange began to snore loudly like a small pig.

"Solange, really!" Françoise woke out of her dream in disgust.

"Well, he *was* snoring!"

"I was not." Pierre was still cross. "Leave me alone." He sat
down on the bench beside Uncle Paul and glared at them. "I was
reading Lenin," he added smugly.

"Oh ho, he was reading Lenin. Let us pray," said Paul with mock
solemnity. "But how could you possibly fall asleep in the presence
of the great man? This is serious. When boys fall asleep while they
read Lenin in Russia, they are whipped."

"Are they, Papa?" Solange opened her eyes wide and looked at
Pierre thoughtfully.

"Don't pay any attention to him, Solange. He's only teasing."
Colette had climbed up into the apple tree and called through the
branches, "Hand me a sandwich, somebody. I'm going to have my
tea up here."

But she climbed down again much faster than she had climbed
up, because she saw Jacques leap over the hedge—no gate for him
—running toward them. Now for the first time Françoise included

herself in what was going on. She gave Jacques his tea—he sat in the grass, plied on each side with sandwiches by Colette, by Solange. Françoise stood by them a moment and then sat down at a little distance. There was something brilliant, dazzling about Jacques. He was so very brown and hard, and his eyes so very blue, and when he laughed he looked like a wolf. "A magnificent animal," Paul thought to himself, admiring the clean line of his chest through his open shirt. But Françoise, speechless, sitting outside the circle, thought of him as one of Tolstoy's wise and saintly peasants, a hero.

Now they were all gathered, they were all together, Mélanie sighed. Saturday afternoon, no more business, no more town till the day after tomorrow. She was home. She looked from one to another. What fine dear children. And bursting with happiness, she leaned over to whisper to Bo-Bo that Solange was ravishing in that pink dress.

"Colette," she added aloud, "you have circles under your eyes. You've been reading too late. When did you put out your light last night?"

"At nine, Mamie," Colette answered truthfully.

"That's too late, darling, much too late," she remonstrated gently.

Why was it always so easy for Colette and Solange? Françoise wondered. "When I was their age my book would have been taken away," she said aloud.

"'*Autres temps, autres mœurs*,' my beauty," Papa answered lightly. It was true, they had been much more severe with her.

All the sandwiches had disappeared; Jacques patted his stomach appreciatively and got up. The little ones had some secret they wanted to show him, and they ran off together.

"Come for a walk with me, Franci," Pierre begged.

"No," she said shortly. Pierre flushed. He was always rushing in like a great bumbling puppy, quite unaware of what other people suffered.

But Françoise hardly noticed him. Jacques hadn't asked her to go with him. All he wanted was an excuse to find Lou-Lou in the kitchen. She knew. And she hated them all, hated the green garden that felt like a prison, hated her father and mother who saw so much, who wanted her to be so much, who expected her to be good and generous and gentle when it was all she could do to keep from hitting everyone, hitting the world—if that were possible. How did people go on living when it was so hard?

Mélanie was upset. "No, Françoise, you really are impossible," she said severely. "Pierre asks you nicely to go for a walk and you are simply rude. I won't have it. What is the matter with you? We love you. We want to help you. And you behave as if we were all tyrants, as if something were fearfully wrong."

"I'm sorry," Françoise said shortly, without looking up.

Mélanie felt baffled. Quite unconsciously she always raised her voice now when she spoke to Franci, as if she could batter through the wall by shouting. It was exasperating, humiliating—and she could feel Paul, sitting opposite, go stiff with disapproval. She was not going at it in the right way, but now she had begun she couldn't stop.

"When Hans comes, I shall expect you to be polite. Hans is a stranger, a guest, and the son of your father's dear friend Gerhart Schmidt. I want to see a change in you before next week," she finished, piling up the cups and saucers with finality. "I shall expect it," she said in her general's voice. But now she herself was near to tears. What was wrong with everyone? With herself?

The little ones came back to break the tension, running across the meadow, flinging themselves down in the grass, out of breath.

"Jacques has mended the bad place in the fence," said Colette possessively and proudly, as if she had done it herself.

"Has he, my treasure? That's wonderful."

"And he's in the kitchen now, spooning with Lou-Lou," Solange added mischievously. "We tried to sneak round under the window to see, but——"

"But *you* giggled. Haven't you any self-control?" Colette asked severely.

Wherever they are it's light, and wherever I am it's dark, thought Françoise with despair. Now her mother would be waiting for some gesture she couldn't make, wouldn't make. She watched Solange climb up into her mother's lap to be covered with kisses and got up silently, praying that no one would notice her. But her departure, which she imagined was invisible, fixed their attention as if she were an actress making a dramatic lonely exit. She did not turn. She would have none of them. She persuaded herself that she was invisible.

When she had gone they talked about her, as in this family they talked about everything, analyzed everything. It fascinated Pierre. At home his parents never discussed anything. They just seemed to live along.

As if Mélanie guessed his thought, she interrupted the conversation to ask, "Have you written your parents, Pierrot?"

No, he had not written. He was bored with his parents. They bothered him. They seemed to him good people, but unimportant, hopelessly bourgeois, having no idea what life was really like. They did not understand Marxism. They expected him to be a good Catholic. It was unendurable.

"You'd better go and do it now. Run along like a good boy and write them a long letter."

"All right," he said obediently, "but what is there to say? They know where I am——"

He's such a peasant, Paul was thinking, a pretentious little peasant. What would become of him? Parents and children, children and parents—the real war, the war that never stopped, was the war between the generations. And the older generation had to lose, that was what Mélanie couldn't bring herself to admit. She was telling the little ones a story. There, at least, the conflict hadn't begun yet, but what would happen when it did? How did one learn to let one's children go? For a moment he felt the family as a weight, as a burden, and went in to take refuge in his study.

When Bo-Bo too had gone, when they were alone in their perfectly intimate world, Colette turned to her mother.

"You know, Mamie, you are too severe with Françoise. She's unhappy. Last night she cried."

"Do you think so, my treasure?" Mélanie was constantly amazed at this child's perceptions, at her wisdom. She herself—oh, she knew it well—was not wise, too imperious and dominating. But one could learn from one's children, and she would learn. "Perhaps you're right," she said thoughtfully, stroking Solange's hair.

"How can she know you love her?" Colette asked earnestly.

"But, *darling,* how can you ask such a thing?" Mélanie's eyes filled with tears. She looked over the two heads, one so fair, one so dark, at the goats, at the red gable of the house. Love Françoise? Why, the children were part of herself.

"She's lonely."

"She has us," Solange piped in her clear flute voice.

"Still she's lonely. Don't you think so, Mamie?"

And we are lonely for her, Mélanie was thinking. We are shut out from each other. We are all lonely and trying to make the connections. Paul, myself——

"Maybe so, my treasure, my wise one. Your Mamie will try to behave better." She said it lightly because she was deeply touched.

"Thank you, Mamie." Colette slid down and, suddenly a child again, lay down in front of one of the little goats and rubbed her nose against its furry forehead, caressing it as if she were a goat herself.

Solange, whose head Mélanie had been stroking absent-mindedly, was half asleep.

The little ones went in to supper; Mélanie sat in the garden, alone. For once she felt tired, far outside her own house, far off from them all. She could see Françoise bending over her drawing board on the closed-in veranda. Mélanie got up and went in. She felt herself quite empty-handed. She stood at the door, filled with longing to take this great girl in her arms, enfold her, cherish her forever and ever, knowing that that would never do.

And then the miracle happened. Françoise turned to her with one of her rare beautiful smiles and asked:

"Is it all right, Mamie? I'm having trouble with the daisy—it looks too delicate somehow."

"Mmmm," Mélanie said, drawing back critically, "try some black. Try more shadow, darling."

It was all right. They did not need to speak of the afternoon. Mélanie, life flooding back into her, full of praises, stopped at the landing on her way upstairs and looked down at the garden, at the great spreading pool of shadow under the willow, at the darkness on the ground and the shimmer of light on the tops of the trees. Now she was in the house again, looking out. She was safe.

What perils one moves through in a day! Sometimes she felt a real terror that she would not be able to manage, that she would never be able to make it—port, or the evening, or wherever the ship of the day was making passage through so many treacherous currents and unknown rocks and shoals.

But to the little ones who found her standing there, one arm up against the window, she looked serenity and poise itself, their mother, their fixed, inalterable star—beautiful and steadfast. They sat down on the window ledge, their legs dangling down over the stairs, and looked up at her. It seemed somehow magical to be gathered here in the middle of the stairs. They did not want to go. So they sat, dangling their legs, talking, making plans for to-morrow.

Pierre, on his way to the bathroom, heard the murmur of their voices and looked down from the third-floor landing. He could see their three heads in the dusk and the bare swinging legs. He could see Mélanie's round white arm and the curve of her back. He wished passionately that she were his mother, that he could run down the stairs and bury his head in her breast and tell her how much he loved her, how his whole life had changed since he had known her, how he would do something great in the world for her sake.

"What are you doing on the stairs?" he called almost angrily. And the spell was broken.

Chapter II

Summer was the children's world. The minute the old car had backfired and roared its way down the driveway, the minute they had waved and heard the last bang and pulled the gate shut, the garden was theirs, the world was theirs, the summer world. They could pick cherries, or go for a walk in the forest, or out across the fields to the brickkiln or to one of the farms; they could build secret houses in the trees. Françoise might pick one of her mixed bunches of flowers to paint and then take it up as an offering to her father's study. Pierre might sneak up there and sit for hours on the floor reading books of philosophy and history. The day was theirs. They were masters of the garden and the goats, small imperious gods, each with his special devotion, and, like the gods on Olympus, squabbling a good deal among themselves.

But before they were quite free, each had his appointed task. The little ones ran up to help Bo-Bo make the beds. Françoise swept the downstairs rooms (Lou-Lou was alone now, so the housework had been divided up). Pierre went to the kitchen to dry the dishes.

He and Lou-Lou had long heart-to-heart talks about love (Pierre was, if possible, more sentimental than she, so he made a sympathetic audience) and about Marxism. She could not tease him as all the Duchesnes did. She was properly impressed, even though she didn't understand what he was talking about and crossed herself frequently. They were good friends, he and Lou-Lou. It eased his sense of inferiority to show off to her, and she felt that he was more her own kind than the Duchesnes.

But this morning Lou-Lou was out of sorts. She called him "Clumsy" angrily when he dropped a dish, even though it didn't break. She behaved like a grownup who doesn't want to be bothered with children.

Pierre brooded on being called clumsy and tried to think of something that would make her pay attention to him.

"What's the matter with you this morning? I bet it's Jacques again!"

"You be quiet!" she answered savagely. He had drawn blood with the first prick. Lou-Lou looked as if she were going to cry. She was not a handsome girl. She was strong and coarse-looking, but she had beautiful deep blue eyes set far apart, and her full bosom and air of sexual vitality, of great reserve energy in repose, was the sort to make boys whistle when she went past. More than anything she wanted to get married. But everything always seemed to go wrong.

One young man had moved away and never answered her carefully composed sentimental letters. Another had left her when she refused to sleep with him, for Lou-Lou was a good Catholic and would go only just so far. And now there was Jacques, whom she loved fiercely and wanted more than she had ever wanted anyone, so she bit her pillow at night and felt dizzy when she thought of him.

"What's the matter, doesn't he love you any more?" Pierre went on relentlessly and crudely, as only a fifteen-year-old boy avid of experiences he doesn't understand can be crude and relentless.

Lou-Lou burst into tears. She ran out into the court at the back and left him feeling very foolish, with the dish towel in his hand. "Oh well, women," he said to himself.

Lou-Lou was ashamed of herself. She washed her face at the pump and came back, dignified and silent. It was a shame to have given way before that silly fat little boy. What did he know about love?

"I'm sorry, Lou-Lou," Pierre murmured, blushing furiously. He would have liked to put an arm around her but he didn't know how, and he blushed because he was thinking about putting an arm around her.

To his great astonishment she slapped his face.

"And keep your eyes where they belong!" she said savagely.

It was true, he had been looking at her breasts, but how did she read his thoughts like that? What was happening to him? Pierre would have liked to fall through the floor, vanish. Instead he dried the dishes meticulously, keeping his eyes fixed to each one as if his life depended on it.

Lou-Lou was thinking, All men are the same. All they want is to lay hands on you, without love, without tenderness. What do they know about how a woman feels, she asked herself, about how a woman wants children, about how a woman wants a man, for life, for always, not dirtily under a bush for a thrill? What did Jacques want of her, always laughing and teasing and trying to get her into a corner? He thinks he's too good for me, that's it.

"Run along now, Pierrot," she said with sudden tenderness.

And Pierre was glad to go, glad to take refuge in his books up on the third floor, glad to be by himself and not to think. Or rather to think about the revolution and how he would be a hero when he grew up.

But he was routed out by the little ones who ran up to get him to work in the garden. Croll came only two days a week now; he was getting old, and the Duchesnes were having to cut down everywhere on expenses. Besides, the children were old enough to take on some responsibilities. They worked very hard in the garden. It was in the family tradition. They had watched their mother doing it for years, and they wanted to be like her. Sometimes Colette went quite white when they had finished carrying the pails for the evening watering, but this was morning and everyone full of energy. Even Solange for a little while worked quite hard, earning a word of praise from Françoise, who, when she was alone with the children, imitated her mother.

"Well done, Solange. You can go and play now," she said. "Pierre, you're doing nothing—you haven't even got half through the row. Look at Colette's row."

Pierre hated working in the garden. He was sweating already. The children had no respect for him. They were all as hard as nails and he was so white and soft. He was no good at games and cried when he lost.

"I'll help you, Pierre," said Colette magnanimously. She had been reading *Little Women* and wanted more than anything at the moment to be good like Jo and Beth and Amy. And then she loved Pierre. He wanted to be a poet; she never told him, because she didn't dare, but she had decided to be a poet too. She kept a little book of poems addressed to the fairies for whom she made nests and houses all over the garden. Colette believed in fairies with an unshakable belief that no teasing changed. She was quite certain that there was a plum-tree fairy and a willow fairy with long green hair; the goats knew it too. She had seen them shy when a fairy sat on their backs.

Françoise felt happy this morning. She took one look at Lou-Lou at breakfast and decided that something had gone wrong with Jacques. That was enough to make her feel happy. But then she was pleased with her painting of the daisies. The black had helped. And for once she felt eased of the struggle against her parents. Perhaps everything would be all right.

The sun poured down on them. Pierre thought he would die if they didn't stop soon. He took off his shirt. Solange made up a song about weeding; it turned into another about how fat Pierre was, and then she stopped because Colette frowned; she stopped and dissolved in wicked, delighted giggles. Though there were only two years between her and Colette, she seemed like a baby, wanting nothing so much in the world as to be loved, only unhappy if she were left alone. At night she stroked and even sucked an old shawl which she would not be parted from. At seven she was having reading difficulties still. Everyone took it for granted that she would not be brilliant. She was just to be the darling, the cherished, the baby. It didn't matter whether she learned to read or not. That was Paul's feeling, and even Mélanie and Bo-Bo found themselves slipping into it. But Mélanie wondered sometimes what she would become.

Pierre sat down between the rows of carrots and wiped his face and neck with a huge handkerchief. It was really hot. Even the birds were quiet in the blaze of noon. The trees didn't stir. The air seemed to have a pulse, as waves of heat beat up from the earth. Françoise decided they had done enough.

The three girls ran panting to the willow and lay down on their backs under it, and Pierre finally pulled himself together and followed them. For once they were all silent.

"I wonder what Hans will be like." Colette chewed a piece of grass thoughtfully.

"Sale petit Boche," said Solange in the tone of voice she had heard Lou-Lou use.

They all laughed, and then they were silent. It was not quite nice somehow to hear Solange say those words. It made them feel uncomfortable.

"Whatever you do," Colette admonished earnestly, "you mustn't say that to him."

But Solange had to try it once more. *"Sale Boche,"* she said again, with evident relish.

"Stop it, Solange! I'll slap you." It was clear that Françoise meant what she said.

"Why does he have to come here in the first place, that's what I want to know?" Colette broke in angrily.

To them all it seemed a menace, an end to their privacy and freedom. With Mamie away all day, they would have him on their hands. They would have to be polite.

"His father is a friend of Papa's—a prewar friend," Françoise answered in a very grown-up voice. "Besides, he's a guest. He'll have to behave himself."

"He's a German."

"And just what is wrong with being a German?" Pierre sat up. A pack of silly little girls, silly little bourgeoises, ignorant and prejudiced.

Colette stopped chewing her piece of grass. Solange rolled over on her stomach and looked at him with amused indulgence. Françoise resented his tone.

"They're the enemy, that's all. They invaded Belgium in 1914."

"They killed Lou-Lou's mother and all her brothers and sisters," Solange broke in excitedly.

Pierre spat with conviction, with so much conviction that it reached all the way from where he was sitting to the path. For a moment they were so lost in admiration of this feat that they almost forgot what they were arguing about.

"Old wives' tales. Do you still believe all those atrocity stories? Nothing but Allied propaganda. Everyone knows that. It was a war for markets, a war of expansion, that's all. Only Germany had the hard luck to want to expand after everyone else had grabbed the plums."

"They killed Lou-Lou's mother," said Solange. She was in a rage. "They killed Lou-Lou's mother," she screamed at him, standing up and stamping her foot. "I hate the Germans—hate them—hate them," she chanted. She was red in the face.

"All right, you hate them," he said wearily. But when she had quieted down, he went on. "You're an ignorant little puss," he said, tickling her leg with a piece of grass. Solange giggled before she had time to remember she was angry, and regretted it at once. "I don't care what you say," she said, lifting her head a moment and then burying it in her arms, "when Hans comes I'm going to put a frog in his bed."

"A lot of good that'll do us," said Colette grimly. Everything seemed all mixed up and difficult and sad all at once. The day was spoiled. She felt ashamed of Solange but she couldn't decide just why. She was only repeating what she heard. But it had sounded horrid.

"Aren't you ever going to forget the past?" Pierre asked earnestly. "Can't you see we'll never get anywhere in this Godforsaken little country unless we're part of something bigger, unless we work with people everywhere all over the world for the revolution?" For once they were too absorbed by his own conviction to pick up the word "revolution" and fling it at him. The revolution was Pierre's King Charles's Head.

"The Left is stronger in Germany than it is anywhere else in the world. They are our best friends. Jaurès knew that. Jaurès believed in the German working people. If he had lived——"

"Who was Jaurès?" Colette asked. She always wanted to know everything. Françoise did not want to listen. It bored her. And now he would go on for hours.

"Jaurès, my child, was the great French socialist and labor leader. If he had lived, there would have been no war."

Françoise had had enough. She got up and yawned.

"Where are you going?" He was talking to and for Françoise. Colette was too young to understand these things. "If you listened to me once in a while you might learn something."

"I'm not interested in politics."

"What are you interested in?"

"Art," she said crisply, and walked away, her head high, looking very handsome and self-assured.

But Pierre was not to be pushed aside. "Art, art," he called as he got up heavily and trotted after her. "My God, Franci, who's going to have a chance to be interested in art or anything else if we have another war?"

"Another war? Impossible! Mamie says it is impossible."

She was infuriating, illogical. "You're impossible. I don't know why I bother to talk to you."

"Why do you?" They were standing under the arbor at the front door now.

"I hate you," he said passionately. "All you Duchesnes. You think you know everything. I hate you! I hate you!" he shouted as she went in and closed the door behind her.

The day was spoiled beyond repair. Colette gave it up. She felt tired. Why did they always pull at each other? Why couldn't they ever sit and talk quietly like grown-up people? And then she remembered even grown-up people couldn't talk about these things quietly. The fairies never argued or got angry. They were always very quiet and happy, living their lives. She would go now and make a bower for a fairy out of marguerites. She would weave a tiny little crown for a fairy and leave it in a secret place, far from any spiders or grasshoppers, perhaps up in the cherry tree.

Chapter III

Mélanie never got used to the wonders of having a car, a little flying sofa on which she and Paul sat every morning whisking through the cool green alleys of trees, coming out into the great lawns and the artificial lakes of the park, watching the sun filter its way through shining layers of leaves—all green, all light, all shadow. Brussels never looked so beautiful as early in the morning when they turned out of the forest into the great avenues: servants were out flinging pails of water down the stone steps, washing the sidewalks; all the windows shone in the light; the city seemed to have an airy elegance, to be made all of light and space. But it was, after all, an intimate elegance, the elegance of a provincial drawing room where one was well known. Sometimes they saw the King out for his morning ride, looking like a kindly professor; this sight, so familiar to thousands of citizens who smiled and said, "See, the King," and lifted their babies up to get a good view, seemed the very signature of home. There was the King, at home in his capital, loved, honored, taken for granted. People felt happy seeing him ride past. All was well.

All over the city people were getting ready for business, the waiters taking the chairs off the tables, the florists unpacking baskets of flowers to set up on the small street stands, the tobacconists standing in their doorways waiting for customers, and Mélanie's heart sang to be part of the city, to be part of this innocent gay morning world. Always, every morning, she had the feeling that something wonderful might happen. She ran to open the mail, convinced that there would be good news. It was absurd to be so optimistic, she knew, but she felt happy. How could she help it? It was ever so much better to have the weight of the big house off their shoulders. And then Paul was with her now. Paul would be upstairs all day making his fine drawings, standing at the big drawing board, whistling, reciting poetry under his breath. They had never been so close. They had never been less in love, perhaps that was why. "He's my good friend, my dear," she thought happily. Would it be like this always? Had they really come to port?

Summer meant a lull in business and a chance to catch up. Mélanie had time to draw up inventories, make plans, time to breathe and enjoy, time to run upstairs and see how Paul was getting on, time to do the show window herself. There was nothing she liked better.

In the smaller place there was more intimacy between the Duchesnes and the people who worked for them than there had ever been. Mélanie brought cold lunch in a hamper from the country, and Paul sometimes went out and got a bottle of beer, or the Jeans brought up hot soup or coffee, and the whole family gathered for an informal picnicky lunch in Paul's studio. Sometimes friends dropped in, Francis or the ebullient fantastic Maurice, director of the theater, and an old friend. The business felt ten years younger in the new place. They weren't making any money, but who cared? As long as they could keep going, times were bound to change.

Every day palaces were going up in the Avenue des Nations, embassies, great houses built by rich importers from the Congo. There were big orders just around the corner, and meanwhile what fun to be making a window, all blue and white with the modern pewter Mélanie had invested in.

"Hand me the big platter, mademoiselle. See, that will just do it."

Mélanie was so busy and pleased with what she was doing that she didn't notice Mademoiselle's monosyllabic answers. Mademoiselle had arrived very late and been properly scolded. Perhaps she was still a little upset. When Mélanie climbed out of the window and back into the shop, a little out of breath with the effort, she turned to her and said, "*Allons,* am I forgiven? Am I really such an old tartar, mademoiselle? Friends?"

"That's better," she said as Mademoiselle shook her outstretched hand. But now she had a chance to look her in the eyes, it was clear that something was wrong. That man again, I suppose, Mélanie thought angrily. Mlle. Louvois had been living for years—everyone knew about it—with one of the big couturiers in Brussels. And for years she had been going through one crisis after another, incurably romantic, incurably sentimental.

She was getting older. She wore too much make-up. Her hair had gotten a brighter and brighter red. It couldn't go on forever. And what was to become of her then?

When the bell tinkled and a shy young girl came in to ask if by chance they needed another salesgirl or typist, Mélanie talked to her to give Mademoiselle a chance to pull herself together. And soon Mélanie was making all sorts of promises, calling up friends, determined to get the child a job.

Paul was reciting the *Nuit de Mai* when Mlle. Louvois came in; he had arrived at his favorite passage:

> "*Ils tracent dans l'air leur cercle éblouissant,*
> *Mais il y pend toujours quelque goutte de sang,*"

he declaimed, surrounded by little pots of paint and the fine Japanese brushes he used for his designs.

Something in Paul's voice and the majesty of the poem, its grandiose self-pity, broke down all Mlle. Louvois's defenses. She did not want to cry. It would ruin her make-up. But she couldn't help it.

Paul was never surprised by violent emotion. It was so evidently there in everyone, just under the skin, waiting to leap out. Looking into people's eyes as they walked along the street, he saw it—murder, despair, violence, just under the skin.

"The beautiful and the mondaine like you, mademoiselle, should never cry," he said quietly without moving toward her. Curious creature, he was thinking. This is what happens when a woman imagines that love can be everything.

"Idiot! Idiot!" But now she had begun, she was lost. There was no stopping the tears of shame, of despair, the ugly female tears, the tears of the betrayed. They tore at her face and through her whole body as if they had claws.

Paul nodded his head sadly. Poor woman. Poor woman, he thought, and he came round and sat on the arm of the chair opposite her.

"Tell me the whole story, old friend," he said kindly. "We've been through a lot together here. Tell me," he said, pouring out a little glass of brandy from the cupboard and handing it to her.

The brandy nearly choked her, but then it crept through her veins like consolation. She looked at him with great grateful eyes, still full of tears. "Oh, monsieur." But little by little the story came out, the petty sordid story of the middle-aged man tired of his mistress, keeping her on out of pity, going to see her once a week, once a month, forgetting her, taking a young girl to work for him, going to bed with her. Old old story, Paul thought. And yet it was not like that. Because at the bottom of it was the helpless, devouring need to love, to love through everything and in spite of everything, beyond humiliation, beyond despair. Only children and the very old know this love, understand it, love naked without hope, without anything to sustain it, without anything to help it through the bad times as marriage does, as physical passion does—the impossible, Paul was thinking. And against his thoughts the broken, childish counterpoint of Mademoiselle's story poured out.

"I know I am getting old and ugly," she said harshly, "but I love him. I have loved him for twenty years. Does that count for nothing? He's not young himself. He won't find a young girl who can love him as I do—we have all our lives behind us—the things we remember, the little things——" But she could not go on.

"That would be true if you were his wife, my poor Louise."

She made a gesture of abnegation. She blew her nose. "I know," she said simply and with dignity.

Paul was a comfort to people just because his view of life was pessimistic, because he was never surprised or indignant. He was comforting because he suggested that there was nothing to do but accept. The outward change would not happen, so the inward change was necessary. He could be truly objective, as if at such moments there were no blood in the mind, as if it were crystal-clear and crystal-cool, a machine for calculating human emotion, not feeling it.

"You must go on loving him."

"I can't help it," she said quietly.

"But you cannot expect him to come back, to be the same, to change now. He won't change. Because in the absolutely pure abstract sense there is no such thing as enduring love, enduring passion. Love changes inevitably; the intensity changes; no two people ever stay at the point of romantic love forever—but that is where you have wished this to stay, where it had to be to exist at all. It was love in a vacuum."

"But then," she asked passionately, "what's the meaning? What is it all for?"

"Ah, my poor Louise, that you have to answer for yourself. The meaning is in you. After all, for you it is the same as it always was.

For you it is there, as it always was. It is he who has lost you, lost all he felt for you, and that is a great loss. He has lost his youth, his constancy—he has lost the meaning."

Outside the window a flock of white pigeons wheeled and turned and settled one by one on the ridge of a red-tiled roof. Paul and Louise both turned at this rush of movement in the air outside and watched them. She felt calm now, calm and relieved, as if she had laid down a great burden she had been carrying alone. And she turned from the pigeons, from the blue air outside, to Paul and looked at him with a sort of wonder. Madame was lucky to have such a husband. He would never falter. He would never change.

"What is it, Louise?" he asked gently, seeing the mask of suffering close down again over her face which had looked so pure, so serene a moment before.

Jealousy, the most degrading human emotion, what did one do with that? For the physical images which Paul's gentle words had dissipated had seized her again. Horror and degradation. And all that had been pure and violent between her and Charles turned to something filthy. For the first time in her life Mademoiselle used an ugly word.

"Ah yes, ah yes, they're not easy, these little tortures we set ourselves to suffer, to surpass. We live through them—we shut our eyes and grit our teeth and live through them blindly. Or, if we are sensitive, aware like you, we open our eyes and stare at them, stare at them until we have seen and understood everything, examined it, possessed it. The possession of physical suffering in silence, in acceptance, that is something. And do you think that a single human being lives through his life without some horror, some humiliation, some ache in the flesh, some such torture? Nonsense, we're all on the rack in one way or another."

What can he have suffered, she wondered bitterly, with his wife and three beautiful daughters, his whole natural life? Not, like her, shut away from all normal joys and sorrows, shut into this prison where the light was never turned off, where one must endure the blaze night and day, day and night.

"No," she said sharply, "you don't know—you can't know——"
and then, catching herself up, "I'm sorry, monsieur. I don't know
what I'm talking about."

"Look into people's lives. Look into anyone's life. There is always
a nightmare somewhere."

He was standing at the window looking out. What would he
say next? Where was he leading her?

"Yours?" she asked.

For a moment she thought he hadn't heard. He stood so still
looking out. Then he gave a little bitter laugh, a mocking laugh,
and came over and sat down opposite her.

"Mine? To be a failure. What do you think?" His voice had
turned to acid, all the gentleness gone out of it. "To be caught between two worlds without the strength to live fully in either—to
want the purest possible life, to want to live in and for the idea,
to want to go far out where no one has ever been, into the stratos-
phere—and to want to be understood, to be listened to, to be published, what? To be a success—yes," he said harshly, with hatred
in his voice, "I admit it: to want those second-rate barterers and
grocers, the publishers and editors to want my commodity, to
want what I have to sell. Idiotic, isn't it? And the result, mademoiselle——" He got to his feet and walked up and down, now as
if he were enjoying himself, like an actor on a stage, playing some
dramatic scene of self-revelation for her; and she thought. They're
all children really. Even he. What a child he seemed to her suddenly, what a boy.

"The result," he went on—"that I am nothing, a poor father, a
poor husband—yes, I *am,* inconsiderate, selfish—and a bad philosopher. Ah, you don't know what it is to come here day after day
and feel satisfied when I have made an adequate design for a desk,
to see the gratitude in my wife's eyes because now at last after all
these years I am of some use to her in the business, to see what it
means, and at the same time to know that I am compromising
what I really mean, that I am getting farther and farther from the

life I meant to have, from the things I meant to do——" He stopped and went back to his desk and stood there leaning on it looking at her. He had never looked at her before, and for one moment their eyes met and each shivered with the contact as if each had seen more than he meant to see, given more than he knew he was giving.

Mélanie came in. "Where is everybody?" she asked, looked from Paul to Mlle. Louvois and understood at once what had been happening. Paul will have been comforting her, she thought gratefully. He always knows what to say.

"It's time for lunch, my children, and we have a most delicious potato salad, if I say so myself—and cold ham which Jean somehow inveigled out of his friend down the street."

She sat down on the arm of Mademoiselle's chair and put one arm around her. *"Allons, mademoiselle, un peu de courage!"* she said with that commanding warmth they all depended on.

Mademoiselle, who felt she had been carried way out into some new sphere, saw the familiar world click back into place again.

Chapter IV

When Hans finally came early in August and turned out to be brown and fair and shy, they all loved him at once. Mélanie had always wanted sons. Now she called Pierre and Hans "My two boys," and if she had asked them to do some heroic act they would have been overwhelmed with happiness; as it was, Hans worked like a beaver in the garden, waiting at the gate for her to come home, longing for a word of praise, homage in his heart. Pierre wrote her rhapsodic poems in Flemish addressed to some heroic earth-goddess whom Mélanie did not recognize as herself.

Back from the office in the evening, surrounded by her troop of

children, Mélanie felt: This is how life should be, standing bare-
footed by the pump, pumping water into Colette's pail which was
handed on to Solange and then to Françoise and then to Pierre
and finally to Hans, who poured it over the cabbages one by one,
and then the carrots, the onions, the beans. It was hot. They were
all tired after the day. But the rhythm of arms swinging the pails,
the heat, the laughter, all had the air of happiness over them. How
lucky they were to live in the country, to be a houseful of children,
to be safe, to have drawn the magic circle of home around them—
this was the only security that mattered, the security of love, the
security of the family—beside it the peril and insecurity of the business, the way in which they could go on, send the children to university, pay the bills, was a small light peril. With one's bare feet
touching the cool hard earth in the garden, it seemed quite unreal.
With the air full of "Hurry up, Mamie, another pail!" "Time to
change hands—Hans at the pump, all move up one!" or "Oh,
Mamie, I'm too out of breath, don't make me laugh," from a small,
red-faced, giggling Solange who held everything up while she
dropped her pail.

The children did not examine happiness. They lived in it as
fish live in water. It was splashing water from the pump over your
body when you were hot. It was the lovely relaxed tiredness of fin-
ishing the job and lying down on the grass, feeling your heart
pumping violently all through your body. It was hunger and waiting for the supper bell. To Solange it was the gold hairs on Hans's
hard brown arms. It was summer and friendship and home. It was
Papa throwing open his window and leaning out to call down a
greeting.

And to Hans it was superlatively the Duchesnes, all of them, all
of them together and the house and the garden and the goats and
the ducks. At home everything felt very still and stuffy. He had
never known a family like this. He could not make them out. Their
business seemed to be going on the rocks, and nobody cared. They
were familiar with servants; they did their own work, and yet they

behaved like aristocrats. They didn't seem to want anything they didn't have. They didn't worry all the time. And they talked so much about everything, things he had never heard talked about: Lou-Lou's love affairs, history, the characters of all the children. Everyone was treated with respect, as if his opinions mattered, even the children's. Everyone seemed to be responsible for himself. More than anything, none of them seemed afraid. It was that, perhaps—the absence of fear. What made it? And why was it so different at home?

"Hans, hurry up, you'll be late for supper!"

He went in slowly.

"Our engineer is late," Mamie teased as she ladled out the soup from a great tureen. With such a large family, the little breakfast room was abandoned; they ate their meals in the big formal dining room, cool and delicious in summer, looking out into the French garden. "Our engineer is taking his time."

He had told them his dreams of being a dam builder, of going to America to study the great new dams there. So now he was the engineer and Pierre the poet. Mamie behaved as if they were already established in their professions. She talked to them seriously about literature, about engineering, as if they were men.

"What shall we have after supper, children, *Nils Holgersson* or poems? Papa said he would read."

"Poems, poems!" they shouted like birds opening their mouths and vociferously calling for worms. Solange would fall asleep, of course; she always did.

It was still a little difficult for Hans to follow French poetry, and sometimes they asked him to read from Goethe and Schiller. Or Pierre would bring downstairs his precious Karel van de Woestyne, the great Flemish poet, and defy them all to find greater poetry in any language.

And sometimes Colette curled up beside Hans and leaned her head on his shoulder. Then he stopped breathing, he was so happy. The magic circle really closed around him. He was inside.

Pierre's fierce defense of Germans seemed triumphantly vindi-cated. For wasn't Hans a German they could all love? And did anyone even remember how they had talked that afternoon two weeks before?

He himself, plunged into this new atmosphere, still tingling with the shock of it, like a diver changing from one element to another, responding to the shock of water, had had no time yet to catch his breath. He was simply splashing around happily in a new life. He listened; he observed; he adapted himself so that he might be-come as much as possible a Duchesne. He had the lover's madness, the wild desire to please, and the special awareness which made it easy to please. The summer seemed an enchantment, and his let-ters home were long paeans of praise, "Today we cleaned out the duckpond and laughed very much at the lazy Pierre who fell into the muck; yesterday we went for a long walk to the big farm. These farms are built around a court and all the manure piled up in the middle, but the peasants are good people, though I don't know how they can stand the smell." . . . "Today I had a long argument with Pierre about Marxism; he has read a great deal; he talks about Rosa Luxemburg—could you send me a book about her?" . . . "Today Tante Mélanie said I had cut the hedges very well; it was a hard job and my wrists are sore from holding the big shears. I am learning a lot here." . . . "Colette showed me a poem today. It was very good. She is a funny little girl; she believes in fairies; she looks like Greta Garbo; she seems very old and very young at the same time. I think she is a genius." . . . "I have gained ten pounds."

Mélanie and Paul, driving into town, often talked about Hans and his parents. Mélanie especially held him up as an example of a well-brought-up boy, disciplined, able to handle himself, and compared him with Pierre, the always-late, lazy individualist, selfish and spoiled. "Of course Pierre is an intelligent boy," she would add, "but what a pity that Emile and Suzanne have no idea how to bring him up."

But as the long, hot August days shimmered on the edge of autumn, as the grass turned brown except under the trees, and every now and then the heavy thud of an apple falling startled the goats, and the terrifying summer storms began, the tension in the air, playing on the children's nerves, changed the honeymoon atmosphere they had lived in for weeks. It was nothing tangible—Solange still climbed up onto Hans's lap and whispered secrets in his ear; Colette brought him her poems; Pierre and he went for long walks, arguing about politics and life and religion; Françoise withdrew almost completely and had a long bout of painting every day for hours, so she had by the end of August a whole set of flower pieces, so beautiful that Mamie had them framed and hung in the dining room. Everything seemed the same and they did not know themselves what was happening. But there were tiny incidents. One day Hans found Croll evening up the hedge he had clipped a few days before himself.

Lou-Lou in the kitchen heard him shout at the old man, "Stop that, you old fool. That's my job. I did it last week," saw Croll obstinately shake his head and go on quietly. For anyone could see the pure line of the hedge was gone. It must be flat as a table, cut with an unerring eye and knowing hands.

She stood in the kitchen window with her hands on her hips and saw the whole scene played out, saw Hans snatch the shears out of the old man's hands and stamp his foot. She had been waiting for a long time for the German to show himself. Now she was glad. She ran out, her sabots clattering on the stone court. She would show that little Boche how decent people behaved.

"Do something else. The hedge is my job." Hans was standing imperiously before the helpless old man like a young troll, on fire with pride and anger, brandishing the shears.

Lou-Lou walked up to him and slapped his face, took the shears out of his hands, and gave them back to Croll. "Don't pay any attention to the boy, Croll."

"Who do you think you are?" Hans was blazing now with anger and humiliation. "How dare you touch me?"

"Here in this house we don't treat anyone as you just treated that old man," she said, and walked off.

"You're nothing but a servant. I'll tell Madame," he shouted helplessly after her.

But this was too much. Lou-Lou came back and faced him.

"Oh, so you'll tell Madame! Go ahead and tell her, then. She'll be furious; Croll has worked here for twenty years. No one has the right to speak to him as you did—or to me either, for that matter. Go ahead and tell her, you little——" She paused here as if she couldn't quite bring out the word. "You little German!" she said with pure hatred.

So that's how they really feel, Hans thought, burning with shame, with anger. So that's how they really feel! It seemed then suddenly as if all the happiness of the last weeks were a sham, a beautiful stage-set put up for his benefit over the reality—hatred. He went up to his room and walked up and down, cursing. Of course Tante Mélanie would take Lou-Lou's side. Wasn't she a Belgian? Weren't they all Belgians?

But when Mélanie and Paul came home, Lou-Lou didn't tell them. Nothing was said. Nothing had changed. Everyone loved him. He was part of the family. And if the servants behaved that way, well, they were servants. Who cared about them? He and Lou-Lou avoided each other, and that was that.

Lou-Lou hadn't told Madame because she was a little ashamed herself, but she told Pierre, and Pierre was shocked. Hans was his friend. Well, perhaps it was the heat and he had lost his temper. Anyone might do that, Pierre reasoned, but he found himself observing Hans with a new detachment, wondering about him— perhaps a little glad in spite of himself to discover the flaw in everyone's hero, to guess that there might be a flaw.

Pierre and Uncle Paul were always having long discussions about

Belgium, and one evening when they had sat outside under the apple trees until it was quite dark, they were deep in argument. The little ones had long since gone to bed. For once Françoise was sitting leaning against her father, enjoying the coolness, pleased with herself and the world. Hans lay on his back in the grass watching the lights come on in the house and the figure of Bo-Bo moving back and forth from the window, half listening as Uncle Paul's voice rose and fell, a human accompaniment to the steady song of the crickets.

At first it had astonished Hans—now he had grown accustomed to this constant criticism of one's own country, "dense, heavy little country," as Uncle Paul called it, "narrow provincial little country." Now he was talking again:

"Don't you see, Pierre, that your Flemish movement is only an exacerbated provincialism, the apotheosis of provincialism? Culturally no one denies its reality and its importance. Politically it just doesn't make sense. It's a little like the Catholic Church—as long as you look at it as a mystical experience it is all very well. No one wants to deny anyone their little ecstasies. But the minute it becomes a political power, a political power which must by its very nature defend property, defend privilege, it is simply a menace and must be fought as a menace. As a Belgian I must say I cannot see as practical anything which divides the country—the proof is how useful it was to Germany during the war. Who made the University of Ghent into a Flemish-speaking university? The Germans," said Uncle Paul with a shrug.

In the grass, where he had lain so relaxed, Hans began to listen attentively, the hair on his neck prickling. Germany, Germany, would they never stop thinking and talking about Germany?

"Just because Germany used a strong inner compulsion, used what was already there, doesn't mean it was bad. I don't see that," said Pierre, warming to the argument.

"No, but the fact remains that many Belgians, because of their being partisans of one group within the country against another, found themselves playing the German hand. And that, I suggest, is a weakness."

"Well, a great many Belgians now play the French hand or the British hand, and that seems to me just as much a weakness, then, from your point of view."

"They happen to be civilized peoples, my dear Pierre." They had forgotten Hans for once.

"And we, you infer, are not civilized? Is that it?" His voice came up at them out of the dark icily.

"Well," said Paul gently (he had no desire to make anyone unhappy; it was far too peaceful an evening), "well, you were never conquered by Rome, you know."

Hans sat up. "And you're proud of that?"

"Perhaps it civilized us," Paul answered gently, yawned, and got up to go.

They won't even talk to me, that was what flashed through Hans's mind. I'm a barbarian to them. The hot, helpless anger flowed through him. I hate them all, he thought bitterly. He had never really been in the magic circle. They had never really included him, only pretended to. All the time they held themselves apart. But I love them, he said to himself. I love them. It isn't fair, he said, feeling intolerably lonely now everyone had gone in and left him, even Pierre. They were there in the lighted house going quietly to bed, clothed in righteousness, and he was outside, lying in the grass in the dark, in the wrong. A German. What did it mean to be a German? Suddenly he wanted to go home, go back to his father and mother, to the quiet house in Frankfort, to be safe from criticism, from doubt. To be a German again and proud of it.

But when he went upstairs to bed he met Mélanie coming from the bathroom in her wrapper and he flung his arms around her and held her so tight she laughed. "You'll strangle me, Hansche."

"I love you," he said in a strained, thick voice.

She rumpled his hair back and looked at him tenderly. "Of

course you do. I love you too, little Hansche. You have become a part of the family. Run along now to bed," she said, pushing him gently, with just the simple authority in the touch of her hand which could heal any child.

It was something in the air. They felt the difference, the slight hostility around them, nobody's fault, nobody's intention. But there it was. All except Mélanie. She refused to believe such things. Hansche was her own boy, the faithful worker in the garden, and she hated to think of his leaving.

Paul made an effort now to draw Hans into their discussions. He even asked him and Pierre to come up sometimes into his sacred study and listen to the radio. And one evening he made a great effort to get Munich, so that they could hear Adolf Hitler giving a pre-election speech.

"I'd like to hear him once—he must be a very powerful orator," Paul had said at dinner. But he was out of temper before they finally got through. Mélanie tiptoed in in her wrapper to listen. The boys sat on the floor; Paul bent over the radio, testing dials and cursing quietly.

"Can't we just hear Big Ben first?" Mélanie asked innocently. That was what she liked best of all, to hear Big Ben ring over the air, making England seem so close. Better than any words. Solid and safe.

But Paul answered irritably, "I've been trying for half an hour to get through to Munich—— There, at last," he said, settling down to listen as a Strauss waltz burst on them loudly. Mélanie vanished into the hall to waltz happily by herself.

"It's just ten. He'll be on in a minute."

Hans waited eagerly for the German voice. He was thrilled thinking of Munich. He had heard his family discussing Hitler contemptuously, but he had not been particularly interested until now. They didn't know anything about politics, his feeling was— and at school one of his best friends was an ardent National Socialist.

And then it came, the flood, the full force of the German language used as a spellbinder, traveling through the night to all the corners of Germany and even here to find a solitary boy sitting on the floor of a Belgian house.

With a movement of sudden shyness before the force of his own emotion, Hans slid over to where he was hidden behind the desk and no one could see him.

"We are not, have never been, defeated. This is the beginning of a new Germany—Germany is great. Germany is powerful—Germany—Germany—Germany——"

Hans was tingling all over. The tears came to his eyes. Germany. The thing to fight for, to die for. Who could understand the flood of love, of passion that the word "Germany," as it was shouted by that voice of a people, could do to a German? It was life pouring in, breaking over like a great wave. Beside the shock of it, the exhilaration, the long intellectual arguments of the Duchesnes, their detachment, turned to dust. This was wine, intoxication, power. His life, his power.

"Paul, I can't stand this. What ranting!" Mélanie went off to bed in disgust. This is not Germany speaking, she thought, just some madman, some hysteric who will be defeated in the election. It was too wild and fantastic to be taken seriously.

Paul smiled. It was interesting psychologically. The man undoubtedly knew how to talk to Germans. After a moment, curious to see its effect on Hans, Paul got up and looked behind the desk. He was met by a flushed excited face, the glare of tear-filled eyes, which blazed at him defiantly, as if to say, "This may be funny to you. But to me it's deathly serious."

Pierre too was fascinated. And yet there was a striking difference in the two boys' faces. Pierre was judging what he heard. He frowned as he concentrated with the effort to understand each sentence in a foreign language. He half shook his head once and looked to Paul for his reaction.

And he was eager to discuss the whole thing with Hans when at last it was over. He called over to the desk gaily:

"Well, Hans, what chance has he got? Tell us the worst."

Hans shook his head like a dog shaking off water. What had Pierre asked? He felt ashamed of his emotion, ashamed and exhausted. It seemed unreal now, a sort of nightmare. "Of course the man is a fanatic," he said condescendingly. But inside him a voice seemed to answer, You are betraying Germany when you say that. He was upset. He wanted to be alone, and, leaving them to wonder what was going on inside him, he went upstairs to bed.

But there, lying in bed, he had the sensation that his bed was a ship and he was sailing away very fast, sailing away from everything here, but he wanted to stay. He didn't want to go. He didn't want to be carried off. He wanted to have time to think, to be himself.

"This is all nonsense," he said, getting up and turning on the light as if to banish a ghost. "The man will never be elected. That's impossible. All reasonable people like my parents will be against him. How could I have been so moved by a screaming hysteric?" He took down a volume of Rilke's poems and after reading here or there, as if to find a talisman, touch it, and go on, he fell asleep.

Downstairs Paul was writing to Schmidt. What did he think about a speech like that? How many people would take it seriously? What was happening in Germany? In spite of himself he felt a deep anxiety, and a pen and a piece of paper seemed poor things with which to try to pierce the darkness. The letter ended:

You must come here for a visit soon. I simply must talk to you, old friend—in spite of one's disgust at nearly everything, one cares about this old Europe.

Your son has given us great pleasure. He is charming, intelligent, and, as Mélanie constantly says, "so well brought up." But I was interested and perhaps a shade alarmed to see what a powerful effect Adolf Hitler's speech made on him. Is there much talk of National Socialism among his school friends? Surely we are not going to become the slaves of incantations and witch doctors?

Your faithful old

PAUL

Chapter V

For once Mélanie was sitting on the back seat because they were taking Françoise to town for the day and she was sitting on the front seat with her father. It was still early enough for the coolness to be in the air, and it flowed past like water, bathing their faces, in the open car.

There they were just ahead of her, her husband and her eldest, their voices lost in the roar of the motor, so there seemed an invisible barrier between her and them, as if they were faces on a screen and she an audience watching, detached, forever close to them, forever separated from them. Françoise had wedged herself as far to the right as she could and was looking out coolly, not giving her father an inch; Paul was evidently talking to her tenderly, consolingly, drawing her to him with the magnet of his love, saying, "Open to me," wooing this elder daughter of his, as he was always impelled to woo every female creature of whatever age. How can she resist him? Mélanie wondered in admiration. I never could.

But from the time she was a little girl Françoise had resisted her father, resisted and fought her way out of the net of tenderness he flung over her, tore her way out fiercely over and over again, would not be touched. That was it, Mélanie said, a fierce chastity; against it Paul's desire to possess a soul, to penetrate to the very inmost core of a person, seemed a sort of rape. Who would win in the end? Could it go on forever? Now, at the end of summer, Mélanie feared a crisis. She had noticed it before: the end of summer is a dangerous time. The children were getting on one another's nerves. Solange had a tantrum the other day over nothing at all; Colette looked listless and tired (was she suffering already at Hans leaving next week?). There was emotion in the air, in the dusty leaves, in the screams of the birds.

And then Lou-Lou. Lou-Lou was becoming a problem. She was

obviously head over ears in love with Jacques, but did he want to marry her? Was there anything in it besides the gossip of the little ones? Lou-Lou would make a devoted wife, and she was a good girl, responsible, honest, but Mélanie had a queer feeling that the last thing Jacques wanted was a devoted wife. He was charming; he was an excellent worker. Monsieur Plante could hardly do without him at the shop. And yet what was it about Jacques? He never seemed quite grown-up though he was nearly thirty—as if there were a blank space, a blasted space somewhere where nothing would grow, as if he had learned to live on air because the root was blasted. But Lou-Lou could not live on air, on charm, on flirtation. Passionate, reserved—she waited. She suffered. She looked bruised, like a fruit stained by its own ripeness; it was time she married. I must have a talk with Jacques, Mélanie thought.

So she surveyed her world, in the morning, on the way to the business, on this late August day. She was sending Françoise over to M. Plante's to look at a children's chest that she had decided to let her decorate: her first real job. The car slowed down and stopped, and they all poured up the back stairs laden with packages. Then Françoise had to be greeted, embraced, told how lovely she looked by the two demoiselles. She did look lovely in a raspberry-colored linen dress, her eyes shining. One wanted to pop a raspberry into her mouth and make her smile, make her laugh, make her fall in love. Someday she would be the patronne; she would run the business. This was taken for granted by everyone. It had always been inevitable, as if she were the crown princess of a reigning dynasty. The business had gone down from mother to daughter, and so it would proceed. Françoise herself had no doubts about this and no conflict. It was what she wanted too. So that every time she came into town she was looking ahead at her kingdom. She plied everyone in sight with questions. She liked nothing better than to be given a job, sorting samples out—or best of all to go with her mother to some client's house and be asked her own opinion about curtains, colors, textures.

But today was even better than the usual days and more exciting. Today she was on her own. Today she would have a chance to do something original, to be entirely responsible. Her head was full of birds and flowers and arabesques of trees, of elephants and monkeys and all the creatures she planned to paint on the doors of the big toy box for a child.

"There, my big girl. Now run along. M. Plante is expecting you— only be back for lunch at twelve." Mélanie gave her a kiss and turned back to her desk.

"Only no flirting with that handsome friend of yours," Paul called maliciously after her. Françoise ran down the stairs blushing. Her father was uncanny. How did he know? How had he found out? It was terrible to have such a father.

Yes, Jacques would be there. And for the first time she was armed. She was going there as Mélanie's daughter, as an artist, as a part of the business. She did not even have to talk to him. He would see how grown-up she was and how serious and how little time she had for him.

But oh, it was a queer thing to have one's knees go back on one like this. She stopped to look in at the lingerie, salmon-colored panties and slips in the windows of the Maison Charme. Françoise looked at each strangely impersonal piece of feminine underwear. What would it be like to have a lover? No, she said to herself, as if she were closing a door firmly, and walked on. People turned to watch her go past—the long swinging stride, something self-absorbed, splendid—wondered who she was, where she was going —not today, but in the end, for life.

"Ah, mademoiselle." M. Plante bowed as he opened the door to her. He was a little old man and he wore a green shade to protect his eyes. "Come in. We are waiting for you. You will see what a beautiful job we have done for you." Françoise hardly listened. She was intoxicated by the smell of wood and chips and sawdust, by the steady hum of a mechanical saw and the sweet shrill scrape of a plane. Carpenters have blue eyes, she thought idiotically, for M.

Plante did indeed have very clear pure blue eyes that looked strange in his wrinkled, ugly old face.

She looked at everything and was disappointed that much of it seemed ugly. Did her mother really have to sell things like that to make a living?

Out of the corner of an eye she saw Jacques bending over a workbench, doing something that required great concentration. He didn't look up. Was he even aware that she had gone past? M. Plante noticed the shadow that had fallen like a curtain over her face. "Mademoiselle is not pleased?"

"Oh yes," she breathed, and knelt down to open the doors. It was all just as she had dreamed it would be, with a secret drawer at the back and a leaf that slipped out to make the chest into a desk. "It is beautiful."

M. Plante nodded his head and ran his hand over the surface thoughtfully. "Not bad, not bad at all. Jacques is turning into a fine workman."

"Jacques?"

"Jacques Croll, one of our young workmen. I'll have him come here in case there is anything you want changed. I'll send him in in a moment, and meanwhile use the desk there. There is paper and anything else you may need."

It was not at all the daughter of the patronne, but the hindside of a little girl, with her head entirely hidden in the chest, whom Jacques found when he sauntered in.

"Hi there," he said as she backed out. "Like it? You look like a donkey in his stall."

"It's perfect," she said in a husky voice. She looked as if she were on the point of tears.

"Well, if it's perfect, you don't need to look so sad about it, Franci. I made it for you," he added with a dazzling smile. "Did you find the secret drawer?" He sat down cross-legged on the floor beside her. "What are you going to paint on the doors?"

"Maybe an elephant, monkeys—I thought Bagheera—an illustration for the Jungle Books, with maybe the white seal inside and the jungle stories outside," she said solemnly. She was too happy to smile. This was life, her life. And Jacques was part of it. They were making something together. It would always be like this. Now they were talking about something, now there was a subject between them, she felt safe.

"What are the Jungle Books?" he asked.

"You don't know the Jungle Books? Oh, Jacques." And then it was all pouring out. She could talk, and, having found her voice, at last able to talk to Jacques, she couldn't stop. She told him the whole story of Mowgli as they sat on the floor, looking into the chest. And while she talked, he watched her. He remembered the jade rabbit. He remembered her as a little girl for whom he used to fly kites. He was sorry for everything. He would have liked to stroke her cheek as if she were a kitten, scratch her under the chin, make her laugh.

"You're looking very grown-up today," he said when the story was finished.

"You weren't listening." Perhaps she had bored him. Perhaps she had talked too much. She fell desperately silent.

"Oh yes, I was, but I was looking at you. I was thinking what a beauty the little girl I used to fly kites with has grown into. I was remembering my sins," he said lightly.

She looked straight ahead, waiting, waiting for something to happen, she didn't know what.

He felt the lightness was wrong. You couldn't talk to Françoise the way you could talk to other girls. Queer little creature. So still and so wild. He saw the pulse in her throat beating, beating. It pierced him all through, as if he were holding a bird in his hand, too much life in too small a space. He would have liked to take her in his arms and rock her and quiet her as if she were a little girl again. Someone, he thought savagely, will break her heart. His hand closed over hers, tight, as if he would crush it.

"Franci," he whispered, "darling."

This was what she had been waiting for, this—a great blaze of fireworks inside her, spreading all through her as if the crimson tree of her blood were on fire.

But what Jacques saw was a young girl, too young, a wild creature caught in his hand, staring straight ahead, severe, frozen. He had done the wrong thing.

He stood up and lit a cigarette.

"I must be getting back to work." He inhaled deeply, and she watched the smoke come out of his mouth, not smoke any more, just a breath. It seemed like magic; everything he did was magic now. "And you, my girl, must be getting to work too." He gave her a last blue look, amused, tender, imperious. "You might tell Lou-Lou that I'll be round tomorrow night," he added, unconscious of the havoc he left behind him; a lifetime compressed into a stroke of lightning when in a few seconds all was illuminated and then all blasted. In the darkness the child towered into a woman.

It is not, after all, the fearfulness of what each person has to meet alone and in himself; it is this set in counterpoint against daily living. It seemed for a while simply impossible for Françoise to go back and face having lunch with the family.

What right had families to know what was going on inside their children? It seemed to Françoise indecent. How could you live so close to people unless you could feel quite solitary and free, be allowed one place, your own soul, to withdraw into? Would her father never understand that? She couldn't pretend that nothing had happened. It must show. It must be blazing on her face. But she could hold up a shield, protect it, keep it hers.

"Hurry up." Mamie leaned out of the studio window and called down to her in the street. "The soup will be cold." Hot soup on a day like this! It seemed the last straw.

"Well, were you pleased, my treasure? Is it what you wanted?" she said, holding her at arm's length and looking at her proudly, and Françoise answered from her dream, from her mask:

"Yes, Mamie."

"Papa has cadged a bottle of beer to celebrate your first job."

Françoise could escape to wash her hands and come back only when they had started eating and she could seem to be absorbed in drinking her soup.

Paul was in one of his gay moods, teasing the two demoiselles. "Beware of this drink," he said, handing Mlle. Zumpt a tiny glass of beer, "it is very strong. You will find yourself writing thousands of francs instead of hundreds on the account books."

And they laughed, the beautiful innocent laughter of grown-up people, people with whole hearts.

"Françoise is silent. Françoise doesn't smile. Françoise cannot believe she has such a foolish papa. Françoise is thinking about the beautiful design she will make for the chest." Her name was like an invocation as he spoke it and as they drank to her.

Only Mlle. Louvois, with her clear blue eyes, looked at Françoise and turned the conversation away. The child was suffering, that was clear enough. But the strange thing about families is that they are so concealed behind prefabricated ideas about each other that the obvious escapes them. Françoise was often moody, silent for no reason, and it was Mélanie's habit to ignore the moods. They always passed.

"Oh, I *am* hungry!" she ejaculated now, putting as much energy and zest into eating as she did into everything else. "Have another roll, Mlle. Louvois; you're eating nothing."

"Maurice was here this morning," Paul said, "as full of fantastic ideas as ever. But he told me the theater was doing marvelously —they have cut the debt down to a hundred thousand francs, a mere bagatelle," he said solemnly, for it was well known that Maurice had absolutely no idea of the value of money. "He is putting on *Dr. Knocke,* and I could see that all the time he was talking he was wondering what pieces of furniture he could make off with for the set. I felt impelled to get up from that chair you are sitting in, Mlle. Zumpt, so he could really look it over."

They all laughed at Maurice, but it was impossible not to love

him. He might have been covered with spangles. He always came
into a room as the clown enters the arena in Paris, the serious
clown, the sad clown all in spangles, with a white face, who
stretches out his arms as the trumpets blow and waits for the
applause, a glittering and tragic figure.

They stopped laughing to listen to steps running up the stairs
three at a time. Speaking of the devil, there he was.

"Hello, old man; forgive me, Mélanie—mesdemoiselles"—he
greeted them all effusively and hurriedly—"forgive my interrupting.
I just wondered if I could possibly borrow that chair—it is just
what we need——"

He was interrupted by a gale of laughter and stood there,
delighted to have been amusing without knowing it, his head
cocked on one side. His face was so mobile that no one remembered
exactly what he looked like—one remembered a vermilion tie,
very black hair, little crinkly eyes, and the famous devilish eyebrows
with pointed tufts that gave him the look of a faun.

"Here you are, you devil. You have no conscience. What do you
think Mademoiselle will sit on now? Stripping us of our last
stick of furniture for a paltry play, turning people out of house
and home!"

"You shall all have tickets, a box, anything you like." He had
now grasped the chair and stood in the doorway holding it against
his stomach. "You know the play? A little marvel of wit—and a
perfect part for me. I'm in heaven!"

"Well, as long as you're in heaven, all's right with the world,"
Paul bantered. There was always an edge in his banter with
Maurice.

"Cabotin," he added under his breath as Maurice crashed down
the stairs. "Hé!" Paul called down, "you can have the chair but not
the whole building with it."

But all the answer they got was a whistle and then the loud purr
of Maurice's racing car.

"What a madman," sighed Mlle. Louvois.

"Well, he enjoys himself," Paul answered cynically.

Françoise looked at her father with a flash of hatred. She adored Maurice. If she could have chosen to be like someone, it would be to be like him.

"He has so much fantasy," Mélanie broke in enthusiastically, "and look what he has done for the theater."

Paul drifted over to his standing desk with his coffee and looked at the drawing on it critically. "Yes, yes," he sighed, "he has a sort of genius. He plucks a nettle and wears it like a laurel wreath." (Maurice had been a failure in Paris and then came back to Brussels and succeeded in creating his own theater.)

Mélanie looked at her husband critically. There was always the stain of acid in his appreciation of anyone's success.

"Monsieur is a cynic," said Mlle. Zumpt, with her genius for the obvious.

"Well, well," Paul mocked her, "you have been with us for twenty years, mademoiselle, and it dawns upon you that I am a cynic. Bravo! What discrimination, what perspicacity!"

There it was again, the edge, the cutting edge in his voice.

"You are impossible, Paul," said Mélanie, laughing at him.

They did not take him seriously. They did not really take him any more seriously than they did Maurice. Only, thought Mlle. Louvois, he has a different way of showing off, that's all.

Only Françoise took him seriously, and as he met her level judging gaze he felt uncomfortable. He went over and put an arm around her, feeling her whole body go tense against him.

"My little girl does not approve. My little girl thinks her papa is a disgrace."

"Yes, I do," said Françoise coldly. Mélanie looked at her in amazement.

"What is the matter with you, Franci? Why are you so glum? Papa is not serious."

But mercifully the bell rang downstairs, and with cries of "A customer, *en avant,* children!" she and Mlle. Zumpt went downstairs, leaving Françoise to clear away.

This was what she had dreaded, to be left alone with her father. She knew, she waited for the change in his voice, the tearing tenderness, the ache of love that would attack her.

"My treasure, what is it? What has happened?" he said, watching her pile up the dishes.

With an immense effort she looked up and smiled.

"Nothing, Papa," she said, and made her escape.

Paul was in the mood to talk. He wandered up and down, erased the penciled letters under the India ink, looked at his drawing, hummed a little tune, went to the window restlessly and looked at the row of pigeons making their everlasting murmur, bobbing their necks in and out at each other, swelling their breasts. The fact is, he thought, I am envious of Maurice. How wonderful it would be to be an actor, to give full rein to one's personality, to be involved in an art and not a science, to be able to use oneself instead of painfully eliminating oneself. "Yes, yes," he sighed, and then called down to Mlle. Louvois. In the last weeks he had come to depend on her. His temptation had never been physical infidelity, but he could never resist exploring a soul, getting down to the naked place of intimacy, of understanding with any woman. He did it with the purest intentions. It was always to help, and he had helped many women with his power to analyze and synthesize experience. It was not a temptation to sin, but to use the real power he had been given, the power of understanding. It had never occurred to him that it was forcing a way into the most closely guarded places in each human being, and that must be dangerous, involving serious responsibility. He had the daring of the amateur where a professional psychiatrist might have hesitated. And quite unconsciously he took it for granted that his "patients" would finally focus their emotions on him.

Mlle. Louvois already felt that some invisible screen which stood between people was removed where she and Paul were concerned. She could talk to him as she had never been able to talk; she discovered things in herself that she had not known were there. She was learning a great deal about marriage that she had never suspected, and it made her a little uncomfortable with Mélanie that she knew so much. It seemed not exactly disloyal, but as if she were looking through a keyhole. Once, as Paul was talking on about his wife, she had interrupted him. "Don't say it."

"Why not?" He had been startled. He didn't know what she meant, didn't seem to feel that he was a man and she a woman, that there are things about women that it is better not to say about one to another.

But today he was anxious to find out what was the matter with Françoise.

"Your daughter is in love."

"Nonsense." Paul was walking up and down as he did so often, his hands in the pockets of his corduroy jacket, pacing up and down as if he could never rest, never sit quiet, never live as other people did, without straining every minute after some invisible quarry. "Nonsense," he said again. "She's a mere child. She's moody, shut up in herself. She has violent crushes like any girl of her age—on Jacques, for instance. My dear Louise, you are incurably romantic," he ended impatiently.

She lit a cigarette and puffed a few times thoughtfully. She was sitting in a leather chair and it felt cool against her back.

"I shouldn't be up here at all, you know. I should be downstairs finding something to do." But she didn't move.

"There's nothing to do on a day like this. Too hot. Who would even buy an ash tray when the sidewalks are like ovens? Stay here and talk to me. I'm bored. I'm restless. Will there be a storm?" He went over to the window and looked out critically, as if he were judging the sky and found it wanting. It was perfectly blue and hard, like the roof of a huge tent, shutting the heat in.

He smiled as he thought of Emile. "Emile is so frightened of thunderstorms that he gets under the bed."

"Not really?"

"Yes, really. That's what it is to be a natural man. Now you,

for instance, might be terrified, but you would never have the
audacity to get under the bed, to admit to yourself how frightened
you were." But before she could answer he turned his back on
her and asked crossly, "What makes you so sure Françoise is in
love?"

"Oh, the way she looked when she came in—I don't know."
What was it really? She couldn't tell exactly why. "She looked
dazzled and hurt and terrified that anyone would notice her. She
made an effort not to show anything. You can't explain these things,
but I knew right away. Is it Jacques?"

Now suddenly Paul seemed to come to life, to focus on the
situation.

"You don't mean it seriously, Louise?" The intensity of his voice
made her hesitate.

"Well, my dear man, I am not a mind reader." She shrugged her
shoulders. "That was my impression. I may be wrong."

"But Jacques is nothing, a lame duck we've helped along. A nice
boy, to be sure——"

Paul was upset. This was the last straw in the middle of all the
heat, at the end of the summer, to have Françoise get into trouble.
She was too young, much too young.

"You mean he's not suitable?" she teased. It was amusing to
see Paul so upset.

"Suitable! Well, of course it's nothing but a childish infatuation.
Suitable! Why, she's much too good for him."

"Well, don't get upset. She has to grow up sometime. She has
to fall in love. It won't last."

"You don't know Françoise. You don't know what a whole
person she is, how serious. Why, a thing like this could blast her
life. I won't have it!" he said passionately. "It's all wrong." And
then, "I don't believe it anyway. I'll go and speak to Jacques. I'll tell
him to mind his own business." He really looked as if he were
going to run out of the building without another word.

"Are you crazy, Paul?" She was sorry now that she had told him.

But how could she know he would take it like this? "For heaven's sake, don't do anything at all. You're the one who will blast her life if you rush in like that. Give it time," she implored him, "and besides, I may be wrong. I am incurably romantic. You said so yourself."

"I must speak to Mélanie. I must talk to my wife." He was all impatience, all fire.

"She's having a business conference with Mlle. Zumpt. It looks as if that new order would go through, half a million francs, not bad."

"Go and get her."

"Oh, Paul, you know I couldn't interrupt her. She'd be furious."

Yes, that was true. Mélanie concentrated on whatever she was doing completely. And in the daytime the business was sacred. "For a philosopher you certainly behave badly," she added.

"This isn't philosophy. This is life. This is my daughter. Can't you understand?"

"You can't stop her heart from beating."

"My dear Louise, she's fifteen."

"Yes, that's what I say. It isn't important. It won't last. Why get so upset about the inevitable? You wouldn't have her unfeeling, insensitive, would you?" she asked pointedly. He had talked enough about the price one pays for awareness. Was he unwilling to have it paid when it came close to him?

Suddenly he sat down as if he were tired of his own violence, as if he dropped it off like a cloak and became again the Paul she had had long conversations with all these weeks.

"I was taken by surprise," he said quietly. "I had no idea——" For once he wasn't able to articulate it in those beautiful flowing sentences as if he were dictating a book. (Often she had wished she could write down what he said exactly as he said it. But now he was a human being, troubled, vulnerable, she loved him as she had not done before.)

Now above all he wanted his wife. He wanted to talk to Mélanie. He felt tired and old. What did Louise know about having children? About how one felt about one's own child? Now it was unbearable that she should suffer—and shut one out of her suffering. For now he was remembering Françoise's face, the fold of her lips, the brilliance of her eyes. Why hadn't he guessed? Why had he let her go?

Louise smoked silently. With all her heart she wished she could help him. But this was a wife's business, and she was no one's wife. When he got up and went to his desk and set himself silently to work, she slipped out.

He didn't even know that she had gone.

Chapter VI

The boys were to leave the next day. Already they were turning the house upside down looking for a misplaced pencil or a pair of rubbers, followed everywhere by the little ones, who were near to tears and got continually in the way. Everyone was jumpy and on edge. And everything here in the house smelled of parting. "Shall we have a *last* game of *Le Nain Jaune?*" "Shall we climb the cherry tree for the *last* time?"

So Bo-Bo finally gave her consent: yes, they could take a picnic lunch and go to the forest. That would get them out of the way and into new surroundings. At once they became wildly gay. Françoise, working in the veranda, angry with the world, heard them stampede past, up and down the stairs (for a compass, for a jackknife, for the rucksacks) like wild Indians. It seemed impossible for any one of them to speak in a normal tone of voice. All was screams and shouts and loud hilarity. And Bo-Bo thought she would never get them out of the kitchen without damage. They had to stuff the hard-boiled eggs, wrap up salt in a little piece of paper, make endless lettuce sandwiches, apple-butter sandwiches, put milk in a thermos, pack the rucksacks—and Pierre insisted on taking several books in case they should want to read. Then when the two boys had selected walking sticks from the stand in the hall and stood ready like mountain climbers, full of responsibility—then the sun went under a cloud. Would it rain? Must the little ones take raincoats? Bo-Bo finally compromised on sweaters tied around their middles. They were off.

"Don't go too far," Bo-Bo called after them. "Take care that Solange doesn't get tired. Don't sit on the damp ground without something under you!"

The gate clicked behind them. They were gone.

Now they were really off and on their own, the four children, who had been so hilarious a moment before, fell silent. They had to walk down the whole avenue to the main road before they crossed over and the adventure really began. The forest stood before them, very still and huge. Once across the car lines, they were in an entirely strange new world.

There were no paths in the forest, or so it seemed, because the brush was all cut out and the tall, straight beech trees rose up on every side, making thousands of alleyways, shedding bronze leaves in the autumn so the whole floor of the forest was a golden carpet. High, high overhead, if you looked up, you could see tiny pieces of blue sky, clouds; the surf of the wind in the tops of the trees never stopped. It was like being underwater, far down below on the earth.

"I'm scared," Solange said in a small voice, holding very hard to Pierre's hand. It was like Little Red Riding Hood's forest: there might be wolves.

"What are you scared of?" Hans teased.

"Wolves," she answered truthfully.

"Wolves, eh? Well, if we see a wolf I'll kill him with my knife and give you the skin for a rug."

Hans was in his element. He whistled happily and loudly, as if he didn't hear the hush all around them, the silence of the forest which made whistling seem an impertinence.

"Shh, Hans." Pierre was bringing up the rear and already would have liked to sit down.

Hans turned. "Why?"

"Because we can't hear anything," Colette answered for him. Hans and Pierre had been on the verge of fighting for days, and she didn't want that—not on the last day.

"Like what?" Their feet sounded very loud on the leaves, now he had stopped. Solange tried walking on tiptoe, but it took too long and didn't seem to help.

"Like a bird," Colette answered dreamily. They went on in silence. It was very cool now they had left the road, cool like a cave. But there were no birds singing. It was all still, silence suspended around them, and they the only interruption.

"Let's sit down and listen," Pierre volunteered. But Hans insisted on going on. They were making for one of the small ponds deep in the forest, a pond where one might find frogs' eggs in the spring. They had often been there with Mamie on a Sunday armed with nets and bottles.

Hans was whistling again.

"Stop it, Hans," Colette said impatiently.

"I'll whistle if I want to," he said crossly, and began again. He was whistling "Deutschland Über Alles," but luckily none of them recognized it.

"Oh, the beautiful moss!" Colette cried and ran to the foot of a tree. There were fat round cushions of pale green moss, thick and firm. She pressed her hands on them with delight. Solange lay down to feel one against her cheek.

"Can't I take some home?" she begged. "Just wait a minute, Hans." It was what the fairies liked better than anything, but she was afraid Hans would think that was childish.

"All right," he said importantly, looking at his watch.

Pierre sat down and looked up at the trees, at their long green trunks. Now they were deep in the forest, and the gray trunks had

turned green, a fine film of moss covering them. High, high up
overhead the leaves were beginning to turn. Here and there a gold
branch waved among all the green. How could he leave all this? Go
home to study in the family living room under the evening lamp,
his mother sewing beside him, his father making drawings of
specimens, pressing flowers, looking at him with gentle deep eyes,
asking, without ever asking in words, if he had gone to confession
this month. It's not my life, he was thinking. It's not what I want.
He felt too big for his parents, too powerful, as if he would knock
into the furniture in the little house, as if he were a prisoner of
their gentleness. There was the gold branch among all the green
leaves, the summer gone already. He felt very sentimental and full
of pity for himself.

Someone was throwing leaves at his face. They got in his eyes
and down under his shirt collar. "Stop it," he said angrily. "What
is this? Leave me alone." That Hans, what a nuisance he was,
always trying to run everybody.

"That's not funny," he said as he pulled himself up. The little
ones were laughing at him. They were stuffing leaves into the ruck-
sack. "Stop it!" he said, in a passion of anger suddenly.

"Hurry up, we're only halfway there." Hans marshaled them off
again. And Pierre deliberately fell back so he could be by himself.
Since they all thought him so funny, they could go on ahead.
Solange was out of breath. No one paid any attention to her. Hans
and Colette just kept on silently, side by side, as if no one else in
the world existed.

They had started out cheerfully, but now something in the stillness made them feel sad and lonely and a little cold.

"Are you sure we're on the right path?" Pierre shouted from far
behind.

"Of course," Colette and Hans called back.

They had left parting behind them when they set out; now here
it was again, all around them in the forest, in the stillness.

"Wait for me," Solange cried, suddenly panic-stricken. She had seen something moving in a bush, or so she thought.

It seemed as if they had been walking for hours, for days, as if they could never go back all that way, but finally they came out into a clearing, to the dry bed of a brook, to the little stone bridge, and knew that the pond was just a few yards away. Pierre caught up, and everyone felt cheerful again, at the prospect of eating. They spread the sweaters and rucksacks out on the ground to sit on, and Hans made a pile of dry leaves for Colette. They were ravenous. They were excited to be so far from anywhere, all by themselves. They laughed very loudly and then, in spite of themselves, half listened for an echo. They wanted to be as close together as possible.

"You've already had one egg and a half, Pierre. That's no fair."

Pierre, as usual, was absent-mindedly eating everything in sight.

"I'm sorry. Here"—he offered Colette a half-eaten egg—"you can have the rest."

Hans was already up and looking for stones to skip across the pond. His idea of an excursion was to do something every minute. Pierre, on the other hand, just wanted to sit and talk, to lie on his back and dream.

"Hans," he called with his mouth full, "come back and sit down. We want to talk."

"Oh, all right." He came back and lay down gracefully on his side. He looked very handsome and self-assured, as if he were on the best of terms with his own body, and Solange and Colette watched him attentively while they ate their sandwiches.

"What shall we talk about?"

"About what we'll do next summer," Solange suggested. Of course they would all be together again. Hans and Pierre had both been formally invited.

It seemed like a safe enough subject, and they embarked on it eagerly. For lately they had come to realize that there were unsafe subjects, subjects they had better keep away from, subjects that made Hans and Pierre go for each other like two dogs with their hackles raised.

"Next summer," Hans was saying thoughtfully, "we might build a house in a tree."

"That's childish." Pierre didn't like climbing trees. He was afraid of falling.

"It's only because you're scared that you say that."

"We'll have a fire at the end of the garden and cook potatoes," Colette interrupted quickly. But Pierre was determined to be irritating.

"Well, maybe I *am* scared. I don't think physical strength is important one way or another. You despise anyone who's weak or scared, but it's the weak often who accomplish the great things in the world."

"You're not weak, you're just soft," Hans said, digging a hole viciously with a stick.

Solange moved over to where she could hold Colette's hand. It was not nice suddenly. It was not a conversation at all. It was this thing that happened now whenever they were together, like a shadow over the sun when nothing came right.

Hans and Pierre felt it too. They didn't either of them want it to be this way, but they were drawn into the orbit of hatred as if it were a magnet. Ever since Lou-Lou had called him a German in that contemptuous voice something had been happening inside Hans. He watched everyone for signs of their real feelings; the only two people he really trusted were Tante Mélanie and Colette. And because he was ready to be slapped with a word, he was always looking for a chance to slap someone else first. Especially Pierre. Pierre was easy to tease because he was clumsy and fiery all at once and because he too was an outsider. Hans sensed the shade of condescension in the Duchesnes' attitude toward Pierre.

"All right, I'm soft." Pierre sat up and glared at Hans.

"Don't, Pierre," Colette begged. "It's our last day."

But they were spoiling for a fight. As well try to stop a thunderstorm. Pierre went on, "But at least I'm not taken in by hysterics like your dear Adolf. At least I'm not a sick and sickening nationalist like you."

The forest seemed to whirl round Hans's head. He was black with rage. He wanted to kill him. He sprang to his feet and stood looking down at Pierre, who was frightened now and showed it.

"All right, let's fight it out."

Colette stood up too and grasped one of Hans's hands. "Oh no, Hans." She turned imploringly to Pierre. "No, Pierre, please don't." She was near to tears.

"You stay out of this." Hans pushed her away savagely. "Will you fight or won't you? You coward!"

Pierre had gone quite white and looked shockingly scared. He stammered slightly, "If we f-fight you'll win, but that won't mean I'm wrong and you're right. It'll only m-mean that you're stronger." While he spoke he got up.

"I thought you Belgians were supposed to be brave, but I guess you're only brave when you have plenty of allies behind you. You won't stand alone." Hans was watching him narrowly. This was his chance to get back at them all. He'd show them who was strongest, who was brave. He'd lick the pants off that fat boy.

"Stop it, Hans!" Colette screamed. "Stop it! You're crazy!" But she didn't go near him. He had drawn a circle of anger around himself like a wall.

Only Solange rushed at him in a passion and beat him with her fists. "I hate you! I hate you!" she cried, tears streaming down her face, choking with rage.

He couldn't hit her. He flung her off roughly and went up and punched Pierre on the nose. He was taken completely by surprise. He couldn't see for a moment, but when he did he lunged at Hans and closed in. Pierre had never been taught to box and he was soft, but he was heavier than Hans and he fought by no rules. He fought because he had to and because he was mad. He kicked and bit and wrestled like a savage. There was no sportsmanship in it. Once he had Hans down, but the lithe boy wriggled out and twisted Pierre's arm. To Colette, to Solange, it looked as if they would kill each other. Pierre's mouth was all bloody. He looked terrifying. Hans was still cool and angry like steel. There was never any doubt who would win in the long run.

"Pierre, oh, Pierre," Colette whispered as if it were a prayer.

Hans hit him hard in the eye with a fist, and Pierre began to bawl loudly, hitting out with both arms blindly, but on the defensive now.

"Hit him back, Pierre. Hit him!" Solange screamed.

But Hans got in another punch on the mouth. Pierre was reeling.

"Have you had enough?" Hans asked grimly.

Pierre sat down, weeping unashamedly. "Yes," he sobbed. "Leave me alone."

Colette went behind a tree and was sick.

Hans went off to wash his face in the pond. His shirt was torn and he had a big scratch across his chest.

Solange sat down beside Pierre, crying as if her heart would break. His head was hidden in his arms. She didn't dare touch him.

"Help me pack the rucksacks, Solange," said Colette when she came back. She said it stiffly, as if she were coming back from a long way off. They would never say anything about it, but they were both terribly ashamed of Pierre. Solange's tears were tears of shame.

It was Hans who brought back a wet handkerchief to wipe Pierre's face. "Here," he said shyly, "use this."

He had won, and he had had to fight and win, but there was no triumph in it. He felt achingly sad and lonely now. Colette and Solange ignored him as if he had ceased to exist.

They walked back in silence as fast as they could, only to get out of the forest, which had become a nightmare, a hostile place, a place to be forgotten as quickly as possible and never gone back to again. It was the place—though none knew it—where each had become involved against his will in conflicts far larger than himself, had been forced out of love into old hate, had been seized with passions hardly his own, had been violently *used*.

It was true that each knew himself betrayed: each sick and exhausted and dazed, like soldiers after a battle.

From far off they could see the sunlight at the edge of the forest, the safe normal trolley car rattling past, the familiar horn, and they ran to reach it as if the whole forest were marshaled against them and they were making their escape.

Once in their own avenue again, they slowed down. Colette and Solange walked hand in hand; Hans, a little ahead, alone; Pierre, as usual, in the rear. Now, for the first time, they drew together. Whatever had happened was their own business. They must keep it from the family. They agreed to say that Pierre had fallen and hit his mouth on a stone. Hans would sneak in the back way and change his shirt.

No one must ever know. They themselves would forget it, pretend, if they could, that it had never happened.

Chapter VII

It was extraordinary how empty the house felt now the two boys had gone. Like lovers who have not had a chance to be alone, the family were shy, especially at mealtimes, to find themselves face to face, with no strangers. The little ones were embarrassed when their mother talked on about Hans; and Françoise, everyone knew, was suffering, so they must all try to be gay and matter-of-fact as if they couldn't tell she'd been crying again. The magic circle was failing them: there were gaps. There were windy places, frightening dark places, even here back in the little breakfast room under the evening lamp.

Like a change of season, there was a change in the family air.

Only Bo-Bo seemed more than ever the same, unchanged, a rock. She said, "Lou-Lou is out of her wits. She forgot to put the laundry to soak last night"; she said, "We must have the chair covers in the salon cleaned before they are put away, madame"; she said, "The hens are laying again, thank heavens." Everyone made appropriate responses, thankful for Bo-Bo, with whom each had his own unchangeable relationship, Bo-Bo who saw and knew everything and could be counted on to behave as if she saw and knew nothing.

It was a relief when the chairs grated back and the family could stop pretending it was a unit and disperse.

For once Mélanie and Paul sat at the uncleared table long after everyone had gone.

"Hello, my dear," he said after looking at her a moment, as she sat leaning on one elbow, her cheek on her hand, meditative, astonishingly young.

Silently they tasted each other's smiles, across the apple peels and the empty glasses, hardly needing to express what each knew the other was thinking. But when the smile had gone, sadness passed over Mélanie's face like a visible shadow. She got up and began to clear away, saying as she did so:

"Jacques is coming tonight. I'll speak to him while Lou-Lou is changing her dress."

"What are you going to say to him?"

"I don't know."

Paul was playing the piano on the table, his long nervous hands tapping out the rhythm in his mind. "Yes, yes," he said to himself. It meant, Yes, yes, we are getting old. It meant, Yes, yes, we are helpless to help our children even though we may try. And then he got up, for he didn't want to see Jacques at all. He went over and stopped Mélanie with her hands full of dishes, lifted her chin, and looked at her half humorously, tenderly.

"Well, old lady, you know best," he said, and went upstairs. They had talked so much about the whole matter that these half sentences were all they needed now to communicate. At first Mélanie had refused to believe that Françoise was in love with Jacques. Like Paul, she was too surprised, too unused to the idea that the child was growing up. It seemed fantastic. Besides, Jacques (they all knew it and teased him about it) was obviously courting Lou-Lou. She shied off from admitting that it could be serious— and if it were, Françoise was really a child. She would get over it She would have to.

Paul and Mélanie had decided not to push her, not to try to penetrate her silences, to leave her alone. This they had done for almost a week, but it was hard, almost impossible, to live in the same house with this silent suffering and not put out a hand. For Mélanie it had been a fearful week. Her flesh ached to hold Franci in her arms and rock her, to say the tenderest words, to tell her that she would come through, that they all loved her, that she was their dear, their eldest. It was against her whole nature to sit passively and be a witness to suffering.

Eventually they would have to talk. They would have to break down the dam. We can't, she thought, go on living like this, strangers to each other, under the same roof. But for once Paul, sensitized, fully awake to his daughter's nature, had been adamant. She must be absolutely free of pressure, free to suffer if she must, free to be herself. But oh, it was hard—it was hard to do.

A half hour later Paul looked down from his study window into the dusk and saw Mélanie and the tall, handsome boy walking up and down, up and down the paths, arm in arm, her emphatic right hand punctuating her speech. She is stronger, more selfless than I am, he thought. She moves by instinct so surely, so simply. She is my wife, he thought, and suddenly, as if his heart had opened to an irresistible flood, he turned and went up the stairs to Franci's room. It was not a conscious transition, a conscious avowal, only in his heart he recognized that Françoise and he were somehow of the same kind and Mélanie another kind. And seeing this, he knew he could help her. But when he reached her closed door he stood outside, hesitating, stood a long time, not daring to knock.

Down in the garden Mélanie was talking about Lou-Lou.

"She loves you. She wants to marry. Don't you think, Jacques, that it is time you made up your mind?" she said abruptly, breaking the easy rhythm of their walk. His hand pulled out from her arm. He stood in the path, facing her but looking down so she couldn't read his eyes.

How handsome he is, she thought.

After a moment he shrugged his shoulders and smiled a dazzling brilliant smile with no feeling in it:

"You see, I don't want to marry."

What did it remind her of? That tone of voice? That look? Years and years ago, sitting on the steps at his father's, the first day she found him, when he said, "I don't like work." Yes, that was how he looked then. But it had not been true.

"You don't want children? A home?" she asked gently. "You want to go on forever living in other people's houses? Playing with other people's children? I don't understand you."

For a moment Jacques looked as if he would run away. Instead he drew her arm through his and they walked silently down the long path away from the house, into the dusk. She waited for him to answer, but he didn't answer. Only in the gentle way he held her arm, in the very slight pressure of his hand, she felt that he was trying to tell her something he could not express, trying to tell her that he knew she was his friend.

"You know how fond I am of you, Jacques. I've watched you grow from an irresponsible boy into a man, from a boy who said he hated work into an expert craftsman—you remember how you ‾felt about going to work? And now look at you! Perhaps this feeling about marriage is just as false, just as much an idea of yours——"

She waited, but still he didn't answer, only walked a little faster.

"Are you in love with Lou-Lou?" she asked directly.

He stopped to light a cigarette. They were standing near a bench under the cherry tree, and Mélanie sat down and looked up at him earnestly. How impenetrable he seemed! What was going on in his mind? Not Françoise? The thought crossed her mind with a fearful dread. Not Françoise!

"I don't know," he said, sitting down beside her abruptly. "Am I in love?" he asked ironically. "I suppose so," he said without enthusiasm. "But marriage—forever—well——"

The arrogance of men, Mélanie thought, suddenly angry.

"Well, you had better make up your mind before you break someone's heart," she said coldly. It was nearly dark now. In the distance she could see Paul's lighted window, the only light on in this side of the house. From somewhere the summer wind brought the scent of stock, drenching the night air. An owl cried far off.

"That's an owl." Jacques sat up, delighted at any interruption.

"Pay attention to what I'm saying, Jacques. This is serious."

But instead of saying anything, she fell silent. They sat in the dark, and Jacques wondered why smoking in the dark was no pleasure. He was waiting for something to happen. He thought of Lou-Lou somewhere far off in the house, the woman waiting for him, the woman he wanted. He threw away his cigarette.

"But what do people talk about when they get married?" he asked suddenly.

Then they both laughed. It sounded absurd. And yet that was what stuck in his mind. He could imagine going to bed with Lou-Lou well enough, too well. He could imagine her cooking the supper and washing the dishes, bearing his children, standing so handsome at the ironing board. But he could not imagine what he would find to say to her all his life, or she to him. The idea terrified him. And in his laughter Mélanie heard the terror, the gasp of being caught.

"My dear," she said, taking his hand in hers in a firm clasp. "Lou-Lou will never mind if you don't talk at all. She'll talk for both of you. That's the least of your worries."

It struck them both suddenly as howlingly funny. They laughed uproariously, until the tears were rolling down Mélanie's cheeks. They didn't know why they were laughing except the relief of having got down to this single practical difficulty, this absurd sudden shyness.

"I'll give you one of the apartments in town for a year as a wedding present," Mélanie said when they were comfortably walking back again toward the house, at ease now, delighted with themselves. "That'll give you a chance to get on your feet, to buy some furniture." She couldn't afford it, of course, but who can afford happiness? She felt immensely happy.

As they reached the front door and stood under the arbor in the dark she kissed him on both cheeks. She looked at him gravely a moment. "This is the right thing, Jacques. I hope you will be happy." And then they went in together.

It flashed through Mélanie's mind that it had been almost too easy. But surely it was the right thing for Jacques now to settle down? And Lou-Lou loved him, really loved him. She would build the marriage on a firm foundation. She would know how to construct a life for them both with her strong peasant nature, her inherited standards of what a family should be. Something in Jacques she would never touch, the wildness, the scream of emptiness—could a person ever fill that? Answer it? Besides, Mélanie was learning that it was not what was given but what one brought to a marriage that was important. The gifts were never equal, the gifts of self at least. There was no absolute communion. Only one person was willing to go out much farther to meet the other, and once this place of meeting was established, they could build. For the time being, at least, Lou-Lou and Jacques would have no difficulty in finding a meeting place. Passion would take them there. And for the rest, who could ever tell?

When Paul finally knocked on Françoise's door she was lying on her bed in the dark. She thought it was Colette, who often came in to kiss her good night. When she saw her father standing there she was too startled for a moment to pull on her dressing gown.

"What is it, Papa?"

"May I come in and sit down for a moment?"

"Of course."

Paul came into the room and looked around. He was amused to see how impersonal an atmosphere Françoise made around herself even here in her own room. There were two rows of books—schoolbooks and a few books of her own, Katherine Mansfield, Tolstoy, Romain Rolland, three or four of the early Colette's—a desk which she never used except for lessons, as her drawing board was downstairs; over the desk a newspaper photo of Lindbergh, an enlarged snapshot of Swiss mountains, and in a small leather case two very old battered photographs of Mélanie and Paul, one a passport picture.

"Where on earth did you dig up that awful picture of me, darling?" he said, sitting down at the desk in the window. It had been taken shortly after the war, and he looked like a frightened convict.

"I found it years ago when Mamie was clearing out her desk."

Françoise had not sat down. She was standing by the bed in her slip, intensely still.

All her quills are standing straight out and ready to prick like a little porcupine, Paul thought to himself. It was quite impossible to make small talk with Françoise. She forced people, by her intensity and complete lack of social grace, to meet her directly or not at all. She could not play any game with anyone, not even with her father. And she resented this quality in herself more than any other. What a lot of anguish she would save herself if she could smile now and tease him about his convict's face. But she couldn't. She could only murmur something about liking the photo; she could only wait like St. Sebastian, tied to a tree, for the arrows to pierce, the arrows of tenderness, of love, the arrows that went to the heart.

Paul refrained from looking at her. He picked a Colette out of the bookcase and leafed it over.

"You would like to get away, I know," he said suddenly. He could feel her mind as if he were a doctor feeling out fracture in a bone. He put his hand unerringly on the truth. That was what seemed so terrible. For all her life Françoise had instinctively hidden the fracture, hidden the wound. Comfort, understanding, which to most children would be a blessing, was to her an agony. Once things were known, explored by someone else, her own secret things, she could no longer deal with them. Her roots were nourished on silence.

So now she winced.

"Why should I?"

"Darling, you are not happy. It doesn't take any very extraordinary perception to see that. And when one is unhappy one imagines that one can leave unhappiness behind by moving to another place. I wish we could afford to send you to England to school, but we can't." His tone of voice was practical; she felt reassured for a moment and sat down on the pillow at the end of the bed.

Paul lit a cigarette.

"You want to be alone," he went on, as he always did, inexorably exposing her to herself, "because something tremendous is happening inside you and you feel that everything here threatens it. With us you are a child, our little girl. And now you are growing up, you feel stifled by the little girl, by all our ideas about you. You want to be yourself and you think that is impossible here. Isn't that it?" he asked, turning and looking at her keenly for the first time.

"I don't know," Françoise answered in a flat, dull voice. She was holding herself back with all the power and the passion with which she would one day give herself wholly. But not to him, not to him. That would be to lose everything, lose her own soul and get nothing in return.

"Do you mind if I go on talking a little, talking to myself as well as you? Perhaps we can help each other," he said gently.

This seemed to Françoise such sophistry that she didn't answer. He would go on anyway, whether she answered or not.

She looked extraordinarily handsome, sitting very straight on the bed. She had always had dignity as a child. Now there was something more fiery and absolute that made Paul want to talk to her as a woman.

"I'm going to tell you a story about myself," he said after a moment. "Long before I met your mother, when I was still at the Lycée, a cousin of my father's came to stay with us for a month. She was ten years older than I. She played the piano professionally, and all that month I sat in the next room to her in the afternoons after school, when I was supposed to be studying, and listened. She played Bach magnificently. It seemed to me while I listened that my whole life was clear before me. I suddenly understood all sorts of things I had never even glimpsed before. I would come out of my study at dinnertime on fire, waiting for a look, for a word from her.

"I had never known any women. I had never been in love before, and now what I felt was so intense that I wondered how I could live from day to day."

It seemed as if Paul had forgotten his daughter as he talked. And Françoise breathed more freely, relaxed, wanted to hear the end of the story. She had always thought of her father and mother together. It was strange, a little disconcerting, deeply exciting to know there had been something else, long before she was born, another life—her father's.

"I spent all my pocket money on violets for her, and she was, I see now, charming to me. But at the time everything she did was cruel because of course she couldn't love me—I was a mere child—and I did love her."

There Paul stopped, puffing his cigarette, as if he had finished. "What happened?"

"What happened? Oh, she went back to Lille after that month was over, and a few years later she married. I never saw her again." Then Paul got up and came over and sat on the bed like a student, leaning over, his hands between his knees.

"But you see, Franci, that isn't really what happened. That's what I wanted to tell you."

Where was he leading her? Into what trap? Françoise was torn between wanting desperately to know and the terror of being caught suddenly. But she finally asked:

"What happened, really?"

"I grew up. In that month I learned everything one can learn about love, love in the purest and most passionate sense, love in the abstract, detached from life, in its essence. And that was because she didn't love me. I never learned anything about her, but I learned a great deal about myself. So that when years later I met your mother, I was ready to live all this knowledge in reality and not just in my imagination. You know, Franci, it is infinitely harder to love *someone* and to be loved than to understand all about it in one's mind."

"Yes," she murmured, blushing fiercely, "I know."

"But one grows up in a day through the other things. In this last week you've grown up. You might be able to hide that from us, but you can't hide it from yourself. It doesn't matter who it is who has opened all the doors for you like a great gust of wind, but they are open. All that I want you to know, my darling," he said, getting up and standing beside her while she bent her head in an agony of shame, "is that this that looks to you now like nothing but pain and nightmare is only the beginning of your real life and not the end—the beginning of love and not the end."

He went out quietly and closed the door behind him.

The end? The beginning? What did it mean? Everything seemed unbearably long and difficult and everything had the power to hurt. Franci turned over on her stomach and wept.

Maybe she would forget Jacques someday, but not now. And now was where she was, *now*. How could she live through tomorrow and the next day and the next, forever and ever? Stay here in the family, have to endure her father's eyes, her mother's eyes, the eyes of everyone she loved and hated, day after day?

"I can't! I can't!" she sobbed, not caring now who heard, who came.

Colette sat up in her bed on the floor below and listened. Papa had been up and then come down again, and now he and Mamie were talking in his study. What was happening to Françoise? What had he done to her? The dark seemed full of suffering and terror, the night full of weeping. But although she was frightened of the dark (there had always been a polar bear in the hall just outside the door, ever since she was a tiny child), she must get to Françoise before something awful happened.

Somewhere between the child world and the grown-up world Colette moved, registering shock like a sensitive instrument for registering earthquake. So much one was never told—like the day before when she had found a pail of bloody cloths in the bathroom and run out screaming into the hall, thinking someone had been fearfully wounded. And then Bo-Bo had come and talked to her about how women bore their children and every month went through a period of bleeding and that this was nothing. It was all so frightening and full of mystery. She wanted to grow up, and know, and not be frightened any more. Tonight the house was full of grown-up suffering and mystery, where she did not belong.

But she braved the polar bear, crept, trembling with fear, up the dark stairs and flung herself on Françoise, whispering desperately:

"You mustn't cry, Franci. You *mustn't*. Everyone loves you. They *do*. You aren't alone. I'm here." And then, as Françoise turned and buried her face in the pillow again:

"Franci, everyone loves you."

"That's just it," the broken voice sobbed, "that's just it."

But just because Colette couldn't understand, she was able to comfort her sister. They went to sleep together, curled into each other's arms.

Chapter VIII

This was Lou-Lou's wedding day and it was raining, so all the plans for a collation in the garden had to be changed at the last minute. Already, early in the morning, before breakfast, the house was a hive of activity.

For once Lou-Lou herself was not allowed to do anything at all: Colette took up her breakfast on a tray, a rose covered with raindrops, which she had run out at the last minute to pick, lying across the napkin. And Lou-Lou looked like a rose herself, a rose covered with raindrops, for she wept continually with happiness and when she saw Colette burst into loud sobs.

"You mustn't cry, Lou-Lou; it's your wedding day," Colette said shyly. She had very rarely been in Lou-Lou's room and she was shocked to see a bleeding heart hanging over the bed, a rosary at the foot, and a pink-and-blue statue of the Virgin standing in a shell on the dresser.

Lou-Lou explained in a stifled voice that she was going to miss them all. The fact was, she had not imagined leaving this house, the children, all the known familiar world; she had not imagined that marriage would be a terrible parting as well as a meeting.

And Colette was embarrassed, standing by the bed shyly telling Lou-Lou that of course they would come and see her often.

"And now," said Colette firmly, in a very good imitation of her mother, "you must eat your breakfast, Lou-Lou."

Then she ran down the three flights of stairs and arrived breathless in the kitchen, where Solange and Bo-Bo were sitting, surrounded by all the silver, cleaning it fiercely. There never would be time for all there was to be done today.

"She's crying, Bo-Bo," she said, as if she were a courier bringing a report from a battle.

"People always cry on their wedding day," sniffed Bo-Bo. There would be enough sentiment floating around without her adding to it today. "You grind the coffee, my treasure; we have to have breakfast anyway."

Colette thoughtfully poured coffee into the cup of the grinder, held it between her knees, and struggled to turn the stiff handle. She strained and pushed till it seemed impossible to move the handle, but finally it made the right sound—a steady crackling of coffee beans—and slowly the little drawer at the bottom filled with fine coffee powder and its bitter strong smell, the morning incense. Colette decided, as she emptied the drawer, that she would never marry. How could she leave Mamie and the house? What would they do without her?

Mélanie, in her sabots, was out in the *potager* picking lettuces. The wet earth smelled delicious, the cool fresh lettuces, and even the rain running down her face and neck was warm and gentle, like a promise. She was proud of Françoise, who had refused to go to a friend for the week end, insisting that she wanted to help. My brave girl, she thought, my fine brave girl.

Ever since Mélanie had told her that Jacques was getting married Françoise had somehow got hold of herself. All this week she had been working on the designs for the chest, talked gladly of their plans to send her next year to the Academy of Design, seemed in fact like a different person. She had got through this alone. Mélanie was proud, proud and—yes, admit it, she said to herself, pulling a snail off a lettuce leaf—a little sad. She had hoped for some confidences, for some communion with her child. But that had not happened. She was to be admired and loved from a distance, like a stranger. How, Mélanie asked herself honestly, will I ever bear it when she gets married?

She stood up and looked round at this garden where she had spent so many years, at the earth she passionately loved; with the rain leaking into her sabots and her wet dress clinging to her legs, she stood, a stout, indomitable woman, her hands full of mud and small green lettuces, and felt the life go out of her in a flood, leaving her empty. What is it all for? What does it mean? If she should die, the garden would turn into a wilderness in a couple of years. All that backbreaking work, all that love and care would go for nothing. What was left when one died? What did a life mean? What made one go on?

Mélanie rarely indulged in such speculations. For one thing, there was no time. But when she did, like everything else she did, her whole being was involved. She was shaken to the roots. Where is Paul? she thought wildly.

But, of course, it was breakfast time. He would come down in a little while. She was not alone in a meaningless universe. She was responsible for all these lives. And Jacques, dear boy, was getting married today. Whatever the abyss, the emptiness within, life doesn't stop; life, which seems such a burden, is really the bearer, the support, the lifter of hearts. Mélanie wiped her forehead with a muddy hand and called in through the kitchen window:

"*Allons, les enfants*—it's time to ring the bell for breakfast!"

Françoise, standing at her window, half listening for the breakfast bell, looking out at the purple and black leaves of the maple, listening to the steady drip of water from the eaves (the gutters must be choked and the water spilling over), Françoise was hardly thinking. She had been in a state of intoxication for the last week, intoxication at being herself. When Mamie had told her the date for the wedding, she had wondered how she would bear it, how go about the world so naked and blazing and alone. And then this extraordinary thing had happened. The pain stopped—stopped like a tooth that stops aching for no reason. Some blessing had come to her, all unasked, unexpected. She felt full of power, the power to do her work, power to live and to be herself. When she woke up now, the first thing she thought of was the design for the chest; next week she would start painting it. She hardly thought of Jacques at all. That was finished. It had been a major operation. Now she was completely well, so well that she could even move among the family without getting all tied up in knots. It was so simple to love her mother, her father, and to know herself loved and appreciated. Why had she never been able to know this before?

Everything gleamed and glistened around her. Even the rain this morning seemed to her beautiful and appropriate. I am myself, she thought, walking down the stairs like a princess. And it meant, I am saved.

Never had there been such a morning of cleaning and cooking and preparations of all sorts. Paul opened the door to his study and flooded the house with music, a whole hour of waltzes—so Mélanie waltzed along the halls with the mop; Solange and Colette finished all the silver and laid the big table in the dining room, counting and recounting the guests, and Bo-Bo was busy in the kitchen, calling out when there was a spoon to be licked or, best of all, the saucepan with chocolate sauce to be scraped.

Lou-Lou refused to stay in her room, she was so nervous and frightened, so they let her do what she wanted—which, it appeared, was to slosh down the tiled floors downstairs one last time. So there the bride was, on her knees, squeezing out the old rag, working away in her first really happy moment of the day.

Françoise had retired to the veranda to make place cards for everyone.

And then, before they were half ready, it was time to dress. The wedding was to take place in the little church in Jacques's village, Paul driving them all over in the car.

"Hurry up, Mamie. We have to wash," the little ones pleaded outside the bathroom door. They had put on their best white corduroy dresses. What would Bo-Bo say if she knew they were going to wash their black hands and faces *after* they were dressed instead of before?

Mélanie at the last moment couldn't find a whole stocking and had to borrow one of Bo-Bo's.

Paul was sitting in the car blowing the horn at regular intervals and trying to keep the rain out of his coat collar.

Lou-Lou had been ready for hours. Her shoes pinched her feet terribly. She was entirely occupied with trying to manage her long dress, her floppy hat, and her bunch of roses, which was just as well, as it gave her something to think about.

They must find the umbrellas—tell Bo-Bo to keep the cat out of the dining room. Where is Françoise? There, at last, they were all settled in the car, Lou-Lou and Paul in front, the rest of the family squashed onto one another's laps in the back.

Bo-Bo waved from the front door. For an hour or two she would have the house to herself. The roast should have been in the oven a half hour ago! Heavens, where are my wits? I wouldn't be marrying that rascal, she thought to herself, not for the world. Bo-Bo had seen a lot of marriages in her life, and she had come to the conclusion that they were hardly worth all the trouble they caused. It was her private opinion that any woman who saw what she was getting in for would run away at the church door. But then they never do know, she considered, and perhaps that is just as well for the future of the race. . . .

In the rain the village looked somber, all black and gray, black umbrellas, black Sunday suits, black dresses and shawls, and the dark gray of roofs and light gray of stone houses.

"Well, Lou-Lou," Paul said as they pulled up in front of the church in a murmur of "There she is! There's the bride!"—"well," Paul went on, "it's your last chance to change your mind."

The awful thing was that now she was in for it, Lou-Lou's only emotion was terror. She had forgotten Jacques's kisses, his blue eyes—she only knew that she was marrying a stranger, someone who might be cruel, violent, in some unknown way terrible. She clasped her rosary and prayer book and prayed, "Mary, help me."

And then she was being embraced and teased by her uncle from Brussels, the only member of the family who had been able to come and who would give her away. He was an enormous red-faced man with a stubble of gray hair; he earned his living as a masseur and quack doctor in the popular quarter of Brussels.

The whole village was pouring into the church now to see old Croll's son get married. Many stopped to light a candle at the small shrine of St. Joseph; in spite of the rain—a penetrating drizzle like a cloud in the air—the outer porch and steps of the church were crowded, and Mélanie was soon deep in conversation with La Grande Louise, while Paul went in with the children.

Solange and Colette pinched each other's arms convulsively as they recognized people. Solange would surely have the giggles before the service was over, and then what would she do? Colette wondered.

They had been brought up to hate everything about the Catholic Church, so now the smell of incense, the altar, the statues of the saints, and the large gory painting of the Crucifixion over the altar fascinated them as if they were in the presence of some pagan sacrifice.

"Look at the Virgin," Solange whispered loudly.

"Shh," Colette answered. Would they know when to kneel?

Françoise waited. All of this had nothing to do with her. She was outside it. She was herself. She was startled when someone tapped her on the shoulder and she turned to face the two demoiselles from in town. They smiled and nodded and she smiled back. When would it begin? She felt her father beside her, knew he was wondering how she would manage, shivered slightly at the idea that he might take her arm. Like Lou-Lou, she wondered desperately why she had ever come.

But Paul was not thinking of her, as a matter of fact. Always and in spite of himself he was deeply moved in a church. Always he questioned himself when he was in the presence of faith. Was it arrogance, intellectual pride that kept him from taking this overwhelmingly simple answer to all his questions? There was such a tiny line between himself, sitting there outside it all, and the woman just in front of them, on her knees, her face in her hands. At any moment, anywhere in the span of one's life, it could happen, the gesture could be made, the abnegation of oneself, the surrender.

What held one back? What in all these images and symbols was the impossible? The bleeding heart, the suffering man on the cross, the everlasting compassion of the woman in blue? Was he so superior to these symbols that he could stare at them coldly, unmoved, and not recognize his deepest longings there? Was it possible at all to come to faith, to life through reason, holding the heart back at the door of revelation while the mind climbed slowly and painfully to the same final place?

But if Paul prayed, it was a prayer to suffer and struggle to the end in the way he had chosen. It was not to yield. It was to keep the mind pure and stern, even in agony, even in love.

Jacques and Lou-Lou were kneeling now at the altar, and all over the church the women wept in an ecstasy of remembrance, of compassion for their own lost youth, for the solemnity of innocence, for the pure moment of happiness given to them once more —noting at the same time how thick Lou-Lou's ankles looked bulging over her tight shoes, noting how she trembled and how Jacques did not.

At last it was over. Lou-Lou tripped on her dress as she walked down the aisle, triumphant, blushing, the traces of tears making her eyes smile brilliantly—and everyone loved her for tripping, for being clumsy and quite unconscious with relief and happiness.

But Jacques was eagerly searching the crowd for someone—and when he found her he shamelessly winked at Françoise. Before she knew it she had winked back. It was so unexpected, so charming— it made a pact between her and Jacques. It said to her, "You know, this is all nonsense." It was the only thing that could have touched her to the quick, made her blaze again with happiness, with the sense of infinite things to come, of the whole future opened out. It was like a miracle.

And Mélanie, who had lost her family in the crush at the door, was amazed to be met by a laughing, radiant Françoise, pulling the little ones after her, giggling excitedly and calling:

"We must hurry, you know, or they'll get there before us!"

This time Paul would take the wedding party back in the car— Lou-Lou and Jacques, Croll and the uncle and the uncle's highly rouged enormous wife. The children and Mélanie would walk to the streetcar and go home that way with the two demoiselles. At home M. Plante and Simone and Francis were to make up the luncheon party.

The rain had stopped; a weak watery sun was trying to shine through the low gray sky.

The little ones jabbered on. "Didn't Jacques look handsome? . . . Did you see his white carnation? . . . Why is there so much blood on the statues, Mamie?"

And Françoise smiled to herself, tasting and tasting again the look in Jacques's eyes, the mischievous look, the companionable wonderful wink he had given her like a present on his wedding day.

The luncheon went off splendidly. Paul kept the whole table roaring with laughter. The children enjoyed themselves running back and forth to the kitchen as waiters; Bo-Bo was made to come in for the champagne and the speeches, laughing in spite of herself at the uncle's broad jokes at Lou-Lou's expense.

Simone and Mélanie exchanged tender amused glances. Simone thought, "What a genius these people have for living, for making happiness around them." It was all so simple and natural and human, Paul putting everyone at his ease, complimenting the women, going the uncle one better when it came to his turn to make a speech, enjoying to the full this preposterous combination of people, outrageous in his humor, delighted with himself.

"The groom! The groom!" They shouted noisily as the champagne was passed once more by Françoise.

"A-hum." Jacques cleared his throat theatrically and threw down his napkin. They waited expectantly. Just as he was going to speak, Lou-Lou's aunt belched quite loudly, and this was greeted with roars of laughter and applause which only increased in volume when she said very formally:

"I beg your pardon, I'm sure," not certain whether she should be angry or not.

Jacques waited for silence. "Give him a chance, now he is on his feet!" roared the uncle. "Come on, young man!"

"I would like," Jacques said quietly, and the murmur of laughter stopped as they felt the sincerity in his voice, "I would like to propose a toast to M. and Mme. Duchesne. I would like to speak of them first as our patrons—for my father, for myself, and for Lou-Lou. I would like to go back ten years, when I first came here as a returned soldier, and try to tell you something of their kindness, their understanding."

Mélanie looked down at Croll's gnarled, short-fingered hands lying on the table—it was strange to see them without a tool, a watering pot, a young plant in them. He had sat beside her silently all through the luncheon, only the bright eyes in the old face gleaming now and then as everyone else laughed aloud. And now he had laid his hands on the table, one on each side of his plate as if he had abandoned them.

She looked up at his face and was moved to see tears in his eyes. Was he at last proud of his son? Or was he remembering things long ago, going back to his own life? She would never know. No one would ever know. But she was glad, after all these years of bending beside him over the garden, to sit beside him now and drink champagne.

She had missed some of what Jacques was saying, as the table applauded loudly, smiling at Paul and Mélanie. What was that?

"This house, these splendid children," Jacques went on. The champagne had made him eloquent. "The life here. No one could tell what it has meant to me."

Lou-Lou was weeping unashamedly by now and needed a handkerchief. Paul began to be a little uncomfortable. This was not the right key for a wedding breakfast, but once he had begun, Jacques had a great deal to say.

"I have not yet spoken of our patrons in business. Here M. Plante, Mlle. Zumpt, and Mlle. Louvois will bear me out—it would be impossible to find an atmosphere more friendly than the Duchesnes have created at the Maison Bernard. That is what we who have had the honor to work for them know in our hearts. But what the world knows is that the Maison Bernard has done something for Belgium, has proved what Belgian craftsmen and artisans can do, has filled innumerable Belgian homes with beautiful things, has set a standard in price and quality of which we can all be proud."

"Hear, hear," called Francis in English. He was delighted with Jacques. What a fine boy, how handsome and self-assured!

"I give you," Jacques finished, "the Maison Bernard and M. and Mme. Duchesne!"

Everyone rose to this and clinked glasses solemnly and then sat down in a murmur of appreciation. "A fine speech," "A fine young man."

Lou-Lou's aunt, who had become quite flirtatious by this time, pressed his hand and said, "You should go into politics."

"Yes, yes," said Paul half to himself, and grinned at Mélanie. "Well," he said to the company at large as he pushed back his chair, "no more champagne, no more speeches. My friends, it's time we sent the young couple on their way."

It was high time if there was to be anything left of Lou-Lou, who, now she had begun to cry, found it impossible to stop.

The taxi was waiting to take them into Brussels. Bo-Bo ran out into the kitchen to get a handful of rice: it might as well begin with all the proper trimmings, even if it was to end badly.

Jacques pulled Lou-Lou over to where Croll was standing, looking very glum, in a corner.

"Wish us luck, Father. Embrace your daughter," Jacques said gently. But Croll was too deaf to catch what he said. He stared at them with something like anger, made an awkward gesture toward Lou-Lou as if he were going to kiss her, and then instead, as if

that would suggest more emotion than he could muster, growled:
"Take care of her, you good-for-nothing."

Françoise was not there to see them off. But nobody noticed that. She was in the kitchen stacking up dishes, biting her underlip fiercely to keep from crying. It was all over. There was nothing more to do.

"Well, that's over, thank heavens," Bo-Bo said dryly when she came back. "We're going to miss Lou-Lou. She was a good girl, a good worker," and Bo-Bo sighed.

She sat down stiffly by the kitchen table. "Oh, my old bones," she said. "They're not much good to me any more," she said crossly. "Come here, Franci, come here and be a sensible little girl," she said firmly, and Franci, impelled by this familiar voice which had talked to her in that tone since she was a baby, came until she was close enough for Bo-Bo to pull her down on her lap. "Sit on Bo-Bo's lap and have a good cry. There, there, that's better," she said, rocking the great girl as if she were a baby. "That's right," she said as Françoise dissolved into tears, crumbled into tears, into childhood again, buried her face in Bo-Bo's neck, clung to her passionately.

"I'm so lonely, Bo-Bo. I'm so lonely," she cried.

"There, there, my treasure, my beauty," Bo-Bo crooned, "my little soul."

The little ones bounded in from the garden and stopped still in the doorway, looking at Franci with frightened, earnest faces, tiptoeing away as Bo-Bo signed to them over Franci's head.

"What's the matter with her?" Solange asked, still whispering when they were out in the garden. "Is she sick?"

"I don't know." They walked hand in hand to the far end of the meadow, as if they had a secret, and when they had talked about it a little they decided to pick Franci a bunch of flowers.

"The poppies are all spoiled by the rain," Colette said in a desolate voice.

"I could give her my red shawl," Solange said in an ecstasy of self-sacrifice.

"She wouldn't like it," Colette answered sensibly. "Besides," she went on sadly, "a present won't help."

In the house Mélanie and Simone could at last have a heart-to-heart talk. It seemed years and years since they had seen each other—for Simone had been in Geneva all the winter before and away at a seaside resort all summer. As Mélanie seemed more and more rooted here in the house in the country, Simone was moving out into the world. They presented an almost complete contrast as they sat in the salon—Mélanie sitting forward in the low armchair, her knees wide apart so the long heavy cotton dress fell in wide folds, her hands clasped between her knees in an almost masculine gesture, the bare feet in sandals showing below her skirt and her brown lined face lit up only by the intent brilliant eyes, her hair pulled back uncompromisingly by the round comb—everything about her straight, honest, like a statue of an early saint carved out of wood.

Simone lay on the chaise longue, delicate, swathed in gray, carefully made up, a lace ruffle setting off her throat, a sapphire ring flashing on her perfectly manicured hands, almost impossibly elegant and finished like a porcelain figure, down to the slim aristocratic ankle, to the silver buckles on her shoes. What could these two women have to say to each other?

Everything—simply everything, for always at every meeting they were astonished by the shock of love. They loved each other deeply, so they could scold each other like two sisters, disagree passionately, and never break the bond. Whenever they met they recognized at once that they had been starved for each other. And now they were already deep in.

"But what a rich life there is here, Mélanie! Whenever I come here, I feel it. The children are wonderful, so absolutely different one from another—it must be a daily excitement to watch them growing." It was Simone's answer to a depression she felt under Mélanie's words, as if she were tired, as if for a moment she had lost her sense of proportion.

"The children are everything," Mélanie said. "I live absolutely through and for them."

"And they adore you."

"Yes." But Mélanie was thinking something else as she admitted it.

"What it is? Paul?"

Mélanie winced at this. "Paul? I don't know. I know nothing about Paul these days. We have both been troubled about Françoise—she is really far beyond her age emotionally, you know."

Simone nodded in agreement. She had always thought Françoise a remarkable child, and now she looked out of the window, wondering. She was not a child to whom Mélanie's standards of goodness, of duty, purely ethical standards, could mean much yet. She was certainly an artist like her father.

"But," Mélanie went on, thinking aloud, "apart from that communication we have about the children, he has walled in his own anxieties and conflict completely as if he had determined not to let me know—ever since he came into the business. We hardly talk to each other any more."

"And yet"—Simone turned toward her now those marvelous clear gray eyes—"yours is one of the few real marriages I know."

"One can get lost, far away from each other, even in a real marriage," Mélanie said quietly.

"My darling, you've always wanted the impossible, believed in the impossible, haven't you?"

But Mélanie flashed out at this, "Is it impossible to want to share one's husband's life, to feel included in it?"

"For years at a time, yes. I can't imagine having perfect communion with anyone on the deepest level for more than moments now and then."

"I feel such a failure," Mélanie said with fierce pride.

"Nonsense, don't be a goose." Simone could be quite tough when necessary. It was this toughness at the center that always surprised people who were deceived by her fragile appearance.

"You don't know." When Mélanie looked worried and stubborn, unlike most women, she suddenly looked very young.

"Any woman who has three magnificent daughters growing up around her and has managed to make life possible for an irascible, temperamental genius of a husband and kept a business going has no right to use the word failure. I'm a failure if you like, but it would never occur to me to think so," she added with a mischievous smile. "You are a goose, my dear, a little goose," she ended firmly.

"Oh, Simone, it's been such a strange summer!" Mélanie burst out, brushing aside all that Simone said.

"Why strange?"

"Full of emotion."

Simone laughed aloud. "You think that because you live out here in the country all by yourselves that you can somehow shut out emotion. What's wrong with emotion? *You* shouldn't certainly be afraid of it, my darling."

"No, I'm not afraid. But all this summer we have been getting more and more isolated from each other. The children are upset and don't tell me what the matter is. Colette has looked ill for days at a time. Françoise imagines she is in love with Jacques."

Simone leaned forward at this and said, "Ah," softly, as if that explained something she had wondered about.

"Paul——" Here Mélanie stopped so violently it was as if she had put a hand up to her mouth.

"What about Paul?" Simone asked quietly. The very tone of the question was healing.

"Well, he spends hours and hours up in the studio in town talking to Mlle. Louvois. He's not in love with her—at least I don't think so—but," Mélanie said in the cold dry voice of a person determined not to cry, "it's so humiliating that he can talk to her and not to me. It's that," she said, making a helpless gesture, letting her two hands fall into her lap with a sort of despair.

Simone looked away, out of the window again. Colette and

Solange were throwing green apples at a mark on a tree—their feet must be soaked through in that long wet grass, she thought.

"Yes," she said out of the silence, "that's hard. But you know, of course, that one can never talk to the person one loves most. They're too involved, too easily hurt."

"It shouldn't be like that," Mélanie said fiercely.

"It shouldn't, but it is." Simone shrugged her shoulders.

"I shall never accept it."

Simone looked over at her humorously, "No, I don't expect you will," she said dryly.

"But what is it all for, Simone?" Mélanie asked earnestly, like a schoolgirl, with all that innocence and fiery purity that was in her. "If you can't share the important things with your own children, with your husband, what is there left?"

Simone threw up her hands. "Oh, don't ask me that. You know far better than I, my darling, for you really live out all these questions, live them out with genius." She looked at Mélanie thoughtfully, as if this speech, which had sounded a little formal, was only to make way for something more. "But, darling," she went on, "you mustn't live absolutely through and for the children, as you said just now that you did."

"Why not? Isn't that what mothers are for?"

"You can't possess the children, Mélanie."

"I don't want to," Mélanie said quickly.

"I wonder."

"Oh, you don't understand anything," she said crossly. And then, because Mélanie was too honest to let that stand, she added, with a rueful smile, "I guess you're right. Oh, Simone, how hard it is to live the good life!"

With that they both laughed. For a wild moment Mélanie wished passionately that she was elegant and slim and had silver buckles on her shoes, that she did not have to get up at five in the morning, that there was no mortgage to meet, that she did not have her own life at all. She got up and stretched, and as she got up, caught sight of Solange, sitting in the wet grass feeding the goat green apples. She pushed open the window and called imperiously,

"Solange, you'll catch cold. That's very naughty. You promised not to get wet when you went out. *Saperlipopette!*"

"I refuse to be very worried about you, Mélanie," Simone said, catching her hand and pulling her down beside her on the sofa. "You're too deep in the midst of life."

Mélanie turned and hugged Simone and smiled. "You mean," she said, "that there is no escape?"

Upstairs in Paul's study, among the clouds of smoke, Francis was sitting on the desk swinging his legs, trying to get a word in edgewise as the torrent of Paul's eloquence poured out. As always when he had been with people, Paul was excited, full of ideas, way up in the air. He had been walking up and down for the past hour, talking as if he might die tomorrow and he must tell Francis everything that was in his mind.

Finally, exasperated, Francis broke in angrily, "My dear man, please let me finish one sentence before you interrupt me."

Paul flung himself down in the leather armchair and took a long puff of the excellent cigar Francis had given him.

"All right, I'll give you five minutes, but don't ask me to believe anything you say."

Francis threw a matchbox he had been playing with down on the floor.

"You're impossible."

"All right, I'll be quiet, but while you've been rushing around to Geneva, to Paris, to Berlin, I've been sitting here in this room listening to the radio. I have been listening to Mr. Musso and Mr. Adolf and their friends and companions and to our Flemish nationalists here."

"But surely you don't take *them* seriously," Francis broke in impatiently. He never could understand what it was about Paul that forced him to listen—after all, he was a crank. That was clear enough.

"They are symptoms, my dear Francis, and it's by studying symptoms that one learns about a disease. The disease is an exasperated nationalism which can only lead to war," Paul went on coolly.

But this statement seemed to enrage Francis. He got up and shook his fists in the air, in a passion of anger and disbelief, and shouted, "No!"

"We can all shout 'No,' Francis, that is easily done." Paul was amused. He loved Francis dearly. He enjoyed making him angry, but, as usual, they got nowhere. The leopard doesn't change his spots even if you throw a bottle of ink at him. And Paul recognized perfectly that it was men like Francis, who believed and fought for the impossible, who made an inch of progress possible—though they must always think in terms of miles.

Francis lifted his hands over his head, open now, as if he had abandoned the fight, and let them fall.

"All right, have it your way. I'm not going to argue with you." Then they laughed at each other happily as Francis sat down again on the desk, because, after all, these arguments were the breath of life to them both, taking them back to schooldays.

"Yes, yes," Paul said, "yes, yes——"

"You haven't told me a thing about yourself, Paul." Francis turned to him earnestly. "What are you working on?"

Paul blew a smoke ring, then another, watching them, with great interest, float up into the air and get wider and wider before they vanished.

"See," he said in a mocking voice; the harsh lightness, Francis knew, was Paul's armor, the shield he held up when he was troubled in mind.

"Yes, I see—a very pretty little trick. What of it?"

"It's the perfect image of my work, a ring of smoke in the air. You can put your finger in the hole for a moment and then it isn't there."

"I don't know what you're talking about."

Paul shrugged and smiled a thin smile, the fine mocking smile of a stage cardinal. "I'll try again. Imagine a tightrope walker who has got it into his mind that he will be able to do his whole act without a wire, in the air. He is obsessed with this idea. He becomes a virtuoso on the high wire because now he imagines all the time that it isn't there at all—and yet he can't bring himself to make the attempt. The trick is faith. Without faith he will fall and be killed. You see?" Paul grinned.

"No," said Francis crossly.

"Oh well, let it pass. I can't talk about my work. It only exists here," said Paul, tapping his forehead. "Lunatics believe they are Napoleon. I have the illusion which you kindly call 'my work.' The truth is I haven't done anything, written a word for four years." Paul was still smiling, still holding up the shield.

"But you will, my dear Paul, you will." Francis looked puzzled and at a loss, and then went on, glad to have thought of something definite and practical. "You have no idea how your reputation is growing, in spite of your obstinate refusal to help yourself in any way—in Paris the other day Percheron, of the Academy, spoke of you in the warmest terms."

"He's a kind old fool." And then Paul threw down the shield and got up and faced Francis. "Don't you see, Francis, old friend, the struggle is with myself, against myself? I don't care what people say. The part of me that matters doesn't care. It's in here," he said, hitting his head now with his fist. "There is the agony and the emptiness and the defeat. Oh, Francis, you don't know, you can't imagine what these years have been. The only thing that's kept me sane has been the business, making myself useful, helping Mélanie a little after all these years."

"Yes." Francis brightened. He was really enormously sensitive to suffering. It was out of his sensitivity to it, his fear of it, that he was such an optimist. "That is wonderful, Paul, really wonderful."

"In one sense wonderful—in another, a nightmare. For I've

wasted these years, thrown them away, as far as my real life is concerned. They have been nothing. Mélanie knows, of course—and that only makes it worse. Because I can't talk to her."

"Why not?"

Paul shrugged. "Why make her suffer? She can't help me there. And nothing is harder for Mélanie than to see someone suffering and not to be able to help them. Her whole life is based on the idea that one can and must help, that it is failure not to be able to. Can't you see how impossible it all is?" he asked angrily.

After a moment Paul went on more quietly. "You see, from Mélanie's point of view I have done the right thing and therefore I must be saved. I must have peace of mind. What she will never understand is that there are regions of the mind where ethical standards become simply meaningless, at least ethical standards in the sense of rules for the 'good life' she is so fond of talking about." Paul looked up and caught a fleeting expression, a troubled expression on Francis's face (what an endearing fellow he is, Paul thought). "Oh, I know, I shouldn't talk about Mélanie like this. She is a fine woman and I love her. That simply has nothing to do with it. That is the plane of living. That is all very simple and clear. I love my wife. We have three beautiful children. We have an interesting business which manages to keep us alive, more or less. All that is concrete, positive. Then throw in X, the unknown quantity—this crazy compulsion to think." Paul laughed to himself. "Yes, to think—it sounds innocuous enough, doesn't it?" he asked savagely, but Francis interrupted him before he could go on.

"What I don't understand, Paul, is why you can't do both—why does it have to be one or the other? Why must a normal life exclude philosophy? Surely other people have managed—Spinoza——"

At this Paul sat down despondently.

"Yes, yes, you're quite right, of course." He turned to Francis half humorously. "Do you think I'm crazy?"

"Maybe you are. But you know, Paul, what always strikes me

when I come here is how much life goes on in this house. You said something about 'the good life' just now, as if the good life excluded conflict, was some calm port of arrival like Fra Angelico's Paradise. I have an idea that it would be nearer the truth to define it as a life lived always close to the point of conflict."

"In that case," Paul sighed, "I am a saint, and I think that even you, Francis, would not bring yourself to admit that."

That night, after everyone was in bed, after the long exciting day, with Lou-Lou safely married, and all the dishes washed, with the house settled down again and Paul creeping in to bed at midnight, there was in spite of everything a great feeling of peace. He reached over for Mélanie's hand and held it gently in his own. She was already asleep.

"Yes, yes," he said to himself.

PART THREE

Autumn: 1936

Chapter I

Mélanie's head was whirling; she might have had arms and legs of lead, so heavy did she feel when she woke up. But she couldn't be ill—that was quite impossible with Bo-Bo leaving and so much to be done. And if she couldn't be ill, she must be well. So she got up even earlier than usual and pampered herself by making a cup of tea before she went out into the garden. She was glad to be out of bed, where she had lain for an hour, wide awake, with a pit of loneliness in her stomach and her head on fire.

Of course it was only right that Bo-Bo should be leaving—the children were grown-up: her work as a governess was finished and they could hardly expect her to stay on as housemaid and cook, which is what it amounted to. But Mélanie, looking out into the garden, lost in mist, felt desolate. It was as if a sister, a close member of her family, were dying.

She unlocked the heavy front door and stood for a moment under the arbor. She shivered, but it was not only the cold breath of the early morning mist that made her shiver, it was the magic of the garden. Everything close to the ground was lost in swirls of white mist, only here and there the shriveled stalk of a Canterbury bell stood above it and quite close to her in the near bed a single deep red rose, like the rose in a fairy tale, a rose with a spell in it, had flowered in the night. The bushes, the trees had melted away into ghosts of themselves. This was one garden, but then when she lifted her eyes there was a whole other garden high up in the air where the sun caught the treetops—a clear, brilliant garden of leaves and the light on pale yellow and deep gold. The mystery and the cold breath of autumn vanished up there into a radiant morning.

The goats and ducks heard her sabots on the path and interrupted these reflections with loud whinnies and quacks. "I'm coming. I'm coming, my beasties," she murmured, clattering across the stone court behind the kitchen to start the business of the day.

An hour later the autumn ravages in the garden were fully illuminated in the sun and Mélanie was hard at work stacking the bean poles, with piles of rotting stalks and leaves around her. Every time she stopped to catch her breath she saw something else that needed doing—it was time to rake the leaves and cover the flower beds before the hard frosts. Perhaps one of the children would find time for it this week. They did their best to help her, but now they were all three studying very hard at school—and Croll had died the year before. Poor old Croll. He really died of grief because he had had to stop working. His rheumatism kept him in bed. It was autumn then too. And she had tried to cheer him by asking his advice about the garden in great detail, but he had only shaken his head and shut his eyes and growled something she could not hear. The fact was that he couldn't bear to think that it would all go on without him, that they could actually manage by themselves though he had poured his life into every tree and bush and plant for thirty years. He would have liked it better if she had come to tell him that everything was going to ruin, a jungle, a desolation——

Mélanie rubbed an arm across her forehead. She was sweating very much and out of breath. What is the matter with me? she thought. The garden was suddenly huge and ominous, as if it would swallow her up, conquer her at last. Even the spade felt heavy, and the sunlight hurt her eyes. A crow cawed noisily and persistently somewhere down the road. She felt for a moment so dizzy that she leaned gratefully on the spade; its worn handle was the one solid object in a world that whirled and dissolved all around her.

She thought rapidly, "It's Thursday. If I can hold out until Saturday, I can take a day in bed on Sunday," and with this promise she forced herself to walk quickly and normally to the shed and put away the spade. She scratched Moïse's head. "I feel awfully queer, old lady—we're not as young as we were, not as nimble, eh?" The cold nose felt delicious in her burning hand.

The children were grown-up now. It always came to her as a little shock to have to look *up* at Françoise, a head taller than Mélanie herself, and although Colette and Solange were still called "the little ones," they were big girls, Solange as pretty as ever, with the pinkest cheeks in the world and the bluest eyes, clear, clear blue eyes which always seemed to be dreaming and never did quite concentrate on the business at hand. And Colette tall and thin and pale, a little straggly, a little too serious—Mélanie saw to it that she got an extra portion of everything. She had been having headaches lately—perhaps she had grown too fast. Perhaps she was making too great an effort to be the head of her class.

The minute Mélanie came into the house she was greeted by cries of: "Mamie, may I pick the rose for Bo-Bo?" (from Colette), and, "Mamie, look! We've wrapped up the gloves in a magnificent package—we stole the red ribbon from your box, is it all right?" (from Solange), and, "Mamie, do you think I can give her the panel unwrapped?" (from Françoise, who had painted a water color of the view from Bo-Bo's own window). "Mamie! Mamie! Mamie!" their voices cried, high-pitched with excitement, covering her with morning hugs and kisses, pulling her this way and that to see and approve first one thing and then another.

And then, "Shh! She's coming!"

"Well, children"—Bo-Bo gave a very good imitation of impatience to hide her emotion—"you are making enough noise to rouse the dead this morning. Is this a menagerie?"

The little ones howled with laughter. "Is this a menagerie?" The phrase had sounded through their childhood. Everyone was shouting and laughing a little louder than usual to cover up the hole, to put off the heart-bursting grief of Bo-Bo's leaving.

They were almost relieved when Papa finally came down in a fearful temper and forced them to be quiet. For a moment they sipped their coffee in silence while Bo-Bo picked up her beige gloves to admire again or looked at Françoise's painting. In six years she had aged. Her bright blue eyes looked out of a wrinkled face. Her hair was as frizzy as ever (for she put it up in curlers every night), but it was almost white, and she had to move slowly, she who had always run everywhere.

They had begged her to stay on, but she was too proud to stay— in a house where she had always carried a great burden of work— and be unable to maintain her own standards. And then—she had not confessed this—she looked forward to resting. All her life she had never stayed in bed for breakfast. She had never been spoiled; she was looking forward to certain small comforts at her sister's. She would miss the children more than she dared to imagine, but she would sleep late in the morning. In six years Bo-Bo's fiery will had been tempered by pain. She was an old woman now, and for the first time in her life she weighed love against comfort and was glad to choose comfort. For the first time in her life she would live for herself. She would enjoy not through the pleasures of others but through her own. Instead of mending stockings in the evenings, she would be able to read. She would read philosophy and poetry—she would even read novels. With these thoughts Bo-Bo had armed herself against the wrench of leaving—and of course she would be coming back very often to see them. This was taken for granted.

"You'll come on Sunday, Bo-Bonne," Mélanie pleaded.

"And scold us for all the things we've forgotten!" Solange added mischievously.

The sun poured in on the breakfast table. It was a temptation to sit and sip the big cups of coffee slowly, to linger as if it were a Sunday. But Paul was already impatient to be off.

"Is your trunk ready, Bo-Bo?" He looked at his watch. "We have to leave in ten minutes."

Solange and Colette ran upstairs to sit on it, to pull the worn leather straps tight and carry it down. Françoise started to clear away, and Paul walked past the windows muffled in scarfs, wearing a thick leather jacket like armor. Soon the explosions, the whines, and hopeful put-put-puts of the old car trying to get started warned everyone to hurry.

But Mélanie was still sitting at the table and so was Bo-Bo.

"Hurry up, Mamie," Françoise called as she dashed through to collect her brief case. Every morning it seemed as if they could never get off in time, and by the time the whole family—complete with books and pencils and coats and gloves, with packages of vegetables from the garden for the two demoiselles and the Jeans— were packed into the car, Paul was usually in a fury and everyone's heart was beating fast. It was a drama they all secretly enjoyed, which started the day off at a proper pitch of excitement— excitement which rose in a crescendo until they got into the car, and gradually ebbed as one child after another was dropped off at school. The car was backed out of the garage now, and Paul blew the horn loudly. This was the second phase of his impatience, the danger signal. Usually it would have galvanized Mélanie into action—the little ones went past the window dragging Bo-Bo's trunk behind them and Paul got out to supervise its strapping onto the running board. Françoise called, "Wait for me!" from the bathroom window.

And then Bo-Bo, who had gone out into the hall to put on her hat, came back. "I'm not going."

"But, Bo-Bo . . ." Mélanie protested weakly. For the last half hour she had felt too ill to hide it any more.

But Bo-Bo paid no attention. She pushed the window open and called out:

"Never mind about the trunk. I'm not going."

The two children dropped the trunk in amazement as Paul muttered, *"Sacré nom d'un,"* and got back into the car.

But by that time Bo-Bo was out in the yard. "Madame is ill. You run along, all of you, and I'll stay here—never mind about the trunk. It can stay where it is," and before they could protest she had slammed the door of the car and shouted, "Hurry up or you'll be late for school!"

Three anxious faces looked back and waved through the little window at the back. Paul turned to Françoise in the seat beside him and asked:

"What is the matter with everyone this morning? Has Bo-Bo gone crazy?" But no one answered him. It was better to be silent, safer.

But a few moments later he turned to Françoise again and asked anxiously, "Do you think Mamie is really ill? I didn't notice anything."

Mamie ill? It seemed quite impossible. She had never been ill in her life, not really ill.

Solange was desperately going over her Latin lesson with a last hope that she might be able to remember about the ablative case.

Colette looked thoughtfully at the mass of gold and bronze leaves in the gutters. The day which had started so well had gone all queer. She felt sick to her stomach.

But at home Mélanie was lying in bed with a thermometer in her mouth and a delicious hot-water bottle at her feet, so glad to be able to lay down the burden of her body that it seemed the most exquisite happiness just to be lying still in a soft bed and not have to move.

"Oh, Bo-Bo," she said with a sigh of contentment, "I believe

I'll go to sleep." And then, as Bo-Bo's impassive face registered nothing of what she read on the thermometer, "Well?"

"Four degrees of fever, madame. When will you learn to take care of yourself? Out in the garden this morning working with a fever like that!"

Mélanie smiled. "I didn't know what was the matter with me."

"Well, now you know, you are not going to try to get up until the doctor says you may."

"The doctor? Is that necessary?"

Bo-Bo laid a cool hand on her forehead, cool and dry as a piece of wood worn smooth by the sea.

"Go to sleep now," she said softly, and for a second Mélanie felt and saw her mother so vividly behind her closed eyes that she did not want to open them. She just murmured, "You spoil me, Bo-Bonne," and then she must have fallen asleep.

For when she woke up the afternoon sun was streaming through the closed green curtains so that the whole room seemed to be under water. Her legs ached and there was a weight on her chest, but she felt inexpressibly happy and at peace, so much so that she began to weep. She had been dreaming about her mother.

For so long, for years, there had not been a day when she could remember this sort of relaxation and peace, when the images of the past could float up into her consciousness—that it seemed almost as if illness were a kind of healing. She had needed to lie still. She had been cut off from whole layers of herself, the layers of experience and remembrance which nourish the present.

Now, between sleeping and waking, uninterrupted by Bo-Bo's silent attentions, the hot bowl of soup, the fresh hot-water bottle, the knowing cool hands plumping up her pillow—she abandoned herself to the necessity of daydreaming. On the roof the doves cooed persistently or flapped noisily down to the window sill. A streamer of sunlight lay across Paul's bed through the slight crack in the curtains, but she was far away in the sea-green gloom, her open eyes looking inward.

To go back into her childhood was a rest, not because it was childhood (which has never been a restful time in anyone's life) but because she was a child in a peaceful world. School had meant passionate friendships which took her to Switzerland, to Italy, and England for long romantic summers. She and her friends had a sense of personal destiny, of being exceptional people who could build for themselves exceptional lives—and politics was only part of the great hope of her youth. For hadn't they all taken for granted and believed that the nations were moving naturally toward world socialism? Of course it had to be fought for—reforms were needed everywhere. She had worked hard for workmen's compensation, for free clinics, but all these things would come to pass in time. War was unknown—progress was inevitable; while all over Europe young people like herself, on fire for justice, plunged into the struggle.

Remembering the sweetness, the extravagance of it all, she thought of her own children with a fearful tenderness. They had grown up in a world savage with hatred and spiritually and economically depleted.

And what had she given them with which to endure and make a life in this world? Character, perhaps. Yes, they were hard workers, all three, even Solange, in spite of her intellectual problems—and in Françoise a kind of indifference. For Françoise was throwing her whole nature into her ambitions as a designer now. She refused absolutely to be drawn into any discussions at home. She simply fled to her big table in the veranda and went to work painting flowers or, since she had entered the school of design, on one of her architectural projects. She had reacted to the uncertainty and trouble of her world by simply shutting it out. And she could do this because she had a real talent, a talent which would possess her. But she was not, Mélanie thought compassionately, a very warm or considerate human being.

And Paul, of course, had for years withdrawn into his work; given up any effort to change or take part in any change outside it;

fastened his whole mind to metaphysical exercises; nailed himself down to a set of spiritual problems which had as much connection with daily life as algebra.

Mélanie turned over on her stomach and laid her cheek on the cool pillow. These reflections which had begun so peacefully and sprung from the heart were taking her into a maze of conflict, were taking her to the harsh unsolved centers of life.

She was suddenly very aware of the stillness of the house. It stood all around her, the walls, the ceilings, the big staircase outside in the hall, the sturdy brick walls and the tiled roof—steadfast, supporting her as the bed on which she lay supported her, and she alone vulnerable and alive. One could try at least to build and maintain a framework of certainty, of security for the children, like a house; and then wasn't it matter of living from day to day?

It seemed a curiously conservative end to the wild dreams of her youth—to be content to build her life within this house, within this garden, to feel so supported by them. But she wondered sometimes if her dreams had not been a man's dreams—and even her young life of passionate free attachments to women, a young man's life. And now she was a woman and this was a woman's life.

After a whole day in bed, it was idiotic to feel so tired.

And then she heard the children's voices in the hall: they must have come back early by trolley to see how she was. They were tiptoeing up the stairs, and she called out:

"Come in, my treasures!"

They came in, subdued and anxious, with a bough of crimson maple leaves for her to see. And she thought with a pang, They look shabby—I really must manage to get them each a new suit this winter.

"I have been having a wonderful lazy day, sleeping and being spoiled."

"Bo-Bo says you must stay in bed at least a week and we are not to let you get up." They looked absurdly troubled.

"I'm not really ill, you know. Just a little fever, probably grippe. It's nothing. Sit on the bed and tell me about school."

Solange burst into a long story of the whole day, how miraculous it was that she wasn't called on in Latin because she had forgotten everything, how she had passed her math test (but *just,* which seemed much more triumphant somehow than if she had had a high mark), how Mlle. Treillère had stopped her in the hall and complimented her on her theme about autumn in the garden.

But Colette was silent, observing her mother with quiet attention.

"Come along," she said when they had been there about a half hour. "Mamie must rest."

Yes, it was foolish to be so tired after a whole day in bed. She could rest again as the shell of the house filled with the murmur of voices; doors banged; the rake scratched far off in the garden; there was water running in the taps again; a plaintive mew dragged Mélanie out of bed to let Fifi, the daughter of Filibert, in to find a soft place in the bed and purr and dig her claws into the eiderdown ecstatically. Soon Paul would be home. . . .

But downstairs nothing seemed right. There was an awful emptiness in the kitchen, where Solange was peeling potatoes. The animals were crying for their supper. With Mamie everything seemed easy and fun—the evening chores were a game they played together. Now they were just chores. It was lonely in the kitchen, lonely in the garden, lonely everywhere, as the pigeons seemed to repeat relentlessly over and over.

"Colette, come and help me," Solange called. But her voice came back from far off:

"I have to finish raking this path. You feed the animals, Little— and milk the goats, will you?"

It was cold and almost dark when Solange went out into the court and clattered across it to the safety and warmth and the close animal smell of the goat shed. What if Mamie were to die? She stopped milking and leaned her head against Moïse's warm flank. Of course that was not going to happen—she knew it her-

self. But in the last few hours she had been aware for the first time
of how much Mélanie held the whole fabric of their lives together.
Without her, the garden, the house, the animals, the meals—everything seemed to have lost its reason for being. There was panic
and emptiness and darkness instead of life and warmth and safety.

What would Mamie think if she knew I had so little courage? she
asked herself, and went back to milking, quickly and deftly, for
Solange had a sure touch with animals. Moïse would never stand
as still as that for anyone else. When she went back into the house
with the pail of warm milk and saw Bo-Bo standing at the stove
stirring the soup, she felt ashamed of her moment of wild grief.
In the bright light of the kitchen, she saw it was foolishness.

But in the shed she had realized something about their lives that
she had never had to face before: someday Mélanie would die;
one's parents do not live forever; eventually one must stand alone.
And she felt fearfully unprepared. I must grow up, she said to
herself. I must learn many things I don't know. I must be ready.

"What's come over you, Solange? You look so serious all of a
sudden." Colette noticed at once that she had changed as they sat
peeling potatoes in the small dining room.

"I've been thinking about our lives."

"What about them?"

"Well," she said, and then stopped, because now it was to be put
into words, she didn't know exactly what she had been thinking;
it had been a sensation of loneliness and independence, and how
did people speak of sensations, except in poetry? "I was thinking
about growing up—how hard it is," she added lamely, and blushed.
It was unusual for Solange to reveal anything of her inner life. She
was the clown and the baby of the family, and she had accepted
her role passively until now, partly because she enjoyed it and
partly out of a deep lack of confidence in herself. Colette was so
much more articulate and intellectual. "I was thinking about
Mamie," she went on as Colette waited for more. "We must try
to help her more than we have."

Colette nodded quickly. "I wish we were older." She understood so much more than she was able to do now. She was tied down by lessons; there never seemed to be time for the real things any more—poems and reading and gardening and the long talks they used to have with their mother about ethics and conduct and what was right and the meanings of things. "There seems to be so little time for living."

"Mamie wanted to be an actress when she was a little girl," Solange said apparently irrelevantly.

"What made you think of that?"

"I was just thinking how differently people's lives turn out from what they plan."

"Oh." Colette leaned her chin on her hand and looked off through the walls of the little orange room and out into the darkness beyond. She herself did not know what she wanted. Once she had wanted to write poems more than anything—now she was not sure. There was so much to be done in the world—how did one have the right? She had lost the beauty she had as a child—she looked sallow and worn beside Solange's rosy fresh color. Her serious mouth, her deep thoughtful eyes, would come into their own much later. But this autumn was an autumn of conflict for Colette and she felt tired all the time.

Just as she was about to speak they heard the roar of the car and ran out to open the doors of the garage and help Paul unload.

"Hello, Papa, did you have a good day?"

"Hello, my birds, how is Mamie?"

"She's been sleeping all day—she has a fever."

They watched him pull off his gloves and blow on his hands, as if he would never be really warm, and then turn to the car with a sigh and hand out one bundle after another.

"Where's Françoise?" Colette asked.

"Oh, she called to say she was staying to work at school until late tonight. Run along, you'll catch cold. You've no business to be here without sweaters on."

It was the same as always, and yet it was different. When Mamie was there, the evening arrival semed always the end of all sorts of adventures, the end of a real journey; there was always so much to tell. It was the gayest and best moment in the whole day. There was always a surprise or a joke—an extra something for supper, a cake or a half pound of ham, or something wonderful or amusing that had happened and with which Mélanie would regale her family. Now they finished unpacking in silence, having paid no attention to their father's remarks about cold.

But when he had come in and extricated himself from the heavy leather coat, the scarf, the hat, and blown once more into his thin frozen hands, he looked at them tenderly and patted their heads.

"My good little girls, my angels," he said gently. And once more the evening folded round them and they were safely home.

Paul stood at the end of the bed and looked down at Mélanie. She had flung an old white cashmere shawl that belonged to her mother round her shoulders, and as he stood and looked down, talking to her tenderly, he felt ashamed. How long it was since he had talked to her like this or felt so romantically and passionately about his wife!

And she on her side felt as shy as a young girl, too exposed before his gaze, so she moved uneasily in the bed and laughed a little self-consciously.

"I'm not your swan. I'm your goose, my darling—your silly goose to get ill like this just when there is so much to do."

"It's time you learned that you're not indispensable. You'd be astonished to learn how well we got on without you," he teased.

"I don't want you to get on well without me," she said, frowning like a peevish child.

He came and sat down on the bed and stroked her forehead and told her that the whole world would fall to pieces without her and all the cities vanish in the winking of an eye and there be nothing left at all—and this, just this, was what she wanted to hear. "My darling wife," he said, kissing her smooth forehead, and then, as she had been doing all day so foolishly, she began to weep.

"Don't pay any attention. I've been doing this all day. I'm so happy." It didn't make much sense, but he understood. He understood, as he would always understand everything, because it was his genius to understand.

"You're tired—I'd better go."

"No, don't go," she pleaded. "It's so long since we've sat and talked." Her hands followed the buttons on his waistcoat, and he stayed. After a moment he said thoughtfully, "I had a letter from Schmidt."

"A good letter?" she asked absent-mindedly, for she was thinking of him and wishing they could go off somewhere together. But of course it was impossible. It had always been impossible. But looking up at his face, she saw the change in it. "No, not a good letter," she answered herself.

"Well"—he got up restlessly and began walking up and down, picking up first the brush on her bureau and then the little box of lace and putting them down—"it sounds as if he's in trouble."

In a second the safe walls of the house, the love and the tenderness and the security in which she had been cherished all seemed to fade away and her mind pushed out beyond the Belgian frontiers into the darkness and evil across the border, so near and so far away across the night. One shut out the suffering in order to be able to go on living, but it was always there, just across the border, like conscience itself.

"I wonder if the time hasn't come," Paul went on, "to try to get him out."

"Out?" Mélanie sat up. "Out of Germany—for good? He wouldn't do it, would he?"

"You'd better read the letter, Mélanie. I didn't mean to bother you with this tonight," he added, but the fact was that Paul had been unable to think of anything else all day. He handed her the letter apologetically.

"But, my dear, of course." She sat up to read. It was dated a week before and had been mailed in Brussels.

DEAR PAUL,

I am giving this letter to a friend of mine who is coming to Brussels on business. I have not been able to tell you of my difficulties here. No doubt you can imagine what it is to a professor of philosophy to be ordered to eliminate Spinoza and Erasmus from his teaching, as well as all foreign-born philosophers. I must confess that in order to be able to go on teaching I had compromised already to the extent of offering a course in the history of German philosophy which I thought would pass with the "authorities." I had misjudged the extent to which we are already poisoned. I have resigned my position at the university, and that means that in the course of time, though perhaps not immediately, my life may well be in danger. From now on I shall be watched. I have stayed until now partly because I have been able to help several Jewish colleagues to escape by being here. Now there seems no reason to prolong the agony of separation from my country, my wife, and my son. Hans is a convinced Nazi and now at an S.S. Elite training school. My wife will not leave her son. You can imagine that my decision has been a difficult one. But now it is made, the sooner I am able to act on it, the better for everyone concerned. I do not yet know what will be possible—there are changes in the regulations every day. But it is probable that an invitation from the University of Brussels to give a lecture on a "safe" German philosopher like Nietzsche would get me a passport. If this fails, I will have to rely on more dangerous means. Here all is pain and confusion and growing darkness. My dear friend, you and yours are to me at this moment literally light. I think of the evening in your parlor, of your three daughters, of your splendid wife. I hesitate to place the burden of my destiny in your hands. But I do not see any other way of going on with the things in which we both believe and for which we live. Please don't worry about me if you don't hear again for several weeks. I have still some good friends here. Fear is the greatest corrupter but it has not touched all Germans yet.

Believe me, your always devoted

GERHART SCHMIDT

Mélanie laid the letter down on the sheet. "Oh, Paul——"

"Yes, it's bad."

"It's frightful—to have to give up his wife and son. Oh, Paul," she said again. There were no tears in her eyes now.

"What can we do right away?" she asked then, sitting up as if she would get up and dress and put on her hat in an instant.

"Lie down, darling," Paul said, coming back to the bed. "The awful thing is that short of the invitation from the university, which I saw to this afternoon—they were most co-operative, by the way; perhaps old Terborch isn't such a dried-up fossil as I have always imagined him to be—short of that, I don't see anything to do but wait."

"Think of him, that quiet gentle man. What he has been through—— What monsters!" she said violently. And then more quietly, "Oh, Paul, the children——"

"Yes, the children," he said harshly. "Our little Hans, whom we thought so well-brought-up and well-disciplined, is now learning the most advanced methods of sadism and torture."

"How will he stand it? How *can* he?"

Paul stood at the window and looked out into the darkness of the garden. "The trouble is that it's far easier to stand it than not to stand it. It's far easier to torture than to be tortured—and the pressure on young boys in Germany now must be unbelievable. I wonder how many suicides there are: it would be interesting to have the figures."

Mélanie watched his intellect at work with a kind of amazement. Even in a moment like this he moved instinctively toward the abstract.

She was thinking, if it were my child—what then? What if Hans were her son, as she had so often half pretended that he was. What would one do?

I must get well. I must be about, she thought in sudden panic—as if there were hardly time now to prepare her own children for the future. One must ask more of them than ever. They must grow up strong and free and powerful in love—for what a weariness of hatred lay ahead she was beginning to understand, though she did not yet name it "war."

Paul had gone back to his study and opened the door so she could hear Beethoven's "Seventh Symphony" broadcast from Berlin.

Chapter II

But Mélanie's moment of panic and resolution was swallowed up in the week to come by the many things that happened while she was in bed. Afterward she looked back on this week of convalescence—it was, after all, only a slight attack of flu, but she stayed in bed because she had a few degrees of fever every night—as a sort of vacation, in which, just as if she were on a journey, she could sit back and enjoy her family without any of the responsibilities of the household.

Every evening the little ones brought their lessons up to her room; she heard Solange's recitations for her and then read aloud to them for an hour. Sometimes, if there were a good concert from London or Berlin, Paul opened the doors and they all listened together, and then even Françoise would come up to join them.

Best of all, Paul had talked to her one whole afternoon about his new book and what he hoped to do. It was a long time since he had been willing to let her know at all what he was thinking about, and she had not even known that he was planning a new book. That was the best news of all. All these things pushed Schmidt into the background—at least until the university should have an answer to the invitation to lecture. They could do nothing until then.

Then she also had a chance to read—a new biography of Mme. du Deffand, several volumes of Sainte-Beuve's *Causeries du Lundi,* which she had missed, and a life of Horace Walpole in English which Paul found for her in a secondhand bookstore. They all vied with one another to invent things to amuse her and spoil her: Simone arrived one morning with a basketful of goodies, a whole cooked chicken (such luxury!), a tongue in a glass jar, and two pounds of *pain à la grecque, speculose,* and other specialties which they used to buy in quarter pounds when they were at boarding school and hoard in their bureau drawers.

They munched them now, spoiling their lunches completely just as they had used to do, and had a long gay talk about the old days. But in spite of everything there was a distance between them, however hard they tried to re-create their perfect intimacy by remembering it. Was it simply that in spite of her understanding and wisdom Simone's life was too different from Mélanie's? She did not have any of the Duchesnes' material difficulties to face, and sometimes it seemed to Mélanie as if these were the very foundation of everything. Whatever she had managed to accomplish had been done *in spite of* there being no money and no security. So every day of peace was snatched out of peril, and that made it doubly precious. You couldn't talk about these things—it would have sounded absurd—and yet the lack of such preoccupations and triumphs in Simone's life made her seem far away, on another planet. And then she had no children. This added to the slightly rarefied atmosphere in which she moved.

"You know, Simone, it is awful, but I have so little time for reading or just thinking now—it's years since I've lain like this for hours, doing nothing—that I sometimes think I am becoming childish for sheer lack of using my mind!"

Simone had been talking about Gide, whom Mélanie hardly knew.

But that, of course, was nonsense, as Simone made quite clear at once, pointing out that it would be quite impossible for Mélanie to live as she did, working on all sorts of practical social problems, without knowing very well what she was doing and without thinking out one situation after another. Only last month she had had a long session with the judge at the children's court about the problems of delinquency.

"Well, it's different—that's just coming to certain practical conclusions to meet certain specific situations. Oh well, I don't know what I mean, darling—give me one more of those heavenly *pains à la grecque* and tell me more about Gide. We are way off the point."

But then Simone wanted to hear all about the children, and Mélanie all about Francis. She had expected him to be in the depths of depression, but to her surprise Simone laughed ironically, with a shade of criticism in her laughter, and said:

"Yes, you would think so. But do you know, Mélanie, he has persuaded himself that Hitler doesn't want war." She shrugged her shoulders. "That is what happens to men when they have an *idée fixe*. Peace is Francis' *idée fixe,* and he simply will not admit the reality. I knew it long ago—I think I knew it on the day of Briand's funeral. Certainly the crowd then, that silent dumb crowd which felt despair rather than grief, mourned for peace as well as for Briand—they knew."

"Knew there would be another war?" Mélanie's throat felt so tight and dry she could hardly say the words.

"Yes."

Until now, until the other day when Schmidt's letter came, she had refused to believe it possible. And even now she had a superstitious feeling that one must not believe—or it would happen. Perhaps that was what made Francis behave as he did.

Once more, as she had the first day she was ill, she felt unspeakably tired as if she were made of lead. And when Simone had left she lay for a long time without moving and wondered, as sick people do, how she would ever make the strength to climb back again into the struggle, now that it led surely and inevitably into darkness.

Later she decided that she must speak to the children. They must know. And one evening when Solange and Colette were curled up on the bed like cats and Françoise came up to show them her plans for a modern study, Mélanie decided this was as good a time as any other.

"You know, children, there is something I think we should talk about as a family." Françoise sat down gingerly on the end of the bed. She hated family talks and she still had a lot of work to do.

"Shall I get Papa?" Colette asked.

"Papa is working. We'd better not disturb him."

But all these preliminaries had made everyone nervous.

Had the business gone bankrupt? Colette wondered. Or was it that one of them had done something so awful that it must be discussed in public?

"Don't look so solemn, my little owls," for their six eyes were fastened on Mélanie's face as if they expected some doom. "It's not as bad as all that." And then she told them quietly that they must fill these next years as full as possible of all the things they most wanted to do and to be, as there might quite possibly be war. "I feel," she ended, "that our responsibility to store up all we can for the future is very great. This applies to the garden, for instance —we must get in supplies of seeds now, and we must clean out the old hives and try to get hold of a swarm of bees. We must gradually become as self-supporting as possible. But it means also, for you children, that you must think ahead." Now that she was talking about it, it seemed quite unreal to Mélanie, and for a moment she wondered if she had been foolish to frighten them.

But instead of being frightened they were delighted. They had always loved to make plans, and now here was a chance to make real ones, necessary ones. Solange burst out with the question she had been storing up for months:

"Do you think, Mamie, that I could work on a farm next summer? Then I would be ready to help." She was blushing furiously, having at last given away her most intimate secret.

"Oh, Solange, you are wonderful," Colette said spontaneously.

She herself could think of nothing. She felt confused. For everything she wanted to do seemed to take such a long time.

"I wonder"—Mélanie's own eyes were shining now with the possibilities this emergency opened up—"I wonder, darling," she answered Solange, "if it wouldn't be better to go for the summer to the School of Agriculture—they have a model farm and you would learn new methods."

Solange groaned humorously. A school sounded very different from a real farm. Nobody wanted to go to school in the summer.

"I tell you what. We'll get Papa to drive us over there and you shall see for yourself."

"A picnic—a picnic on Sunday!" Colette cried happily. It was years and years since they had had a picnic all together.

"Only we must ask Papa—perhaps later, as he is working so hard now. Perhaps in the spring." Their faces fell.

"In the spring there may be war," Solange said decidedly. They had accepted the idea of war already. It was part of their vocabulary. "We had better get everything settled now."

"Oh, my darlings, I didn't mean that it would happen as soon as all that!"

Françoise got up to go. She had been hearing talk of war all year at the school; there were constant fights among the boys—some of them ardent *Flamingantistes,* already inoculated with Nazi propaganda. ("Who wants to fight for France?" they said defiantly.) She had long ago accepted the fact. It seemed rather naïve of her mother to bring it up now. And besides, how would it change her life to think ahead to the war? One must go on as one had started. There was nothing else to do.

"Don't go, Franci," the little ones begged. "We want to talk."

"I have to work," she said shortly.

"You're just like Papa," Solange said accusingly.

Françoise turned at the door and smiled at them; they all three seemed to her like children, "You settle the world, my friends—I have to work."

Solange shook her head. "She works all the time. I can't understand it." Mélanie and Colette laughed.

"No, I'm sure you can't understand it," Colette teased, "lazybones."

"I hate school," Solange answered without malice, "and she's doing what she wants."

Colette looked thoughtful. She played with the fringe of her mother's shawl. Finally she turned to her mother shyly.

"Mamie?"

"What is it, my treasure?"

"Do you think"—it was frightfully difficult to ask, now she had come to the point—"do you think I could somehow go to England next summer?" Now she had begun, it all tumbled out. "I could work my way. It wouldn't cost much, only the fare to get there."

"But of course, darling, if that's what you want to do."

What a wonderful evening it was! All the things Colette and Solange had secretly hoped and prayed for seemed to be suddenly possible—and all because there was going to be a war!

"What I want is to be responsible for the animals," Solange went on decidedly. "I think we should have sheep. Then we can have the wool and also meat when the lambs come."

But Colette was dreaming about Keats's house, about great forests, about cathedrals, about Katherine Mansfield's country and Shakespeare's country—England; the word was magic. She would live there. She would see the clipped hedges and the cottage gardens full of flowers, and the green rolling hills and the great oak trees. She climbed over the bed and hugged her mother passionately.

"Oh, Mamie, I'm so happy," she said. "You can't imagine."

That is being young, Mélanie thought, seeing all her terrors for their future meaning for them only a great adventure.

But in her bed that night Colette lay wide awake and couldn't sleep. She felt ashamed of having asked to go to England. If Solange were away at a farm and she went away too, who would help Mamie in the house? And then if they must really think now

about the future and what they wanted to do and how to be prepared if the war came, going to England was just a luxury.

For the last year Colette had hoped that something would
happen to decide things for her. And now it had come, but it
didn't make it any easier. Solange, she thought, was really a saint
—she wanted so little in life. She was perfectly happy as long as she
was allowed to be with animals and plants or helping in the house.
She seemed to have no personal ambition.

But her own life was nothing but confusion these days. For a
year she had hardly written, and her little notebook lay at the back
of a drawer because she couldn't bear to look at her last year's
poems—they seemed so childish. Whatever she wrote now she tore
up. She had become extremely critical. And then, whenever she had
a free hour, there were so many things in the garden and the house
that needed doing. She thought sometimes that her conscience had
grown too big for the rest of her. As a doctor I know I can be useful,
she said to herself, but how do I know I can ever write a really
beautiful poem?

Sometimes it seemed as if she could never make up her mind
unless she could get away from home, get away from her parents,
get away from her awareness of their problems and their relationship. And so England had become an escape, a dreamworld, a place
where she could be her real self again, where she could be quiet
and released for a while from the immediate pressure of this enormous decision. England was, in a way, poetry. And that was why
now, lying awake, she blamed herself for having seized at the
opportunity so selfishly.

Her head was bursting. She felt that in a moment she would
scream or throw herself out of the window. It really did occur to
her that that would solve everything, and she was in a cold sweat
with terror that she would do it. So she ran out of her room, bump-
ing into the door in the dark, and slipped down the stairs, trembling
violently. There was a light under her father's door. "Papa is working." How often through her childhood those words had meant,

"No, we can't go on a picnic," or "Don't talk so loudly in the hall."
Above all, they meant he must not be interrupted. The linoleum
was icy under her bare feet; she was shaking so much, she was
afraid she'd knock against the stair rail and startle him. Now she
was this far, it seemed impossible to go back. Should she instead
creep into her mother's warm bed and say she had had a nightmare? No, Mamie needed to rest. That would be worse.

Finally she scratched at the door very softly, like a mouse, and
waited. There was no sound from inside. So with a sudden movement, brought on by cold and fear, she pushed open the door and
closed it softly behind her.

He was sitting at his desk, back to her. "Hello there." He turned
and welcomed her as if it were the most normal thing in the world
to have his daughter appear in the middle of the night in her nightgown.

"Do you mind, Papa, if I just come and sit here a little while?—I
won't disturb you. I'll just put on your wrapper." His beautiful
Jaeger wrapper, bought long ago in the good days, hung on the
door.

"Of course, my bird, my treasure." He got up and helped her
thin arms into the long sleeves. "There, now you look like a monk.
Did you have a nightmare? Come and sit on Papa's lap and get
warm."

She buried her face in his neck, smelling his delicious smell of
shaving soap and tobacco, and clung to him passionately, whispering, "Oh, Papa," over and over, and he rocked her as he had rocked
them all through their childish griefs, on his thin pointed knees.

After a moment he lifted her chin and looked at the intense face
before him. But she did not want to be looked at. She buried her
face in his shoulder and clung to him tightly, remembering the
peril she had been in.

But after a moment she got up and went over to a little stool and
sat on it.

"You see, Papa," she said gravely, "I am stuck about my life."

He lifted his eyebrows slightly. "Your life, eh? What about your life? I admit that one's life is apt to look a little strange in the middle of the night."

"I don't see any way out, Papa." She was frowning now, the dark frown which screwed up her face.

"Well, we have lots of time—let's talk about it."

She explained then what they had been told about the war and that she had wanted to go to England.

"All that seems to me very sensible, my dear. What is troubling you, then?"

She was, he thought, an amazing child. He wondered, counting back rapidly, how old she was exactly—for in her ability to analyze herself and others she seemed far older than sixteen.

And yet, crouched over on her stool, she looked like a little girl, the little girl who had made nests for field mice and fairies all over the garden, the little girl who wrote poems and was always full of secrets. But she did not talk like a little girl.

"How is one to decide, Papa, between serving poetry and serving life itself?"

Paul laughed; the pointed thrust of this question hit him right in the center of his own life.

"That's a pretty big question to try to solve in the middle of the night. I don't wonder you were frightened."

"Oh, I wasn't frightened of the question. I was frightened because it seemed impossible to decide without betraying something. I mean, I have always wanted to be a poet. But lately I can't write any more, so how can I *know* any more? How can I know what is right, Papa?"

"Don't you think, darling," he asked gently, "that it's perhaps a mistake to try to force a decision now? You're still very young. Many people write poems when they're your age and then stop as they grow older."

"But I don't *want* to stop!" She besought, not him, but her destiny itself. "That's just what's so terrible."

"No one is forcing you, are they?"

"I don't know. I feel lost." Her fists were clenched with the effort of explaining. "You see, I want to be useful."

"Yes, yes," Paul murmured. He understood her struggle so well, but he was surprised that she should have come to it so young. This was the crisis he had been through only ten years ago, when he was thirty—when he had decided to try to help Mélanie in the business. At Colette's age most young people would be thinking of expressing themselves without too much sense of responsibility to the world at large. This was Mélanie's doing, of course, with her high standards of behavior, her uncompromising ideals. He did not like it. "Yes, yes," he said again.

"If I am not a poet I want to be a doctor—a children's doctor, and if so, I would have to begin choosing my courses at the university for that, next year. You see, I *do* have to decide," she ended, waiting for him to speak. "And then when Mamie said the war might come I thought: I want to be ready."

"I think you mustn't worry too much about the war. I think we shall have to go on living as if there were to be peace—there is nothing else we can do. And, my darling, life doesn't stop for a war. There will be plenty to be done afterward, and perhaps it is for that you should be getting ready. We can't accelerate our lives now beyond the normal. That would be false, and perhaps even fatal. No, what you must come to discover is where your own deepest need lies—that is hard enough."

"Yes, Papa."

"You wouldn't be a very good doctor, you know, if you only did it out of a sense of duty without a real vocation."

"I know. Oh, Papa, if I only believed I could be a poet!" she said passionately.

"It's not as black and white as that, Colette," he said, for the first time severely, because he felt that here he was combating Mélanie's absolute ideas. "We live by faith in the end, not by reason. If you are a real poet you'll never be sure—there'll always be the enormous risk to take, the risk that you are following a will-o'-the-wisp, as my father used to say. And you may not even know when you die, whether you had the right to take the risk. I don't expect to know," he added with a bitter smile.

So there was, after all, to be no answer tonight.

Paul looked at Colette observantly.

"My darling, come here, come to Papa." The magnet of love pulled her back to sit once more on his knees, safe in childhood. "You mustn't try to solve these things with your hard-working little mind any more. You must really have a little faith in life itself. When the times comes," he said, stroking her soft straight hair, "you'll know what is right. Something will tell you—and until then try not to worry too much. You have time, my bird, you have all the time in the world, years and years. I want you to go to England as you planned next summer and enjoy yourself, and not worry any more."

"I'll try, Papa." She felt much better now. But still there was no answer.

When she had gone, Paul sat looking at the stool where she had been sitting and realized that a child was a witness, and Colette, more sensitive than the others, had always been a silent and tormented witness of his struggle with Mélanie, pierced by it as a child might be haunted for a whole lifetime by a single scene of violence. But he and Mélanie lived out their conflict—it was in a sense the very basis of their marriage, the rock which split them but on which they stood firm though there might be an abyss between. But Colette had only received the impact of the conflict like a bruise—she was trying desperately to be both her mother and her father in one person.

Every flaw, every hesitation, every compromise in him or in Mélanie he saw now was reflected in Colette's enormous eyes as if they were an enlarging mirror.

And then he remembered Louise. He had thought of Louise as his own problem. Now he realized that any problem of his became imperceptibly the children's problem as well; consciously or unconsciously they stood as witnesses to his life. He sat with his head in his hands for a long time, knowing the whole of his responsibility and what he felt to be the whole of his failure.

But upstairs Colette was already fast asleep.

Chapter III

If Mélanie's illness left a hole in the life of the house in the country, at least she was there upstairs, ready to comfort and give advice, to be waited on and cherished. At the business in town everyone felt themselves listening in vain for the sharp commands, the passionate exhortations, the drama which created a climate for them all. Now the ice age seemed to have set in. Nothing was right. Mlle. Louvois and Mlle. Zumpt had a tiff. They were not on speaking terms and communicated entirely through Jean, who got so tired of running up and down stairs that he tried several times to give notice and had to be calmed down by Monsieur.

Paul himself had a lot of work to do on the new order. He wanted only to be left in peace at his drawing board, making minute calculations and drawings, and to recite poems while he worked. Instead he found himself drawn into the stupid quarrel downstairs and finally blew up in a rage and ordered the demoiselles to make it up or leave. He stayed, grimly, until he had seen them shake hands, and then went upstairs and banged his door as if to say, "Just dare come up and disturb me again!"

It made Mlle. Louvois very nervous to have to make decisions on her own. The curtain material Madame had ordered was out of stock in dark green. Would gray be just as suitable? Would gray be just as suitable? She asked herself stupidly over and over, and finally hesitated so long that the wholesale house hung up on her. And Mlle. Zumpt, who had of course been listening, smiled. By the end of the morning Louise was close to tears.

She was no longer an attractive woman. She wore a turban now to hide her graying hair; she had stopped dyeing it and it had not grown out, so it was a hideous particolored mixture. Her heavy make-up seemed only to emphasize the oldness of the face. Only her clear blue eyes looked incongruously innocent and young, so she reminded Paul sometimes of a Siamese cat. He pitied her so deeply that his pity was very close to tenderness. She had, of course, fallen passionately in love with him and now nursed this hopeless love as she had once nursed and lived by her long love affair.

Mélanie was shocked that he had allowed such a thing to happen. She didn't seem to understand his side of the affair at all.

What she didn't know was that he had given so much of himself to Louise, had talked to her so intimately of his own problems, that he was himself indebted to her. A real intimacy had existed between them, an intimacy based on their equal unhappiness, and they were bound together by what they knew about each other. He blamed himself bitterly for having fallen into the whole thing. What a sentimental fool he had been!

But after all, he asked himself then, could he have done differently? A man with a divining rod in his hands cannot help it if he is thrown to the ground by the force of the current when he is led to it. He had a very real power to understand and to help. Could one deny this power, refuse to use it when a human being was in trouble?

He was annoyed with himself for thinking so much about her. He was aware of her downstairs all the time she was working and waited half impatiently for her to knock at the door. When she finally did it was nearly time for lunch.

"Sit down, Louise—and have a cigarette. I'll be with you in a moment. I hope Mlle. Zumpt and you have come to your senses."

"Oh, it's been a fine morning." She laughed ironically. "Madame will be in a fury when she comes back and finds what a mess everything is in."

In six years they had grown used to each other. And for Louise the best moments now were these, when she could sit quietly whiie he worked, and smoke a cigarette in peace. At such times she felt herself keenly alive—she thought of many things which never came to her mind when she was alone. For she was a woman who would never be completely herself except through another person, within a relationship. And for all its outward slightness, this was a real relationship and one which fully occupied her heart.

Strange, she thought as she inhaled deeply and felt the slight disturbance, the pain, and then the intoxication of the smoke in her lungs, looking out as she had done a million times on the red tiled roofs opposite and the row of pigeons—six years of her life were framed by this static scene—strange how in a novel it would be inconceivable that she should still be sitting here. No writer, she thought, half amused at the idea, would dare to hold two people in such suspense for so long a time. Once, on some warm spring evening, he would have kissed her; or, more likely, the tension would have exploded finally in a quarrel and she would have left the business, as indeed she had thought of doing many times.

But a real life was so much longer and more obscure than a life in any novel, for the novelist inevitably looks to the few moments of crisis to illuminate his characters, whereas, she thought, character is really developed and matured in the interminable spaces between. In six years Paul's children had grown up from babies to young women, and still she sat here looking at the red roofs and the pigeons, waiting for him to finish his drawing and talk to her, as she had done years and years ago. And still the suspense was there, the bubble of excitement in her throat when she knocked at the door, the sense of something imminent between them which might at any moment in all the years have resolved itself—and yet, she saw now, would never never do so.

"What is Jacques doing?" she asked suddenly.

"Oh, I don't know," Paul answered indifferently, still absorbed in what he was doing. "He's got a little shop of his own now and makes a good living mending old furniture and making an occasional piece. He has become a satisfied paterfamilias—he has settled down." His tone mocked the words as if nothing could be more stupid and fruitless than Jacques's life. "We never see him any more." And then, as he washed out his brush and licked it into a point before laying it down, he added, "What made you ask?" and sat down with a sigh opposite her, thinking, as he did so, We are getting old, my poor Louise; for she did indeed look badly this morning.

"I was wondering about Françoise."

Paul shrugged. "Oh, Françoise has forgotten all that. That's ancient history. At her age six years is an eternity."

"And at our age?" She smiled a little sadly.

"A moment—an interminable moment, which is quite a different thing. We haven't changed—or hardly—but Françoise is a different person."

"What is she like? I never see her any more."

Paul smoked for a moment in silence. He was thinking of how little he really knew of his eldest daughter. "She has succeeded admirably in divorcing herself from her family—she lives with us, but that is the most that can be said. She is charming, gay, ready to talk about her plans and her work, but as for what really goes on inside her—you know as much as I do. He smiled with a trace of bitterness. "She has made her escape."

"Is she happy?" Louise asked innocently.

"A perfectly irrelevant question—no one is happy at twenty-one —she's fearfully ambitious. She is determined to be graduated *'avec la plus grande distinction.'* I have an idea that she has wrapped her emotional life up in a sort of cocoon for the time being—but how do I know?" he added. "She never brings any of her school friends home any more. All sorts of things may be going on."

"And that doesn't worry you—and Madame?" Louise couldn't imagine Mélanie not knowing what was happening to her children. Everyone spoke of the Duchesne family as the closest, the most

intimately linked of any family they knew. It had often been discussed downstairs—that and the almost total lack of sophistication
of these brilliant children.

"Well," Paul said quietly, "you know it was a battle for years. But
then Françoise won. After the business about Jacques she never
confided in us again. She's a strong character, stronger even than
her mother, because she is more personally ambitious. And even
Mélanie finally understood that Françoise had won her independence, not by moving out, by going away—which I'm sure she must
have considered—but *within* the family. That is quite a triumph,
eh?" he ended, as if he enjoyed the triumph immensely himself.

"You are generous, Paul."

"No, I'm not generous. Not a bit. I should be fearfully jealous
of any man Françoise loved. Which is, I suppose, why it's a good
thing that I am unaware of that not impossible he—if he exists."
And then he added as an afterthought, "Mélanie *is* generous."

"Yes, she is." On that they were silent for a moment. Speaking
of Mélanie made them inevitably think of themselves—Louise,
especially, with her divided loyalty, could never hear the name
without a sharp pain.

And feeling the emotion in the silence, Paul was drawn in spite
of himself to speak, to explore the wound, to put a new dressing
on it.

"It's not been a very gay six years for you, my poor Louise," he
said gently.

"I don't know," she said, looking at him steadily with her clear
glance, "not gay perhaps. Not empty either. At least," she added
half humorously, "I haven't settled down."

Paul got up and began to pace the floor. He was irritated with
himself for going on with this, irritated by his own lack of courage,
with his holding on to her love, because in some way he needed it
now. If she were not there, in that chair, for an hour or so every
day, he would miss her fearfully. And in return he gave her so
little and that so negative, little more than this irritation, this rest-

lessness—and then whatever went on in her imagination. Not answering her look or what she had said, he laughed suddenly.

"Madness and craziness," he said savagely. "But you know, Louise, you have somehow or other built yourself into my life."

Now that he had said it—so much more than he had ever been willing to admit until today—she realized suddenly that this was the last thing she wanted to hear. As long as she had been sure that nothing would happen, that she was locked safely into the impossible, she could enjoy these hours on which her life depended without guilt, without torment. The last three years had in some ways been the happiest, the richest of her life, just because she had stopped believing in the possibility of anything more.

"Nonsense," she said with surprising vehemence. "I won't hear of such a thing. It's not true."

"Yes," Paul said gravely, "it is true." And then he went on, apparently irrelevantly, "You know, Louise, I am working again—at my own work. I have begun a new book."

"Paul, that is wonderful. That is *good*." How many times he had told her that he would never write again, that it was perfectly pointless to try to express his ideas, to go through the fearful labor of condensation and clarification again, since there was no one to read what he wrote. And always she had believed, always said he would have to write again when he once more had something to say, and when the ideas were fully matured, they would demand to be expressed. "What did I tell you?"

"Yes." He came over and took her hand in both of his and kissed it. "You believed in the impossible. I can't imagine why, but you did."

But she would not say again that she loved him. She would not, whatever it cost, exploit this moment for more than what it held in itself. On this point she had in the last moments come to a final understanding with herself.

"I love you." The words were spoken before he was aware of what he was saying.

Gently she pulled her hand from him. "No," she said quietly, "I have been useful. That is enough."

And for the first time in this strange conversation he looked at her, for herself and not for himself, in amazement.

"What has happened to you, Louise?"

"I don't know."

"You've changed. Since we've been here this morning—you've changed. What is it?"

For a moment, as it is said a drowning man sees his whole life spread out before him, she saw her whole life spread out. But she was not drowning. She was coming into the fullness of her real self.

She laughed. "I suppose, Paul, that I've grown up. Do you think it is possible that at my age one can suddenly grow up? It sounds ridiculous, I guess." But her voice betrayed that it was not ridiculous at all. This, then, was the harvest of those six years in which nothing at all had happened. It would take her a long time, many hours of solitude to explore fully the significance, the total gift of the last few minutes. But for the moment it was she who must dress the wound, not he. Because her wound was healed.

"You have been a good friend to me, Paul," she said at last. In spite of herself, it sounded like a farewell.

Chapter IV

Two weeks later the university still had no word from Schmidt; the absence of news had become a tangible part of Paul's and Mélanie's life. It was the last thing they talked of before they went to sleep, and when Mélanie got up at seven, in the dark, and wondered why she felt so anxious, it would sweep over her again. By now he might be in hiding or—this she steadfastly refused to admit—already caught, trapped, and shut up in a concentration camp. Her thoughts turned to his wife, whom they had never seen, of whom they knew nothing except that she had chosen to stay in Germany. Was she doing it only for the sake of her son, in the hope that he would change and eventually come back to her and then flee with her to join Gerhart? Or was it a real divorce, a divorce in the mind? *Could* she be a convinced Nazi?

In the early morning, at seven even, it was still quite dark; the autumn rains had begun; and Mélanie had at times a feeling of claustrophobia, as if the immense darkness of Germany hung over them and would swallow them up. It was a relief when the dim gray dawn came and one by one the familiar trees and shrubs of her garden made their appearance and the natural day chased away the spooks. Anxiety was to become from now on, she foresaw, a permanent part of their lives. It was all very well to remind herself that the aftereffects of grippe were known to be fatigue and melancholy; she could push them away violently by an effort of will and by keeping busy, but the fact remained, anxiety had taken up permanent residence in the bottom of the heart.

The radio, Paul's great source of relaxation, had now become a Cassandra they must live with every day, the loud repeated voice of terror, bringing bad news and the presence of evil into the house. Mélanie wished sometimes that they didn't have a radio. Perhaps if they did not listen or hear the loud voice of the Nazi, they would be able better to keep in touch with the voice of Germany, the gentle heroic voice of Schmidt and all the others whose silent struggle, whose silent suffering Mélanie felt she was listening to and trying to reach all day long.

Paul talked now of going into Germany himself to find Schmidt. He would be quite capable of doing something rash and crazy, of getting himself killed, which would be no help to anyone. So every morning Mélanie hoped against hope that there might be some word. If the telephone rang at the office, her heart was in her mouth. Wouldn't Schmidt be able to get some message through somehow, soon?

The days of this autumn had become interminable.

So it was a relief when their old friend Emile Poiret turned up one rainy day under a big black umbrella to ask them to help him —it was a relief because Emile's trouble was a human and practical one that Mélanie could help to solve. Here was something she could *do*. It was, of course, about Pierre.

They had seen very little of Pierre in the last years. They knew that he was writing Flemish poems, had even published two small books, and that he had spent two months in Russia and come back an enthusiastic Communist. But the few times he had come out to the Duchesnes' on a Sunday, he had made a very bad impression on them. He wore cheap flashy suits—he threw his weight about a good deal. He had become, in fact, an intellectual snob, surrounded himself with an adoring group of young Flemish enthusiasts, and would take no criticism from anyone about either his life or his work.

His articles on Russia had made quite a sensation in the Brussels *Soir,* and on the few thousand francs they brought in, he had set himself up in a hotel and made a fool of himself by taking prostitutes up to his room not for the usual purpose but to convert them to Communism, and because, incurably romantic, he had some idea of saving them from their sordid lives with his flaming and nebulous ideas. Most of this the Duchesnes had already heard—it was common gossip. Pierre had graduated with honors from the university in the field of comparative literature (he had amazing facility with languages), and he was not one to hide his light under a bushel. Whatever he did, he was anxious to do publicly.

He favored his parents with an occasional visit—they had a little daughter ten years old as well as the grown-up boy—showed his contempt for them and their ideas openly, borrowed money from them whenever possible; but they actually knew very little about his life.

It had been a terrible shock to Emile and Suzanne when they were faced with debts amounting to three thousand francs, three or four months' salary to Emile—a sum which it would be crushingly difficult to pay. But it was not the money; it was, as Emile said, not even the criminal tendencies this pointed to; it was "the lack of heart." It had come to him like a stroke of lightning that their son, their brilliant and adored son, did not love them. And he took this to be his own fault.

He sat now in Paul's studio—he had not even taken off his overcoat—with tears pouring unashamedly down his cheeks. Paul and Mélanie looked at each other, exchanged one glance of complete understanding, and then Paul said, going to the little cupboard where he kept a bottle of brandy for just such emergencies:

"First of all, drink this; it will make you feel better."

Emile made a wide gesture of despair, as if this were the final and worst misunderstanding.

"But, Paul, you know very well I do not drink wine."

"This is medicine," Paul answered firmly, and handed him a small glass, which Emile drank as if it were medicine, in one gulp, and then shook himself like a dog and blew his nose on an enormous blue handkerchief.

"I feel it in my chest." He beamed as he polished his glasses.

"Secondly," Paul said, taking out his wallet, "and before we consider the serious aspects of the affair, here is three thousand francs." And, as Emile made a gesture of protest, "It happens that we are rich today, enormously rich, because we have just been paid a hundred thousand francs by a skinflint factory owner——" He did not mention that all of this and more was owed for mortgages on the two houses and bills, but anyway, they had enough to give to Emile, and that was the main thing. Here Mélanie interrupted:

"And of course, Emile, this is a loan to Pierre. We shall expect him to pay it back himself, little by little."

"Now," Paul said, sitting down opposite Emile, "now, my dear man, take off your coat and let's talk about the thing that really matters—Pierre himself."

The Duchesnes had always dazzled Emile. He looked at them in amazement. They acted with such speed and efficiency in any emergency that one hardly had time to realize what was happening. He looked from one to the other and shook his head.

"You are good, so good," he said gently. "I cannot refuse."

"What does Pierre say to all this himself?"

"Oh"—Emile stammered slightly in his anxiety—"he doesn't know, of course, that I've come to you. He would be furious."

And once more Mélanie and Paul exchanged a wordless communication.

At that moment Pierre himself was walking in the park near the Palais Royal, trying to make up his mind whether he dared to go to Tante Mélanie and make a clean breast of the whole business. He had gone back to his hotel room after breakfast to find that he was locked out for unpaid bills—and, far worse than that, that the manager had got into touch with his father, who must by now be on the way. The idea of meeting his father in the lobby of the hotel in front of the supercilious clerk was more than he could face, and he had simply run away, hatless, in a light raincoat. Here at least no one would look at him—for there was no one here. He walked aimlessly, looking down at the pebbly path and the sad crumpled leaves, and, as the violent emotion of the first half hour left him, began to think.

He blushed to the roots of his hair as the whole humiliation swept over him—how he had swaggered in and out of the hotel, been insolent to the clerk, and all because he wanted people to know he was someone important, Pierre Poiret the journalist, Pierre Poiret the Flemish poet—and all the time they had no doubt been snickering behind their hands, knowing it to be all false, false armor that he wore to hide his sense of inferiority. Now his father was probably already at the desk, weeping and wringing his hands and making humble apologies to the manager. At this Pierre ground his teeth. For the insane part of the whole business was that it had all happened through a petty miscalculation in his accounts. He had simply made a mistake anyone might make over a few thousand francs—careless, perhaps, but hardly criminal. It was crystal-clear that if he had been some bourgeois wine merchant the hotel would never have acted as they did. They would have reminded him gently that his bill was overdue. They were putting him out because they had been waiting for a chance to do so for weeks, ever since he started bringing Jeanne and Suzy and Marie-Ange up to his room. They were putting him out because he was a Communist. When he had got to this point, Pierre began to feel better. So—he was really a martyr to the cause. In that case, he need not feel ashamed or humiliated. He lifted his head and looked critically at the great chestnuts all around him. Lines of poetry rushed to his lips: "In the day of my humiliation, I walked under the dying chestnuts, lonely." He fished around in his pockets for a pencil and wrote the line down on an old envelope, shifted the position of "lonely," and then buried the envelope in his pocket again like a squirrel with a nut.

He felt elated—he would leave the country, get the *Soir* to send him to Czechoslovakia or Finland. His head buzzed with plans. In the end this might be the best thing that had ever happened to him.

And then in the distance he saw a small stout woman walking toward him fast: Tante Mélanie! In his state of excitement it seemed possible that she was looking for him, that she had come like conscience itself to find him and humiliate him in a far deeper way than the clerk at the hotel could do. The woman came nearer and nearer; he found it impossible to run away. He walked steadily toward her until he saw that she was somebody entirely different —an old crone with too much make-up on and a squinting eye. He was astounded to realize that he was almost disappointed that it was not Tante Mélanie.

I hate them, he muttered to himself, I hate them. For the last few years all his efforts had one unadmitted purpose—to make the Duchesnes respect him and take him at his own evaluation of himself. They must admit that he was a genius, an exception to all their rules. They must come to him and confess that they had been wrong in their opinion of him, that they had misjudged him when they called him selfish toward his parents, because he was serving a great destiny. When his first book came out and Paul wrote him a long detailed letter of criticism he had been furious. What does he know about what I am trying to do? he had shouted to a group of his admirers. What does he know about poetry? And he had never answered the letter, though for some reason he had carried it in his wallet ever since and reread it often. Ever since he had been a small boy his attitude to the Duchesnes had been ambivalent. On the one hand, the house in the country was his promised land, the one place he could remember where he had ever felt at home. On the other hand, it was the scene of his humiliation—for always, and quite without intending to, the Duchesnes had made him feel inferior. They had taught him manners, and that in itself, meant so kindly, was a fearful humiliation. They criticized him constantly, as they did their own children, and all for his own good, but he was not their own child, so the criticism seemed barbed and rankled afterward.

He had determined never to see them again until he could see them on his own terms, but now he was so filled with tenderness when he thought of Tante Mélanie that there were tears in his eyes and he was on the point of running to her the moment the least thing went wrong.

He felt cold and terribly lonely and thought with distaste of the few places where he could go, the disorderly dirty apartments of student friends, or home. Home, he thought bitterly, to face his father's gentle forgiving gaze? His mother's tears and protestations? It would be better to ship out as a common seaman on a freighter for Brazil.

The terrible thing was that this one little slip, this mathematical error, would now stand up and seem to prove that there was something wrong about his whole life. The injustice of it! The meanness of human nature! But what was he to do? All his clothes were locked up, his typewriter, his books and papers—without three thousand francs his hands were tied. The only people he could imagine having that sum on hand were the Duchesnes. "I can't, I can't," he muttered aloud, clenching his teeth.

And then he had an inspiration. He would ask Dupierreux to send him to Spain—true, no one yet had sensed the significance of the war in Spain. They still talked about it as if it were a local affair. It was a tremendous chance for a reporter. He would come back covered with glory.

But when Pierre got to the office of the *Soir,* he was told that Dupierreux was in conference and could see no one until tomorrow. The girl at the telephone desk looked him up and down, and he realized suddenly that he must look like a wild man, with the water running down from his hair, his collar soaked. With her uninterested glance his whole plan collapsed—they would never give him the chance. Dupierreux would smile sweetly and tell him that they were of course sending seasoned reporters to the front. A mere student with three articles on Russia to his credit could not be considered. Pierre was glad to be out on the street again, where at least he was invisible, where no one would look at him appraisingly and inevitably read his distress.

He looked at his watch. It was half-past eleven. If he hurried he could be at the Maison Bernard before the gathering at lunch time.

Now he had made his decision, he did not think of what he would say when he arrived. He thought of nothing except that now he was on his way to the one place in the world where he wanted to be.

Panting—he had run the last four blocks—sweating, drenched, he burst into the studio upstairs and found the last person he had expected—his father.

Before Emile got up, before anyone could accuse, forgive, demand, do any of the things Pierre had imagined would happen at once—Mélanie had walked over and kissed him on both cheeks.

"You're soaked," she said severely. "Come along to the bathroom—take off your coat and hang it where it won't ruin the furniture. Where *have* you been?"

She had meant to be angry, but now that she saw him she couldn't be anything at first except glad to see him—and her question meant really, "Where have you been all these years? We've missed you."

"You see"—Emile turned to Paul warmly—"you see, we all turn to you as soon as we are in trouble."

"Yes, yes," Paul sighed, and then added mischievously, "but in that case it would be nice if you came to see us a little more often when you are not in trouble—eh? It's awful how we never see each other any more, Emile."

Mélanie was looking at Pierre critically—he had grown much thinner, let his hair grow too long, and looked, she thought, like a caricature of a poet. But his wide-apart clear blue eyes had not changed, nor the sullen expression in the eyebrows, drawn close together and quite heavy.

And Pierre, who was stripped now of every hope of playing a part, since his father had told them the whole story, let himself be propelled back into the studio without a word.

"Hello, Father," he said with a sheepish smile, and sat down heavily in the nearest chair.

"The Duchesnes have generously given me three thousand francs to pay your hotel bill," Emile began clumsily.

"Oh." Pierre was not surprised, nor even, it seemed, particularly grateful.

"You might at least thank them," Emile said gently.

"Thank you very much," Pierre answered, like a child repeating a lesson.

"Our lion is as meek as a lamb," Paul teased. "Not a growl, not a roar, Pierrot? Why, we had heard you were a swashbuckling terror of a man, the Flemish Byron at very least—and now you are cast down for a tiny little debt? Come, come——"

But Mélanie saw that the boy was close to tears.

"No, Paul, don't tease him. Look, I suggest that we talk about all this later. It's nearly lunch time. You'll stay to lunch, Emile, of course?"

Pierre's last hope vanished as his father accepted the invitation.

"You will want to talk," Mélanie added, and took them into the little study-bedroom next to the studio, where Paul sometimes slept when he stayed in town. "There, my children, make yourselves comfortable; we'll call you in half an hour."

The door closed behind her. Pierre was alone with his father. The room was like a prison cell. There was nothing to sit on but the bed—the single window opened onto a court and was, for some reason, barred. Emile sat down. Pierre went to the window and stood with his back to his father. Let him begin.

But Emile was silent. He knew that it was a terrible thing for the boy to find him just here just now—that it must seem a betrayal— for the Duchesnes had been *his* people, *his* friends always—and one reason Emile had seen little of them was not to trespass on this center of his son's life.

In his innocence, Emile could wait, forever if necessary. But Pierre, in his guilt, turned after a moment and said with an aggressive intonation:

"Well? Aren't you going to say anything?"

Before the naked hatred in the boy's eyes, Emile dropped his own.

"Pierre," he asked in a perfectly detached voice, as if it were a scientific question, "why do you hate us so much?"

This was the last question Pierre had expected, penetrating as it did with frightful honesty to the very core of his confusion. It took from him his only arm. He blushed to the roots of his hair.

"Why do you ask me that?"

Emile was sitting forward with his hands clasped between his knees, a familiar gesture, one which had always irritated Pierre, for it was exactly the position of a workman on the trolley cars.

"Because," he went on with the same quiet voice, "I never understood you before. I never understood this fact in your life—that you have always hated and despised us. It's a tragic fact, Pierre. And I blame myself that I have refused to recognize it until now."

The man is so terribly good, Pierre said to himself. Why then had this goodness always irritated him?

"Why do you hate us, Pierre?" he asked again. There was going to have to be an answer.

Downstairs Pierre could hear Mélanie's voice and then Mlle. Zumpt laughing. Outside, just outside the door, was the whole normal world, but here he was caught in sickness and death.

"You are an intelligent boy," Emile went on. There was not an ounce of sentiment in his manner. The tears, the gentle suffering which always set Pierre on edge, seemed to have vanished. "You must have thought about this a great deal in all these years. I think you will have to try to answer me, Pierre."

Pierre turned his back on his father and stared at the window.

If he answered now, he would be tearing up the very root of his life, his pride. The long war with his father would be over and his father would have won. But he knew very well that he would never have the patience to be silent. His father's own interminable patience had come to an end, and the silence now was an absolute vacuum, a suspense which no one could sustain forever, certainly not he. Some violence, some rush of emotion would have to fill it. Pierre felt as if the tension in his head would burst it open. And Emile waited.

When Pierre spoke, he spoke to the barred window, without turning.

"You were always trying to make me do things that I didn't believe in."

"I never forced you to do anything."

Now Pierre turned savagely on him. "No, that's just it. You sat there and looked at me until I wanted to kill you. Why didn't you force me? Why didn't you?" he said hysterically.

Emile smiled one of his rare illuminating smiles. "My poor child."

"Don't pity me," Pierre answered furiously. "Don't you see? It's a way of life I don't believe in. I don't believe in your saintly compassion. I believe in violence. I believe in revolution. I hate your church and your Christ!" He felt as though he were shrieking.

"And what else?" Emile asked, as if it were the most natural thing in the world for a young man to deny God, as if it had hardly shocked him.

"I felt that home was a prison—I had to break away from you or be swallowed up, destroyed. It was I or you, don't you see?"

For a moment Emile was silent, as if he were weighing evidence quietly, and then he said, "Sit down, Pierre. Sit down," he said again, and Pierre sat down with his head in his hands, abjectly. He was beginning to see for the first time that under his gentleness his father was strong, deeply strong, and in his heart he was glad.

"This is my failure, Pierre, not yours. And it is for me now to beg your pardon."

"No."

"You were always brilliant, and I was always afraid that this brilliance would lead you away from the human things. I did not impose my will on you—no, I did worse than that. I tried to be your conscience. You are right. I made your home a prison." Here Emile knocked his forehead with his closed fist in a gesture so violent for him that it betrayed itself in his voice. "I have been stupid."

Pierre put his head in his hands and wept convulsively. What a waste the years behind him seemed, an interminable waste he had dragged along after him, a waste of pride, a waste of hatred—since it was ending now in this abject state, in his weeping in his father's presence.

Emile had not moved. He sat still with his hands clasped between his knees.

At this moment of failure he had communicated with his son for the first time in years. His words had actually penetrated, moved the boy. Here, when he had been wholly cast down, he was mysteriously lifted up by the Divine Compassion. He had

come to understanding. The inexhaustible miracle of life filled
him with joy.

But although Pierre had been for a moment touched by his
father, a moment of illumination (which he thought of as weakness
the next day) does not change a life. At first he sank back gratefully into being once more a child of the Duchesne house. For
they had insisted on taking him back to the country with them
for an indefinite stay. He was to take his time. He was to work
at the novel he had begun and have the long quiet autumn days
to himself in the empty house—and in return he was to help in
the garden.

In these days what struck him most was how little anything
had changed here. Every morning he got up in the dark, went
down to the kitchen to get a pot of hot water to shave with, dressed,
and threw his bedclothes together in a semblance of order. There
was the ritual of breakfast, the noisy ritual of the family's departure for town, and then silence and solitude. From his window
over the garage he looked out on the black earth and frozen cabbages of the *potager,* covered with frost in the morning so they
gleamed moon-like in the dark. He sat for hours watching the poplar trees tremble and sway and the leaves fall one by one. Everything in the house was as he had remembered it—the three blue
plates on the shelf in the breakfast room, the melancholy portrait
of Paul as a boy, the Sunday smell of the salon, the familiar book
of French nursery songs open on the piano, the dark green linoleum
in the front hall, so cold underfoot—and the gay sunny veranda
where Françoise painted at her high table. Nothing had changed.
It was all just as he had remembered it a thousand times, on a
slow train in Russia, in his dingy hotel room, and on his long
walks by himself through Brussels. And more important than
the things themselves, the atmosphere of the house was exactly the
same—the enormous amount of life going on, the violent argu-

ments, the scenes of reconciliation afterward, the precious warmth of the evening "good nights" on the stairs. He had come home. He was so happy that tears filled his eyes a dozen times a day. He had no desire to see any of his old friends in town. His life for the past two years seemed to be blotted out from his memory like a dream. He composed a long tender letter to his father and mother, asking their forgiveness and promising to think deeply about the future and to try to be worthy of their trust. And having mailed it, he forgot all about them too, as if nothing whatever existed except the Duchesnes and the house and the garden.

But after the first days he began to be aware that there were changes, that there was a difference after all, that it was no longer quite the same. Was it that he had forgotten how hard everyone worked here? Of course in the old days there had been Bo-Bo and Louise and Marie, and, in the garden, Croll. Now there was no one, but—no, it was not only that. In his hours of hating the Duchesnes he had often reminded himself of how enclosed they were in their own corner of the world and accused them of intolerable smugness. Their Olympian attitude, he had told himself a hundred times, was only a kind of escapism. And Françoise, whom he disliked intensely, still behaved as if the world around her was none of her concern, still refused to be drawn into political arguments, still scorned his offers to inform her.

But of course for him the heart of this house and the reason for his rooted attachment to the family was Tante Mélanie. And it was in her that he began to notice the change. She still rallied herself and everyone around her to the daily tasks as if each day were a battle into which one plunged with zest. She still loved to sit at the table after supper and talk endlessly of everything under the sun, from gardening to Dostoevski and from Fascism to Picasso. He had never surprised her in a moment of lassitude or doubt. And yet there was a difference.

Six years ago she could not have possibly kept herself from taking a high moral attitude toward his own escapades, for instance. But to his enormous surprise and uneasiness, no one had scolded him or insisted on "a heart-to-heart" talk; they seemed simply as happy to have him back in the fold as he was to be there. Uncle Paul, of course, teased him incessantly about his debts, about his poems, about his political stand, and about his insistence that he would go to prison rather than serve a year in the army. But that was very different from the inquisition he had expected and steeled himself to meet. When after a week nothing at all had been said, he began to wish to explain himself, all unasked.

He realized with a flash of self-knowledge that disturbed him, that he had been fighting a war all these years with something in the Duchesnes which no longer existed. At my age, he said to himself, I take absolutely for granted that in six years I shall be a different person. But it never occurs to me that a grownup will change. One expected grownups to be one thing and not another, to have been finally molded into the shape in which they would die. It was quite a shock to Pierre to find this was not so. They *do* respect me, he said to himself. They really can accept me as I am, without humiliating me. The fact filled him with shame. He saw himself now as unbearably crude and narrow.

And the person he chose to confide in was Colette, Colette who had shared the secret of writing poetry with him when they were both children, Colette who was now unlike any girl he had ever seen, in that she seemed absolutely untouched sexually and years older than her age in understanding. She puzzled him and he was very curious about her. But it was hard to get her alone—when she came back from school she was always doing lessons or running out to the garden. And when he followed her out, she seemed strangely impersonal, telling him what to do to help but not particularly interested in what he had to say. Once he asked her if she wrote poems still and she answered "No" with such finality that he didn't dare pursue the matter any further. Once he asked her if she were in love and she gave him a look of complete scorn and said, "Of course not," as if she had more serious things than that to worry about.

Finally one warm Sunday afternoon he persuaded her to come for a walk—"Just to the end of the road where we can see the fields."

They walked quickly, as if they were on an errand and had little time.

"Do you think I've changed much, Colette?" he asked after a moment, because this seemed as good as any other way to begin.

"I don't know. I haven't thought about it." She gave him a mischievous sidelong look. "You're much thinner."

"You've changed," he said insistently.

"I expect so," but she would not give him an inch.

"Why do you treat me like this, Colette?" he asked in exasperation. "After all, we're old friends—we used to have fine talks. Don't you remember?"

She kicked a stone forward with her right foot and seemed entirely absorbed in following it up and kicking it on another few yards. They had used to play this game for hours, and for once Pierre moved quickly and got ahead of her. "Pay attention," he went on angrily as he kicked it a good ten yards.

"I *am* paying attention," she answered, running ahead. She was laughing at him quite gaily, and as he caught up with her he pulled her arm through his and adjusted his step to hers.

"There, that's better." What did she think of him really? He wanted to know that suddenly more than anything else in the world.

"Is it?"

"More friendly. Now we can talk," he said happily. She had not drawn her arm away.

"I don't want to talk."

"You're a funny girl."

For some reason they stopped in the middle of the road and stood there, silently, warily, facing each other.

"If you really want to know," she grinned, "I think you're awful."

"Why?" he grinned back.

"Well"—she walked on alone, frowning thoughtfully—"as far as I can see, Pierre, you're completely selfish. That's one thing."

"Have you read my poems?"

"I don't see what that has to do with it."

"It has everything to do with it," he shouted angrily. "Don't you see?"

"No," she answered with another sidelong look. It occurred to him that she was simply teasing him and none of this was serious. "As a matter of fact, I *have* read your poems. Most of them seem to me rather loose and romantic and very much like you," but now she blushed because she felt she had gone too far, farther than she meant, seeing him collapse before her eyes so visibly as if she had put a pin into a balloon. "I'm sorry, Pierrot, that was mean. I don't know what I think," she said, suddenly skipping like a little girl and picking up a crimson maple leaf from the black road.

All Pierre's old anger and frustration filled him again. What made these people so damnably sure of themselves? Only because they didn't know anything of the world; had no idea what the real conflicts were; didn't realize that the banks of Belgium controlled its politics and, for one step forward, forced the legislature one step back; knew nothing of Russia, of Spain, of anything but their private lives and their absurd old-fashioned ethical standards which drove them to try to be useful without ever going to the root of the matter, to work in clinics or against child delinquency without ever examining the political framework behind them.

He walked on ahead with his head bent, his hands shoved into his pockets, raging.

"You think *that* because I'm trying to say things in my poems that will reach the masses, things that have never been said before. I'm pioneering," he shouted back at her.

She ran to catch up with him.

"Besides," he went on more quietly, "all you're doing is repeating what you've heard your father say."

"Perhaps I am, but I think my father is a very wise man. Don't you?" she asked directly.

"He has all the faults of the pure intellectual," he said pompously.

"Namely?"

"First of all, complete detachment. He doesn't know what is going on. He lives in an ivory tower."

Colette was frowning now—always these same questions came up wherever one turned. It was awful.

"But, Pierre," she asked seriously, now they were really talking, "if you believe that nothing is possible without the revolution, I should think you would work for that, really work, not by writing poems, but through the unions, or whatever one does—by going directly into politics——"

"One must use the talents one has. Mine is for writing, so I try to put my writing at the service of the revolution."

At last he was given a chance to explain himself, and Pierre was wildly happy. He sniffed the air. He looked around at the small closed château they were passing.

"I bet you don't know who lives there."

"No, I don't."

"You see," he said in triumph, "you don't even know your own neighbors."

"Summer people," Colette said with perfect contempt. "We know the people in the village."

"Touché," he admitted. "No"—this is what he had wanted to talk about all along—"I can't define your family really. Your father and mother are the best people I know. I love them more than my own parents."

"Well, then," Colette asked gently, "what's wrong? Why do you always fight us?"

"Because"—he threw up his hands in a gesture of despair and giving in—"because if I didn't I would have to change my life, everything I believe in, begin again from the beginning——"

"I don't see that. Why does everyone have to be alike, do the same things, believe the same things in the same way? That's Nazism. Why can't we be ourselves and you be yourself? Why do you take our mere existence as an attack on yourself, Pierre? It's so strange," she said passionately.

"Because," he exploded, "don't you see, when I'm with you I don't believe in myself any more."

Colette saw suddenly what anguish and self-torture there had always been behind his boastfulness, and she remembered the fight in the woods, the horror and shame of it—it came back vividly, and she understood that they had been cruel to Pierre that day, had not backed him up as they should, had despised him because he was beaten—whereas instead he had shown the purest kind of courage, the courage of the weak in the face of the strong, the extreme courage of the coward who makes himself brave by an act of will.

"We're a horribly critical family," she admitted, slipping her arm through his.

"Oh, Colette," he murmured in an agony of self-pity, "I've been so lonely always."

But what he didn't tell her, what he hadn't quite the courage to confess, was, "I've been so wrong all these years."

They were coming to the end of the avenue, where the rough pavestones gave way to a dirt road, where a last avenue of maples ended in open fields. On one side stood a white summer villa, the windows boarded up for the winter, and on the other, black plowed hills, rolling off gently one after another to a wide, far-off horizon. Here Pierre and Colette stood together and breathed in the space and the distance.

"How I love this country. I love it passionately," Pierre said after a moment. "Oh, Colette, I want to be useful."

But she didn't hear him. She was sniffing the wind like a colt, her eyes shining.

"Be quiet, Pierre; the larks are singing."

Each was lost in himself, lifted up in an ecstasy of wind and sun and space. "I want to be useful." Never had Pierre said those exact words before. He was amazed at himself.

"You're a family of magicians, Colette—you are dangerous people. One is not safe within a mile of any of you," he broke out as they turned back to houses and people, to the crowded trees and darkness of the avenue.

And Colette laughed, though she had no idea what he meant.

Chapter V

It was strange, Paul thought, sitting at his desk on a Sunday morning not long after Pierre had come to stay—it was strange that the state of the world drove them all inward rather than outward. This autumn seemed above all a season of evaluation and self-questioning, in which each in his own way set his personal life against the huge pattern of terror—even Pierre. Outside, it was a still, sunlit morning, gentle and radiant after the long cold weeks of rain. The cat stretched herself out on the window sill, her two front paws laid meekly on either side of her tummy while she licked it passionately, lying flat on her back in a most abandoned position. Fifi was far more attached to Paul than Filibert had ever been and so, perversely, he was far less interested in her. He tolerated her presence, he teased her mercilessly, and he pretended not to be flattered when she wound herself round his legs purring loudly.

"Cat," he said to her severely, "you distract me. You make it quite impossible for me to concentrate on anything but the superior quality of the fur on your stomach. You are not *'L'amie des amoureux fervents et des savants austères'*—you are a little devil."

But still he watched her and sighed, "Yes, yes."

The truth was, he had found it impossible to do any real work since Schmidt's letter. It created an inward suspense, as if he were hung up in the air in a vacuum. Now Francis was pulling wires to try to find out if Schmidt were still in Berlin, and Mélanie had written to his wife, a perfectly normal letter telling the family news and asking for news of them. They should have an answer to this in a day or so. Something must give them an inkling soon of what had happened and what might be done.

"Yes, yes," Paul murmured again, picking up a sheaf of papers, glancing at them absent-mindedly, and then laying them down again. With the future so uncertain, the past had become extraordinarily vivid. He found himself looking back to his student days more and more, turning backward as if to discover something he had missed. He and Mélanie had been young in a way his own children—even Solange, with her funny little air of responsibility as she went out to take care of her animals—had never been. They had had no chance to be extravagant, to have their favorite books bound in expensive special bindings (he remembered the bindery where he had spent hours as a young man, choosing a fine leather and examining the hundreds of designs, the smell of morocco, the delicious cool parchments), to go for week ends to Paris or to London. His family had never been really rich, and yet, as he looked back, his student days seemed to him extravagantly free and rich by comparison with Colette's for instance. Much more had been asked of her at an early age. Was this a loss? Or a gain? It would take another ten years to begin to know, and by then they would be plunged into the utter dislocation, anguish, and terror of another war.

Because of this certitude of disaster, everyone was driven down into his deepest self now. And because of this, time had assumed a false importance. There was no time. A child like Colette actually weighed whether she ought to spend a summer in England—it seemed fantastic—at sixteen!

Fifi, having licked her fur into flat wet decency, now stretched, sighed, and closed her eyes.

"Cat," Paul said to her, though she was not listening, "you are emancipated from the past and from the future—emancipated from time, lucky creature. You live in the eternal present of the true mystic."

For must one not try to be at every instant the whole of what one would choose to be for eternity? To fail now, to be less than the utmost possible, was perhaps to fail for all eternity. And if I should die tomorrow, Paul asked himself, what should I leave behind me? Three dead books, three living children, and somewhere in the deepest part of me a sense of utter failure, a sense of loss: the absence of faith. For all I have done all my life is to ask questions, to push one step further down a long black tunnel with the hope, with the desperate conviction that there must be a light at the end. But what if there were not? Could one live and die in darkness?

Emile did not. Mélanie did not. Far away from him, as far as if he breathed a different air, they moved in light. They lived by faith. In other words, they are sane, and I, he said to himself, am insane; driven by a demon; longing above all for love and for true brotherhood, and shutting out even my old friends like Francis, like Emile, because I pretend to see and to know more than they do about things which after all one can only feel, not seize with the intellect.

In the last years he had been increasingly lonely, depending almost entirely on Louise for companionship, but when he did have an afternoon with a friend, he felt chiefly a desire to escape. He was relieved to be alone again. They did not really know what he was talking about, and as a result, in an effort to explain himself, he talked too much, and badly.

In writing, in setting his ideas down with the utmost precision, so they might have the abstract beauty of a geometrical figure, he had only been doing what the poet does when he takes the infinite pains to express his admiration of his lady's eyes in a sonnet. It came back to him vividly how in 1919, in his first book, he had had the sensation of writing a letter to Schmidt, a letter that couldn't be written until the means of communication were open and the barriers of the war down. And everything he had ever written had perhaps been written in a desperate desire to communicate what he always failed to communicate through living itself. They had been a long apologia for his failure toward Mélanie, toward the children, toward Emile, Francis, and all the others, toward life itself.

"Oh, how you startled me!" He turned to see Mélanie standing in the door.

"I'm interrupting."

"No, no," he said, looking at her as an explorer who has spent a year under the glare of snow and sun might look at a green tree. "Come in. I've only been asking myself all the old questions that have no answers—and talking to Fifi," he added with a smile which said better than any words that he was truly glad to see her.

For even after all these years she never approached him with any feeling of certainty, always with the same inner trembling that it would be the wrong time or that, for some unknown reason, she would not please him.

She gave a shy little laugh and confessed, "I felt lonely. I don't know why."

"What a strange autumn it is," he said as she sat down in the comfortable armchair. "Here we have been living along more or less quietly for five or six years and suddenly it seems as if a crisis were at hand. I can't work." He shrugged. "Even the children feel it. Colette looks as if she sat up half the night thinking. You, my dear, say you feel lonely; Pierre turns up in a mess, expecting us to be able to solve his problems for him—heaven knows why. What is it in the air?" he asked meditatively.

"I have a funny feeling," she answered, and he was struck with the parallel to his own thinking, "that everything is getting sifted down to its essence. I feel myself changing. It's peaceful here, Paul." She looked at the neat desk, the rows of books, the broad beam of sunlight crossing the room with motes of dust dancing in it. "I wish we could sell the business," she said suddenly and violently.

"Why not?"

"Well"—Mélanie frowned—"there is Françoise and her future. We can give her a chance to design on her own, give her a start. Then," she added as if she were a little ashamed, "I think of our people, the two demoiselles, how would they live? And the Jeans? And M. Plante? Things are not going to be easy for anyone now. Paul, I just can't see turning them out."

"It's Schmidt's letter, isn't it, Mélanie? It's that—the shock, the crisis—strange——"

"I don't think it's strange at all," Mélanie answered indignantly. In a second she was her old self, matter-of-fact, forthright. "After all, it's a sign that there is no hope for Germany—at least the good Germans are once more not going to have a chance. We know now that there will be war."

"I told you there would be war ten years ago. I've always known it."

"You've always known it intellectually—but here is a fact that pierces us where we live. It's different. It's no longer an exercise in political dialectic. It's what we're going to have to live, Paul. Oh, don't you see the difference? Why doesn't Schmidt let us know what to do?" she interrupted herself impatiently.

"We're none of us very good at living in suspense, are we? And yet that will be our element from now on."

"There's never been any real security—not since before the last war—but there's always been hope, I suppose that's it. Now"—she laughed at the image as she thought of it—"we're rather like Noah before the flood. We have to think of something to do."

"There's nothing to do."

"Oh, Paul"—she got up and went to the window, looking down on the little orchard, on the white table and chairs under the apple tree, on the goats, on the pattern of paths laid out at her feet—"how can you say that?" (She, for one, must see to it that they got a hive of bees; and how the apples needed pruning!) "There's your work. That has to be done. Those are the things that count, that really matter now. That's what I meant about the business—it doesn't seem to matter." She came and put one hand on his shoulder, tenderly. "I suppose that's why I felt lonely—for a long time it's been little more than a means of keeping us going financially. I never could imagine doing something I didn't believe in." She was like a tree that has suddenly lost all its leaves in a blast of hurricane wind. The hopes, the faith of twenty years, lay strewn around her.

Paul took her hand in his and warmed it as if she were cold.

"That's what you meant about an end," he said gently. He got up and put an arm around her, so they were both leaning against the desk looking out.

"I suppose so." She let her head rest on his shoulder. Here was rest, love, peace—here and nowhere else in the world. For a moment she let herself rest in it.

"And the beginning?"

"Oh, don't ask." She turned from him to hide the rush of tears. "I don't know. There's no giving up the business, Paul. It will have to go on for another five years or so." Everything would go on as before: outwardly there would be no change in their lives. Only inside the frame they would have to change, grow, build new faith to meet the new and terrible future. How did one do that?

"But your book, darling." She looked him full in the face, not hiding her tears now. "That's what is good, deep, lasting—what we can build on. I believe so much in what you are trying to do, Paul. In the last weeks I think I have come to understand it as I never did before—I have sometimes not understood, I know. Partly because quite literally I couldn't follow you, but more because . . ." Here she hesitated, and Paul interrupted:

"Because you wondered if the critics were right and I had been pursuing a chimera of my own all these years."

"No." Again she frowned the characteristic frown which all the children had inherited, as if thinking for her and for them were a physical as well as a mental process. "No—I can't say it," she ended, smiling. "I don't quite know myself. Isn't it true, Paul, that we have missed a great deal of each other all these years? Can we ever catch up?"

Standing before her, he took her face in his hands, exploring it with his fingers, the straight low forehead, the deep-set eyes, the small stubborn nose and the beautiful sad mouth; delicately he traced it with his fingers and then he said:

"I've missed you, Mélanie. I've missed you."

All these years their beds had touched each other in the night; they had slept side by side; they had lived side by side; they had loved each other deeply and silently. And yet there had been a sense of parting, a profound loneliness, as if there were some fundamental misunderstanding. Could it be dispelled now, literally like a mist burned off by the sun?

"I haven't loved you enough," he went on, kissing her hungrily and lightly wherever his fingers had touched her face.

"We're middle-aged, Paul—and I feel so young, it's absurd." She drew away from him to look at him and she was blushing deeply.

"Nobody knows a damn thing about love until they're middle-aged. That's one thing I'm sure of."

"And now, *darling,* I've got to feed my family. Heavens, it's nearly one!"

And as she left him Paul sat down at his desk, trembling with eagerness to go on with his work.

It takes a long time, all one's life, to learn to love one person well —with enough distance, with enough humility, he thought—and he was flooded with happiness, thinking of the years ahead.

Chapter VI

It was true, as Paul told Louise, Françoise had forgotten Jacques—or, if she had not forgotten him, he meant the final shame of childhood, the last time she would ever expose herself to grownups, the last time she would give herself away. When, standing at her high drawing table in the drafting room at the art school, she sometimes remembered the wedding and what had happened afterward, she bit her lip and worked with a ferocity of concentration which the other students noticed. One made the experiment of teasing her; a curly-headed handsome boy put an arm around her and said so the whole room heard it:

"Françoise is in a mood. Françoise is thinking of someone."

Françoise turned like a flash and slapped his face. It was a savage, hard slap; the laughter which greeted it was both astonished and admiring. After that they left her alone when she was moody.

She had soon learned what that wink of Jacques at the wedding implied. It was not the dear and secret comradeship, the silent understanding she had believed it to mean. It was something quite different, shameful, wrong. For the next time they had met, when she was sent to M. Plante's on an errand, Jacques had kissed her full on the mouth. She had never been kissed before, and this strange tongue forcing itself into her mouth filled her with horror and revulsion. Nothing of the fire and ecstasy of that one moment by the chest weeks before was in his kiss. It seemed to her filthy, and afterward she had wiped her mouth over and over again, as if she would never get the taste of tobacco and beer off her lips. It had disturbed her profoundly, as if a delicate equilibrium inside her had been smashed. It had made her dizzy with fear, and she had decided there and then that she would never let another man come anywhere near her.

The boys at the school sensed this fierce guarded quality in her at once and left her alone. She never did belong in any of the gangs which set themselves up, fought among themselves, gathered in the park near the school at the lunch hour, and had their private jokes. Her friends were a gentle Argentinian Jew who adored her silently and would never dare to tell her so, and a tough angry Flemish girl from the Lower City in Brussels, whom Françoise respected because she was talented and because she laughed at the boys. With these two Françoise relaxed and enjoyed herself, but she never asked them to come home. They were part of her life at the school, but neither was part of her real life. Once Antonio had taken her to a concert, but she had been distracted from the music by his presence and afterward preferred to go alone. Music had become her one real passion. She spent all her pocket money on records and concerts—listening to music, she felt released from all the tensions. She became fully herself.

One night as she got off the trolley and entered the pitch-dark of the avenue she had had an impulse to turn back. It was always an ordeal, the final quarter mile in the dark. Every time a leaf rustled, her heart jumped. Often she stopped and stood still, transfixed with terror, only to run wildly, her heart in her mouth, until at last she could click the gate behind her—safe.

But her freedom to come home late at night alone was worth the terror. That was what she told herself on the particular night when she had for some reason wanted to turn back. And then, when she was only a hundred yards from home, a hand had suddenly been put across her mouth and she was grasped fiercely across one breast. She bit the hand so hard that she tasted blood on her mouth, tore herself loose and ran blindly, weeping with terror, hearing a guttural drunken curse behind her. Her clothes were drenched with sweat when she finally got to her room and turned on the light. She lay on her bed, cold to the marrow and without the strength to undress. Later she rinsed her mouth over and over and still it tasted of blood.

But she did not tell her family what had happened. The next time she went to a concert she took an umbrella with her. In the fierce determination to keep her freedom, to keep her inner life intact, she found the courage to face the terror alone. It was a tremendous victory, and when she thought of it she felt elated— at least in the daytime. At night the smell of the man who had seized her haunted her—she would turn on the light fifty times during the night, imagining that he had somehow got into the room.

The only thing she shared with Mélanie and Paul was her ambition and her work. When she had finished a design for furnishing a child's nursery, for an exhibition room in an art gallery, for a workman's recreation hall, she always brought it home to be criticized and talked over. She trusted her mother's judgment more than that of any of her teachers—and Mélanie was not slow to criticize the academic point of view at the school.

But there was one ambition she had not discussed with her parents, and that was her ambition to be a stage designer. She had not told Paul and Mélanie that there was to be a contest for designs for *Peer Gynt* at the school—and she did not bring her ideas and plans home. The anxiety about Schmidt and the talk of war had touched her very little. She worked late every evening at the school and fell into bed when she got back. Her terrors, her dreams were all her own.

Maurice, the quixotic, extravagant Maurice of the Brussels Theater, was to be the judge, and it was rumored that if he liked the designs he might give the winner a chance to do a production for him at the theater. The competitive spirit, always strong at the school, ran high.

Françoise had helped hang the exhibit of drawings, winnowed down now to ten, of which Maurice would choose the three best. Hers had not been among the first choices of the judges from the school, but among the last. She herself looked at her designs, now they were up, with a feeling of despair. They were so bare and understated compared to the others. She had been praised for her ingenuity in using four set pieces which could be shifted around for all the outdoor scenes, but she had felt disappointed to be praised for mechanical rather than imaginative reasons. Beside the Argentine boy's rich colors and fantastic baroque sets, they looked queerly bare and undramatic. Of course the lighting would have to do everything—Maurice would know that. It was one of his pet theories that people were lighting modern sets with the most old-fashioned and unimaginative techniques. He had come back from a visit to Russia full of enthusiasm: "You've got to suggest, rather than state. The motion picture, the film can state more completely than any theatrical set—but it cannot suggest. That is for us," he had said last time he was at the house in the country, and Françoise had listened, rapt.

Now today, for the first time, he would see her work and judge it. Françoise dressed in clean clothes from top to toe, as if she were going to be examined by a doctor; she put on her best gray suit, a suit she had had made two years before with her first real money; she ironed her one ruffled blouse, a Christmas present from Paul's brother in the lingerie business; she brushed and brushed her straight dark hair until it shone and then braided it over her head. She wore no make-up, but her eyes shone and her cheeks were pink with excitement. The family viewed these preparations with amusement and curiosity. Solange and Colette plied her with questions, but she just smiled and said:

"Oh, it's nothing, some sort of reception at the school."

But Françoise had a fine contempt for all social occasions and would have worn her oldest clothes on purpose if it were only that. Solange and Colette winked at each other and determined to find out somehow.

And Paul surveyed her with a smile and added his observations:

"Your Argentinian must be making headway after all."

"Nonsense, he's nothing but a boy," she answered without self-consciousness.

But Mélanie held her at arm's length and kissed her and said simply, "Well, whatever the secret is, you look beautiful, my darling, and we wish you luck." She kissed her on both cheeks.

"It's terribly important!" Françoise called back as she made her escape.

In the course of the afternoon they forgot all about Françoise because everyone was waiting anxiously for the postman. Surely there would be an afternoon mail—surely there would be a letter from Frau Schmidt? Solange swung back and forth on the green gate for hours watching for the dark blue cap and big bag to appear around the corner, listening for the horn in the distance—would he never come? Had he just given up the avenue for the afternoon?

"He'll never come if you watch for him," Colette called from the shed where she was chopping kindling.

In a corner of the big studio where the designs were hung, Françoise giggled with Antonio out of sheer nervousness. They had some joke which would not have seemed funny at all at any other time but now convulsed them both. The room was full of people, talking loudly and self-consciously and keeping an eye on the door.

But unlike the postman, who seemed to have no sense of responsibility, Maurice strode in exactly on time, his vermilion tie, his crest of black hair, his baggy English tweeds making an amusing contrast to the director of the school, correct in his pin-striped trousers and afternoon coat.

"He looks like a funeral-parlor director," Antonio whispered in Françoise's ear, and she put a handkerchief in her mouth to keep back a shout of laughter.

As Maurice stopped before each set of drawings and model, the student who had made them was introduced and given the chance to "defend" his project.

It was impossible not to love Maurice; as he talked to each student, the perspiring drawn faces broke into smiles, the clammy hands relaxed, the stammered "Yes sirs" gave way to good talk. Everyone felt the difference between the man who was an artist himself and the pompous director who, if he made a criticism, always seemed to be about to write down a grade in his little black book.

With instinctive tact, Maurice did not greet Françoise as an old friend but looked at her designs exactly as he had looked at all the others; if anything, he was more severe with her. Françoise was not

a bit shy now that she was speaking of her work. She spoke passionately in defense of her bare stage, of what could be done with
lighting, so much so that the director intervened.

"That is adequate, mademoiselle. You need not go on," he interrupted. "You are to answer questions, not deliver a lecture."

Françoise glowered at him, blushed to the roots of her hair, and
shut up like a clam. But she felt better when Maurice gave her arm
a gentle squeeze as he passed on to the next drawings. "Stupid old
fool," Antonio whispered, and that was comforting too.

How she hated authority! How she longed to be out of school
and doing her own work!

It was time for the students to go into another room and wait
for the results. As soon as they were seated in the small theater, the
buzz of subdued conversation rose to a roar. Boys and girls shouted
across to each other; a disagreement in one corner turned into a
fist fight. In the middle of the noise, Françoise sat very still in a
knot of anger and pride. How angry Mamie will be, she thought,
when she hears what that old monster said! She couldn't wait now
to get home and tell them.

In an amazingly short time the director, followed by Maurice,
looking artificially solemn as if he were playing the part as well as
he could, walked out onto the stage and the director raised his
hand for silence. Like magic, the roar ceased and there was absolute
stillness. The wild animals became in an instant an attentive host of
young, upturned human faces.

"Ladies and gentlemen," he began, and coughed deprecatingly,
"we cannot possibly express the deep satisfaction and pride we
feel in having had the distinguished assistance of our most cele-
brated man of the theater in helping us to decide the various
merits of your designs."

Someone in the back of the hall coughed deprecatingly in a
perfect imitation of the director, and a gale of laughter swept the
theater. Françoise watched with delight how Maurice swallowed a
smile as if he were swallowing a piece of chocolate. The director

flushed, brought his hammer down furiously on the stand before him, and shouted in a completely different tone of voice:

"I must ask you to restrain your levity. This hysterical atmosphere is hardly appropriate to the solemnity of the occasion."

The laughter made itself felt now like a physical earthquake— soundless, but shaking shoulders and chests with violence.

"You are savages," the director went on icily.

The savages now engaged in an epidemic of nose-blowing, innocent coughing, and squeaks quickly suppressed in sneezes. Françoise began to be frightened. It was really too much. They were going too far.

"I will wait for appropriate behavior from you." The director looked as if he were about to have apoplexy and sat down, crossed his legs, and put on a patient face as if it were a mask he had just taken out of his pocket.

For a second hysterical laughter and chastened silence hung in the balance—a single giggle might have tipped the affair over into open revolt. They had laughed at the director so much behind his back that this outbreak in public was intoxicating—but on the other hand, they wanted to hear the results. Curiosity won just in time. As quickly as it had come, the laughter passed over; for an eternity the students sat once more in strained silence. Wrist watches ticked as loudly as grandfather clocks. The director waited.

Finally he rose and announced, as if he were meting out punishments to the unworthy, that Mr. Maurice Bernard had named Jacques Français first, Françoise Duchesne second, and Antonio de Marco third in the contest. "You are dismissed," he said quite unnecessarily as the shouts and applause rocked the hall.

Françoise, smiling, triumphant, wearing her success like a rose in her mouth, pushed her way out of the crowd of hands and arms, patting her, embracing her, shaking her two hands, and made her way to the stage.

Maurice jumped down to throw his arms around her and kiss her on both cheeks.

"To think of it—that little Françoise—that little Françoise—and I never dreamed!" Delight poured out of him. He dressed the world in magic. "Here, let's get out of this—come along with me and celebrate."

It was all like a dream. Françoise found herself sitting beside him in the racing car, being driven with careless grandeur, the horn blowing, *"Malbrouk s'en va-t-en guerre,"* crazily down the wide avenues, to one of the big cafés on the Avenue Louise. Maurice never stopped talking, praising, admiring, laughing loudly over the students' demonstration against the director.

"Oh," he said happily, "I like this country. I love these people who never will take any kind of authority seriously—what a splendid gang of boys and girls. What spirit! Ah yes, one must know how to laugh in this world, Françoise—and to cry, eh?" he said, turning to her solemn and radiant face and almost knocking down a policeman.

She had always adored Maurice. He was the antithesis of her own family, perhaps that was one reason. She had heard his sins recounted often enough: irresponsible about money, full of fantasy as a child, and with a child's amoral nature. He was in debt—he had made his wife unhappy—he was not to be trusted—and yet— and yet—the very people who seemed to relish his misadventures loved him in spite of themselves. "He's an artist," they would end with a shrug, as if that explained everything. "He's a genius—what can you expect?" The Duchesnes, critical as they were of him, always ran to meet him with cries of joy whenever he came. And always when they were children he had come laden with presents—the kind of presents no one else ever thought of—an immense teddy bear when everyone else considered Françoise too old for toys (she still kept it always on the end of her bed), a living white rabbit for Solange when she was still a tiny child.

"Do you remember the rabbit you brought Solange years ago?"

"Remember *Ubu Roi?* I should think I do remember him."

"And how Solange cried when he disappeared—it was awful."

Never, never had Françoise imagined she would be talking like this to Maurice; walking with Maurice into a café where the head-waiter bowed and scraped and murmured, "This is an honor," and gave them the best corner; Maurice ordering, as if it were the most natural thing in the world, a *Châteaubriand aux pommes frites,* a cress salad, a bottle of Château-Neuf du Pape—and Françoise felt almost frightened when she saw how much it would cost. They had been brought up to be as frugal as birds—a dinner like this in a big restaurant was unheard of. Oh, what she would have to tell when she got home!

"What are you thinking about, eh? With those great shining eyes?" Maurice twinkled.

"I was thinking how jealous the family will be."

"They won't be worried? You hadn't better phone?"

"Oh no, I do what I please," she said rather grandly.

And again Maurice looked at her, amused and delighted. "Oh, you do, do you?"

"Well, I'm grown-up, you know. I graduate next year." Yes, she was grown-up indeed, with a waiter gravely pouring wine into her glass, another waiter whisking her plate away and putting in its place a perfect round succulent steak covered with *sauce Béarnaise* and with a mound of tiny thin fried potatoes beside it.

"Yes," Maurice answered with appropriate gravity, "you seem very grown-up. Your scene designs are extremely good, Françoise, did I tell you that?" He lifted his glass and looked at it speculatively, while Françoise, her fork suspended in mid-air with the first heavenly mouthful of steak on it, waited breathlessly for what he would say next. "Let's drink to doing a play together one of these days—only first you will have either to eat your mouthful of steak or to put it down."

Françoise put it down with a smile and raised her glass. They drank silently.

"Mmm," she said, "that's good." She was wondering how to ask him more about what he had said—a play at the theater—and when? And what about Jacques Français? It wouldn't be fair if he didn't get a chance. Maurice was eating and drinking with obvious relish and didn't notice her hesitation. He went on, "I have great plans for next season—we'll go to Paris, for one thing. With a repertory of Belgian plays. I want to get a dramatization with music of *Till Eulenspiegel*—how would you like that? How would you like to do some designs for that this summer?"

"But what about Jacques Français? He was first," Françoise wrenched out of her.

"Who's he? What are you talking about?"

"The boy whose designs were best for *Peer Gynt*—they told us that perhaps you would——"

"Oh well," Maurice shrugged, "by next year he will have forgotten all about it. His designs were good, but I am really more interested in you—— Oh, don't worry about that." He pushed Jacques away as if he didn't exist.

Françoise's face, which had been open and smiling a moment before, now closed as if she had pulled a visor down and wore a helmet. She had always heard how it was, how one had to know the right people, make contacts, and often the students had told her enviously that she would never have to worry as she could step right into her mother's business. But the idea was revolting. The violence, the purity in her flashed out suddenly.

"It's not fair," she murmured almost inaudibly, but Maurice saw her dark face turned away from him, the tears of anger in her eyes.

"Why, my dear child"—he threw his napkin down and reached over to take her hand—"don't be upset. Why, these things happen every day. That's life. That's the world. Come, don't be a little goose." He must make her smile again somehow. "You're a little puritan like your mother. I would never have believed it! But, Françoise," he pleaded, "it's my business and mine alone"—he laid a hand on his chest—"whom I choose to design for me. What in hell does a prize at some stupid school of design have to do with it?" he asked in exasperation.

Everything around their meeting had been gay, magical, impossible—— Oh, let it stay like that just for tonight, Françoise said to herself desperately. I am a fool to care. I mustn't let this spoil everything. But she was down in a dark hole and she couldn't climb out. She drank her glass down in one gulp and was surprised at the effect it had almost at once. She began to feel dreamy and pleased with everything, with her steak, with herself—yes, even with Maurice, his eyebrows raised in an amused question as she glanced at him.

"Am I a goose?" she asked thoughtfully. "I suppose I am."

"A beautiful goose, a snow goose, that's what you are." He poured charm over her, dressed her in charm. No one had told Françoise she was beautiful. The boys at school were much too shy; sometimes her father said so, but she knew what he really meant was that he loved her and not that she was beautiful at all.

She was flushed now with the wine and the food and all that had happened. "Oh, I'm so happy," she sighed.

"That's better. For that you shall have an ice cream, a Coupe St. Jacques."

"May I have chocolate instead?" she asked hopefully.

"You may have anything you like—and two demitasses, waiter."

And then to amuse her, to make her go on laughing with pleasure, to make the magic again, Maurice talked for half an hour about the actresses in his company (he was a perfect mimic), about the scenes they made over their clothes, about the plays he would do, about the theater itself, with the mixture of hatred, exasperation, and passion which it always raises in its true lovers. And Françoise listened, delighted, like a child at a play, drinking in the lingo, the atmosphere, learning it by heart.

"There," he said at last, "now I have a rehearsal, and you must go home. I'll have time to drive you part of the way if we can get this turtle of a waiter to bring us a check."

But when he said good-by he kissed her on both cheeks and made her promise to give him some designs for *Till* by the fall, that he would count on her, that she mustn't have any more foolish ideas.

What would the family think?

She was too excited to be frightened on the dark road; she was too full of Château-Neuf du Pape and her own powers to be scared of any man.

But when she got home there were lights on everywhere; and when she burst in, full of her story, she found the whole family moving furniture, her father carrying an armchair up from the salon, Solange with a broom in her hand, Mamie with an armful of sheets and blankets. They leaned over the stairs and, before she could speak, announced:

"Schmidt is coming—he's coming from Switzerland—in a plane —he'll be here tomorrow. Isn't it wonderful? We are making Bo-Bo's room into a study!"

It was a great night. No one got to bed till long after midnight. They praised Françoise's luck, sitting around the table eating bread and pear jam and drinking hot chocolate, and heard the story over and over. Solange asked, "Tell us about the steak again." And Mamie, "He really wants you to design a play?" And Colette, "I wonder if he will like his room."

They were so tired and excited they talked about everything at once. What a lot had happened in one day!

But in her room alone, when the excitement had subsided and the house all around her was dark and still, Françoise felt dissatisfied, jarred, as if she had been floating along on air and had been jolted down to earth. The family had not taken her worry about Jacques Français seriously at all; they had brushed it aside just as Maurice did. It was not her sense of justice that suffered so much as that hard core of independence she had created for herself. She did not want to depend on people's kindness, on their interest, to do what she dreamed of doing. At the school she knew well what would be said—she had been already *"hors concours"* because of her mother's position. Maurice's interest was probably half friendship for her family. She was set apart by privilege—they would be right to say so. Would she never be able to stand absolutely alone?

She lay on the bed with her hands behind her head, staring at the ceiling. No, that was not it at all. It was not that. It was something quite different. It was that she longed more than anything now to be taken in, to be part of the company of her contemporaries, to be accepted for herself, to share in their struggles. In that instant her whole attitude to her own life suffered a violent change. She was so excited by this new idea of participation with others that she couldn't sleep. It was like coming out of prison. Why not do a play with the people at the school? Why not make something of their own?

In the dark still house she was not alone. Each in his bed lay wide awake, burning with expectation, leaning out from his closed secret garden, each in his own way, to embrace the world. The silence of the night was full of longing and of love.

Chapter VII

The next morning everyone, even Pierre, was up before daylight. The children were to be excused from school so that the whole family could go to the airport together—all except Françoise, who could not afford to take a day off so close to the examinations. Their work of the night before was only a beginning—the whole house had to be scrubbed and polished, and all this to be done before eleven o'clock, when they must set out on the great expedition. They worked fiercely, joyfully, in the relief of at last being able to *do* something for Schmidt, to serve him, to show their love and their admiration by making sure that every pane of glass let in the sunlight (it was a beautiful clear morning with a powder of frost on the grass; the garden looked like fairyland), by heating an unheard-of amount of water so that he could have a hot bath, by making his bed with the fine linen sheets from Paul's parents' house. Paul went down to the cellar to bring up the bottle of Quetsch in his honor, and then paced restlessly around his room and up and down the stairs, in an agony of impatience. It reminded him vividly of that afternoon in 1920 when they had first seen Schmidt after the war. But they mustn't overwhelm him—and Paul hurried down once more to tell Mélanie and the children not to shout, to be very gentle and quiet and restrain their affection. They hugged one another to get a little of the exuberance out of their systems. And finally the time came to leave.

Of course they were early and of course the plane was late. They stood in the wind and the sun, half frozen, stamping their feet, blowing their noses. Paul had gone into the restaurant to get warm, but nothing would tear the others from their whole view of the sky. They looked and looked until their eyes ached. Where was it? Could something have happened? He was coming from so far, from so many perils, not until they saw him with their own eyes could they be quite sure, could they quite believe he was safe.

"Remember," Mélanie admonished one last time, "for him this is not the joy it is for us. He has left everything—we mustn't be too happy."

And then, as they tried to take the smiles and hide them somewhere (but nothing could dim their shining eyes—and Pierre had gone quite white with emotion), at last they saw it, a speck on the horizon, so tiny it could never have crossed the mountains, and then suddenly larger, roaring over their heads so they waved madly and shrieked and all the rest of the crowd wondered whom they could be expecting—a brother, a sweetheart?

Clumsily, like a big bird, unaccustomed to land maneuvering, the plane which had looked so small and light hummed heavily across the field.

Now they were silent as Paul ran out of the building pulling on his gloves, shouting excitedly, as if they couldn't see, "Well, there it is!"

And there *he* was, smiling too and waving, and looking so perfectly natural, so like himself, that everyone forgot about not being happy and they swarmed around him shouting, "Hello, here we are!"

Mélanie threw her arms around him and kissed him warmly. He shook Paul's hand. He turned to Colette, hesitated, and asked, "But this is not Françoise?"

"No, it's Colette, the middle one, and this is Solange our youngest. You will see Françoise tonight. And this is Pierre Poiret, Emile's son—you remember Emile?"

"Of course. How do you do, Pierre?"

Now that he had arrived, it seemed to take an eternity before they could bundle him up and carry him off, take him home. The passport official was as slow and stubborn and hard to convince as every passport official would be from now on. He examined every paper in Schmidt's wallet, and in his brief case, slowly and methodically. He turned the passport itself over and over in his hands.

"You understand that you can only stay here for six months?"
"Yes."

"It is forbidden to take a job during that time."

"I understand that."

Mélanie and Paul stood beside Schmidt; Mélanie kept her hand firmly on Paul's arm to prevent him from exploding with anger.

"Have you friends in Brussels?"

"We are responsible for Herr Schmidt," Paul said stiffly and formally, but he looked as if he would kill the man gladly.

"And who are you? Identification papers, please."

The Duchesnes now had to submit to a cross-examination. How long had they known this German citizen and under what circumstances? What was Paul's profession? When he said "philosopher," the passport official raised his eyebrows cynically. "You earn your living as a philosopher? Why are you not connected with a university?"

"That is none of your business," Mélanie broke in angrily.

"I asked your husband a question, madame."

"I have private means," Paul answered shortly.

"We're in business in Brussels, the Maison Bernard," Mélanie interrupted. This seemed to annoy the official extremely.

"Oh, so you're in business. Well, why didn't you say so at once?"

"I am going to report you for rudeness," Paul said icily. "You behave like a Nazi. This is Belgium."

The man turned red. "I'm sorry. I shall have to have further guarantees. It is my duty to make sure that everything is *en règle*. You will have to wait."

"But he has a visa from the Belgian consulate in Geneva!" Mélanie protested.

"I'm sorry." The official disappeared into an inner office with all Schmidt's papers.

"Don't worry. I am used to this. This is nothing, my dear friends. Please don't be angry," Schmidt said gently.

"It's outrageous!" Mélanie stamped her foot with anger.

"Petty officialdom, bureaucracy," Paul muttered. All their joy had vanished. It was too humiliating. Here was a man who had given up everything, family, country, profession—everything—to come to freedom, and now he was being treated like a potential criminal! And they were helpless to do anything.

But Mélanie had an idea. "Paul, telephone Francis at once. He has influence. For heaven's sake, get us out of this. Tell him to come here if necessary."

"What is happening, Mamie?" asked Colette anxiously. The children had been waiting half an hour in the car.

"It is not," Schmidt said quietly, "a very honorable thing to be a German citizen this year. He is quite right, your Belgian official."

"Oh, this is awful!" Mélanie said bitterly. "Run along, Colette, we'll be there as soon as we can. Papa is telephoning Francis."

An hour later Schmidt's passport and papers were handed back to him but with regret. The official seemed thoroughly disgruntled.

"I'm only doing my duty," he said angrily and as if he had hoped his duty would involve sending Schmidt back to Switzerland.

"You do it in an intolerable way," Paul answered.

All the way home he was too angry to speak. He drove grimly while Mélanie and Schmidt talked about the children and the business and the garden. She felt forced to talk about these safe subjects because they could not yet ask Gerhart about himself. In the back the children sang to keep warm. But as they turned into the avenue, everyone fell silent.

"This is it. This is your avenue, is it not?" Schmidt asked.

At last they had him safe. They were opening the green gate.

"Run ahead and light the fire in the salon," Mélanie called to the children.

And Solange called back, "You can have a hot bath at once. We heated lots of water this morning!"

At this everyone laughed, glad to have something to laugh about.

"He looks quite clean," Paul said.

An hour later Schmidt sat drinking a glass of Quetsch, smoking a cigar, as he had done years before, with the children gathered around him listening to him as if he were an oracle, Mélanie sewing in the big armchair, Paul stretched out on the sofa. Silently Schmidt tasted his liqueur.

"Yes, yes," Paul murmured half to himself. He was thinking how sixteen years before Schmidt had broken down and told them it was terrible in Germany. And now?

"It seems unbelievable that you're here." Mélanie looked up and smiled at him warmly, and then she added because she couldn't wait another moment, "How did you manage? Do tell us, Gerhart, tell us the whole story."

He smiled deprecatingly. He smiled a great deal, just as he had always done, and almost mechanically, as if it were a form of politeness and not hard to do. But always as if it were something to be done, not a spontaneous communication from the heart.

"Well," he answered slowly, "once I had made the decision it was surprisingly easy to get away. I had a doctor friend diagnose t.b. and arranged with a sanatorium in Switzerland. Officially I shall be in Davos for the next six months."

After all their visions of his wandering alone through woods, hunted by the Gestapo and perhaps crawling over the border at night!

"Oh," Solange said with such obvious disappointment that Schmidt laughed aloud, really laughed for the first time. He turned to her then earnestly.

"Things are not to be imagined—you see, life is at the same time so perfectly normal and so perfectly abnormal. I was in great danger, as a matter of fact, but the danger was intangible—it never materialized." He waited a moment, unconscious of their bewilderment, choosing his words with care, speaking a little stiffly as he always did in French. "You see, the danger was inside. In me. I couldn't make up my mind to leave. The danger was in the decision—once that was made, the physical business of getting out just meant a little ingenuity, a little courage—yes, I confess that at the Swiss border I was badly frightened for a moment—but that is nothing. Of course if I had stayed two weeks longer it might have been impossible. I had to decide," he said again, painfully, half to himself.

The whole family listened in silence. Pierre, who burned with questions, felt that he had no right to speak. They were awed by this experience, more strange, simple, and terrible than any they had known.

For the first time Schmidt's face showed his inner agitation; he rubbed his forehead with one hand, back and forth, back and forth, as if he were rubbing away a knot inside.

"You can't imagine what it is to leave one's own country," he said almost in a whisper.

Mélanie was quick to protect him. "Don't, Gerhart—don't talk about it all now. You must be so tired. We have all the time in the world."

"I want to tell you," he said earnestly, "but I am tired."

It was all empty around him—they felt it, the emptiness, as if there were a chill in the air. Subdued, silent, Solange and Colette went out into the garden hand in hand. Schmidt went to rest in his room and unpack his one small valise, which Pierre insisted on carrying upstairs for him.

Mélanie slipped an arm through Paul's; they stood and looked out at the familiar battered white table and chairs under the apple tree.

"Oh, Paul," she murmured, "how lucky we are."

"Yes, yes," he sighed. It was, for once, a perfect clear day; the leafless branches of the trees shone like golden wire against the pale blue sky.

"I *couldn't* leave this," she said suddenly. "I couldn't—leave you. the children, all my life——"

"He did," Paul answered simply.

"Poor man, poor man," she repeated; "poor man."

"We don't understand yet what is happening in the world—we don't know."

He went softly upstairs, leaving her alone in the salon. Mélanie was glad there were things to do, the roast to put into the oven—yes, it was high time. She had managed to get a roast of Australian beef. Once more she felt tangibly supported by the framework of her life, by the house, the table to be set, the things to be done. She hoped, incongruously, that Gerhart would enjoy his dinner. But after a funeral the sensible Irish eat a great deal, weep themselves out, and then eat and drink mightily. Could they help Schmidt back into life with these simple things: food, the family, work in the garden? It seemed the whole reason of their existence at this moment to try to do so.

And Mélanie poured her concern for him, her ache for the world itself, into cutting the beans into thin, thin slices, into seeing that the oven was just hot enough, into marshaling the children to their holiday tasks.

And Schmidt, lying on his bed, tense, exhausted, relaxed as he heard her voice call:

"Hurry up, children, the table must be laid—I need your help," and Colette and Solange's flute voices answer from far off:

"We're coming!"

When the bell rang for lunch he was fast asleep. He woke with a start, wondering where he was, suddenly hungry.

They each had a tiny glass of beer (two bottles were divided among them as a celebration) and behaved as if its effect were that of champagne. The chill, the emptiness seemed to have been driven away by the Australian beef. Solange, whose irrepressible laughter could never be held in check for long, convulsed them all, including herself, with an imitation of her hated mathematics teacher whom she called by a series of vegetable names, "Old Onion," or "Old Potato," or, worst of all, "Old Salad."

And Schmidt insisted that Paul do his imitation of a concert pianist, which he had not done for years but which the children had clamored for when they were little. And that led them to speak of Bo-Bo, to all sorts of humorous and tender memories.

"But where is Françoise? I am longing to see *her*," Gerhart said as they got up to go into the salon for coffee. By now he was firmly established in the family as "Uncle Gerhart." "She must be quite grown-up."

"Oh, she is," Solange teased, hanging onto his arm, looking up at him, and shaking her curls. "She's very grand and grown-up. We never see her any more. She works all the time."

He had already admired the set of flower paintings in the dining room and now wanted to hear all about her and what she was doing. And when he had heard he stirred his coffee thoughtfully and turned to Mélanie with a bitter smile.

"She is making these beautiful paintings and scenery for the theater—and you see, Hans"—they had been careful not to mention Hans, and everyone stiffened as his name was spoken—"Hans is being trained now in the arts of oppression and violence. Yes, he is being taught systematically and scientifically how to beat up the Jews."

"No, it's not possible," Mélanie said fiercely.

He nodded his head. "It does not seem possible, but it is so. You see, you cannot imagine," he said softly. "No one can imagine. We Germans ourselves do not imagine. My wife, for instance, does not want to know what Hans has become. She refuses to admit it, *in her mind*. She has shut it out because it is too painful." He was speaking passionately now, though he never raised his voice, but he had clenched his fist and it trembled as he spoke. "You see, when he comes home he looks so fine and strong, and he is a handsome boy, brown and tall, holding himself well—and he is gentle with his mother, a good boy at home. He tells us that he is helping to make a new Germany, and she sees him fine and flaming before her, and she does not visualize what this means. She will not believe it."

"She doesn't believe you?" Mélanie asked tentatively.

"She hasn't seen the things I tell her *with her eyes*—she has seen Hans, and he is better and dearer to her than any argument. Here you have already heard many terrible stories, I am sure. You think of Germany as a place of great suffering, intolerable brutality and suffering, and it seems inconceivable that people do not protest. But you must understand that these stories are not heard in Germany. Oh, one here perhaps, one there—but it is so easy, when one doesn't want to believe, to slide over an isolated case, to put it down to individual enmity or brutality—in every country the police are apt to be brutal. There is always some excuse. And each time one has made the excuse, silenced one's conscience, it is a little easier the next time. So that now, after three years, things that no one could have accepted in the beginning seem almost inevitable."

"But there must be many people like you who are not like that?" Colette asked.

A spasm of grief, pain, bitterness passed over Schmidt's face, as if her words had been a physical blow. "That is what one would have hoped." He shook his head from side to side miserably. "It is so difficult to tell you, to explain, what it is like—— If we professors could have got together at the very beginning, taken a stand together—but we were not organized. Many were unconvinced of the necessity for action. And then it was too late—the few who dared to resist openly disappeared. Their families disappeared. It was as if they had never existed." He hesitated a moment. "It was easy to persuade oneself that it was better to go on existing, to do what one could secretly, and otherwise to conform. Two of my colleagues committed suicide. Two escaped at the beginning— one a Jew—they are in America now. One died in a concentration camp last year. At first I stayed because I could help friends who needed my help—my oldest friend, the lawyer Jacob Goldstein, was shot while trying to get over the border. We believe that he must have been denounced." He was speaking rapidly now, feverishly, as if he wanted to tell them everything as fast as possible. No one spoke. They listened. They felt the wind of fear in the room, the taste, the smell of fear. Just a hundred miles away, just across an invisible border line, these things happened. Life was like this.

"Would Belgians have behaved like this? Frenchmen? Swiss? That is the question I have asked myself over and over. The shame —the shame of it——" he said, covering his face with his hands as if he were unable to look them in the eye.

"But the *people* are not like that. I don't believe it," Pierre broke in, his eyes blazing. "The trade unions, the organized Left——"

"I don't know. I don't understand, myself," Schmidt said quietly. "But it does not happen all at once. It is not white and then black. The choices are never so clear. The people have been slowly poisoned until they don't know themselves what has happened. They don't want to know because they have been given a faith, and that was what they needed.

"You must not forget, Pierre, that in Germany freedom, democracy, meant starvation for many, misery of every sort, shame, defeat, despair. Now we are slaves in Germany, yes, but the Nazis will tell you we have hope, we have pride, we have full employment, we have food. These are a kind of freedom. And then," he went on, speaking directly to Pierre, "there is no such thing as the People. There are in a time like this only individuals and individual consciences. The strongest and the bravest were the first to go—hundreds are dead already or already broken. You *can* break the spirit—that is what is so frightful. I have seen it happen."

Solange got up and went over to her mother, sitting on the end of the chaise longue, stroking her mother's feet. She was on the brink of tears.

Before he went on, Schmidt got up and shut the door, an involuntary gesture of which he wasn't even conscious. Mélanie understood now suddenly why he had been speaking so softly—he could not realize yet that there was no danger of being overheard.

"I came to you so full of love—and here I am, poisoning the air," he said as he came back. "It might be better to be silent."

"We have to know," Colette said sharply.

"Yes, dear child," he said gently, "you are right. You do. I will tell you a story of someone I knew slightly and afterward heard much of. I believe that I must have made the decision to leave as a result of this man. He was also a lawyer, an Aryan." He smiled. "You see, one falls into the Nazi terminology in spite of oneself. He had the courage to defend a Jew in a small case of robbery, and though he lost his case, his defense was an impassioned plea for justice and so an attack on the Nazi courts. Shortly afterward he was tried for sedition—this was two years ago. He was given a mild sentence, and this so enraged the Party that he was taken out of prison before his sentence had elapsed and sent to Dachau. He was there sixteen months. Oh, they were much too clever to let him die there. They sent him back alive to Frankfort, alive and apparently sane, an old, white-haired, broken man. He is very gentle now. He doesn't bother anyone. He can be seen and pointed out sitting in the sun on a bench reserved for Aryans in the park. His presence is a constant reminder of what opposition to the Party means."

For a moment Mélanie wondered if she would not ask the children to leave. The tears were rolling down Solange's cheeks, silently, though she was making an enormous effort to hide them. But no, they must know the truth. They must be given this weapon of knowing. She had no right to protect them. Colette seemed frozen into thought, hunched up in her chair, her chin in her hands.

"I wanted to be able to go on fighting," Schmidt went on. "You see——"

"But if everyone leaves, Uncle Gerhart—what will happen?" Colette asked.

"Nothing will happen in Germany for a long time, I believe for many years. The Nazis will be there for a long time, perhaps a century."

"No." Mélanie dropped the sock she had been darning. "That is impossible, Gerhart."

"The alternative is war."

"Yes," Paul answered quickly, "I know."

"And no one but the Nazi is prepared for war," Schmidt went on. Then he saw Solange crying.

"Oh, my little one," he said in German, *"liebchen*—we must not despair."

The sobs that Solange had held down until now burst out, and she threw herself onto Mélanie's breast, crying bitterly.

"She is too young—I am so sorry, so sorry." He turned to Mélanie, his troubled eyes dim behind the glasses.

"No," Solange sobbed, "no, I'm not too young."

"No, she is not too young, Gerhart. You must forgive her, mustn't he, darling, for lacking self-control? We must learn to face these things, to be able to face them, Solange dear. That is the least we can do."

"I—I'm sorry." She got up and ran out of the room and Colette followed to comfort her.

"I hate the Germans!" she cried when they were safe in the nursery, "I hate them. Why are they there, always there?" she cried in a passion of rage. "Ever since we were little it's always been the Germans, the Germans. Why can't they leave us alone?" She was in a real fury, wanting to break everything in the room, tear up, destroy, and there was nothing to throw but the pillow which she hurled on the ground.

Colette waited for the tantrum to be over, brought her a wash-rag to wipe her face on, and then sat on the bed beside her with an arm around her and said:

"Uncle Gerhart is a German and you don't hate him."

"Yes, I do," she sobbed. "There's no peace anywhere." She felt as if their whole life had been invaded by evil and terror and that it would never be the same again. "They'll come here. They'll kill us all—they'll put us in concentration camps," she sobbed.

"We have to be ready," Colette said severely. "We have to have courage. Mamie is right."

Solange embraced Colette with all her force, clinging to her passionately. "We'll stay together. Nothing will part us ever, will it, Colette?"

And Colette answered, "Of course not." But she was thinking—having made her decision in the last hour—I'm going to be a doctor. Next year at the university I can begin. It was an enormous relief to have decided that once and for all.

Pierre came in, for once subdued, and sat down on the end of the bed.

"I feel ashamed of my whole life," he said. Colette looked at him in amazement. She resisted the impulse to say coldly, "It's about time."

From the window, if they had looked out, they could have seen Mélanie with her pruning knife, up in the apple tree, and Paul and Gerhart, wrapped up in coats and mufflers, pacing up and down, up and down the garden paths in the sunlight, talking philosophy. Gerhart was quite unaware that he had already made a revolution in the house. It was true, their lives would never be quite the same again.

Chapter VIII

Now, after two or three weeks of fine weather, St. Martin's little summer faded and the interminable cold and damp of a Belgian winter set in. The sky closed down like a lid. The garden looked desolate, and everyone wore sabots outside because of the mud. The excitement, the emotion, and the great decisions raised up in the first week of Uncle Gerhart's visit settled down and life had once more its routine pattern. Paul was apt to find excuses to stay at home in order to be able to continue his endless discussions with his friend; Gerhart himself, who had been unable to work seriously for a year, set himself to writing a short book on Nietzsche—a defense of Nietzsche against the Nazi appropriation of him. Pierre worked fast and carelessly at his novel—he was no longer interested in it, but hoped to make a little money on it. And then he had decided to go into the army as an officer's candidate. In the morning the men had the house to themselves.

In the evening, when the whole family gathered for supper, they sat around the table for hours talking. It seemed as if Uncle Gerhart had always been a member of the family—they took him for granted. They teased him about his admiration of Françoise, who had always been his particular friend; they saw that he had the best cut of meat and the largest egg; they included him in their lives and they were unaware of his own private difficulties and growing sense of exile.

In making the decision to come, he had still been wrapped up in Germany—it was his relation to Germany which had forced the decision. He had not imagined what the new life he was embarking on would be like, what it would be like once he had left, to know that he would probably never go back. His safeness here, the cherishing atmosphere and the influence he saw that he had on the Duchesnes, bringing them their first direct experience of Fascism— all only served to set in relief his inner loneliness, his sense of loss, and the question of what he could do in the end.

In his talks with Paul he always emphasized the importance, the necessity for work of a philosophical and spiritual nature. He believed deeply in what Paul was trying to do and respected his solitary effort. But the book on Nietzsche was an exercise rather than anything else, something to do, until he should have come to a decision about his own real life. More and more he felt a need— and it was strange and against his nature and all his habits to feel it —a need for active service of some sort. He was nearly fifty and ill equipped for anything except a professorship: it was possible that the University of Brussels would offer him a visiting lectureship for one year. Paul was pulling wires to bring this about. But, although Schmidt had responded gratefully to the idea, in his heart he was reluctant to undertake it.

He had begun to keep a notebook, jotting down a sentence or two every day, as if he were keeping a record of an illness, a chart of his progress as an exile. Perhaps much later it would be useful to others—or, if not, it gave him at least the illusion that his suffering might someday serve. His terror was that, now he had taken the huge step of leaving, it would prove to have led nowhere. Anything active he undertook now would risk endangering his wife and son. To force them to suffer for his own beliefs when they did not share them, and when he himself was safe, seemed practically impossible. He would have to take another name, bury himself in a life so different from his old one that he would not be traced. He slept badly. The fears he had mastered while he was

in Germany attacked him now. He woke up several times screaming hoarsely, dreaming that he was being tortured.

Of this conflict he said nothing to anyone, only jotting down in
his notebook short sentences:

Exile: in its obsolete meaning the word is defined as "To devas-
tate; ruin."

The spiritual severance and the spiritual attachment—to despise
what one loves; to be ashamed of one's own country. All negative,
all destructive, poisoning the power to act.

The physical malaise—this no one can imagine who has not experienced it. The very smells are strange; the food in one's mouth;
the language. I used to enjoy speaking French. Now I find it a great
effort. I am tired after our discussions in the evening—tired by the
fact that I have expressed myself badly. I feel here almost never
wholly myself. There is something missing.

The children ask me all the time about Germany. They are fascinated. They listen as to an evil fairy tale. And it becomes more
and more painful for me to talk. At the same time I myself come
back to the subject and am more savage than I need to be, out of
fear of not facing the whole truth. The whole truth? Where is the
responsibility? How far is the witness of a crime guilty? When
Pierre says, "The German people are not to blame," can I honestly
agree with him? In the answers to these questions lie my future
and the future of many others, perhaps whole peoples.

The temptation to feel oneself an exception and so separate, having special *rights*. The exile has no rights. He has only duties and
opportunities.

Never to forget that given the choice of martyrdom or exile, one
chose exile. This places a great responsibility on the individual. He
must, in a sense, *justify* his choice.

To seek out the levels and the conflicts where the struggle, which
is perhaps already lost for several generations in Germany, can still
be won. Spain? America? As far as I can find out, in Spain there is
acute awareness of the magnitude of the struggle, of the international nature of Fascism. In Spain it is open war; in America,
should I go there, I would be again a teller of fairy tales to children.
I am nearsighted, sedentary, completely untrained for a life of ac-

tion. How far is this persistent idea of Spain an escape, a quick violent means to solve a problem of conscience? How far is it a cool decision to go where I can be most useful? But in the last analysis one does what one *has* to do. Forcing a decision now is cowardice. I must be patient. I must think.

Avoid other exiles. The temptation of the past. We do not help each other. The unity of exile is a false unity, a sort of stage-set security where we can act out our play *The True Germany*. So many haven't the strength to do more than this, and who shall blame them who has not known the experience himself? I am protected because I am separated from my family. I am truly free and alone, so my responsibility is very great.

The temptation to despair, to give up because one knows how difficult it was in Germany for an honest man to stem the rising tide. Will he be of any use anywhere else? Are the people of the free countries, so sure of themselves, really so much braver than we were? The worst temptation—cynicism, to justify one's own cowardice by pretending to a superior knowledge of evil, and that evil will always win. To give up before the second battle because one has lost the first. And this is really once more the temptation to be a witness and not a participant, the one who sees all and knows all just because he doesn't have anything to do with the confusion and difficulty of even the smallest *action*.

What one believes is scarcely important; it is, I am certain, how one acts on one's belief. Judge a man not by what he says but by what he does. The people who say they are anti-Nazi in Germany behind closed doors, and have not done anything to prove it, cannot be believed, or rather, their belief has no virtue in it, no creative power. Is this not really the Christian ethic? It is here that the passivity of the Church becomes criminal because it is the living symbol of the truth and yet does not act upon it. A man can say he is a Christian and yet in no way behave like one. But no man can say he is a Nazi and not be forced to *do* something sooner or later to perpetrate or be a witness to positive evil. And it it so much easier to do evil than to do good that the good man must be a thousand times more active, more brave, more consistent, and ferocious than the evil or he will have no chance. In the end it is all almost unbearably simple—it comes down to the individual conscience. And here philosophical inquiry is important, must go on. I suppose what separates me so painfully from Paul is that I feel responsible, am in a sense guilty. It makes a gulf between us. He has a right to go on with his work quietly. I no longer have that right—more than that, it has become spiritually impossible for me to do so.

It was on a Sunday afternoon in late November when Gerhart wrote the final paragraph. As he sat at his desk, looking out at a steady hard rain which the wind had slanted so it looked like the rain on Japanese prints, he felt more peaceful, more truly at peace with himself than he had for a long time. He had become accustomed now to the landscape outside his window; it no longer looked strange and foreign, was no longer to be "looked at," but had become part of his inner life. So he sat, wrapped up in a blanket to keep warm, and lit his pipe.

The tinkling of the tea bell roused him and he went down to find that there were guests for tea, Francis and Simone, whom he remembered as old friends of the Duchesnes. Always now he felt a slight hesitation in meeting strangers, dreading the shock of discovery, dreading the necessity to explain himself once more, dreading pity as much as disagreement. The salon, as he pushed open the door, looked full of people—and he was glad to take the tray out of Solange's hands and so make his entrance as one of the family.

"This is Uncle Gerhart," Solange said proudly, as if she were exhibiting something greatly to everyone's credit.

Francis rose to shake hands, and Gerhart went over to the chaise longue where Simone, as always, was stretched out, to kiss her hand.

"We have been meaning to come to see you, Herr Schmidt, for weeks and weeks. This is a great pleasure," she said warmly.

"Sit down, Gerhart, and have a cup of tea quickly before Francis starts asking you so many questions that you won't have a chance to drink it," Paul said in his teasing voice.

"Perhaps I will ask him so many questions that he won't have time to ask me any," Gerhart said, smiling his formal smile.

The children passed the big plates of bread and butter and jam while Simone and Mélanie kept up a steady conversation about how prices had gone up, about the garden, about the children, about the new Lenormand play Simone had seen in Paris. And then, when everyone was settled, when everyone was supplied with bread and butter and tea, there came a pause, a silence, as if they were all waiting for someone to take the plunge, to come out with it, whatever it might be. For there was something in the air, and Gerhart felt it at once.

"I feel a conspiracy in the air," he said gently, "is it not so?"

Mélanie and Paul looked at each other half amusedly and half guiltily, and Paul turned to Francis.

"This is the most devilishly perspicacious man we have ever had in the house. He had not been here two weeks before he knew all our secret problems and was busily at work helping us to solve them. He is, you know, a sort of St. Nicolas, performing daily miracles."

The tribute was so unexpected that Gerhart blushed to the roots of his hair. "Nonsense," he murmured while the children shouted at his blushes and Solange had to get up and embrace him.

"But it's quite true," Mélanie protested amid the laughter.

"The conspiracy," Francis said smilingly, "if there is one, is that Paul and Mélanie have some crazy idea that you and I are going to disagree, Herr Schmidt. But we will show them that it is quite unfounded."

"Heavens, an examination. I never could pass my oral examinations," Gerhart said. "This is not fair." He looked so much like a frightened schoolboy that Solange felt it necessary to go to him; she sat down on the floor by his chair while he stroked her hair absent-mindedly. She tried to hide her pleasure at this mark of affection by looking as solemn as possible.

"Let's examine them instead," Francis said. "Let's make them tell us why they think we will disagree—— Ah-ha!" he said, as if it were a game, pointing his finger maliciously at Paul. "Now we've got you." Yes, it had suddenly become a game, and yet underneath the children felt the suspense. Françoise was frowning her deep frown of rejection and disapproval whenever political discussions came up.

Mélanie looked at Simone for support and cut through all these preliminaries by stating simply:

"It's just, Gerhart, that Francis doesn't believe there will be war."

"Why discuss it?" Françoise, for some unknown reason, was pink with anger. "If there is, there is; if there isn't, there isn't. And no amount of arguing will affect it one way or another. I am sick of all this talk."

Everyone turned and looked at her in amazement. For Françoise, who rarely spoke in any gathering, it was an amazingly long and passionate speech.

Before Mélanie could scold her Schmidt had interposed gently, "She is quite right, you know. Let us talk of something else."

Again there was a silence and this time an uncomfortable one. It was as if they were under some spell and things couldn't come out right.

"I was in Berlin a month ago," Francis said, lighting a cigar and lighting Schmidt's for him on the same match.

"Ah, then you see, he knows far more than I do." Schmidt was delighted with this chance to escape.

"What was your impression, Francis?" Mélanie asked.

"Well, you know, I've never liked Berlin." It was said half apologetically, and Schmidt answered at once:

"Don't apologize. I've never liked it myself. I'm a Frankforter, you know. What do they talk about in Berlin these days?"

"The anti-Semitism is perfectly deadly, as you all know. I was assured, however, that Germany had no territorial aspirations beyond possibly the Sudetenland—this has not become official yet, but I gather they will start a big propaganda war about it very soon and expect the English to back them up. Everyone told me they were astonished at the ease with which they reoccupied the Rhineland—even high officers had believed that they were taking a great risk. Well, after all, that was inevitable sooner or later."

Gerhart Schmidt listened attentively. With all his heart he wished not to enter into an argument with Francis. It was a far greater effort to him than he ever showed to argue with people, especially in French. And disagreement had always tasted like ashes in his mouth. In this he felt a great sympathy with Françoise. It was one of the things that drew him to her. But at the same time he knew that he had no right to keep silent. Outside Germany as he was, safe as he was, the least he could do was to tell the truth constantly, and never to shirk doing it just because it happened to be a Sunday afternoon and he was for once feeling peaceful.

"Did you hear anything about Spain, for instance?" he asked tentatively.

"I didn't hear anything directly, of course. But I gather that they are very pleased with the behavior of German planes, especially the dive bombers, and that a good deal more help is being sent than will ever be officially admitted. Why?"

Françoise tried to imagine a way to leave the room without being noticed, but gave it up after a while. She was interested in the two men rather than in what they were saying—they were so very different. Francis always looked rosy and clean, as if he had just had a bath and had been singing in it. His optimism, his buoyancy were evident even in his dress, his bright ties, his way of smiling quickly and warmly and leaning forward as he talked, and he talked quickly and emphatically with enthusiasm. Uncle Gerhart, on the other hand, seemed almost absent-minded by contrast, as if he were always thinking ahead to something he was coming to and hadn't said yet. He seemed both wary and tired, and always he spilled cigar ash on his waistcoat and then brushed it away without looking, so that he was apt to brush a clean place and leave the ashes just where they were. But Françoise felt they were both essentially gentle people, friendly people, and under normal circumstances there could have been no antagonism between them. They would have enjoyed each other—they both liked to laugh. But now for the last few years the terrible thing was that people born to like each other got into fierce hateful arguments. It was like a sickness. Françoise wanted no part of it.

Thinking all this, she had hardly listened to the conversation which had moved a long way in the last quarter of an hour.

"You are a pessimist, Herr Schmidt," Francis was saying. He was perhaps a little nettled by the children's obvious rapt attention to everything Gerhart said; for the first time there was an edge of exasperation in his voice. "Don't you see," he went on, "that anything we do now against Germany means war? Don't you see our hands are tied? Surely the occupation of the Rhineland proves that."

"But are they tied in Spain, where Fascism can still be openly fought? Would it be so impossible for us to sneak a few planes across the border and four or five divisions?"

"You are oversimplifying, Herr Schmidt," Francis said, shrugging his shoulders.

"I think he's right," Mélanie said decidedly. "We can't let innocent people suffer. We have a responsibility."

"We have a responsibility to keep the peace—millions and millions of lives are at stake," Francis said passionately.

"Is there peace in Germany? Is there peace in Spain? Or in our hearts here now?" Gerhart answered quietly; but his eyes behind his glasses had narrowed.

"That's metaphysics—what goes on in the hearts and minds of people is a matter for priests and psychoanalysts."

"Why, Francis." Simone sat up in astonishment. "You surely don't believe that. What a terrible thing to say!"

"Well, if you're talking about peace in the heart, you're talking about Heaven as far as I'm concerned," Francis answered sharply.

And Gerhart was thinking, What a waste. What a senseless quarrel. It was time to put a stop to it. It was time to make his own position quite clear.

"Yes, yes," Paul murmured. It was the first time he had spoken.

"Well," Gerhart said, smiling as if he had a secret, "we must each do what we can. That is all. You do your damnedest to keep the peace of Europe and I shall go to Spain."

"You mean that really?" Pierre asked excitedly. Colette and Solange looked stunned. It was like a sudden change in weather, a violent frost, a blight. No, he could not be going away! That was impossible!

"Yes, I have decided. It is what I must do."

"But, Gerhart," Mélanie said, as if she were scolding a child, "no, you can't do that. Why, you're not a soldier. You'll be no good to them."

"Yes, Gerhart, what is this romantic idea?" Paul asked.

"You'll never get papers," Francis added, as if that were final.

"I think he is quite right," Colette said emphatically.

"Darling, no one asked your opinion." Mélanie was shocked at her air of authority.

He was going to leave them! But he had become part of the family. Solange curled around where she was sitting on the floor so she could put a hand on his knee. "Don't go, Uncle Gerhart, we need you here. We need you," she said passionately.

"I'll come back, my bird. As you all know, I'll probably be put to some perfectly safe job like censoring, as I'm afraid it's true that I would not be a very good soldier."

"But, Gerhart"—Paul was angry himself now—"what an utter waste! How can you think of burying yourself in such perfectly useless work when you are a philosopher? How can you abandon all that you have begun in the last twenty years? Other people can do clerical jobs. No one can write your books."

"I can't help it, Paul. I've got to be part of the struggle somewhere. I didn't leave Germany and my family to settle down comfortably and give up the fight. Can't you understand that? I could not live with myself. I could not write. I'm sorry to distress you and to have said this so suddenly without preparation," he said, turning to Francis with a mischievous smile, for now he had come out with it, Gerhart felt very happy. "But somehow or other our discussion forced it out of me." And then he got up and took Mélanie's hand. "You have been so kind, so wonderfully kind," he said gently. "I think I will go upstairs now if you will excuse me."

The children rose in a body, Françoise first of all, and followed him without a word, as if they were attending a funeral.

"Yes, yes," Paul murmured.

"We must be going too." Simone felt that it was time they left. The Duchesnes obviously wanted to be alone.

"What a tragedy!" Francis sighed. "A man with so much to offer——"

"Do you really think it such a tragedy, Francis?" Paul asked ironically. "You know, I envy him. He has reached a place we still have to reach. He has made peace with himself."

"Oh, Paul, you sound so sanctimonious," Mélanie broke in. "All that will happen is that he'll get killed by some senseless Italian bomb, and what good will that do?"

Once more there was a great rift in the security of the house and the garden and of all their lives—and through it blew the cold wind of fear, of desolation, the wind that was gathering power, that would become hurricane. And what did they have to pit against it?

PART FOUR

Winter: 1940

Chapter I

Now it had come, the war which entered the children's hearts long, long ago on a summer day in the forest when Pierre and Hans tried to settle their differences in a fist fight, which accompanied them through adolescence so that its presence was as familiar as winter or the frost on the grass in the early morning. Now it was here, intangible in reality as it had been as the ghost of their childhood. Belgium itself was an island like the house on the avenue—entirely surrounded as it was by countries which, although they were formally in a state of war, seemed reluctant to wage it, so that already it had a name—"the phony war," the war all were reluctant to fight; the war with no death and no honor, to prevent which France and England had been willing to throw Czechoslovakia to the wolves; the war the Left everywhere hated and denied; the war of false promises, of doubts, of confusions; and in the middle of it, Belgium and Holland, the neutral islands, armed to the teeth, waiting, hoping, hardly believing they would escape in the end.

The death was a death of the spirit, locked in winter, like the landscape. For many who had put their hope in the great experiment in Russia now were bewildered to find themselves automatically allied wtih the Nazis in Germany since the Nazi-Soviet pact; and many who had put their hope in Spain saw now that although the brave and the free might go forth to battle, "they always fell." And many who had believed Fascism must be fought openly and bitterly in battle saw their fire and faith worn down in what seemed to be a dismal play at fighting while Germany went calmly on devouring the countries of Europe one by one and Franco and Mussolini triumphed over the heroic people of Spain.

For Mélanie, for Paul, for the three girls embarking on the adventure of work as grown-up people—as autumn turned into winter in 1939, as St. Nicolas, and Christmas, and the New Year, came and went, and it was 1940, and still the huge suspended armies waited and the generals reviewed the Maginot Line and the Siegfried Line and nothing happened—for the Duchesne family it was a time of great activity and furious work. While there was still time, there was so much to be done!

The real crisis, the crisis of fear, the crisis of acceptance had been lived through three years before in the autumn, when Gerhart escaped from Germany. Mélanie often thought of it; since then she had lived from day to day as gaily and well as possible for the sake of the children; more, perhaps, for the sake of life itself. From that time on she had known and accepted that they lived on the edge of an abyss. It is strange how one can become accustomed to such a position!

For Paul the deep crisis had come just before the Loyalists capitulated, when they learned that Gerhart had been killed in a bombardment of Madrid. That was two years ago, just two years ago. Paul had gone through months of inward revolt, of passionate protest. But Mélanie, with her instinct for heroism, could not agree with him. "It was what he would have chosen," she kept saying. "It was what he knew would happen."

"It was suicide," Paul answered bitterly.

There was so little to do at the business that he and Mélanie

took turns going into town. He had always been a solitary character. Now he was lonely, and loneliness became like a sickness.
He wrapped himself in it and sat at his desk doing nothing or
listening to the furious bombardment of propaganda over the radio
with cynical amusement. There had been months of this, until
Mélanie wondered if he would ever come out of it, ever find the
way to cure himself, ever seem to be part of his family again.

And then in the autumn, when war was declared, he had suddenly begun to write, to write as he had done after the last war, a
letter to Schmidt, a cry of despair and recognition across the silence.
Once more he had been saved by his work.

The New Year of 1940 began for the Duchesne family with a
great blazing fire in the salon and Paul reading his book aloud;
Pierre, now an officer in the cavalry, was there and Pierre's parents
and Francis and Simone; even Bo-Bo was there. And Mélanie, in
her chatelaine's dress, beamed. It was almost like old times. No
one spoke of the war. Now that it was here, it was curious how no
one wanted to speak of it. Instead Paul told humorous stories and
teased everyone; the shabby old salon was full of laughter; the
three girls had never looked so beautiful, so full of life. Here in the
familiar room, surrounded by all that they loved, it seemed as if
they were an island of light in a great darkness. Here in spite of
everything life could still go forward, nourished by the past, intimate and breathing its blessing on them.

Emile and Suzanne were absurdly proud of Pierre now that he
was an officer; and Pierre himself was absurdly proud of his uniform and his shiny boots and his orderly whom he could lecture
to for hours on political matters and who had to listen. He was
still writing poems and publishing them, much too fast; he was
still unable to take any criticism. But he was tough and lean now
and ardent in his praise of the army—and he basked in the approval of his family and friends. He was even a little condescend-
ing to Solange and Colette, which amused them no end. Well, if

the war has done nothing else, it has made a man of Pierre, they agreed when they were alone.

Emile had brought with him a portfolio of drawings of the plants of his beloved Ardennes, which Françoise greatly admired and Paul insisted on keeping, in order to try to get them published; Emile was absolutely incapable of any sort of business transaction.

"It is foolish," he said, "but these people frighten me to death with their talk of percentages, interest, royalties, heaven knows what! I go in there to get my book published and go out finding that I have promised to pay *them* a huge sum instead of their paying me!" He shrugged his shoulders philosophically. "What will you? I just was born without the bump of business. It is not there," he said, feeling his head as if to discover it while everyone laughed and Mélanie said:

"Ah, Emile, you are just the same! You have not changed!"

"I am hopeless," he added, as if he were after all quite pleased to be as he was. "But somehow we have managed not to starve all these years, thanks to Suzanne." In the last years Suzanne had taught domestic science at the village school to give her husband more time for his work. Over Françoise's bent head they smiled the secret smile of perfect understanding.

"Look, Mamie," Françoise interrupted, "look at the columbine —how fine it is!"

Before they left they must all go out to admire the pale green strange beauty of the Rose de Noel. Emile knelt on the damp ground to examine it closely.

"Yes, it is beautiful, Mélanie. It always seems like a miracle, doesn't it?—a winter flower."

For a moment they were all silent. They had talked themselves out and come to the end of the day. Francis looked up at the sky and sniffed the air.

"Snow tonight," he said, and then, breaking the spell, "My friends, we must hurry or we shall miss our tram!"

New Year 1940 was in fact like New Year's Day on all the other years, except that one more layer was added to friendship, except that perhaps they loved each other more than usual, locked on the winter island, in the middle of war.

Solange and Colette were terribly excited because Simone had given them each, as a New Year gift, five hundred francs to have new suits made. Altogether it was a fine beginning to the year— even though they somehow forgot to feed the rabbits and the pig and had to creep down after they were all undressed in their wrappers and go out shivering to do the forgotten chore. They looked at Numéro Trois, the pig, critically while he greeted them with squeals of pleasure and devoured the milk and potato peels they put in his trough.

"He seems to get longer and longer and thinner and thinner," Colette said, moving a flashlight back and forth.

"Poor Numéro Trois, you need more bread and fat, don't you, old man?" Solange murmured. She decided there and then, as her New Year resolution, that they would have to organize forays to restaurant kitchens and pick up scraps regularly for the pig— otherwise he would never fatten. All through the winter, from then on, the three girls took turns riding their bicycles in the coldest, wettest weather five or ten miles back and forth to collect scraps for Numéro Trois.

Solange had finished her course at the agricultural school in December, and now she was going to take an examination given by the Ministry of Agriculture to choose four teachers for traveling schools sent out to educate farmers in remote districts. She still suffered from a lack of confidence in herself and agreed to take the examination only when the whole family bore down and insisted.

"But it's the last time," she said firmly, while Mélanie shook her head sadly.

"You are well equipped for such a job—and you would enjoy it. Come, a little courage!"

But Solange only felt her stomach turn over with the familiar pre-examination sickness. I shall never make it, she said to her-

self miserably, I am so stupid. She was not stupid, but she was slow
and very thorough and not at ease in intellectual work. So she did
very well on all the practical tests—she could kill a pig and make
sausages or cut a sheep's wool with perfect assurance. But the
minute she was confronted with a piece of paper and a set of
questions and that dreadful smell of ink and sweat in the examination room, she felt an absolute blankness come upon her. For days
before the examination she wandered about the house like a lost
soul. Everyone teased and cajoled her—Colette patiently went over
all possible questions with her, so that she too was becoming an
expert on agricultural matters; and on the last evening Paul took
her into his study and talked to her so gently about all sorts of
things, including his book, that she went to bed somehow comforted and slept well.

On the morning of the examination Solange was given a large
piece of cheese with her breakfast and a large slice of *pain d'épice,*
a great luxury in these days, and two cups of coffee; but she could
not eat, though everyone pretended not to notice.

Oh, life is awful! she said to herself. How does one manage? It
seemed practically impossible to get to the examination, let alone
take it. She was quite pale and shivering as Mamie embraced her
and Papa joked. "Above all, restrain your sense of humor, little cabbage. If there is one thing the Minister of Agriculture does not ap-
preciate, it is a sense of humor."

She envied her Flemish classmates who could stop at the church
on the way, light a candle, and say a prayer to help them through.
She envied all the passive people in the trolley whose hearts were
not beating so fast they hurt their chests—and above all she envied
people like the conductor who only had to blow his horn now and
then and never had to take an examination. In another four hours
I'll be on my way home, she thought, but that was small comfort.
The four hours ahead might as well have been eternity, so impenetrable, so thick did they seem, so impossible to live through.

But after all her nervousness, the examination was surprisingly easy, so easy that Solange became convinced that she must have misunderstood the questions, not answered fully enough, or that there must be some trap.

"Never mind, it's over. Don't mention it again," she admonished the family when she got home at last. "Thank goodness I can take care of our animals now in peace and help Mamie with the housework." It was outside Solange's ideas of the possible that she might be one of the four to win and receive a post at "twenty thousand francs a year." There were twenty-seven other contestants, and she put the matter out of her mind.

In late January four of the precious baby rabbits died for no apparent reason. Solange was digging a hole to bury them when the postman blew his horn at the gate and she ran to see if there was any mail. The postman smiled when he saw it was the prettiest and sweetest of the three girls and took a long time fumbling about in his bag so as to have the chance to tell her how pretty she looked this morning, in spite of the bad weather. Solange had always loved compliments; she blushed with pleasure now as the postman finally brought forth a large official-looking envelope and gave it to her with a flourish.

"For you, mademoiselle!"

"What can it be?" she said, frowning. What can I have done? she thought rapidly. Was she being summoned to court for some unknown misdemeanor?

The postman waited, unashamedly curious, while she tore open the envelope; he watched the expression of bewilderment and anguish pass over her face. Then she gave a great shout, "Oh, Mamie! Mamie!" and ran down the path to her house. The postman scratched his head. "Bad news. I wonder what it could be?" A pity that she had run off so fast.

"What is it, my darling? What has happened?"

"I've won. I've got the place!" Solange shouted, and burst into violent sobs as if this were a calamity too great to bear.

"But, my treasure, that is wonderful! Bravo!" Mélanie said, astonished at Solange's lack of self-control. "Here, blow your nose, my precious idiot, and stop crying."

She was reading the notice now herself. "First place, Solange! That is really splendid. You see, how wrong you were to doubt yourself. How pleased Papa will be!"

But the strange thing was that it really took Solange several weeks to realize her good fortune. It was such a complete surprise that instead of rejoicing she seemed stricken for days and went about her tasks in the garden, utterly subdued.

"Strange wild little creature that she is," Paul said to Mélanie one night, "I wonder if she really wants the position."

"No," Mélanie answered, "I don't think it's that. She just has to get used to the idea. She is so humble—she somehow never imagined what it would be like."

Slowly the baby of the family realized that she was grown-up, that of all three it was she who had landed a splendid job all by herself, that it was she who would help support them from now on—and, above all, that this was work she had always longed to do. Soon she was busy as a beaver collecting all sorts of material, folk songs to teach her pupils, collections of paintings to hang up (in this Françoise was a great help), and even old folk dances, for they all agreed that she must try to enrich her agricultural teaching with some folk art and, if possible, to stimulate and revivify the old traditions.

"Think of it, our little Solange," they said, holding her in a new awe. And Colette, who had always admired and believed in her little sister, was the most delighted of all.

After three weeks Solange herself blossomed under this new sensation of being important and recognized. Her hair curled more uncontrollably than ever; she was always laughing—and no one dared to think where she might be, in what distant village, when and if the Nazis decided to invade.

Chapter II

For Mélanie the days
rose now, one by one, as if each were a reprieve, and yet she had
no anxiety. It was as if all that were past, done with, a stage she
had passed through. There was really nothing they could do now
except to live as fully as possible, to root themselves so deeply that
they could not be shaken. It was amusing to see how the three girls
ordered her around, insisting that she let them take over a great
part of the housework; how they had little by little taken command
of the house. They teased her; they covered her with kisses; Solange
and Colette still loved to come and lie on her bed before going to
sleep to gossip about the day; Françoise still burst in with her new
plans for scenery or costumes—and yet there was a difference from
the old days when she felt as if there were a physical connection
between her pulse and theirs. One by one each had withdrawn—
Françoise long ago after the affair of Jacques, Colette when she
first went to the university, Solange just now as she was preparing
to take over her job. A large part of their lives was spent away from
home. It was partly that. But not all that. One had to lose one's
children—she had always known it. And Mélanie watched herself
severely to see that she did not betray her sudden feeling of loneliness, of being shut out from her own deepest life. Of course with
Paul it had always been like that. She had long ago stopped
expecting any change; it was an ebb and flow, and she had learned
that eventually the tide would flow in again. But with the children
it was a final severance, as she knew well.

Mélanie poured her energy and her love into a hundred channels
—into cooking new dishes, inventing a cake or a soup, making a
perfect mayonnaise for the salad; into community work—organiz-
ing the air-raid precautions for the village, taking over the guid-

ance of two delinquent boys whom she talked with once a week; into reading; into the garden and its infinite demands for attention; into the animals, the bees, the ever-affectionate Fifi, poor thin Numéro Trois, and old Moïse, as stubborn and wild-eyed as ever. The only thing she really resented was that she could not put in the fourteen-hour day she had been used to. She got absurdly tired now and went to bed right after supper, sometimes falling asleep over her book. And under it all was strung the unspoken tension, the certain knowledge that more would be asked of them all soon, and that they must be building up inside a reserve power to endure, to survive, and not to be conquered whatever might happen. Once in a while this terror of the future seized her by the throat and she must give herself some extra all-absorbing task to push it away. So on one of those days she had gone over all the linen, mended all the sheets and pillowcases, and torn up the fine old linen ones, too worn to use, into bandages for the clinic. Or she would go out into the shed and chop wood for an hour or two. One could not give anything up, yield anywhere; it seemed necessary now to take on more, and to do it with more complete concentration than ever.

And at the business it was the same. To keep going, to maintain the Maison Bernard at all, meant putting three times as much imagination and energy into it as ever before. There was now the joy of working with Françoise, who was proving herself to be a designer of real talent. But the two demoiselles were getting old and crotchety, and Jean complained every time he had to come upstairs. A hundred times Mélanie had longed to throw the whole thing up, sell the business and settle in the country. But then there were taxes to meet and they must wait six months, or a new order came in and she couldn't resist that, or Françoise designed a nursery so charming that all Mélanie's enthusiasms returned and swept her along through the beastly little accounts and the bills and customers who did not know what they wanted.

It was a matter now of living through—of living to the utmost within the limits imposed upon them. And in spite of all, Mélanie rejoiced in her life, in life itself, and never saw the sun rise over the poplar trees without a lifting of the heart.

The immediate problem on these late January days was Colette: she had been looking very pale and had lost weight. She was working with furious intensity at the university, taking half a dozen courses in anthropology, psychology, anatomy, physics, history of medicine, heaven knows what! It seemed sometimes to Mélanie that she was temporarily losing sight of human beings in her pursuit of knowledge. She had become the least bit pedantic in the last years. What was happening to her? The poet of the family, the most imaginative one of all?

At first she had taken to her work at the university like a duck to water, swimming through her courses with delight, talking a blue streak when she came home, pouring out her discoveries, her face alight. She passed her examinations with "great distinction." She seemed to have good friends in her class. Mélanie suspected that she was in love, but if so, it was not having the right effect. She seemed pinched and locked up in some misery of her own, poor child, when all should have been promise and excitement and joy. And Mélanie did not dare ask her what was the matter. Only she suggested that Colette give up her trips to get food for Numéro Trois. (It is amazing what importance a pig can take on in a family!)

"There is no point in making yourself ill for a pig, my darling— we can live without pork, you know!"

But Colette refused to listen. It was her job and she was determined to do it, and as Mélanie herself would have felt and said the same thing, she compromised by filling Colette's plate as full as possible and by going up to her room and shyly suggesting at eleven that it was time she was in bed.

Finally one day she burst out, "It's the arguments, Mamie," hiding her head in her hands, as if the arguments were going on inside it like Breughel monsters at that very moment.

"What arguments, Colette?" They were sitting round the supper table waiting for Françoise, who was due at any moment.

"You know Ado, the boy I have told you about, the brilliant one who got a first in the examinations? Well, he is a Catholic, you know, and he is forming a group among the students to discuss politics. That is all right, but I joined because I knew what he was really doing was starting a fascist anti-Semitic gang. The Bernstein boy came to me about it. The first meeting was three weeks ago, and I went and kept quiet to see what they were leading to. At the second meeting Ado started talking against the Jews and I had to speak. Then they all attacked me—they won't listen to reason, Mamie. It's as if they were crazy."

"Why didn't you tell us this before, darling?" Mélanie said. She was prickling with anger.

"They said I was in love with Salomon Bernstein—they said awful things. They said women shouldn't meddle in politics."

Paul had listened to this with great interest. If only Mélanie doesn't get all excited and do something passionate that she will regret, he said to himself, for Mélanie was clearly very angry, so he said to Colette:

"My dear child, there have been student fights of this kind ever since there were universities. Pay no attention to them—when your mother and I were in college people fought duels for socialism against the monarchists. *Plus ça change, plus c'est la même chose.*"

"But, Papa, people weren't being tortured just across the border for being monarchists or socialists. Your best friend didn't die in Spain for being a monarchist or a socialist. Now it's the whole world—one has to fight. That is what Uncle Gerhart said."

"She's right, Paul. You know she's right," Mélanie said hotly. "I am going to speak to the rector of the university."

"Oh no, Mamie, please don't. That would only make it worse." Colette turned to her father for support.

"Mélanie darling, a little calm," he admonished gently.

"I won't be calm. We can't have this sort of thing in Belgium."
Paul shrugged. "Ah, ah. We can't have it. But we do have it,
my dear. We do have it. You might as well admit that."

Solange looked from one to the other, her blue eyes troubled. "I
don't think arguing with such people does any good—can't you
get this Ado and the Bernstein boy together?"

"It's too late." Colette shook her head sadly. "It's as if Ado were
poisoned; and then besides, he loves to lead and feel his power.
He has got a whole group started now—he would never go back
on all that. And then you see," she added painfully, "nobody likes
Salomon anyway. He is awfully sure of himself and superior. They
call him the Rabbi behind his back."

"But why, Colette? Why didn't you tell us this when it began?"
Mélanie said again.

Why hadn't she told them? It had seemed so much a student
business, something between herself and her contemporaries for
one thing—and then she had been afraid her mother would plunge
in and only make matters worse. When Mélanie was angry she had
the courage of a lion and did not hesitate to meddle quite furiously in other people's business. And then, besides, she had hoped
to persuade Ado that he was wrong—and then—she liked him
awfully. Until now he had been her best friend and even once
brought her a flower to wear. Everything was all mixed up and
painful.

"I didn't think it would be like this. Ado was my friend." She had
gone quite pale with the effort of explaining.

"Well," Paul said gently, "what does this group intend to do,
Colette? What are their aims?"

"They talk now about forming themselves into a semimilitary
band, affiliated with De Grelle—and then they have decided on a
boycott of the Jewish students. They refuse to sit with them at
luncheon. They jeer them on the way home."

"No," Mélanie said, "that's incredible. Why, they're grown-up
boys. This can't go on, Colette. You must let me do something."

"Your Ado can't really be so intelligent after all if he has been taken in by that cheap little politician, De Grelle."

"Oh, it's not De Grelle. It's just that it's so much easier to hate someone near by. Ado knows that his whole career will be interrupted this spring when he is called up. He says the Jews are always getting out of being called up. He is angry at the world and wants someone to hate—it's all that, Papa, you know."

"He must get it at home," Mélanie said. "We must see his parents."

"Oh, Mamie"—Colette was near to tears—"it's true. It's awful how people talk. They don't know. They don't realize."

"Don't the other students react to this?" Paul asked. "You're not alone, Colette."

Colette looked troubled again. Now that it was being examined and seen through her mother's and father's eyes as well as her own, it seemed even worse than before. "You see, they're afraid. Ado and his group are the most brilliant for one thing—and then they are aggressive and they know what they want. They say I'll only get into trouble—even Salomon begged me yesterday to leave it alone, that it would only make things more difficult for him."

Mélanie shook her head violently. Disapproval filled the air around her.

"I'm going to the rector," she said with such adamant decision that they all knew it was useless to argue. In a way Colette was relieved to have the burden of anxiety taken from her, to feel the strong simple answer in her mother to all the questions. For Mélanie always cut through to fundamentals, cut through to action. It was awful to have her butt in, but it was better than leaving things as they were.

But punishing Ado or even making him see reason would not really solve anything. For the pain of the last weeks for Colette had been to be divided against herself—and of this she could not speak. She loved Ado. In the old days she had always looked first for his approval, waited for his smile at the end of class, enjoyed passionately their arguments about everything under the sun. No one would ever know what it had cost her to defend Salomon, whom she did not really like, against this boy whom she adored, whose presence in the classroom had been enough to make the whole day shine. But she had lain in bed at night thinking and thinking and remembering that this was what Uncle Gerhart had had to do. It was the sickness of the world that now families themselves were divided, dearest friends wounded each other to the heart, and even the very young were forced to align themselves against each other. How often Uncle Gerhart had said it: "Deep belief now means war, means pain. We are wracked with the struggle in the heart. And what the guns do and will do is very little beside what the mind must do."

So Colette had sacrificed Ado, but it did not make her feel well to do it, or happy, or sure of herself. On the contrary, she went through long self-examinations and was full of doubt, and when she felt herself almost hating him now, she wept bitterly. For how, if she and Ado, who really loved each other, could not agree, could not live beside each other in peace—how could nations ever do so? And she would not, could not yet admit that one or the other must be destroyed and that this was a radical division where persuasion, gentleness, and love could not even come into play as creative forces until Ado and those like him were made impotent to impose their way of life.

She did not see yet that the image of Belgium as a neutral island, a place of safety where one might still live in peace, was a fiction— and that there was no longer any such island in the world. Everywhere on every level the war was being fought out—between Francis and Gerhart, between herself and Ado. She felt little courage to wage it, only a great sense of desolation and loss.

"Well, if Françoise is not coming," Paul said with a twinkle, "I suggest that we divide up her omelette—Colette looks as if she could do with another mouthful!"

"Yes, come along, darling," Mélanie responded quickly. "We'll have a little feast—come along everyone, pass your plates."

"Mmmm—I could eat three whole omelettes," Solange said nostalgically.

"Could you, my treasure? Well, someday we shall have all the eggs we can eat—you'll see."

It seemed now as if they were always hungry, and with all her ingenuity, and in spite of the cupboard in the cellar full of jars of beans and peas they had put up in the summer, and the pots of pear butter, and the sacks of grain, Mélanie knew that sometimes her children did not get quite enough to eat. At that moment that seemed a small part of their trouble. They went to bed with heavy hearts, and Paul stayed up very late writing, writing his long complex letter to the dead Gerhart which now sustained him from day to day. For Mélanie it would always be action, quick and fiery, and for him, this other kind of action, slow, and done in darkness like a miner digging coal, the effort to see clearly, to go so deeply into every conflict that one might reach the universal answer, the peace that passeth understanding because it is achieved by love through thought.

Chapter III

It had snowed during the night, so when the family woke up in the dark they were aware of a special silence outside, the snow silence; Colette and Solange were out of bed early, while it was still dark—excited by this new world. It seemed as if the sun would never rise and show them the white meadow and the beautiful fragile trees all shining, all pure, bringing back memories of Russian fairy tales even though it was a mere half inch or so and would melt into mud by noon. Everyone felt gay after the passionate argument of the night before, and Françoise, late as usual—she had come in long after the others were asleep—had to hear the whole story again. Now they were all united behind Mélanie and anxious for her to go to the university as soon as possible. Colette saw to it that she wore her best suit; it was shabby, but at least it did have a Liberty-silk lining which showed when she opened it. Françoise lent her some gloves.

"Only you must promise not to lose them, Mamie," she said severely.

"Perhaps you should tie a string to them as I used to do for your mittens. Oh dear, I am sure to lose them. Do I have to have gloves?" she asked miserably.

"Without gloves," Paul teased, "you would not even be admitted to the rector's secretary." But everyone knew that was a barefaced lie, for she would see the King himself if she had made up her mind to do so.

Now her eyes were bright with adventure and resolution as she and Françoise and Colette went off together through the snow, arm in arm, like three schoolgirls.

"Do you think it will do any good, Papa?" Solange asked as she cleared away the breakfast dishes. Paul was sitting in the sun, hunched up in his wrapper, with the cat on his lap, looking, she thought, like a great cat himself, with his eyes half closed against the brilliant light.

"Who knows, my bird? Who knows? Your mother has great powers of persuasion when she is not too angry to use them. It all depends, I should say, on what sort of man the rector is——"

"Colette is sad," she said, coming back to sit down for a moment, with her chin in her elbows, beside her father.

"Yes, it is a sad, painful business to be at war with one's friends."

"Will there ever be peace, Papa?" she asked hopelessly.

Paul sighed, "When there is justice," and left it at that.

"And you think there won't be justice for a long time?" she persisted, searching for a ray of hope.

But all he could offer was a murmured, "Well, we must try to believe."

Solange got up then and washed the dishes—soap was becoming

scarce like all fats. It would be marvelous to think of a time when there would be plenty of hot water and soap again. But justice, that was something else. Did Christ believe, she wondered, that it would come on earth, or only in Heaven? I wish I knew, she thought, wringing out a wet towel, looking forward now to the reward of going out to her animals with the scraps. They were not troubled by these difficult questions. They were just there, breathing their warm sweet breaths into the hay, waiting to spring up and whinny with pleasure when she came in, to rub their cold noses into her warm hands. With them she felt safe.

After some discussion it was decided that Mélanie had better see the rector alone. She had wanted Colette to go with her, as she knew the whole story so much better herself, but this Colette hated to do. "They'll never forgive me," she said, "if I go with you." She went to her courses, big with this fearful secret, hardly daring to look at Ado, avoiding Salomon, who was sure to come up and ask her what she had decided to do.

And meanwhile Mélanie was sitting on a hard bench outside the rector's office waiting for him to come in. The secretary was already vanquished: Mélanie would be allowed in as soon as Monsieur le Directeur arrived.

"Well, what can I do for you, madame?" He was a little thin man, dressed impeccably, always impatient and nervous, so that now, while she sat down, he shifted papers around on his desk, moved the inkwell one inch to the right, and seemed incapable of looking her straight in the eye and listening to what she had to say.

"My daughter is a student here in medicine, in her first year——"

"Yes, yes, she has done very well indeed."

"I don't know if you are aware, monsieur, that there is a very serious situation among the students, an organization led by Ado Sauveur, which is openly anti-Semitic and affiliated with De Grelle."

For a moment the director stopped fidgeting and frowned.

"Of course I'm aware of it," he said sharply.

"What do you intend to do?"

The director leaned back in his chair and put the tips of the fingers of his two hands together delicately, judiciously. "Nothing, madame."

Mélanie repeated to herself, "calm and gay" several times, but it did not work. She felt her anger rising.

"But surely, monsieur, you cannot allow Jewish students to be persecuted here in the university?"

"Isn't *persecuted* a rather strong word, madame? As far as I know, there has been no violence. It is unfortunate, but the Jewish students will find a certain amount of prejudice against them later on when they leave——" He shrugged, as if she could finish the sentence as well as he.

"And so we are to stand by and allow students to organize themselves into aggressive bands, influence the weaker students toward a completely undemocratic view of life—we are to allow this to go on and do nothing?" Mélanie asked, not hiding now the anger in her heart.

"Precisely, madame." He was looking at her now with indifference, as if the matter were settled.

"If that is your last word, I have nothing more to say. You force me to take steps outside the university."

The director rose and bowed slightly. "I don't think you quite understand. The De Grelle party, though fortunately it has no power, is a recognized party in the state. We have no right to take steps to correct the political views of our students. They are adults. Their political views are their own business. We are not a Nazi institution. Freedom of speech is one of the tenets in our Constitution."

"I think I understand," Mélanie said shortly. "I'm sorry to have taken your time."

He bowed again. "Not at all. A pleasure, madame."

So that was that. Mélanie boiled with indignation. She went to the business to think what to do next and was soon busy telephoning the university to obtain Ado Sauveur's address. She brushed aside the small business matters on which Louise wanted a decision and flew out again, taking a trolley to the other end of town, sitting very straight, staring in front of her, so intensely absorbed in her own thoughts that the man opposite became uncomfortable and moved to another seat thinking she was looking at him. But Mélanie was completely unaware of where she was or what went on around her. She was gathered together into a knot of determination. But this time, she told herself, I must be as wise as a serpent and as gentle as a dove. She did not smile at the incongruity of either of these images as applied to herself.

Half an hour later she was ringing the bell of a cheap new villa in Uccles. It was fake modern, with big plate-glass windows and stucco walls, with the sashes and sills painted a hideous chocolate brown and yellow. Her ring was answered by a series of sharp barks and growls and the door opened by a woman of about forty-five, made up to look a good deal younger, in a yellow negligee. She looked Mélanie up and down as if she were a solicitor or salesman and grudgingly asked her in when Mélanie explained that she was the mother of a school friend of her son's. I shall never be able to talk to this woman, she said to herself. The Pomeranian who had barked was now sniffing her ankles with great displeasure, and Mélanie returned his dislike heartily.

"I'll come straight to the point," she said, after having looked in vain for some support from any single object in the room.

Mme. Sauveur said, "Pray do," and offered her a cigarette, lighting one herself.

"Your son is a friend of my daughter's," she repeated, "and I have come to you about something which is going on at the university. I don't know whether you are aware that Ado has organized a group of students with the avowed purpose of making the lives of the Jewish students as uncomfortable as possible——"

For the first time the pretty blonde woman who had been looking at Mélanie with amused curiosity sat up straight. She flushed slightly and said that Ado had talked of some such group but she had not paid much attention.

Mélanie leaped to her opportunity. "I'm sure that you disapprove as heartily as we do of these activities—which are probably due to excess vitality, nothing more—and I have come to ask your cooperation. Perhaps you could talk to your son——"

"Oh, madame, really, I couldn't do that." The flush had deepened and her slippered foot betrayed her irritation by tapping nervously as she spoke. "Ado is quite grown-up now. I do not meddle in his affairs." She went on righteously and stooped to pick up the Pomeranian and cover him with kisses. "No, my little treasure, my little powder puff, we couldn't do that, could we, my fluffikins?"

"But you do feel as we do about it?" Mélanie asked, somewhat shaken.

"Really, madame, I cannot see that you have a right to ask me that question."

"My child's happiness is involved in this. She has been deeply troubled—in fact she has made herself ill over it. I ask you please to answer me."

Mme. Sauveur seemed only too delighted now to comply.

"Well, to be perfectly frank, I'm afraid my husband could not sympathize with your point of view. We are members of the Rexist party."

Mélanie made a move to get up, but Mme. Sauveur made a motion to ask her to sit down.

"And just a minute. Perhaps as you have come so far I ought to tell you exactly how we feel. It would be better for the Jews if they kept out of the professions which are already overfull of their race. As long as the university has the policy it has, we can do nothing about it, but I see no reason why my son should associate with people there whom he would not associate with at home."

With a great effort of will Mélanie mastered her anger and said simply, "No one is asking him to do so. But that is a long way from forming a group to persecute other students at the university."

"Surely you exaggerate, madame."

"I have the word of my daughter, madame."

"There is really no point in our discussing this, is there?" It was Mme. Sauveur now who rose, forcing Mélanie to get up, smiling sweetly at her with the Pomeranian cuddled into one arm. "We have different points of view. I am sorry that you came this long way for nothing."

"I am profoundly shocked," Mélanie said, looking Mme. Sauveur straight in the eye. "I would not have believed this possible in Belgium."

Paul was right again as he always was. Things were much worse than they had dreamed. Would the papers carry this story? Mélanie feared it was naïve to expect them to. But it was worth a try—and she would have to try to see Francis at his office. He at least would be on her side. Such things can't go on, she said to herself, more determined than ever now to fight this to the finish.

That night, when they were gathered again for supper, she pulled herself out of her depression by acting out the three interviews graphically for them—for when she had left Mme. Sauveur she went straight to Francis's office and had lunch with him. They had to hear the furniture at the Sauveurs' described over and over again. ("Was there really an orange velvet pouf?" "Was there really a china figure of a nymph lying on her back supporting the lamp?") Colette was fascinated to have this glimpse of Ado's life at home. And when that subject was exhausted they had to know exactly what she had had for lunch and all that Francis said. They had to know a hundred things. But when she had at last exhausted all the events and details of her battles of the day, there came a pause. She sat with her arms folded, leaning back in her chair, and looked at her family half humorously, half ashamedly.

"So you see I was able to do nothing."

"Yes—yes," Paul murmured.

"Don't say I told you so, darling"—she turned to him pleadingly —"but of course you were right as you always are."

"No, I'm not right. I'm just a pessimist. Nevertheless, I'm surprised that Francis refused to take this seriously. I do take it seriously—I simply think it is extremely hard to fight."

"What shall we do now, Paul?" she asked with perfect assurance that he would know. At the end, in the final analysis, they always would come back to him and trust his judgment, however much they rebelled in their natures against his detachment.

For once even Françoise was interested and alive to this battle. Her Argentinian friend was a Jew, and once or twice at the school she had caught sly comments, an atmosphere, a hint which suggested that there could be trouble there. When she left the school she had put it out of her mind.

"Yes, Papa," she added, leaning forward eagerly.

In his own way Paul had been absorbed in the problem all day, walking up and down in his study, taking down a book, glancing at it, half reading, half thinking, working a little but with Colette's tense worried face always in the background, asking the same question.

"I would like to ask Ado and his friends to come here to talk it over with you, Papa," Colette said suddenly.

"Yes." Solange, who had been lost in her own thoughts, woke up. "Yes, that is a good idea. I'm sure it is." She could not believe yet that persuasion would not help.

"I wonder," Paul answered (he was immensely pleased that Colette trusted him so much). "From all that you say, Colette, I would guess that I might as well go out and argue with the wind."

"But what can we *do?*" she pleaded. The air was full of this pleading, this necessity for action, immediate drastic action. And Colette loved this boy—that was clear to him now. She was suffering doubly, from her intellectual horror of what Ado was doing and from her wounded affection. Just as Mélanie had suffered when Francis told her that her sentiments were all very true but that nothing could be done, bringing the fact home that they were caught, all of them, and might as well sit still. This is what had happened to Francis when he saw his whole edifice of hopes for peace fall like a house of cards after the Munich Pact. He had not committed suicide. He had given up belief. To Mélanie it seemed worse.

"I wonder," he said again, holding all these thoughts balanced in his mind one against another, "if you shouldn't try to talk to him alone, yourself, Colette? Have you thought of that?"

The light drained out of her face and she had again the pinched lost look they all dreaded to see.

"I'll try, but you see, he knows now how I feel. He thinks of me as an enemy—just as we think of him. Besides," she added as an afterthought, "I'm just a girl."

"And what if there is nothing to be done? What if Francis is right?" Paul threw the question down casually.

But it galvanized Mélanie. She got up and began mechanically to stack the dishes, putting down a few scraps in Fifi's plate, emptying the milk jug into her saucer. The others sat around the table, silent, filled with loneliness and sadness, as if for the moment the world were drawn into this tiny circle where there was still faith and still hope, as if they stood alone.

"No, Francis can't be right. We might as well all die at once," she said passionately. "We can't give up now. Colette is part of the university, and it's her duty to see this thing through—and we must help her. For one thing, darling"—Mélanie turned at the door of the kitchen, her arms full of plates, and the children got up mechanically to help—"you must not imagine you are alone. There are other students who feel as you do. Can't you get a group together and include the Jewish students, go at the whole matter from a constructive point of view? Let Ado and his gang see very clearly that it is they who stand alone."

Already Mélanie felt better. After all, Francis did not matter as these young people did. They were what counted.

"Yes," Paul said without conviction, "she can do that."

"I'll try," she said, though she felt no confidence in herself. For what would a group be without Ado, the most charming, the most brilliant, the one she loved? She rubbed her forehead with her hand as if she had been dreaming and were waking up. She felt infinitely tired. After all, it was going to be her job—Mamie had not been able to help. She would have to go on alone. And all she wanted was to be at peace and study, not to have to worry any more about the world, not to have to do anything heroic yet, above all not to have to engage in a long boring business of talking to students she hardly knew and didn't want to know.

"*Allons,*" Mélanie commanded. "To work, my children. Whatever happens we must wash the dishes and get to bed."

But after all they couldn't go to bed. There was a great restlessness in the house, as if the doors and windows kept being blown open and cold drafts let in—drafts of self-doubt, drafts of anger and the pain of separation. First Mélanie got out of bed and tiptoed out into the hall to Paul's study, then a few minutes later Colette and Solange followed and knocked to ask timidly if they might come in too.

"It's impossible to sleep," Solange said, curling up on a footstool at Mamie's feet. Colette sat on the arm of the big armchair, and Mélanie, seeing that she had come without slippers, warmed Colette's feet in her hands and then made her wrap them in an old shawl.

Alone, each had felt the wounds go deep, had felt it would never come right again. In the dark everything became monstrously difficult. Now, safe in the warm light of the study, they felt better.

"It's so good," Colette said, "to be able to talk, to know that at least we are together."

It's true, Mélanie thought, we are together as we haven't been for years.

And Paul, turned round to face them (he had been sitting at his desk), looked at his wife and two daughters, so different and in some ways so deeply alike, alike in their innocence, their passion for justice, even Mélanie, in spite of all her experience, as tender and violent as a green shoot in spring.

"You do rush in where angels fear to tread," he said half mockingly.

"I can't help it, Paul." (How often Mélanie had said that and always in self-defense.) They had been talking of Francis. Mélanie had now confessed that she had lost her temper with him and left him angrily. She was ashamed—any lack of self-control was against all her beliefs—but she had gone to Francis for a little balm after the first two interviews, gone to him as an old friend for comfort and support, and the shock of finding him as incapable of direct action as the other two had overwhelmed her. "I know I should never have showed how strongly I felt."

"You interrupted a busy morning, rushed in on him, and fairly knocked him down with your own determination."

"I know," she said humbly.

The children instinctively defended her, but she said gently, "No, Papa is right."

"You are all incapable of arguing without making it a matter of life and death—it's a Belgian trait, I must admit. Do you remember how upset Françoise was when she was only about six and we took her to a little restaurant where two men came to blows over Classicism versus Romanticism?"

"What happened, Papa?" Solange was eager to know. People never did tell the end of stories. They always ended, she thought, where they should begin.

"I don't remember. But perhaps, my children, you should try to overcome this weakness—for it is a weakness. Think of Gerhart. He had strong convictions, but he always managed to lay his case on the table quietly and give the other person a chance to express his own point of view."

"Gerhart was a saint. I am not," said Mélanie decidedly.

"But he did say, Papa," Colette answered, "that if we are passive witnesses we are denying our responsibility as human beings."

"Oh, I don't say we shouldn't go on fighting, darling. Only let's be careful and wise. There are different ways to act, you know. Sometimes thinking, thinking deeply to the very bottom, is the hardest and bravest kind of action. Sometimes being silent is the hardest and bravest kind of action."

How many times since they were little children the girls had been present at this same argument and witnessed it in their mother's and father's lives—and as always Colette weighed both sides, torn between them. Somehow or other one must love her mother's way the best but honor her father's. Somewhere between the two she must find her own balance. Oh, Ado, she thought, with a deep nostalgia for someone her own age, if only you could help me now!

Solange, in her simplicity, had no doubt. Her mother might be angry herself, but no one could be angry with her very long. For a moment it seemed to her that they were all making a great deal of something not very important—and then she thought, no, it was like this in Germany. That is what Gerhart said. Each tiny incident seemed unimportant, and each time one allowed it to pass, the chance of righting the whole power of evil that was taking over the country diminished. This mustn't happen in Belgium.

"Anyway," she said thoughtfully, "we must try to help, mustn't we, Papa? Even if we do it badly, we must try."

"Yes, my treasure," her father admitted. "I only meant to say that all this is a symptom of a real sickness, and one doesn't cure a sickness in a moment, or even in many weeks and months. We must be patient."

"I can't be patient, Papa," Colette insisted passionately. "Ado is my friend!"

So after all there was to be no peace that night.

Chapter IV

In the middle of this family crisis Paul finished his book. He finished it with a curious sense of loss, as if he were sad to give up his daily companionship with Gerhart, this long intimate conversation in which for once he had allowed his heart to infuse his ideas with a particular tenderness and warmth; now that it was finished, he was reluctant to let it go. In any case, it would hardly be read. After twenty years of neglect on the part of the public, Paul expected nothing from publication, nothing that he would not know more intimately and directly by reading the manuscript to a few friends. After all, in the last analysis, one writes for one's friends. If others discover these letters by accident, so much the better. Fame is only a great noise around a silence where one listens for one or two discreet voices. They are what count.

"I'm getting old," Paul said to himself, and that, he thought, is a good thing. For it left him free—as if he had cast off the unimportant struggles, the struggles of a man trying to hold up an umbrella against a storm or to find shade from the sun, the struggles outside his power to change—and he was deeply free now to face the real inward struggles. It seemed above all a beginning, this end of his book—a place where he could stand and look about him and where loneliness was the necessity, not the impediment. For in this written work, which he imagined would be his last, he had finally come to terms with his own life. He had accepted it. And the book was a confession, the naked telling of how he had come to accept it, by what difficult steps, with what ardor and what pain. And it was also an answer to Gerhart and Gerhart's decision to move in the opposite direction, toward action, toward identification with the physical struggle of society, toward the sacrifice of his inner life for the sake of the immediate war within humanity.

This is your way and it is not mine. But in the end we are moving together to the understanding that we are each alone, free and responsible all at the same time. And out of this freedom and this loneliness we must choose our responsibility with perfect love, which means perfect detachment.

Nothing that we do will seem to have had any use: your death was in vain. The enormous sacrifice you made of personal happiness, of work, of all that had been your life, led only to defeat and death. My search for truth will have perhaps ended in nothing more than the acceptance that the search itself is a justifiable and beautiful way of life. And yet who knows what invisible roots we may have nourished, what part in God we may have helped to exist— for does He not become small when our understanding of Him is small and great as our understanding of Him grows? And is He not above all the sum of our love when it learns complete detachment?

So the book ended, as it must, with the most important word in Paul's vocabulary, with his deepest act of faith—detachment.

A few mornings later he was standing at his desk in the studio at the business, going over a design, when M. Bernard was announced.

"M. Bernard—M. Bernard?" Paul asked himself. Who in the world is he? But when a lean, smiling man came to greet him with outstretched hands he recognized him at once.

"It's you, old friend," Paul said warmly. "What brings you here?"

He had the extraordinary name of Booz Bernard and was, as the name suggested, a Jew, a man whose heart seemed always to be in his eyes, overflowing with love and good fellowship, always at the service of the arts, always turning up with some new scheme (he had kept a small poetry magazine going for years and printed at his own expense innumerable small volumes by his friends; and he paid for all this by working himself to death as a designer, editor, jack of all trades—which even included a Domestic Bureau for servants). Paul was delighted to see him.

"You're like a djinn, Booz—you come out of nowhere just when I am most glad to see you, when I have without knowing it been longing to see you. Sit down, sit down and be comfortable. Let's talk."

Booz beamed—it was literally true that smiles wreathed his thin face. They seemed to be in the air around him like the smoke from his cigarette.

"What can you have been doing, Paul, that you're so absent-minded? Though I suppose that is the prerogative of philosophers and lovers. You sent me Emile Poiret's manuscript weeks ago, and now, instead of being furious with me for keeping it so long, you've forgotten all about it."

Paul laughed. "It is awful. I had forgotten it. I've been working like an angel on something I've just finished."

Booz rubbed his hands together delightedly. "May I see it? Your book, I mean?"

"Of course, of course—but first tell me about Emile. What chance is there?"

"It must be published, that goes without saying." Booz looked sad as he said it, as if it were a confession. "And I have wracked my brains to think of a way. Of course we could do it by subscrip-tion——"

"Emile would never consent to that. He knows nothing about business. He would call it charity and go back like a wounded bear to the country."

"Dear man, dear man." Booz shook his head sadly. And then he smiled mischievously. "You know, I mortgaged our house to pub-lish the *Anthology* last year. My wife doesn't know it. She would never forgive me. So I really don't know what to do. There is nothing else to mortgage."

One would say there aren't such people. They don't exist. And yet there he was, quite unconscious of the effect on Paul of what he was saying, rubbing his hands together.

"Booz, you're crazy," Paul said severely.

"I am crazy, it's true," Booz said happily. "Why not be crazy, after all? It's better than being bored."

"How much would it cost to publish Emile's book?"

"Fifty, sixty thousand francs—what with the unions, work of this sort has gone up enormously in price."

"The plates would have to be in color, of course." Paul tapped his fingers with a pencil. It was shocking that no big publisher would do this sort of thing, shocking that the pure works (and this work of Emile's was both beautiful and necessary and would be used by students of botany immediately) were always pushed aside, published, if at all, by accident or through the good will of friends. It was all wrong. But certainly there was no point in trying to revolutionize the publishing industry in the middle of a war.

"I tell you what, Booz, I'll pledge half of the sum if you can raise the rest—we might as well be in debt for another thirty thousand francs—we shall be ruined in any case very soon," he said with a light bitterness that pushed aside Booz's eager thanks.

And if his purse was a good deal lighter when Booz went, his heart was lighter too. It had been a good morning. Paul had even promised to come and read the new book to a group of writers and poets whom Booz brought together two or three times a year—one couldn't refuse Booz anything. He always made Paul feel humbler and better than he imagined he could be. So his first instinct had been to refuse (hadn't he decided only today to withdraw entirely from public performance?), and then he had not been able to refuse. His reasons suddenly appeared selfish, ungrateful—he had accepted; he had immediately begun, in spite of himself, to look forward to hearing how the little book would sound, to wonder what effect it might have, to tremble with anxiety and excitement like a boy, as if he had never written anything before, nor heard it fall into a perfectly indifferent silence.

"Yes, yes," he said to himself, and because he felt happy he recited the whole of the *Nuit de Mai* as he finished his drawing.

Mélanie will be pleased, he thought—more pleased even than he, and as happy as he at the idea of helping to publish Emile's book. Paul longed to write and tell him the good news at once and then decided to let Booz have that pleasure himself.

There was a roar of planes overhead; the startled pigeons on the roof opposite rose up in a great flight of white wings, circling round and round in great agitation and then settling again with soft complaints, as if nothing had happened. Paul stood at the window and watched them.

"Stupid little creatures," he thought.

But after all, everyone instinctively watched when planes went over—what the pigeons do we all do, inwardly, these days, he thought. There were air-raid shelters all over the city: at any moment, at any hour, the monster War, growling at the borders, might leap upon them. If only, Paul said to himself, we can get Emile's book through the press before it comes!

It was a morning of interruptions. Françoise came running up the stairs in a state of such excitement and joy that she gave her father a great hug (a most extraordinary demonstration).

"What's happened to you, *ma belle?*"

"Clément's father has given us a truck—a real huge truck so that we can make a tour in the spring with our plays! Think of it, Papa! A truck all our own! We'll go to the villages and put on the plays for the children. Everything we've hoped for is going to happen!" She was radiant, out of breath, panting with the good news.

For two years she and a small group from the school had worked at night to write and rehearse plays for children, Françoise doing all the costumes and scenery herself—how many nights she had sat up till all hours sewing and dyeing, making masks, even building furniture—this had been her answer to Maurice, not to go on alone, but to work with her companions at the school, to begin at the beginning, to make a popular theater of their own. But they had no money to spend, and at first the performances had been poor because they really knew nothing, any of them. Now this year they were just beginning to find their own technique, their own writers —and of course all the older boys were being called up into the army.

"At least we shall have this spring, Papa! You know, Clément has been deferred until he finishes this year at the university. Alfred too. Oh, I am so happy." She sat down like a boy with her legs stretched in front of her. "I ran all the way down the Chaussée. I'm all out of breath!"

She had not given her father a chance to get a word in edgewise, and he was watching her, amused and delighted to see the transformation. Who would have believed the silent, secretive little girl she had been could turn into this wildly expressive and talkative young woman, in the theater, of all things!

"Well," he said half to himself, "perhaps you will have this spring. I hope so." So much, it seemed, must manage to get done this spring! So much life demanding expression, so many hopes and dreams pushing through while there was still a little space left in the world before they must take refuge in each heart and wait and wait for the end of the war, be kept alive somehow until the end of the war.

Françoise got up impatiently. "Oh, Papa, you are a pessimist. We *must* have this spring!" she said passionately to the sun and the pigeons outside.

Yes, they must have it. But would they? Would they?

"And if you don't?" he asked gently, for surely she must be prepared. Always she had pushed the war aside, refused to listen to the talk about it, refused to be drawn into the circle that must eventually enclose her—and all the others—all the world.

"Well," she said defiantly, tossing her head like a young horse, "well, we'll go on somehow anyway."

"Yes," Paul said gravely, "I'm sure you will." For he knew it well, there was iron in this child of his. But he did not dare think what it might cost to "go on somehow." It rang in his mind, that gallant, free "We'll go on somehow anyway," and for once Paul felt a wave of pride in his little country, where after all the books did get written and published, the plays produced, in spite of lack of money, lack of audience, lack of everything except the fire and life poured into them.

Chapter V

But for Mélanie, for
Colette, this was not the morning of joyful news, full of friends
and surprises, but the morning of guilt and secret fear. Mélanie was
now thoroughly ashamed of her impatience with Francis, and
Colette was determined to speak with Ado alone.

Nothing, Colette decided in the night, was worth this parting—at
least she must try once to reach him, to touch him. But the difficulty
lay in the fact that this sense of warmth that crept about her heart
wherever he was concerned had never been expressed. They were
still eyeing each other speculatively, absorbed in the infinite preliminaries to spoken love. He did not know her really, and though
she imagined she knew him well, she had never had a chance to
test her intuition about him: she had never talked with him alone.
She had known his anger and rejection and never his love. But it
was there—of that she was certain. Over and over she rehearsed
the tiny incidents on which she had built this world of sensation
and passion: how he had first smiled at her across the room during
an examination and the smile was a gift, how he had lent her a
book she needed, how once he had brought her a flower—but
that was long ago. And now she had asked herself what it was
about him that haunted her, though she knew his faults so well—
his arrogance, his slightly mocking deference to the professors, the
impression he gave of doing what he chose with a fine indifference
to public opinion—and then, yes, his English tweeds, his pipe (the
other boys smoked cigars), the way he listened with his head on
one side, the way he spoke when he became excited, clasping his
hands together fervently. He had the thing Colette lacked most and
envied—a sort of chic. He was a natural leader. If he stood in the
corridors between classes, a group gathered around him at once,
laughed at his jokes, wanted to be near him. She had always been

too shy to be part of this group—and too proud. So she had hardly noticed what he was saying so excitedly, hadn't realized what he was driving at until he had formally asked her to join his "club," as he called it. And then Salomon had come to her and spoiled everything.

How would she ever have the courage to see him alone? And how to manage it without everyone knowing right away and teasing her unmercifully? . . . But luck was with her that morning. She had had to wait for a trolley and she was late—the corridors were empty when she ran up the stairs and saw Ado ahead of her.

"Ado," she whispered desperately. Would he hear? Would he turn?

"Oh, it's you," he said as she caught up with him. He looked at her angrily. "What's all this about your mother?"

"Meet me after class, somewhere where we can talk," she begged.

"All right—at the far café. I have things to say too," he whispered ominously, and then they were in the classroom and there was nothing to do but live through the next two hours somehow. Colette was furious with herself for being so nervous. I must be detached, she repeated to herself as if it were a charm. But how did her father do it? How, if one loved someone, could one be detached?

"You're a silly girl," Ado said rather smugly when they were finally sitting at a table in the back of the café where no one would see them, drinking bitter coffee out of a glass. "Ugh," he said, tasting his, "all chicory and no coffee."

Colette sat frozen beside him, warming her hands on the glass, not looking at him.

"You take life too seriously. I like you, you know," he said with splendid condescension. "You're bright. But you think you know too much. You want to change the world—that's foolish."

She must say something, but sitting there beside him at last, she felt numb, so divided between anger and love that she was incapable of speech, of decision, of anything but to sit there in the middle of the tempest of her blood, waiting for something to happen.

"What did you want to talk about?" he asked more gently. After all, she was a girl, and she looked awfully pretty sitting there so silent and white. Would she let him kiss her? he wondered. She looked awfully aloof and she wouldn't smile today. He'd never seen a girl who changed so much when she smiled.

"Oh, Ado," she murmured desperately, as if there were some wild hope in his name.

"Well, what is it? Can't we be friends? What is all this, anyway? I know you don't agree with my politics, but after all, this is a democracy—we're all at loggerheads politically. What difference does that make? I like you. You like me—only for heaven's sake, keep your parents out of it," he added imperiously.

"But if it is a democracy, Ado," she began hesitantly, "doesn't everyone have equal rights? The Jews here——" She didn't finish the sentence.

"Oh, the Jews, the Jews! Everyone talks about the Jews." He shrugged his shoulders. "The Jews look out for themselves, believe me. You don't have to worry about that. The Jews do very well indeed."

"In Germany?" she asked, beginning to find her voice and her belief.

"Oh well, Germany—besides, they've all got out, haven't they? They have money in banks all over the world. Belgium is full of rich Jews—it's an inundation," he said dramatically.

"Are you afraid of the Jews, Ado? Are you really scared that they can take your place in life away from you?" Colette was angry now, and she didn't care any more if she never saw Ado again.

"Now look here, Colette, who do you think you are, anyway? I won't take that from you."

"You don't have to. But I won't take your attitude, either, and I'm going to fight you, Ado. That's what I wanted to tell you."

"Oh, so you're going to fight me, eh? Well, that's splendid. The *cause célèbre*—Ado Sauveur versus Colette Duchesne." He laughed mockingly with the theatrical laugh he reserved for his public. All the intimacy had gone.

"There's no point in talking, I guess," Colette said wearily.

"No, I guess not."

They sat, uncomfortably, side by side, drinking sips of coffee, silenced.

"Don't you see, Ado, it's the world!" she cried out of her desperation, and it meant, Don't go away from me. Don't let it happen. Don't let's part like this. "We're all poisoned."

"You may be. I'm not. I am perfectly well, thank you. I just can't see going to war for the Jews, or for France, or for anything else for that matter. Let's clean things up at home. There's plenty to do here."

"But, Ado, De Grelle sent men to fight on Franco's side. He's friendly with Hitler. It's not just this country. It's all locked together, don't you see?" But as he didn't answer she added, "Did you ever hear of Gerhart Schmidt? He said——"

"Oh yes, some crackpot German philosopher who got himself killed in Spain. Those people are just crazy idealists. We've got to be realistic, Colette. They lost, didn't they? Just a lot of romantic nonsense because people are afraid to face the realities at home—so they rush off to fight someone else's war. It makes them feel better."

"The cause of Belgian freedom was a lost cause for hundreds of years. That didn't prevent people from fighting and dying for it."

"Well, we're fighting for it now—De Grelle is a patriot. De Grelle wants to see a strong unified Belgium, and if that means making terms with Hitler, all right. Our business is to protect our own country. You can't change my mind, Colette," he added, "any more than I can change yours. So why try?"

"Because," she murmured, blushing in spite of herself, "because you're the only person I want to be friends with—and now it's impossible."

He tried to take her hand. She pulled it away.

"No, Ado, no," she murmured with tears in her eyes.

"I can be friends. I don't see why you can't. I don't say it's impossible."

Why couldn't they be friends on one level and disagree on another? Oh, why couldn't they?

"You look awful when you screw your face up like that into a frown. Come, have another coffee and forget it——"

"I can't, Ado, I can't," she said dryly, forcing the tears down. It would be the last humiliation if she were seen to cry. She turned her face from him and didn't look at him again.

There was nothing but a little sediment left in their cold glasses. It was time to go.

Now that it had really come to this flat parting, he looked disconcerted, at a loss, like an actor who cannot get the hang of his part. And for once he was silent. They went out together into the damp bone-chilling air; Colette shivered so much her teeth were chattering.

"You're a silly girl," he said half mechanically as she turned away from him with a short "Adieu, Ado," and walked rapidly down the street, aware of his eyes on her back all the way to the corner.

When they might still have found a way to be friends she was close to tears. Now she felt dry and empty and above all tired. Now that it was done she had a wave of revulsion—the whole thing seemed like madness, nothing but a stupid quarrel for which she was paying an enormous price. For weeks the whole world, the very air around her, had been infected, and all for Salomon, whom she didn't like. What good would it do? Now everything would go on as before, except that she would be without Ado and his smile forever and ever. Standing, shivering, at the trolley stop, she felt bitter, bitter, wondering why she had had to be born into a world so wrong, so torn that there was no peace and no happiness left any more, thinking of the days when she was a child and could happily write poems, work in the garden, when the world had been enclosed in the hedge and the green gate, safe and dear.

The wind was cutting now. It whipped her legs. And just as the big square white end of the trolley came into sight a company of soldiers marched across from a side street, blocking all traffic so the trolley was there in sight, and she, kept from its warmth, had to stand, watching the waves of khaki go past. There was no band; they were marching sloppily, and some even had cigarettes in their mouths. Did they feel as she did, caught, unable to be themselves, hating the world they found themselves grown up in, responsible for?

Was this, she imagined in a flash, what lay behind Ado's attitude? Revolt? And all his bravado and conviction whipped up to hide his own confusion? Poor Ado, she thought when she was seated in the warm trolley. We must either become angels or monsters, then; there seems no alternative—and although she looked very little like an angel at that moment, it was quite clear in Colette's mind what she would try to be.

Why was it that as soon as the green gate clicked behind her everything always became so much clearer and easier? Solange saw her coming from the kitchen window and opened the big front door with a sweeping gesture.

"Well, old lady, what happened?" she asked, beaming with delight to have Colette home again.

But Colette's nose was twitching like a rabbit's. "What are you making? What's that delicious smell?"

"Cookies—a surprise for Mamie. I'm glad you're back. It's lonely here all alone."

It was wonderful to be back. Colette sighed with relief and sat down at the kitchen table to eat a piece of bread and jam and drink a cup of goat's milk.

"Where's Mamie?"

"She suddenly decided to go in town and see Tante Simone—— What happened?" she said all in one breath.

"I broke off with Ado. It was all stupid." Colette sounded so weary that Solange dropped down automatically in a chair beside her. "You can't change people's minds once they're made up." She sighed and looked out of the window at the darkening winter sky, and Solange watched her, wishing she could think of something to say. "You know," she went on, "I think more and more now about Uncle Gerhart; how hard it was to do what he did, to cut himself off from all he loved and still to come to that wholeness in himself. I feel so divided—unclear. I want to be happy," she ended half defiantly. It seemed to Solange to have no connection with what had gone before.

"People behave so differently from what they are; I don't think inside himself Uncle Gerhart felt whole. Only he had somehow accepted not being whole as the price for what he believed."

"Maybe." They sat looking out into the garden until Solange gave a cry of horror and rushed to the oven. The cookies were a little browner than absolutely necessary, but they weren't burned. "Thank heavens!" she said, suddenly a child again. Colette, hearing the roar of the car, ran out to open the door and help unload.

Paul went right upstairs, in one of his incommunicative moods. And Mélanie came into the kitchen to kiss the two girls and steal a cooky and wander about as if she had been away a long time and wanted to look at everything at once.

"That old pot needs scouring," she said, and characteristically, her hat and coat still on, her cooky unfinished, went to work on it. Solange and Colette looked at each other.

Mamie was upset. Her face looked harrowed, the line in her forehead between her eyes so deep it might have been a wound.

Solange came behind her and took off her hat, teasingly, tenderly, and pulled at her coat till she could slip it off in spite of protests. Finally, as if Mélanie had worked off some impatience, some despair, she turned to them triumphantly, showing the saucepan's shining bottom.

"There, that's better."

Then she sat down at the kitchen table and, while they all three peeled potatoes, heard the whole story of Colette's talk with Ado.

"I feel I've been wrong," she said then, and it was awful to see their mother so humble. "I haven't helped you, my darling."

"No, Mamie," Colette answered quickly. "Don't you see, I can't like Ado any more. That is finished." Saying it made it true, and in that truth and the acceptance of it she felt at peace with herself for the first time in weeks.

"Simone scolded me frightfully for always rushing in and trying to do something—she's right. Your Mamie is an old fool."

But this time it was Solange's turn to protest, to get up and put an arm round her mother and hug her. "We have to try at least, Mamie. That is what you said yourself. Only we may not succeed, that's all."

"It's not quick. That is what I begin to understand. It's not anything that can be done quickly, to change the world we have allowed to be made around us. It is slow—because it involves a change of heart." And then, with a little characteristic movement of imperious exasperation, Mélanie added, "That woman, that mother of Ado's—I can't see how *her* heart will ever be changed."

"You're home. That's the main thing," said Solange matter-of-factly. "And we must set the table. Papa will be starved. He seemed cross when he came in."

"I made him cross—he had all sorts of good things to tell me about publishing Emile's book, and I depressed him because I was angry with myself."

But now the savory smells were filling the kitchen, and with them everyone relaxed, became more cheerful, and by the time they were sitting down to an omelette and potatoes they were all three laughing again. It was like any one of a thousand evenings when everyone felt so hungry each had to go and taste the supper while it was still cooking until Solange protested:

"There won't be anything to eat if you taste it all!"

Just as Papa came down, rubbing his hands, the front door was pushed open and Françoise burst in with a basket on her arm in great excitement.

The omelette was forgotten. They all got up to see what she was bringing. They guessed all sorts of things: A goose? Butter? *Plain d'épice?* François giggled rather nervously and shook her head each time. Finally she lifted her scarf off and revealed—a puppy. A tiny ball of camel-colored fluffiness, fast asleep.

"No," Mamie said in mock despair, "not another animal—Françoise, we can't. What will we feed him?"

"He can have my share," Solange said quickly. She had taken the puppy onto her lap and was talking to him gently.

"He's beautiful, isn't he?" Françoise looked around in triumph.

"He's beautiful *now,*" Paul answered, "but what will he turn into?"

Was there a hint of duplicity in Françoise's answer, "A pure-bred chowchow"?

"I don't believe it"—it was Colette—"but he is darling," she added quickly. "Look, his ears are still folded in."

"This is all very well," Paul said, "but I am hungry and the omelette is getting cold."

The omelette disappeared almost before it was set down before them—it simply vanished while they thought of a name. (It was finally decided that Hassan would be appropriate.) And then Françoise had to tell them all the plans for a spring tour with her friends in the new truck, and Solange must get up to warm some milk for Hassan as soon as he opened one eye and whimpered hopefully. And then Fifi must be introduced and, after smelling this strange furry creature, showed her acceptance of him by licking his face very thoroughly and then helping him to drink up his milk, which he did with such gusto that he covered her with white spots and she had to wash herself all over to get clean.

Françoise covered the floor of her room with newspapers and insisted that he should sleep with her. "He'll be lonely," she pleaded when Mélanie suggested that the tiled floor of the kitchen might be easier to clean.

"What a lot has happened today!" Solange sighed when the last dish was wiped and the time came to turn out the lights in the kitchen.

"And nothing is decided, but I feel much better," Colette announced.

It was true, the nightmare which they had lived in for the last few days was past. They were waking up, not to heaven, but just to the real world, the simple daylight, their own lives. Once more the magical circle was drawn round them, and here in the old house everything still seemed possible, even to be patient. Going out from it, they moved through the world armed in strength, warmed deep inside, with much to give because they burned brightly in themselves. Even Colette that night slept soundly for the first time in weeks.

Chapter VI

As the evening, when Paul was to read his manuscript drew near, he read it over several times to himself, marking passages, considering what he would tell them, filled with inner excitement. There is such an abyss between a work before it is performed, heard, known and that same work once it has been heard, once it is, so to speak, given away. And this interval, between the writing and his chance to read it to a sympathetic audience, was a time of great tension for Paul. Perhaps after all the whole thing was unreal, a complete illusion of his own, something that went on in his mind which he had not been able to express at all—like a tone-deaf person who believes he is singing the tune he hears in his mind but is really uttering a monotone. At fifty he still had the innocence of a boy with his first poem, so removed had he been from the gossip of literature, from the business of making oneself known, of being seen in the right places, of being talked about. So that now this tiny opening in the curtains of silence seemed a radiant promise. He was eager and humble and full of hope. And the children were amazed to see him struggling with his tie in the bathroom as if he were going to a dance and singing loudly.

"Ouf, you smell of moths, Papa."

He gave Solange a deep bow. "Do you know when I last wore this outfit? Ten years ago, at the opening of Maurice's theater. Your papa has managed to keep his figure tolerably well, eh?"

Mélanie brushed and brushed at the shoulders and trousers, as if brushing would somehow remove the greenish tinge of old age. But when he was ready in his white silk scarf and old fur-lined coat, he did look remarkably elegant—and so handsome, Mélanie thought, giving him a last kiss, patting the brief case, as the three girls called in chorus:

"Good luck, Papa!"

The little hall where these monthly meetings of Booz Bernard's were held belonged to an archery club which met here once a week to shoot clay pigeons. The stage was so small that there was barely room for the speaker and a lectern; and the fifty "Friends of Literature and Philosophy" were packed in like sardines with the long rack of bows and arrows behind them. Paul felt at ease here at once. It was all amusing, gay, young—as young as he felt, though most of the heads before him were bald and there were several white beards. But everyone was smiling, laughing, talking a blue streak as if they hadn't seen each other for years; old friends turned up to kiss Paul on both cheeks and shake his hand many times, as if they could not welcome him warmly enough.

"You must come here more often, old man." It was what Paul himself felt. These were his true friends, men who had gone to college with him, many of them in business now (the law, medicine—all the professions were represented) but these were men who cared about giving their encouragement and attention not to what was fashionable and successful but to the young and unknown, to the old and unknown like Paul—who wanted to feel themselves creatively back of the life of the spirit, a company of true believers.

And in spite of himself Paul was moved by Booz's introductory speech, too long and far too enthusiastic, giving him credit for a reputation which he clearly had never had, but so full of heart— he could not be angry with Booz. For Paul could be violent on occasions like this. Exaggerated praise cut him to the quick, rubbed salt in his wounds. If I am obscure and have fought this solitary battle alone, at least let them give me credit for that and not for an easy fame I have never had, he had said once years before with savage emphasis. Now he was older, saner, and, above all, beyond caring.

He was only glad to be able to pay homage to Gerhart Schmidt, to speak of him now, and to be here among friends. As always, he read beautifully and spoke without notes in such perfectly ar- ranged phrases that there was hardly any difference between what he read and what he threw off in explanation between the written passages. Booz was sitting directly in front of him, and he found himself addressing himself to this one man among them all, as if he were paying him particular homage.

When he had finished there was a moment of silence, and Paul wondered if he had gone on too long. He had limited himself strictly to an hour. Had he bored them? But just as this thought flashed through his mind the "Bravos!" started to ring out and the applause sounded as if the fifty had been multiplied by magic into several hundred, like the loaves and fishes.

In a moment he was surrounded and carried off to the next room where there were jugs of beer and bread and cheese for their refreshment. Many had questions to ask, and Paul found himself talking and talking, amplifying these ideas he had kept in himself for so long, eager to explain——

"But it's you," he interrupted to seize a very old man's two hands. "It's Professor Alard!"

The old man twinkled. "Yes, I'm not dead yet." Oh, how the

memories of the Lycée days came back as he heard again that musical voice, for Alard had been his professor of Greek at school! "And I wanted to tell you," he said, "that your book will be a great comfort to many people in these terrible times," and patted Paul gently on the shoulder.

"If it's ever published," Paul said, smiling gaily.

The old man nodded his head. "It will be published. You see, Paul, this book of yours has heart. You have been always so afraid of showing your heart, eh? But something has happened to you. Am I not right?" The gentle old man talked to him still as if he were a student, and standing before him, Paul felt like a student again, drinking in this praise as he had used to do on the rare occasions when Professor Alard was pleased with a translation.

One dreams of glory, Paul said to himself as he led the old man over to a table where they could sit and talk. (Booz joined them there with Defaux, the lawyer.) One dreams of glory, and in the end it is not glory that matters, it's to have one's old professor of Greek turn up one day, exactly as he was thirty years before, and praise a piece of work wholeheartedly.

"You were always a rebel, Paul," the old man was saying in his musical voice, "and your way of rebelling was that superb indifference, that datachment you were so proud of. Now you are still rebelling against this passionate age, determined to stand outside it, but your detachment has become positive instead of negative. Am I right?"

But it was impossible to talk quietly, for someone tapped Paul's shoulder from behind, someone called to him across the room, and Booz himself bobbed up and down like a jack-in-the-box. So Paul smiled at everyone and suddenly longed to get away, to get home and tell Mélanie all about it.

Now that it was over, he realized how keyed up he had been. He wanted to think over what had happened, to assess it; it had not occurred to him that there was a radical difference in this work from the preceding ones—it had seemed like one more step in the same general direction, a step illuminated by Gerhart's act, so that the darkness all around had been lit up, but it did not put an end to darkness. It did not provide any more answers than his former works and their explorations of the dark passages of doubt, their implacable honesty, their outright denial of any optimism whatsoever. What, then, had happened that for the first time he knew what it was to touch people, for the first time he *saw* a work of his *act,* affect, move an audience? He had often given lectures in the old days, but he had never—he was well aware of it—evoked love, only a cold admiration. Afterward people came to him with questions, but they did not come with simple homage. And that was what had been in Booz's face, in Alard's pat on his shoulder. It was strange——

When Paul came out into the street it seemed as if all Brussels was asleep except for this group of aging philosophical enthusiasts, and their good-bys rang out loudly in the stillness. The white façades of the houses presented black windows to the street, as if they were stage sets without depth. And overhead the sky opened out immense with stars. He walked fast, glad to be alone in the silent city, not feeling the cold, lost in the solitary elation of having given away his idea and at last knowing the gift to be needed, seeing the gift accepted with eager hands. The loneliness in which he had lived until now overwhelmed him—he might have been living on the moon. He had thought he was driving down in himself the longing for fame, but he understood now that it was something quite different—something pure that he could not understand, for he had never known it—the desire for communication. He was no longer talking to himself, justifying himself. He had stepped out of that narrow circle—he had been lifted out of it by Gerhart. It was a humbling realization, and he welcomed it.

But was it all a change in him? Was it not also partly a change in them, a change in the world where now people were being forced to ask themselves the questions they had always pushed aside, the fundamental questions, the simple questions like: "What is the meaning of life? What is important? What is not?" With war imminent each must strip himself down to the essentials. So for the first time there were people ready for what he had to say, just as he was for the first time ready to meet them.

But as Paul walked fast from the trolley down the winding dark avenue toward home, there was an undercurrent to these evaluations which had nothing to do with war or philosophy but with his own life—he was coming toward Mélanie. Soon he would be home. Soon the green gate would click behind him and he would be walking down the path, seeing the gable of the house standing up against the immense sky. And there inside, fast asleep by now, lay his wife.

But after all there was a light in the kitchen, and Mélanie was not asleep but downstairs in her padded dressing gown waiting for him.

She heard his nervous quick steps crackling on the frosty path and ran to open the door (in spite of everything she had been a little nervous about him, it was so late). His face felt frozen against her warm cheek.

"Come inside quickly. I have some hot chocolate on the stove."

"How is it you're still up? It's nearly one——"

"Oh, I've been asleep. But I woke up and you weren't there— so I came down." She tried to sense his inner atmosphere before asking about the evening. Too often he had come back from occasions like this, for all his high hopes, full of defeat, saying only, "What can you expect? No one is interested in thinking these days." But before she could ask him he had told her.

"It was a wonderful evening, darling—wonderful. After all these years . . ." He was sipping the hot chocolate gratefully, and she stood watching him, filled with happiness to be beside him and to see that he was well, safe, happy, drinking the drink she had gotten up in the middle of the night to prepare for him. It was like a secret fete.

"I know, Paul."

"They were moved, Mélanie. They understood. Now at last, when I had given up all idea of publishing or even showing the manuscript to friends, I seem to have said something they need to hear."

He looked ten years younger.

"You can't imagine what it is like—the difference—the sense of being part of humanity again that I have." And then he stopped and looked at her standing there, with tears of joy in her eyes. "My wife, my dear one," he said in the voice that touched her marrow always, "how patient you have been."

"No, Paul, it's you who have been patient."

"Well, I don't know. I think you know that I had despaired— but you never despaired."

But she had despaired, not of his work, never of that, but of him, of his heart, of his gentleness. In the last years she had watched him eaten by acid, as if there were no balm any more in anything that could reach him. She had despaired and wept bitter tears alone, but thank heavens he would never know that she had.

He drew her arm through his, and they walked up the long flight of stairs slowly together, talking softly as they went. At the landing they stopped, as they had so many times before, as if they had arrived at a long lap of a journey, and he kissed her once more and said, "You know, Mélanie, we have to thank Gerhart for this."

"I know."

"We must remember Gerhart in the years to come. We must remember Germany—it is going to be hard to remember. It is going to be said that Gerhart's Germany never existed—and perhaps it never has existed. But it can exist, Mélanie. In a hundred years, two hundred years, perhaps, and to exist it must be believed in."

But Mélanie was not sure; her feet were rooted in earth, and tonight Paul seemed to be flying about all on fire in the airy spaces.

"I don't know, Paul, it only seems to me more and more that this war is taking place in each man's heart and it is there that it will have eventually to be fought out, if not now, then in another generation.

"Look at Colette," she went on. "That is what she has been having to face. And it's not easy, is it, Paul?"

"No, it's not easy," he said, half lifting her up the last stairs.

Soon the house was perfectly still except for the quiet breathing of all the sleepers in it. Mélanie and Paul lay hand in hand, happy and exhausted, having fallen asleep in a communion so perfect that it needed no further gesture than this.

Chapter VII

As the first hints of spring thrust through the winter—the mornings lightening by seven instead of eight, the willow turning yellow, a few hopeful green spears pushing up through the leaves—as February went out and March came in in a burst of warm weather and sunshine, Mélanie was more and more tempted to stay home from the business: the garden seemed much more important. It was essential this year that the early planting succeed, so that they would have supplies of food by May and June—just in case. The air was full of rumors these days, but people had got beyond panic. They were grave, but they were not nervous. Colette was working furiously for her examinations, plunged so deep into her books that even the conflict with Ado was subordinated for the time being. Françoise was in an ecstasy of costume-making and mask-making and rehearsing for the tour—the house was full of scraps of bright-colored cloth, paper, and glue, and finally the salon was completely given over to the theater. From here she emerged disheveled but always happy with her newest achievement, a piece of material which had taken turquoise dye perfectly or a humorous mask with a mustache made of fur. Solange would not start on her job until late May, so she was able to help now in the garden, and Paul rejoiced with them and shared in it all—dashing off to town for whatever there was to be done at the business and supervising the printing of his book with Booz (there were infinite delays and bothers with the printers, but he hoped to have proof in a couple of weeks).

Often as they stooped over the wet black furrows or leaned on their spades, smelling the spring air or crying gladly that the swallows had come back, Mélanie would feel the stone in her heart, the great heaviness of the agony of Greece, of Austria, of Czechoslovakia always there, loading these days with a desperate burden. But there was nothing she could do except make the rows straighter than ever, love her children better and more wisely (and how radiant Solange had become in the last year!), rejoice in Paul's renaissance of spirit—and every week walk over to the village and help organize air-raid precautions.

The days were carried along on a stream of suppressed excitement, like a bubble in the throat, a tension which made every pleasure and every moment particularly vivid—even nature seemed to share in this creative fervor. For never had there been such a spring!

Only Moïse was subdued, she who had always gone wild the first warm days when she was let out from her stall, rubbing her forehead on the trunks of the apple trees as if to greet them, leaping high into the air and shaking her ears happily when she landed, nibbling the fresh green grass ecstatically. This year she lay down a great deal and hardly ever played any of her old tricks; she walked sedately to the meadow and never tried to run away. Even her whinny sounded disconsolate. She was nearly twenty, and the hair round her nose was quite gray. Solange worried about her a great deal and used to go over to the meadow and talk to her and bring her tidbits from the kitchen whenever she got the chance. What would they ever do if Moïse died? If the warm, sweet-smelling stall were empty and no impatient whinny demanded breakfast as soon as anyone stirred in the house?

Solange explained this to her as gently as possible by rubbing her forehead by the hour and whispering in her ears, but she just lay in the sun chewing her cud and cast a weary eye on the world of spring, not at all comforted by Solange's admonishings that parrots and elephants lived to be much older than twenty and there was no reason at all why goats shouldn't.

Every morning now became an anxious time until someone had gone out to the stall with breakfast and reported that she seemed no worse. But she grew more listless every day.

"She has no *joie de vivre* any more," Solange explained to her father, "she who was so gay."

And he answered nostalgically:

> *"Le temps s'en va, le temps s'en va, madame,*
> *Le temps, non—mais nous nous en allons."*

"Perhaps she's lonely," Solange observed. They were sitting at breakfast one Sunday morning.

"Why not get a pair of goats to keep her company?" Françoise suggested.

"Darling, we can't afford it," Mélanie interrupted. There were so many things now that they couldn't afford. Solange needed a winter coat, but that could wait till next year. But she must have some new blouses to take with her when she left.

"I wish we could have a sheep too," Solange murmured dreamily.

Mélanie was melting already. "It would, of course, be practical," she said judiciously, glancing over to see what Paul thought of this sudden extravagance, for the whole family was now eagerly planning all they could do if they had more animals, another pig perhaps—then the present pig could be killed before the hot weather and before Solange had to leave.

But where would they get the cash for such an investment? The fact was that the Duchesnes seemed to have everything except money these days. Whatever came into the business simply melted away in mortgages, the interest on debts, and their day-to-day expenses. Only Françoise was rich, for she had saved all the money she earned for her share in designing for the business and she had just finished a nursery for the royal children.

At the moment Françoise seemed to be entirely absorbed in Hassan, observing his ears with close attention, for it was becoming more and more obvious that Hassan would never by any stretch of the imagination turn into a purebred chowchow—his fluffy teddy-bear coat was turning into straight orange hair; his ears would not stand up in spite of all Françoise's efforts; in the middle of the discussion she turned to the family with a sweet and rather guilty smile and admitted:

"Perhaps after all his father was not a chowchow!"

"Oh, Françoise!" Solange shouted accusingly. "What a liar you are!"

"But you have to admit he is darling just the same. Look at his funny little eyes—and he has the blue tongue of a chowchow, you can't deny that." She was not to be disconcerted as she kissed the top of Hassan's head and set him down on the floor where he could be critically surveyed by the whole family.

His tongue showed its blue tip through his smug little orange face, and he gazed up at her with such plain adoration in his tiny black eyes that they all laughed merrily.

"Never mind, you are a good doggy, aren't you?" Mélanie told him consolingly.

"But she deceived us terribly, and she'll have to pay a forfeit," said Solange severely.

"All right, my friends—I'll pay for a goat as a companion for Moïse, how's that?"

"And a little pig?" asked the inexorable Solange.

"All right."

So breakfast was finished in a hullabaloo of rejoicing while Françoise went upstairs to get two thousand francs from her secret cache.

"Heavens," Solange said, looking at the huge bills with astonishment, "you are rich!" Everyone embraced Françoise admiringly. Who ever heard of so much money? And she had earned it all!

But the rejoicing did not last long. Colette came back from the shed with a stricken face.

"Oh, Solange, come quickly. Moïse seems much worse. She won't eat anything. She just lies there and pants."

Everyone followed Solange out to the shed, not even waiting to put on coats, while Paul still sat at the table playing with Hassan.

Solemnly they gathered round her while Solange stooped over and felt her nose.

Breathlessly they waited for the verdict. But she only shook her head, two great tears falling on Moïse's head.

"She's dying," said Solange quietly.

"Can't we do anything at all?" Mélanie asked. They turned to Solange now deferentially, as to a doctor in a sickroom.

"No."

Quietly, on tiptoe, Françoise, Mélanie, and Colette went back to the house to tell Paul. Quietly they cleared the table and washed the dishes, while Paul put on a coat and went out to see for himself.

"Do you remember when she was little how she used to stand up on the table in the breakfast room as if she were looking for a mountain to climb?" Colette asked. They were filled with memories of the past. Thinking of Moïse and all they had experienced by her side brought back the last ten years vividly. It seemed as if with her a part of their own lives was dying.

"And how she used to frighten Fifi out of her wits?"

"Oh, and do you remember," Françoise broke in, "the time she escaped to the rhododendrons and made herself so sick eating all the best flowers, the great pink ones, as if they were a salad?"

"Mamie sat up all night with her——"

"She loved flowers," Colette said sadly, and suddenly the humor of this remark touched them all and they giggled in spite of themselves.

But how would they ever be able to look out at the meadow on a summer day and not see Moïse lying there in the shade, chewing her cud, flapping her ears against the flies, greeting them with affectionate cries—her eager wild eyes, her quickness, and how she loved to tease them!

Out in the shed Paul was squatting down on a pile of hay watching his youngest daughter. She was sitting in the stall with Moïse's head in her lap, her wise fingers stroking her gently, rubbing behind her ears—all Solange's care for living things, her sweetness poured out in the quiet rhythm of her gesture, back and forth, back and forth behind the sensitive ears. They did not talk. It was enough to be together here, and Solange was grateful to her father. He understood. He knew that she was afraid to be here alone when the time came, when the dim, patient life she was consoling as best she could went out forever.

For a moment Moïse shifted her weight and tried to lift her head—the wild blank eyes looked out at Solange once more with a gold flicker of recognition in them, and then her head dropped down. The glazed look of death met Solange's clear-seeing eyes.

"Oh, Papa," she said through the blinding tears, "Papa." Gently he lifted her up and begged her to come in now there was nothing more she could do.

"No," she cried softly, "let me stay here a little while." So he left her, padding softly in to tell the others.

Now she was alone with death, she knelt down once more and stroked the delicate little hoofs with awe. This is what happened to life, to all life, sooner or later, this inexplicable, this terrible departure—all the fire, all the light in the world turned to darkness, gone. Where? Where did it go? The birds, the flowers, her mother —and Solange, alone in the shed so full still of Moïse's wild smell, wept harshly for all she understood and could not understand, for the sorrows of the earth, for all wildness fled, for all friendship and all love that passes and cannot be held.

There they found her. They all had tears in their eyes, but Mélanie spoke sternly:

"You mustn't let yourself go, Solange darling." And then, "Come, we have work to do: the rabbits are starving. It's late."

But this was just what seemed so terrible to Solange, that life must go on, that the dead are left, forgotten so quickly, and life goes on. In an hour or two she herself would be laughing.

"She was an old lady," Paul said gently, "and she died peacefully."

Obediently Solange got up and came away. Inside, the house was just the same. Hassan had found one of Mélanie's slippers and was busily chewing it to pieces.

"Let him have it, the poor beastie," said Mélanie gently as Françoise stooped to punish him. That was the only way she could imagine to face death, that there must be more life, more life given back somewhere. It was little enough, to let a puppy chew up a slipper—it was nothing, of no consequence—no more than the death of a goat. But each understood what she meant.

Later in the day Mélanie and Solange dug a hole by the rhododendron; they buried their old friend there, without tears. It had been hard digging, and they were flushed and out of breath. They felt full of life.

It's good, Solange thought to herself, that she is safe in the earth now. The knot in her heart relaxed.

But Mélanie, who had showed her grief so little so as not to add to Solange's exaggerated melancholy, felt sharply that this was the end of twenty years. They were buried now, all those springs, those summers, those long autumns and winters, sunlight and firelight, their happiness, the children's growing up, the years of peace— and, patting the earth with her spade, she blessed them in her heart.

Chapter VIII

Now time seemed to
have wings, to be flying past fearfully quickly, as if the weather
itself joined in a great burst of fecundity. Never had there been
such a spring, so beautiful, so capricious, raining down sunshine
and then in an hour casting immense black clouds over the land,
bringing the flowers bursting out so the garden was a glory of
narcissi, daffodils, anemones, tiny pink daisies sprinkling the
grass, and the fruit trees snowed under with blossoms. The birds
never stopped singing. The greens had never looked so brilliant,
and it seemed to Mélanie as if she had the eyes of a child, all was
so fresh, so new, so overwhelmingly full of life—even the slugs
seemed to have multiplied this year! It was like Eden before the
fall.

April came and went, shot through with the agony of Norway,
interrupted in its golden progress by notices that reserves were
being called up. And still life went on. Solange went to market and
came home ashamed, fearful, smiling all over, with not only one
sheep but two lambs and a little pig and a goat. She had spent
all of Françoise's money! But Françoise could think of nothing
but the final rehearsals of the play. They named the sheep Maman
Matelas and decided to sell the lambs later in the spring. They rejoiced in the new life in the old shed. The vegetable garden began
to have its springtime look of a Dutch garden, all neat, all prepared, without a single weed. In the glass frames the cress made
Mélanie's mouth water.

The adventures of these days were small—once the pig escaped
and ate the hearts out of twenty-seven lettuces. Once Fifi caught
a bird. Once Hassan ran away and wasn't found for twenty-four
hours. The plates for Emile's book were in the final stages; one
day in late April, Pierre turned up with a twenty-four-hour leave

and thanked Paul with tears in his eyes for this homage to his father. The Duchesnes were pleased with Pierre. He was growing up. Even Colette was emerging from this painful winter with an occasional bloom of happiness on her cheeks. She swam through her courses at the university like a duck in water.

And then, before anyone felt ready, it was May already; the lilies of the valley spread their pearls under the willow tree; the radio announced that all leaves in the Dutch Army were canceled. No one took these alarms very seriously. There had been so many in the last year. They all turned out to be as unreal as the air-raid alerts.

So when early on the morning of May tenth, Paul shook Mélanie out of a deep sleep and said, "Listen, there's bombing over toward Brussels," she just answered sleepily, "Probably some army exercises," and went back to sleep.

Paul lay awake and listened. It sounded like repeated, violent explosions of thunder, echoing long after the blast. It sounded awfully real. For once he was up first and sitting by the radio when Mélanie came sleepily in at seven to hear the news if there was any.

"The Germans bombed the airfields early this morning and then declared war. It's here, Mélanie. It's come."

She felt extraordinarily calm. As she busied herself with the breakfast she was puzzled by Paul's agitation. Well, it had come. For nearly ten years it had been on the way. For nearly ten years she had been preparing her mind and heart and planning for this moment. She was glad to think how well the garden was started: it would be well now to keep the lambs for meat later on.

Breakfast was like an officers' mess before battle. They decided that Paul should stay at home by the radio—he had taken his coffee upstairs at nine to get another news broadcast. He came down to announce that the Belgian Army was mobilized and already French and British troops were moving across the frontier into Belgium. The King would speak briefly at eleven from his headquarters at the front.

They decided that Mélanie had better go into town and see what cash she could scrape up and decide with the demoiselles whether to close the business at once or wait. Colette insisted on going to the university as usual—she wanted to find out what was going on. Françoise must meet with her group, all ready to start out in a week and now probably all called up as army reserves. Solange wanted to go in with them—there might be volunteer work of some sort in town. They were all restless and excited, wanting to be wherever things were happening, and as they half ran down the avenue to the trolley they sang the "Brabançonne." It is strange, Mélanie was thinking, observing the girls' excited eyes, that however much one knows war is terrible, the hour when it really comes, when a country is called to defend itself, lifts all hearts. There is one moment of wild elation. Already, when they were sitting in the trolley, the moment had passed.

In town a battalion of soldiers, carrying full packs, no cigarettes in their mouths now, swung down the Avenue Louise. Everyone stopped in his tracks to watch them march past. Grave anxious faces, no cheers. One woman wept convulsively into her handkerchief and then waved it with a desperate last gesture as if she were ashamed of her tears.

Some cafés were closed. Men in civilian clothes hurried to the billeting offices: all reserves were called up. In the trolley everyone was talking together by now. They shrugged their shoulders. "Well, it's here," a veteran of the last war assured them. "They won't have it so easy this time, the *sales Boches;* you'll see." The women said nothing. Silently they calculated what reserves of food they could muster; silently they thought of their husbands, their sons. But on the first day of the war the city of Brussels wore a determined air. There was no panic.

And once the girls and Mélanie had arrived at the business they were carried along on all there was to do. Mélanie had first to calm Mlle. Louvois, who was weeping hysterically (like so many others, she had persuaded herself that somehow they would escape). Jean announced that they were calling for volunteers to dig trenches in the park for air-raid shelters, and he and Solange went off together to offer their services. Françoise was dispatched to a factory near the Gare du Nord to try to finish up a mural for which she was responsible. If she could get paid for it they would have a little cash in the house. Mélanie hated to let her go, as the station might be bombed, but Françoise laughed at that. "Our Air Force will take care of them." They didn't know then that the Air Force had been practically completely destroyed by the bombing early in the morning, which the Nazis had carefully accomplished *before* they declared war. Colette went off to the university to say good-by to the boys, who would of course all be called up in the next few days. They agreed to meet again at the business by four o'clock.

And during that day Mélanie decided to keep the business open as long as possible, if only because it seemed the best way to keep up the morale of the two demoiselles, who as long as they could come here would feel some support in the daily routine.

But by evening the atmosphere had begun to change. The first great shock to optimism was the fall of the fortress of Eben-Emael, considered impregnable—the Nazis had taken it by surprise with parachute troops during the first day of the war! The stations at Ghent had been bombed. But at least, they said to each other, the British and French are there now. The British were rumored to have penetrated into Holland. In Brussels itself there was still no panic. Red Cross stations had been set up. The Civilian Defense organizations were in high gear.

Françoise pooh-poohed any danger at the factory and said she would be able to finish if she could have one more day. Booz Bernard came to the office to assure Mélanie that he would get Paul's book through the press somehow—several of the printers' assistants had been called up, but they would manage. It did Mélanie good to feel Booz's firm handclasp, to find him running about his errands as usual. Solange proudly exhibited the blisters on her hands and was in high good humor. "You have no idea how hard the earth is in the park—it's like breaking stone." Jean had given up and come home at midday, leaving her alone, but she had had a good time, elated by the spirit of democracy at the trench-digging. All sorts of people had turned up. She was illuminated with love for her country. "If I could only remember all the jokes. We laughed so much we could hardly work."

It was almost as if people were glad that at last the winter of waiting was over, the frozen winter of the spirit when nothing was asked of them but to wait. Now they could act. Now they were needed.

But two days later the Belgian Army, with the British on its left and the French on its right, was forced to withdraw to the second line of defense. And on the thirteenth and the fourteenth the Germans broke through the French lines north of Dinant, forcing a bitter retreat on the British and Belgian armies, who felt they had just begun to fight.

Refugees began to pour down the roads, bringing rumors with them—at first a trickle, a panic-stricken family in a fast car with a terrible tale of machine-gunning from the air, then more cars, and finally a river of carts piled high with possessions, of old men and women, of tired wailing children, and with it the ghosts of millions of refugees from the last war, the flood of reality and the flood of memory mingling so that suddenly in a few hours, in a day, the atmosphere changed to panic. Françoise came home white, terrified, from her last day at the factory. It seemed unbelievable to find her family there, just as always, drinking tea in the breakfast room.

"Oh, you can't imagine. It's like madness, Mamie. Cars push their way around the carts, knock them over—there's no solidarity any more. It's like madness," she repeated. "Everyone tries to save himself. In Brussels people are closing their houses."

"I know," Mélanie nodded. "In the last day everyone has left the avenue. Mme. Lanoix was kind enough to bring us over a sack of flour they couldn't take with them."

"No wonder," said Paul, tapping with his fingers on the table nervously, "the Germans are at Sedan."

Sedan—the word went down their spines like a finger of ice.

"They say the bombing of the roads is like a holocaust. Where are our planes? Where are the British, the French?" Françoise cried. How many people asked the same question on these terrible days!

"Oh, Mamie, what shall we do?" Colette asked, her enormous eyes fixed on a corner of the table in terror.

"We can't stay here," Françoise answered quickly. "The Germans may be here in a day, in two days—we've got to plan."

But never had Mélanie imagined leaving. It was all too quick. There was no time to think, and once more she desperately commanded her inner self "calm and gay, calm and gay."

"Listen, is that planes?" For a moment no one spoke as they crouched over the table.

"I'm going out to see. I can't stay here." Solange got up. The others followed. What they saw was the farmers' truck from an estate near by piled high with crates of gasoline and trunks and behind it the town limousine, driven by a chauffeur and the whole family of their neighbors packed inside.

"Well, bon voyage to them," Paul said bitterly.

It was such an anticlimax from their terror of a moment before that the tension was visibly relaxed, and Mélanie seized on this opportunity.

"Listen, my children, we must think this out very carefully. Just now we were behaving like everyone else. I felt that hot wind of fear inside me. But we mustn't give in, must we, Paul?" she pleaded. "We must go inside and think it all out."

Something in her was revolted by this picture of the rich people getting out. What would the poor people do, the old, the sick? Were they simply to be abandoned? In one hour had all sense of responsibility vanished? What was happening to the world?

It was, Mélanie felt, a formal occasion, one which demanded

the salon as its frame. Paul followed her, and the children followed him, and they all settled themselves around her. With some instinct she was not even aware of, Mélanie sat down on a stool by the hearth and lighted the fire.

"We might as well have a fire to take the chill off," she said matter-of-factly. And it seemed to do something remarkable for the inward chill as well as the chill in the air when the big log caught the flame from the fagots.

"Now"—she turned to them as she had many times before when family plans were involved—"each must say what he thinks. First Paul."

Paul had been listening to the radio all day. He had perhaps the clearest idea of any of them of just how bad things were. He had already made up his mind earlier in the day that if the Meuse Line could not be held they would be in real danger, so now he spoke rapidly and concisely, without emotion.

"Mélanie, I think we should leave. We have the car and we have ten extra gallons of gasoline. That would take us well into France. We can go to the Didiers' place near Tours eventually. They would be glad to take us in, I'm sure."

"You'd really *leave*, Paul?" Mélanie asked with a stone in her heart.

"What about the animals, Father?" Of course Solange thought of the animals.

"I won't leave without Hassan," Françoise interrupted fiercely.

"All right, Françoise," he said impatiently, "we can settle all that later. We could take the sheep, goats, and pig over to the village."

"We might be able to get the truck and take some of the families of our group with us."

"We can't ask the Didiers to take in a whole army of refugees, Françoise. Be sensible."

"It's so awful to leave everyone like this," murmured Colette. She did not know what she thought.

"If we stay here, we may be massacred," Françoise answered coldly. "That won't help anyone."

"But the garden—the house——" Solange was near to tears as it suddenly came over her what leaving meant.

Mélanie looked from one to the other, trying to read their hearts. Whatever was best for them, she would do. Whatever they chose, she would choose with them. But her whole being revolted against flight. All these years she had been building for resistance, not for flight; she had been preparing her family to endure another occupation; she had planned the garden so they could live. She had invested in another hive of bees. To leave now? She looked from one to the other with her heart clamped down as if it would burst.

"What do you think, Mamie?" Solange asked with a desperate hope in her eyes.

"Yes, Mélanie, what do you think?"

Mélanie clasped her knees with her hands. She was sitting all hunched up on the stool, and now she turned from them to poke at the fire.

"I can't imagine leaving. I—I don't know——" She looked into the fire.

"This is not like the last war, you know, Mélanie. These are not the Germans of 1914," Paul reminded her gently. "Remember what Gerhart said."

"I know, I know," she said, but shook her head as if to deny what she knew, "but think what we risk by leaving—depending on charity, having no roof over our heads. Here at least we are at home."

There was a loud knock at the door. Everyone jumped. Could it be the Germans already?

But Paul, who brushed the family aside to go himself, opened the door to La Grande Louise. She was out of breath and had one hand on her heart, as if to hold down the fearful gasps which tore through her. Her face was bright red and she had obviously been crying.

"Oh, monsieur—monsieur——"

"Come in, come in, Louise. What is it?"

She had never been in the salon before, but now she was led into the salon and Solange ran to get her a glass of water. As soon as she saw Mélanie she went to her and shook her hands with passionate gladness.

"Oh, madame, everyone is leaving," she sobbed. It was terrible to see this great oak of a woman shaking like a child. "The mayor has gone. The six aldermen. The priest left this morning to go to Brussels and has not come back—people are so terrified they are running off with nothing onto the streets, leaving their doors open. There is no one to tell us what to do——"

Mélanie made her drink the glass of water and sit down.

"The avenue is deserted. I was so afraid you had left."

"No," said Mélanie quietly, "we are still here, my brave Louise. Now sit there quietly and catch your breath. I must speak to my husband a minute."

The children looked at one another and nodded their heads. "We'll have to stay now, won't we, Françoise?" Solange whispered. There was no doubt about it in anyone's mind. They could not abandon the village. They were needed here.

When Mélanie came back she had on a light coat and Paul had put on his shoes.

"My husband and I will go back with you," she said with quiet dignity.

When their father and mother had left, the three girls sat around the fire, drawn close together, feeling suddenly responsible and very much alone.

"I'm glad we're staying," Colette said thoughtfully after a moment. "If ever Hans Schmidt should turn up, I'd hate to meet him as a refugee on the roads. Let him come back here and find us as we were. That's as it should be."

And the other two nodded their heads silently.

After a moment Solange got up and went out to feed the animals.

The sky was deep green over the poplars; the birds were singing their evening songs; the earth seemed to breathe peace. And Solange felt that somehow now they were safe and had escaped a great peril. Now they were going to be all right. Because, she said to herself, they can come here and kill us. But they can't make us change our way of life.

Author's Note

Although there were young fascist groups in Belgium before and during World War II the author wishes to apologize for suggesting that such a group might have existed at the University of Brussels. As the novel was written during the Hitlerian occupation of Belgium this fact could not be checked at the time.

May Sarton